Frances Gordon is the daughter of an Irish actor and after a convent education worked in newspapers and the legal profession. She now lives and writes in Staffordshire. She is the author of four acclaimed fantasy novels, written under the name of Bridget Wood, and three previous horror novels, BLOOD RITUAL, THE DEVIL'S PIPER and THE BURNING ALTAR, which are all available from Headline Feature:

'A superior example of the vampire genre... a pleasure from start to finish' *Time Out*
'A chilling, blood-curdling novel' *Peterborough Evening Telegraph*
'A quality novel of supernatural power through the ages... Blending well-fleshed characters and a strong story' *Bradford Telegraph & Argus*

Thorn
An Immortal Tale

Frances Gordon

First published in 1997
by HEADLINE BOOK PUBLISHING

First published in paperback in 1997
by HEADLINE BOOK PUBLISHING

A HEADLINE FEATURE paperback

10 9 8 7 6 5 4 3 2 1

ISBN 0 7472 5485 0

Typeset at The Spartan Press Ltd,
Lymington, Hants
Printed and bound in Great Britain by
Mackays of Chatham PLC,
Chatham, Kent

HEADLINE BOOK PUBLISHING
A division of Hodder Headline PLC
338 Euston Road
London NW1 3BH

AUTHOR'S ACKNOWLEDGEMENTS

My grateful thanks are due to Dr C J Cooper, Consultant Psychiatrist, who patiently guided me through the medical and psychiatric aspects of this book, and to Chris Emery, of William Emery & Sons, who provided such excellent help and information on the legalities and practices surrounding burials and funerals in England.

PART ONE

'She shall fall into a profound sleep which shall last a hundred years . . .'

Charles Perrault, *The Sleeping Beauty in the Wood*

Chapter One

Almost the entire family went to Edmund's funeral. Imogen's father said it was a time for supporting one another, and the aunts all agreed.

'The Ingrams closing ranks with an audible click,' said Great-Aunt Flora tartly, but no one paid much attention because Great-Aunt Flora was often tart. Eloise, Imogen's mother, said 'tart' was a very good word, because Flora had had a great many lovers when she was a girl in the thirties and forties, and it had coarsened her.

'I don't know why she's even here,' said Eloise, irritably.

'I think she's here to be with me.' Imogen said this carefully, because she had been in the car with her cousin Edmund when he crashed it, driving too fast, and if she had been sitting in the front instead of in the back she would have been chopped up as well. She was trying not to think about it too much, and she was trying very hard to forget the sight of Edmund's body. Edmund had been showing off with the new car his mother had given him for his eighteenth birthday. Imogen had not liked him very much but nobody ought to die smearily like that, crushed into his seat and cut to pieces by glass.

'Your father and I are with you,' said Eloise in response to this. 'You don't need that mad old woman as well.'

'Make sure to put a warm coat on before setting off,' said Imogen's father. 'There's a very cold wind today. Haven't you a warm woollen scarf?'

'Yes, you don't want to catch flu again, Imogen. I remember I was prostrate with nursing you last year. Dr Shilling said at the time it was exactly the kind of strain I should avoid.'

'I think we should have got Shilling to take a look at her again. The shock of the crash – I might still give him a ring.'

They did not want Imogen to go to the funeral. They never wanted her to go anywhere. It had been a long time before Imogen had seen that they always managed to block invitations from schoolfriends or suggestions from teachers that she join the school choir or orchestra or drama group. She would quite like to have done all of these, or even just one of them, but in the end it had not been worth Mother's migraines and palpitations and Father's worried frowns, or the aunts' twitterings. There had even been the suggestion of trying for a university place during her last year at school, but Father had not seemed to like the idea, and had had an interview about it with her headmistress. The aunts had all joined in, saying, oh dear, all that way from home, and supposing she was ill again? And then Mother had suffered some kind of collapse and lay around on daybeds and sofas looking ethereal, and Dr Shilling had said she must not be caused any kind of anxiety. And as for Imogen leaving home, well, it was not to be thought of.

The aunts did not want Imogen to go to Edmund's funeral either. There had been worried discussions for days beforehand – 'All that emotional strain straight after the car crash,' said Aunt Rosa who was thin and slightly acidulated and did not believe in shirking facts – and there had been much telephoning and anxious consultations as to what would be the best thing to do.

'Better for her to stay safely at home,' said Aunt Dilys, who was Rosa's younger sister and lived with her in Battersea. Aunt Dilys was short and plump and addicted to sugary puddings and Barbara Cartland novels and a nice gin and tonic before her lunch.

4

'I daresay Royston and Eloise will already have decided that,' said Rosa.

'Oh yes, probably they've called in that nice Dr Shilling. Of course, he's known the Ingrams for a good long while – don't you recall *his* father being called in when Royston's father died? Mother said how very kind he was. And Royston and Eloise are both very careful of Imogen, although I've never seen any signs of . . . *you know*.'

'Neither did Lucienne Ingram's brother,' said Rosa caustically.

'Well, no, but they say she was really quite happy in – well, in that place they put her.'

'Thornacre,' said Aunt Rosa, and Aunt Dilys shuddered. 'And Sybilla Ingram's husband,' Aunt Rosa went on inexorably, 'didn't see any signs of anything out of the ordinary either.'

'Dear me, no. That was Waterloo year, wasn't it?'

'Trafalgar.'

Imogen knew about Lucienne who was supposed to have done something appalling to her brother around the time that Edward VII had been on the throne, and whose photographs had been systematically destroyed by the family so that if you ever looked through old albums you kept coming across unexpected blanks. She knew about Sybilla as well, who looked slyly out of an oval frame in the dining room, and had glossy golden hair twisted into ringlets and a narrow red velvet ribbon round her neck to show sympathy with guillotined French aristocrats. Imogen had always disliked being alone in the room with Sybilla's portrait, especially on dark winter afternoons before the lights were switched on. As she and Edmund grew up, it occurred to her that Sybilla looked at you from the corners of her eyes with the exact same smile Edmund wore when he was about to do something particularly cruel – like the day of his ninth birthday, when he had held the cat over the kitchen range for five solid minutes. Then he had blandly gone into his birthday tea with Mother and the aunts, his jersey still smelling of scorched cat fur and cat sick. Imogen had not been able to eat anything, even though there was strawberry shortcake and cream trifle.

The aunts always beamed on Edmund and admired his golden hair, and said, oh, *wouldn't* his father have been proud if he could have lived to see him, and wouldn't it be rather suitable if one day he and Imogen . . .

'Wouldn't it be rather suitable' meant, of course, that Imogen and Edmund might one day get married. Being married to Edmund would be absolutely the worst thing in the world, and Imogen would have done anything to stop it happening.

Looked at sensibly, it was not really such a very bad thing that Edmund was dead.

Great-Aunt Flora, sweeping into the Hampstead house ten minutes before everyone was due to leave, brushed aside all the ditherings and said energetically that of course Imogen was going to the funeral. 'And don't press your temples and look sorrowful, Eloise.'

Somebody – Imogen thought it was Dr Shilling – murmured something about migraine and the strain of the occasion, and Great-Aunt Flora said, 'Rubbish. The only thing wrong with you, Eloise, is rampant hypochondria.'

Everyone at once looked to see how Eloise would field that one, but Eloise declined the bait. She leaned back in her chair and half closed her eyes, but Imogen thought the headache or the dizzy spell would not develop because Mother had bought a new suit in Knightsbridge earlier in the week to wear today. Aunt Dilys had already commented how very smart it was – 'And so *youthful*' – but Great-Aunt Flora had asked if Eloise thought it really suitable to wear such short skirts at her age.

'She's decked out like a black widow spider,' remarked Flora to Imogen as they set off. 'Silly creature. I told your

6

father at the time not to marry her, but he would do it.'

One of Flora's lovers had been a racing driver and he had taught her to drive at breakneck speeds. They dashed along the road to the church like bats escaping hell, but Imogen did not mind. The funeral was going to be pretty harrowing, but when you were hurtling round bends at sixty miles an hour, at least you were not worrying about minced-up bodies in coffins.

'Cheer up, child,' said Flora as they drew up outside the church. 'There's still the inquest to come. You can dress up to the nines for that – I bet your mother will – that family always did over-dress, everyone used to comment on it. The press will probably be there. You might find you're questioned by a good-looking journalist. Or even a policeman.'

'Father would put a barbed wire fence round me within the hour. Or whisk me out of the country the next day.'

'He worries because you aren't very strong.' If it was possible for Great-Aunt Flora to sound hesitant, she sounded it now.

'I'm strong enough to enjoy being questioned by a good-looking policeman.'

'Oh, you don't want a policeman,' said Flora at once. 'They make frightful lovers, policemen. No staying power.'

She's changed the subject, thought Imogen. But she said, 'Is it true you once had six lovers in one night?' This was the kind of thing you could say to Great-Aunt Flora, although you never knew whether to believe the reply.

Flora grinned. 'You've heard that one, have you? I expect it was the night of the Pineapple Ball in nineteen forty— No, never mind the exact year. And there were certainly six *good* ones.'

Imogen found Great-Aunt Flora a huge comfort.

Dan Tudor had only attended Edmund Caudle's funeral because of two things. One was that the *Messenger* wanted a piece on the funeral and the family, and he was broke; the other was the intriguing nature of the Ingrams themselves.

As the owners of a children's publishing house they were not so very remarkable, but as a family they were slightly macabre. Dan found himself wondering if there was material for a book here. There was the famous cause célèbre of Lucienne Ingram in 1905: the guileless lady who had taken an axe to her brother and, as the idiom of the day had it, attempted to turn him into a female. Dan, researching background beforehand in accordance with his custom, read the report of the case on the *Messenger*'s microfiche, and derived wry amusement from this gem of Edwardian prurience. And there had been an Ingram lady somewhere around 1810 who was supposed to have murdered a straying husband or lover, although the details of this were vaguer. Either the *Messenger* had not had very efficient record-keepers then, or the Ingrams had managed to cover it up a bit more successfully.

'The *Messenger*'s features editor wants something a bit gossipy,' his agent said.

'I'm not a gossip columnist,' said Dan, with extreme distaste.

'No, but they printed that extremely good review on your Le Fanu biography. You owe them something for that.'

'I don't owe them a free gossip column.'

'When did I ask you to do anything free?' demanded his agent. 'It won't be free. Now listen. Dig up the Ingram murders if you can – it almost looks as if there's a homicidal female born about every ninety years—'

'Something nasty in the distaff shed.' Dan found the idea of disinterring skeletons from the cupboard of a family who had just suffered a bereavement a bit unsavoury.

'Yes, the ninety-year interval is probably coincidence, but you might look further back than Sybilla. Describe the present-day family as well, of course, if you can do it without being too litigious.'

'Piers, I'm never litigious.'

'And particularly describe the females,' said Piers, ignoring this. 'Eloise Ingram is supposed to be a bit of a stunner, in a die-away, *Lady of the Lake* fashion.'

'Oh, all right. And the bereaved mamma – what's her name? Thalia Caudle?' Dan supposed he might as well get as much detail as possible beforehand.

'She's Royston Ingram's cousin,' said Piers, and Dan heard the grin in his voice.

He said, 'Do you know her? What's she like?'

'Fortyish. Efficient. Well known in charity circles. She does a lot for student groups.'

'And?'

'And she's supposed,' said Piers, 'to have a robust appetite for good-looking, very young men, although she's fairly discreet about it. But I've heard it said . . .'

'What?'

'That all the charity work she does is simply a way of finding new lovers.'

'I'd better wear my chastity belt and take a rope ladder to escape with. Anything else?'

'Try to drag in the family empire: Royston Ingram's books for tiny tots.'

'Was Edmund Caudle the heir?'

'If he wasn't, find out who was. Basic research, Daniel.'

'Basic gutter-press fodder,' said Dan and took himself off.

The aunts thought that considering the dreadful nature of the occasion, everything was going off quite well.

They had managed to keep Flora and Thalia more or less apart which was always advisable at a family gathering because those two had never got on. Flora had always said that Thalia spoiled Edmund disgracefully but then Flora had always preferred Imogen. It was surely only natural for Thalia to be concerned about Edmund's future. When he

9

was born, everyone had seen him as Royston's natural successor at Ingram's, but lately this had looked a bit doubtful, what with Edmund failing his exams and not wanting to go on to university – 'Not being *accepted* to go on to university,' said Flora – and Thalia apparently prepared to support him financially for as long as he wanted. Of course, she could afford to do it; her husband had left her comfortably off. Nobody knew the precise amount concerned, although Dilys and Rosa had speculated about it at the time, but it was plainly a very substantial amount. And anyway, a great many young men were a bit wild in their youth and settled down later on.

Aunt Rosa thought the choice of hymns had been suitably restrained and Dilys thought the lack of any flowers in the church showed a nice sense of feeling on someone's part. Two unmarried great-aunts of Royston's who lived in Dulwich commented on the excellence of all the arrangements.

'And everyone brought back to Hampstead, with a buffet lunch all waiting for us. *Very* efficient. And so nice to see all the family assembled as well. There are a good many people we don't recognise, but then no one ever makes introductions at a funeral.'

No one made introductions at a funeral. It was this that had been in Dan's mind as he got in his car and drove behind the cortège as it turned out of the church. If you had enough panache you could bluff your way in anywhere.

The house was more or less what he had expected; large and solid and rather complacent. No one who lived here would ever have known what it was like to grind out hack articles because the gas bill was due.

The rooms were overheated almost to suffocation point and there was a scent of slightly too strong rose potpourri everywhere. If this was the way the Ingrams normally lived, Royston Ingram must have to publish an average of one bestseller a month to pay his central heating bills alone. Dan accepted a glass of chilled Traminer from a tray that was circulating, and studied the company. There was a fluffiness of elderly aunts and cousins, as there was at most funerals, and there were one or two decorative females. Dan regretfully but resolutely kept away from them. The elderly aunts all sat together and caught up on family news with guilty relish and smiled on Dan with hopeful curiosity. Dan smiled back with uncommunicative courtesy, and retired to the sketchy concealment of a window seat. The slightly furtive nature of this afforded him a perverse pleasure. Like the Robert Burns line: 'There's a child amang ye, takin' notes, an' man, he'll print it . . .'

His agent's thumbnail sketch of Eloise Ingram had been wickedly accurate: she was pale-haired and slightly languid and Dan had seen her twin in a dozen illustrations of *Morte d'Arthur* or Lambs' *Tales From Shakespeare*. She was the mad dead Ophelia, bizarrely transported from weed-covered, weeping willow-fringed rivers into a fashionable London suburb. For a moment this image was so vivid that it came as a shock to see that she was drinking what looked like a large gin and tonic, and wearing a designer suit.

Thalia Caudle was dark and thin, with huge hungry eyes like burned-out lamps. The Wicked Fairy of the tribe, thought Dan. She had not quite reached the age where she could be described as ravaged, but she was not far off. She looked as if she might very well possess carnivorous leanings towards young and attractive men. Dan finished his wine and reminded himself that Thalia had just lost her only son in a motorway pile-up.

He was just heading back into the room for a refill – the Traminer was very good indeed – when he saw Imogen Ingram.

11

Chapter Two

It was a most remarkable moment, and it would teach cynical writers to jibe at Hampstead and to call houses complacent and make up absurd allegories about wicked aunts and pale, languishing ladies.

In a minute – maybe after another glass of wine, maybe after the entire bottle – Dan thought he might be able to analyse Imogen's extraordinary looks. But in this first crowded moment, he was aware only of dark cloudy hair and a pale, translucent skin with arched eyebrows, and of slender ankles and wrists. All the gifts, thought Dan, watching her. Beauty and charm and, from the look of her, intelligence and humour as well. She moves like a nymph or a faun. Yes, and if she's the heir to Royston Ingram's publishing empire, which she probably is, she'll have his money one day.

Money had nothing to do with it; this was a face to sack cities for and to burn the topless towers of Ilium for. A face you would not necessarily want to take to bed with you but that you might very well want to take into dreams with you. And she's probably no more than sixteen!

There was an appalled moment when he wondered with horror if he had reached the grim stage of finding nymphs – all right, nymphets – desirable, but surely to goodness you didn't start that at twenty-seven? And this did not seem to have anything to do with physical desire. This was nearer to the pure, glowing passions of the Renaissance: Dante seeing the unattainable Beatrice when she was nine and loving her

12

for ever; Petrarch burning with cerebral and celibate ardour for Laura. It was the emotion that dreams were made of and that luminous essays and bright-flame poems were written about, and it was the very last thing Dan had expected to succumb to at a wake in Hampstead. I'd better concentrate on what I'm supposed to be doing here, thought Dan. Spying. No, that sounds dreadful. A chield, takin' notes.

He looked around the room again, and it was only now that he became aware that most people were watching Imogen. There ought not to have been anything very remarkable in that, she was worth watching, but Dan began to feel uneasy. There was something wrong here; there were currents and cross-currents filling up the too-warm room, like a vortex struggling to be born. Plain, straightforward grief at the sudden death of an eighteen-year-old boy? No, it's something more than that. It's something centring on the girl. But surely Imogen was only doing what thousands of sixteen-year-olds did at family gatherings? In Dan's experience it was something most of them enjoyed in a slightly egocentric way; unless they belonged to the shaven-headed, safety-pin-in-the-nose brigade, most of them liked showing how grown-up they were in front of indulgent aunts and uncles. But there was nothing indulgent here; there was no my-how-you've-grown-my-dear mien in anyone in the room. This was more like a roomful of people being extremely wary of an unpredictable child.

He scanned the room. There were mourners and friends and family. Assorted aunts and the occasional uncle – the Ingrams appeared to breed more women than men, or maybe the women possessed a stronger survival instinct. Eloise Ingram was holding languid court to a couple of admirers, one of whom had been pointed out to Dan as Dr Shilling. He was fiftyish, with a well-scrubbed look and an air of low-voiced reassurance. Trust the Lily Maid of Astolat to provide herself with a doctor as part of the frame for her decorative invalidism.

Dan looked across at Thalia Caudle. Thalia was standing against the curtains of the deep bay window, momentarily alone. The red velvet cast a dark shadow over her, pulling a mask down over the upper half of her face and giving her eyes glinting pinpoints of crimson. It was a trick of the light, no more than that, but for an unpleasant second Dan received the strong impression of something malevolent peering out. He blinked, and the odd, disturbing image vanished. But wasn't Thalia entitled to feel aggrieved towards the girl who had come unscathed out of the crash that had mangled Edmund? Wasn't she due a bit of angry jealousy?

As Imogen moved away, one of the aunts murmured that there should always be just one hot dish at a funeral and she believed Imogen had gone to fetch it now. The plump aunt said with guilty relish, 'It's a Westphalia ham baked with cloves and honey, I heard.'

'Trust Dilys to hear that,' said a third with affectionate reproval, and this was so ordinary and so mundane an interchange that Dan felt normality trickle back for a moment.

Then Imogen returned and the tension came back into the room. As if she's dragging some kind of dark force field with her, thought Dan. As if we've all moved over the centre of the vortex and it's starting up, ready to suck us all up into its greedy centre . . . Don't be absurd, Daniel. Yes, but there's something very odd here.

Imogen was carrying a large oval dish with a domed silver cover over its contents. She set it down on the long table that had held the canapés and the ice-cooler, and then glanced across to her father with a cautious smile. She's looking at him for approval, thought Dan. She's half proud of having had a hand in whatever's in the dish – Aunt Dilys's baked ham? – but half guilty at being pleased about anything on an occasion like this. An absolutely normal emotion.

And then Imogen lifted the lid of the dish.

Dan felt at first as if he had received a sharp blow across his eyes, and he could not make sense of what he was seeing. He felt as if every one of his senses had been dislocated, and there was a rushing sound in his ears – the vortex again? – and then everything clicked back into place and his mind ran properly on its tracks once more.

At first he thought that what he was seeing was simply an insufficiently cooked piece of meat, but in the next heartbeat he knew it was nothing of the kind. He forced his mind to pin down the skittering fragments of thoughts. You're a writer, a recorder of emotions and events. Kick your mind back on course and bloody record, then.

At the centre of the dish carried in with guilty pride by Imogen Ingram, its ragged neck jammed hard down on to the spikes, its dead, staring eyes glazed and hoar-rimmed, was the head of a young man with golden hair.

Dan stared at it in horrified disbelief, his mind seething and his stomach churning. The head of Edmund Caudle, served up at his own funeral. It's the funeral baked meats, set before the king, he thought wildly. But the king's going to reject them; in fact from the look of him he's not only going to reject them, he's going to consign the cook to the dungeons and bellow 'Off with her head' into the bargain – oh God, no, not that. It sounds as if somebody's being sick in the corner by the window; I'm not surprised. I hope whoever it is managed to miss the Sheraton desk.

People were getting to their feet, overturning chairs, and someone was screaming, and someone else was saying crossly, 'For the love of God, one of you take Eloise out. And bring a bucket and mop.' Even at such a moment Dan registered that the Lily Maid was swooning decoratively, thus abrogating all responsibility for the terrible thing on the table. Dan finally managed to look at it again. It was still where Imogen had placed it. Well, did you expect it to move? demanded his inner voice. Maybe you thought the poor dead thing might start shuffling itself to the table's edge— If I start thinking like that I shall join whoever's throwing up on the Sheraton.

Two of the aunts – Dilys again and a thin, pointy-faced one with her – had gone to Thalia Caudle's side, but she shook them off. She was staring at Imogen, her eyes like black, fathomless pits, and the two aunts exchanged hesitant looks. Thalia looked like someone who had just taken a skewer in the heart. But she was still on her feet. Dan registered this with a refocusing of attention. This one's taking it on the chin.

A terrible silence had fallen, and every head had turned to Imogen. She was still standing by the table, her face white with shock, and even from where he stood Dan could see how her eyes had dilated with fear and bewilderment. Dan glanced quickly around the room. Everyone was looking at Imogen and on every face was shock. On most was accusation. They all think she's done it, thought Dan, and now his writer's mind was engaging top gear, recording everything. They think she somehow got into the mortuary or the Chapel of Rest and stole the head. They think she's mad – oh, hell's teeth, yes, *of course*! They think she's mad in the way those other women in the family were mad, the one who was supposed to have murdered her lover, and Lucienne, who chopped off her brother's prick. Only this one's chopped off her cousin's head. For God's sake, aren't any of them going to help her? He looked across to Royston Ingram; Ingram's face was an unhealthy grey colour and the flesh seemed to have fallen away from his bones. One hand was pressed to the left side of his chest, and he was breathing with a struggle. Heart, thought Dan, his own sinking. The princess raving mad, the queen retiring to bed with the vapours, and the king having a coronary.

It was then that he discovered in panic that he had crossed the room, and that he had actually picked up the domed lid. Its underside was faintly smeared with a thick, colourless dampness. Brain juices leaking? Don't be absurd, it's probably condensation from the baked ham! There was a teeth-wincing scrape of metal against metal as the lid clanged over the dreadful thing on the dish, and a sigh of relief went through the room.

Dan put one hand on Imogen's arm. 'I think you should go and lie down, Miss Ingram,' he said, and then realised that he was about to look round and say, is there a doctor in the house? He heard with disbelief that he did say it, and almost at once a voice at his side responded. 'I'll get John Shilling,' said the voice, 'he took Eloise out.' And Dan recognised with thankfulness the same capable, slightly-sharp tones that had ordered somebody to fetch a bucket and mop.

Imogen looked at him with an unfocused stare. She was smaller than she had seemed from across the room and more fragile-boned. Her head was level with Dan's shoulder and she had to look up at him, and this added to her air of helpless vulnerability. She was like someone suddenly rocketed into a deep trance; it was impossible to know if she had heard him, or if she had heard anything, or even if she was aware of what was happening.

He realised with relief that Dr Shilling had come back into the room, and that he was putting an arm about Imogen and guiding her to the door. As she went with him Dan felt something unfamiliar and painful tear at his heart. He wanted to put his arms around her and say, listen, it's all right, Imogen. You didn't do this and nobody really thinks you did. It could not be done. One of the aunts went with them, murmuring something about sedatives and hot water bottles. Dan bit down a sudden wish to go with them, to make sure that Imogen really was all right. As the door closed behind them he turned back to Thalia, and sensed every other person in the room doing the same.

Edmund's mother had not moved. She was standing stock-still, but there was no doubt about the malevolence

17

and the black, bitter hatred. And if we're still talking about force fields, thought Dan, this one's the champion magnet.

When Thalia finally spoke, she did so softly, but every single person heard her.

'It looks as if it's happened again,' said Thalia. 'The thing we've all dreaded. The Ingram madness. Lucienne's madness. Sybilla's.'

Her voice was ordinary and down-to-earth. If she had lifted one hand and pointed like some pantomimic Tragic Muse, if she had cried, *'The mark! She's got it! The mark!'* the horror would have plummeted into melodrama and Dan would probably have washed his hands of the whole affair and made a disgusted exit. But Clytemnestras do not stalk twentieth-century drawing rooms in Hampstead, and tragediennes are trapped and held for ever in the timeless lime-lit oblongs of Victorian stages. Thalia left it at that. When she spoke again, it was to Royston, as directly and as intimately as if they were alone in the room. 'You know, I did warn you,' she said. 'When she was born, I did warn you.'

Dan thought Royston tried to speak and saw him fail, and in the same moment someone on the other side of the room began to cry, and someone else said in a whisper, 'After all their care, after the way they *guarded* her – it's too cruel.'

And then Aunt Dilys's voice, 'Does it mean . . .?'

'I'm afraid it means,' said Thalia, her voice as bleak as a January dawn, 'that she'll have to be put away. For ever.'

It had served the whey-faced bitch right to have everyone in the room staring at her with that horrified disgust.

There had, in fact, almost been a moment when Thalia could have felt sorry for Imogen, but it had vanished instantly, and she had been suddenly and violently glad of the creature's humiliation. The spark of hatred that had flared up when Imogen survived in the car crash and Edmund died, was already blazing up into a consuming passion.

Hatred. Vengeance. Who would have thought it would be

such a fiercely satisfying emotion? Thalia, her mind splintered with agony, her world in tattered fragments, had looked at Imogen after Edmund's death, and thought: you smug cat, why didn't you die instead? It had been then that the cold vicious hatred had ignited, and it had been then that the idea of punishing Imogen – of making sure that Imogen could never enjoy her own heritage – had taken root. There had been a deep and fierce delight in laying plans and weaving toils. Imogen must be punished.

Put away for ever . . . The words had had a satisfying ring, even though she had spoken them so softly. This was something Thalia had learned from the tedious committees and the boring charity groups: that it was not the table-thumpers people took notice of, it was the softly-spoken, the unemphatic. The more laid back people were, the more impact they made. There had been impact in what she had said about Imogen, and there would be impact in what she was going to say to the family in the small room Royston called his study, where everybody was gathering to discuss what must be done.

Royston would not be there, but this did not matter. He had been useless and ineffective when they were both children, and he had been useless and ineffective today. He had seen his cherished daughter publicly exposed as a mad thing and he had not been able to face it, which was why John Shilling had had to give him a shot of something or other. Thalia had pretended to be concerned, but she would not have minded if Royston had been left to die of heart pains there on the floor. Royston and Eloise should be dealt their share of punishment. The strong, satisfying hatred welled up in Thalia again. Neither of them would be able to prevent it.

Eloise would certainly not be at the family discussion. She had taken refuge in one of her ridiculous swoons, with that besotted fool Shilling in attendance. It would be nice to think that Eloise was cheating on Royston with John Shilling, but it was not very likely; she was a cold, frigid bitch. The wonder was that she had ever got into bed with

Royston; the pity was that she had stayed there long enough for Imogen to be conceived. Dr Shilling pampered her invalid whims, of course, which was about all he was good for. He had painstakingly administered sedatives to various people today and he had sent for a mix of soda bicarbonate for Cousin Elspeth who was always sick at the least provocation but who might at least have opened the window and done it on the shrubbery.

And Imogen was going to be shut away. Thalia licked the idea greedily in her mind. It was a good thought; it was a *satisfying* thought. It served Royston and Eloise right for wrapping up the wide-eyed little shrew in cotton wool so that no breath of harm should ever reach her – and so that the Ingram madness should be kept at bay. It served them right for wanting to keep Edmund out of Ingram's Books, and for being patronising about his intelligence. Edmund had been as intelligent as any of the family; in fact he had been more intelligent than most of them put together. It was true that he had not bothered with tedious exams and A levels for university, but this had only been because there were more interesting things for him to do.

Thalia came softly down the back stairway, pausing for a moment on the half-landing. Everything dealt with? Yes. She went quietly through the big kitchen, deserted now. All well in here? Yes again. Now for the family. She took a deep breath and paused before crossing the hall with the black and white chequered floor that some mid-Victorian Ingram had put down, and the Benares brass table that Colonel Ralph Ingram of the India Army had brought back. The family were about to go into conclave, exactly as Ralph and his lady had done over Lucienne, and exactly as Sybilla's parents had done. The motto of Ralph's regiment had been something about protecting your own, which was what the Ingrams had always done anyway. Thalia was not in the least interested in protecting Imogen, but she was very interested indeed in avenging Edmund's death.

Chapter Three

Dan had not managed to get into the conclave; he had not even tried because there was only so far you could get with such a thin disguise. He had been unchallenged at the wake but he would certainly have been unmasked at a serious family discussion.

He left the house quietly and inconspicuously, and went back to his flat in Belsize Park where he sat at his desk for a long time, staring out of the window, scanning the mental notes he had made.

What had happened today was something that defied reporting. Dan tried out a few phrases. 'The funeral service of Edmund Caudle, heir apparent to Ingram's Books, took place today, and was . . .' Was what? Marred by the appearance of the deceased's severed, refrigerated head among the buffet lunch? Enlivened by the onset of madness in his sixteen-year-old cousin? Dan stared out of his window at the view of the rooftops, and saw again Imogen Ingram's extraordinary beauty and felt again the dark tanglewood web seething just below the surface of that comfortable house. Better, really, to try to forget the whole thing. There were other ways of paying gas bills, for heaven's sake.

He dragged the cover off his typewriter and forced a sheet of paper angrily into the roller. He would have to turn in some kind of report, but he would be wary. Phrases like 'taken suddenly ill' and 'collapsed during lunch' shaped in his mind.

But all the time he was typing, Imogen's face kept coming between him and the text, and somewhere beyond the slick facility of his article he was aware of an idea struggling upwards.

A story – no, dammit, a full-blown novel! – about a girl who was born under, and lived with, some kind of creeping, encroaching danger. A girl who was somehow cursed from birth, and because of it was guarded and protected so that the curse should never materialise but who was eventually and inevitably overtaken by it on her seventeenth birthday. And then was shut into a walled-up castle for a hundred years until she could be woken by a handsome prince's kiss? jeered Dan's mind. Jesus God, Daniel, that's been done a thousand times, ever since Jacob Grimm said to his brother, 'Wilhelm, let us collect up the fairy stories of central Europe and flog the most macabre as children's entertainment.' Ever since Charles Perrault and Basile and a dozen others. Ever since Disney and his brethren took it into the realms of technicolour whimsy and tweeness.

But the idea would not go away. The Ingram family had caught his imagination, and the notion of a book about them had been forming ever since he had entered the Hampstead house. Now the idea of writing it as fiction – a dark, increasingly menacing tale, peopled with thin, haggardly beautiful widows and Lily Maids and indulgent spinster aunts, with Imogen at the heart – forced its way upwards. It was a ridiculous idea, of course, and yet—

No, it could not be done. I'm not listening to you, said Dan to the idea. I don't want to know about you, and I'm going to pretend you're not there.

This worked for a full five minutes, at the end of which Dan swore loudly, tore the sheet of paper out of his typewriter and threw it across the room, and then tipped his chair back to stare out of the window again. The rooftops were shiny with rain and it was getting dark. This was the time of day he liked best. His flat was at the top of an old

Georgian-cum-Regency house; it was what the estate agents called a lateral conversion, spread across the top floors of two adjoining properties so that the rooms were huge and the ceilings high. When dusk started to shroud London, from up here you could see little clusters of lights coming on, and you could see the long, snaking, bead-necklace of car headlights that were the perpetual rush hour on the Finchley Road.

Since the idea would not go away, he took a proper look at it. How viable was it? Blow viability, how sellable was it? Even romantic novelists had to pay gas bills and eat. And his typewriter was practically an antique. The appalling spectre of buying a word processor loomed.

All of this ought to have been daunting but none of it was. Dan did not really care if he wrote it on a typewriter or a word processor, or with a biro and ruled pad, as long as he did write it. How uninterrupted could he hope to be while he wrote it? There would have to be various journalistic commissions – at least, Dan hoped there would be, on account of having to live and eat and pay bills. He thought these could be slotted in. Oliver was coming to stay during the Oxford half-term, but Oliver had never been an interruption to anyone in his life. If Dan explained what he was doing, Oliver would smile the gentle, unworldly smile that probably drove his female students wild, and half the female dons as well, and say how exciting, and wouldn't their father have been pleased, and it was time Dan took a swing at fiction anyway.

I believe I'm going to do it, Dan thought suddenly, and was conscious of rising excitement. It would not be a serious book of course, at least, not in Oliver's meaning, but it would not be lurid pulp fiction either. One would have to avoid certain influences; the shadow of Angela Carter hovered perilously. Dan tipped Ms Carter a nod by way of acknowledgement, and reached for a fresh sheet of paper. At least let's see how it looks. Let's see if we can translate the original legend into modernity.

A girl born not quite into high wealth, which would be a little too sequinned, but born into reasonable affluence . . . Yes. But born under a threat of some kind. A disease? Well, you can hardly make it a spinning wheel and a dark bewitchment at a christening party, but what about making it one of those appalling inherited things? Was it Huntington's disease that lurked in the system and didn't make its presence known until the victim was thirty? Don't be absurd, Daniel, you're not Dostoevsky or Solzhenitsyn; you can't have a heroine crumbling away from some ghastly terminal illness through two or three hundred pages. In any case, you know perfectly well you're going to make the menace inherited madness. Lucienne and Sybilla Ingram, said his mind, with a satisfied nod.

The minute he started to type, the sentences tumbled out of his mind and rattled across the page. They became paragraphs before he knew it, and the paragraphs became full pages. Hardly daring to breathe in case he broke the spell, Dan experienced the indescribable sensation of seeing a huge, immensely exciting landscape start to unfold before him. I'm about to take a journey, and I don't know where it will take me, and I don't know what travelling companions I shall make, or even what kind of bedfellows I might pick up . . . And, said his inner voice, caustically, if you can possibly manage to avoid all the appalling puns about being sent to sleep by a prick and woken up by one as well, you might make something halfway decent out of this.

It was important to get rid of most of the heroine's guardians fairly early on, in order to leave her entirely vulnerable. Dan considered the methods of murder available to him. How close should he go to the original fairy story? Hadn't there been something about the princess's family – or at least her parents – being cast into a bewitched sleep as well? Would it be possible to recreate something along the lines of the sleeping sickness epidemic of the 1920s? Or could he come up with something more sinister?

Some kind of deathlike trance? Catatonia, wasn't it? He would have to get hold of a copy of the story, and from the look of it a shelf-full of medical tomes as well.

But if he was going to deal out murder and mayhem on this scale, the first priority was to create an archvillain – or perhaps villainess . . .

A villainess. Dan felt his lips curve into a smile. He would have a villainess, a greedy, feisty lady who would wear a false face to almost the entire world, a bland, civilised mask that would stay firmly and undetectably in place until the killings began and the reader felt the spine-chilling breath of evil, and began to catch glimpses of the red tooth-and-claw madness beneath the urbane exterior.

But until then, while the archvillainess planned the killings and spun her evil web and discussed the heroine's plight, the mask would remain firmly and undetectably in place and no one would have the least idea of the truth.

How would she set about the murders?

'What's going to happen to her now the madness has finally surfaced?'

Inevitably it was Aunt Dilys who said it, and most of the people in Royston Ingram's study thought she said it against the combined mental opposition of them all.

The aunts huddled together, sipping the hot, sweet tea that Mrs Scullion had brought, which was kind of her. The sprinkling of husbands had opted for large brandies, and Dilys had joined them.

Nobody had any idea of going home. Some kind of decision had to be made, and it had to be made today. There was an unspoken feeling that probably Thalia would take charge; she was so strong-minded and clever, and of course she was accustomed to meetings and decisions because of all her charity work – she worked very hard for several organisations.

Dilys, whose brandy had been a generous double, was moved to observe that the family had been along this road before, at least twice to everyone's certain knowledge, which had the effect of reminding everyone who might conceivably have forgotten about Lucienne and Sybilla. Cousin Elspeth said Dr Shilling ought to be here instead of fawning on Eloise as usual, and where was Flora?

'Flora's with Imogen, I think,' said Dilys. 'I don't know where Thalia is – does anybody know?'

Nobody did. Several people were secretly rather relieved at Thalia's continuing absence, because nobody quite knew how to treat someone whose son's head had somehow been taken from its coffin and placed on a serving dish. She would recover, of course; she was a very strong lady indeed, but she had to be allowed a little time to get over the shock.

Everyone was still shocked, of course, but beneath that emotion was now running a thin line of curiosity about the unknown young man who had gone to Imogen's side so swiftly. Dilys asked wistfully if he might be a boyfriend of Imogen's they had not heard about, but Rosa said this was unlikely, because Royston would not have allowed any boyfriend within miles of the child. In any case, the young man had been nearly thirty from the look of him – far too old for a seventeen-year-old.

Aunt Dilys, whose own youth had included one or two romantic episodes, was heard to murmur mutinously that age had nothing to do with it.

Flora, entering the room in time to hear this last remark, agreed.

Imogen lay on her bed and tried to push away the thick, clouding mists of the sedative administered by Dr Shilling; she must try to make sense of what had happened today.

She thought she should have been warned when she first fetched the dish from the kitchen and found it cold to the touch, almost as if it had just come out of the fridge, or even the freezer. It should not have been cold at all; the ham had been baked with whole cloves and basted with brown sugar and orange juice and honey. She rather enjoyed cooking, and she had timed it all carefully so that it would be ready to serve at the lunch, along with bowls of salad and buttered rolls. The ham had been left in the half-oven while people were eating canapés and drinking sherry, so that it would stay warm but not actually cook any more. Edmund's head, not cooking but keeping warm . . . Oh God, no!

She had made a lemon soufflé as well, and Mrs Scullion, whose son worked in a fish restaurant in Chelsea, had prepared a whole salmon. Concentrating on preparing the food had stopped Imogen from thinking about Edmund and how he must look inside his coffin, and how the coffin was in the ground now. Burial, not cremation, Aunt Thalia had said. She had been unexpectedly insistent about it.

If Edmund had been cremated today's appalling incident could not have happened. Imogen frowned. Was there a clue there? Could they ask the undertakers who had been into the Chapel of Rest before the service? But could anyone – any of the family or friends – really have opened Edmund's coffin and stolen part of his body? Imogen tried to visualise it and failed completely. Only I can't think properly! she cried silently. When I've slept this wretched sedative off, then I'll think. Then I'll try to reason it out.

If she had checked the serving dish before taking it in, it would not have been so dreadfully dramatic. But there had not been time: Aunt Thalia had come in and said to hurry with serving the ham, everyone was waiting. And so Imogen had hurried, and five minutes later everyone had seen what was under the dish's lid.

They had all been very kind afterwards, but they had all avoided looking directly at her. Even Great-Aunt Flora's eyes had slid away as she had helped her into bed and drawn the curtains against the afternoon light, and switched on the electric blanket – 'Just for a few minutes. Just to help the shock.'

She thinks I'm suffering from shock, thought Imogen. I expect I am. But that's no reason for them to avoid looking at me.

The only one who had not done so was the unknown young man. He had looked at her very directly; in fact he had looked at her as soon as he came into the room. Imogen had been strongly aware of it, and she had wondered who he was. He was rather good-looking, in a dark, damn-your-eyes kind of way. If it was possible to imagine meeting Heathcliff or Mr Rochester at a family funeral, he would fit the part very well indeed. Only you would not meet either of those two at a family funeral; in fact if you lived in this house, you would not meet *anybody*. But he had been rather nice, the dark young man, and he ought to be thanked for coming to help her while the others had been standing about, staring in shocked horror. She would try to find out who he was – Aunt Flora might know – and send him a little note. Was writing polite thank yous to strangers acceptable? Imogen thought it would be more acceptable than telephoning. People at school had giggled over the sending of Valentine cards to boys, or the making of phone calls asking boys to parties or discos, but Imogen had never done it because she never met any boys to do it to. She had been invited to parties over the years, but Mother had a way of suffering migraines or vague nerve attacks on the afternoon of the party, and Father or Dr Shilling generally ended up asking Imogen to stay in – 'Just this once,' Father would say. 'She likes to have you here.' Dr Shilling would say that after all, there would be other parties. It was not asking so very much.

It was not asking much at all, but the trouble was that it had not been 'just this once', and in the end there had not been other parties because people had stopped asking her. You could not blame them. You could not really argue against somebody's illness either, not when the somebody was your own mother, not when she had a habit of clutching your hands and crying and asking you not to leave her while she felt so dreadfully ill, and saying awkward things about being grateful. Dr Shilling had hinted once that Mother's delicate health might deteriorate and Imogen had instantly had visions of nightmare things like multiple sclerosis or cancer. You could not insist on going out to parties when your mother might be dying of cancer, even when it started to be obvious that she never got any worse. It was not something you could very well question, but Imogen had begun guiltily to wonder if she would end up like some ghastly Victorian spinster whom everyone whispered about rather pityingly – 'Poor Gladys, such a waste of a life . . . Never married because of her mother, you know . . .'

Dr Shilling's sedative must have been stronger than she had realised; she was starting to slide down into sleep, which had better be resisted because of what might be waiting on the other side. Edmund might be waiting; what was worse, it might not be Edmund as he had been when he was alive but Edmund as he had looked after he died – squashed and bloody, grotesquely twisted . . . headless . . . grinning from the silver platter between the potato salad and the cheese board, his dead eyes glazed like those of the salmon . . .

It was getting dark and wintry outside, but in here it was very warm. Mother could not bear to be too cold. 'I'm afraid I'm rather a chilly mortal,' she said when everyone else was scarlet-cheeked from the blast of the heating. 'I have to be watchful of my health.' It was disloyal to think that Mother made sure that everyone else was watchful of it as well. Imogen did think it, and then felt guilty all over again.

The ivy that grew outside was tapping against the window, as if it might be twining itself over the panes of glass. It was normally rather a friendly sound, but this afternoon, with darkness closing down, it was vaguely threatening. Like something trying to get in. Like something tapping out Morse. Let me in, my dear, let me in . . .

Imogen's eyelids were growing heavy, a great weight was pressing down on her, and her heart was beating in exact time with the let-me-in tapping. It was necessary to stay awake to avoid meeting Edmund in a nightmare, and it was necessary to stay aware in case the let-me-in creature got in . . . Or was it in already?

It was necessary to fight the sedative and stay alert in order to work out why everyone had treated her so oddly after that appalling event at lunch.

Chapter Four

Dr John Shilling thought he had handled matters rather well on the whole. It had been a nasty business – how on earth had Imogen managed it? – and it had been a delicate business as well. But he thought he had dealt with everything pretty well.

Royston was resting in bed – this was his third or fourth attack of angina pectoris and John had given propranolol along with a mild sedative. There was no undue cause for alarm, and no indications of any myocardial infarction. But just to be sure he would arrange for an angiograph.

Eloise, whose constitution was so exceedingly fragile, had taken a double measure of the phenobarbital John had prescribed last month for her insomnia. He had himself shaken out two of the tablets from the prescription bottle, and Thalia had gone down to the kitchen for the mineral water Eloise preferred for swallowing pills. John had seen Thalia's slightly curled lip at the request. Of course, none of the family really understood how extremely delicate Eloise was. John had never discussed it with the Ingrams; he liked to think of it as a small but perfectly permissible bond between himself and Eloise. Any bond of a more substantial nature was naturally unthinkable, even though it did not stop him thinking about it from time to time. He hoped he would never actually do anything about it and he thought he would not because he did not really want to spoil his vision of Eloise as a pale, untouchable creature. Also, the GMC were inclined to be severe about that kind of thing.

He allowed himself another brandy; he was not on call this evening, and someone could drive him home later or he could call a taxi. It had been suggested that he might stay on to supper and he dwelled pleasurably on this. It was likely that the family would all have left by then, and if Eloise had slept off the phenobarbital, which was probable, she might join him in the dining room. Just the two of them together . . . There was a scenario to fuel a man's fantasies. John Shilling's view of Eloise as delicate and fragile did not prevent some of his fantasies about her from becoming extremely explicit.

It was very warm here in the sitting room – Eloise could not bear the cold, poor darling – and his eyelids were feeling heavy. As well as the brandy there had been an excellent Traminer at lunch; he remembered that he had accounted for at least a bottle of it. His thoughts roamed silkily in certain forbidden realms.

On the outer rim of consciousness he could hear the murmur of voices from the study. The family in conclave, presumably. It was nice of them to rally round Thalia so staunchly. They would probably close ranks about Imogen's macabre behaviour as well, which was one mercy. John tried to think whether Imogen had actually committed an indictable offence, and what was going to be done about it. The idea of Eloise's daughter being publicly punished was unthinkable. But probably something could be worked out – the Ingrams were amazingly loyal. John Shilling's practice was an old family one; his grandfather had actually been summoned on the terrible day that Lucienne Ingram had taken the meat axe to her brother. He had helped the family to cover up the facts then, just as John himself would probably help to cover them up now. Presently he would tidy himself up, sluice his face and hands and comb his hair in readiness for that little supper . . .

He was almost, but not quite, over the boundaries of sleep – the room so warm, the brandy so seductively smooth – and he was allowing himself a brief, delicious daydream in which

Eloise Ingram received him in a clinging silk gown and nothing else, and permitted certain preliminary intimacies. There was a gratifying flicker between his legs – have to quench *that* before supper! – and he was just thinking he would look to see what time it was when there was a crash and a scream from somewhere upstairs.

John was rudely jerked out of his half-romantic, half-lascivious doze. He leapt instinctively to his feet, and there was a moment of sudden sick dizziness. He grasped the mantel to steady himself –that last double brandy! – and turned to the door. Someone was running sobbingly down the stairs and coming across the hall. Whoever it was was panting with unaccustomed exertion or fear, and somewhere on the other side of the house somebody was shouting something.

The door to the warm sitting room was flung open and Aunt Dilys stood there, her face doughy white.

'Dr Shilling, praise God you're still here. Please will you come at once.'

Royston, thought John, fumbling on the floor for his medical bag, remembering it was outside in the hall. Myocardial infarct after all, blast it! He crossed the room and caught irritated sight of his reflection in the wall mirror. He was flushed and pouchy-eyed from drowsiness and befuddled-looking from alcohol. Not good for Eloise to see him like this, not good at all. Still, no time to think about that. Got to get to Royston, poor old chap, see what's to be done. He found his case and made for the upper floors, almost colliding with Thalia on the half-landing.

'What the devil's happening? Is it Royston?' He sounded just surprised enough to cover any faint slurring.

Thalia clutched his arm. 'Oh God, John, it's appalling. I didn't think she was capable of— And there's nothing to be done for either of them, absolutely nothing. But you'd better see it for yourself.' She led the way to the large double room at the house's rear.

As John stood in the doorway of Royston Ingram's room, he had the confused impression that he was standing on the threshold of a stage set. The warm coppery stench of fresh blood filled the room, and there was a dull malevolent light as well, a red, smeary light . . . He blinked and forced his mind to focus.

Royston Ingram lay on the big double bed, Eloise beside him. Her skin was the colour of cold pale marble, but the marble was streaked with red where the blood had soaked into her ivory silk robe. Stabbed? When? By whom?

As he bent over the bed, John had the really appalling thought that it was not ten minutes since he had been visualising her in just such a robe – clinging and sensuous – leaning over a table, pouring a cool wine into his glass . . . Sickness rose unforgivably in his throat, and he swallowed hard and forced himself to take note of everything.

On the side table, near to Eloise's hand, was a small cut-glass tumbler, and John thought: the mineral water for the phenobarbital. The double measure I told her to take. Had it been sufficient to render her unaware while this – this *butchery* was happening? The terrible poignancy of it struck him like a blow – the last thing I did for her!

From the look of Eloise she was certainly dead, but John had to make sure; above all, he had to behave profession-ally. He noticed that a thin sheet had been drawn up over the lower half of the bodies.

Royston's skin was faintly blue-tinged, and there was a dribble of vomit over his chin. He might well have suffered the infarct before he was attacked, or he might have suffered it while he was being attacked. He was certainly dead; they were both certainly dead. You did not lose blood to this extent and survive. And Royston had been sedated as Eloise had, which meant that neither of them could have put up much of a fight.

John moved unsteadily forward. There were things you had to remember in cases of violent death; you had to remember not to touch things, to determine causation as far as possible until the police surgeon arrived—

Police. The word hit his mind and broke into splinters, and each splinter was etched with a different word. Investigations. Questions. Scandal and gossip. Newspaper reports. His mind was blurred by brandy and wine and numbed with shock, but he could see the headlines very clearly indeed. *Maniacal double murder . . . Publishing mogul dead . . .*

He felt for a pulse at wrist and neck and found none, and he managed to focus a light on to the pupils of both the victims' eyes. Nothing again. He was dimly aware of Thalia explaining about being sure they were both dead but sending Dilys for him anyway.

Of course they were both dead. It was unbearable but it had to be borne. He dare not let himself think of things such as coma states, somatic death . . . His shiningly beautiful Eloise was dead. Stabbed, quite obviously. He thought he said this aloud. 'And I must – examine them. I must find the – the wounds.'

'Yes, of course.'

Examine that body about which ten minutes earlier he had been fantasising. Peel back the thin silk, not in the way he had for years imagined doing, sensuously and intimately, but coldly and clinically, for no purpose other than to expose knife wounds, areas of trauma; to show up mutilations to that flesh around which he had woven those shameful, exciting dreams. His stomach betrayed him in earnest this time, and he had to make a dash for the adjoining bathroom. He hung over the washbasin, retching miserably. Disgusting.

When the spasms finally stopped, the mirror gave him back an appalling reflection. He was grey and blotched with grief and panic, and his eyes were bloodshot.

'I can't make the examination.' He met Thalia's eyes at last. 'I simply can't do it. They're both dead, and they've obviously both been knifed. Or something. Royston probably died from coronary shock.' He looked at Thalia. 'But I

35

can't examine Eloise,' he said. 'You'll have to call in someone else.'

'I understand.'

'It's a job for the police. The coroner—' He stopped short, and then managed to say, 'Who did it? Was it Imogen?'

'Oh yes,' said Thalia very softly. 'Yes, it was Imogen.'

Thalia took a seat behind Royston's desk, and saw at once how everyone turned gratefully towards her, like obedient children waiting to be told what to do. Good. She took a quick mental inventory. Flabby-minded people like Rosa and Dilys and flabby-stomached people like Cousin Elspeth could be dealt with; that besotted fool John Shilling could be dealt with as well, and with far greater ease than Thalia had hoped possible. He had come with her to the study but he had taken a chair a little apart from them all; he was grey-faced with grief and his eyes were slightly unfocused. A faint aroma of brandy clung to him. Good again. He would be no trouble.

The scattering of spouses would be no trouble either; they would do what they were told, just as all Ingram spouses did. This was not a family where females married strong-minded men.

There remained Flora Foy, and Flora might be difficult. She was unpredictable and unconventional, and she had always had that ridiculous preference for Imogen. But even Flora, with her scandalous past and riotous youth, could not deny what had happened today; she would hardly want Imogen to become known as the young woman who had stolen a corpse's head and served it up at its own wake. She would certainly not want the child charged with the murder of her own parents. But she might be a bit of a stumbling block.

The only other stumbling block was that unknown young man who had so unexpectedly taken command and summoned John Shilling to attend to Imogen. Whoever he was – a colleague of Royston's perhaps, or representing some decrepit and distant cousin for the day – he had apparently left the house. This might indicate extreme diplomacy or it might indicate something quite different. He might very well need to be traced and somehow silenced.

She said, 'We can't have any squeamishness about this. We know what's happened, and we know who's responsible for it. And as far as we can, I think we should protect her.' She paused, and then said, 'Royston wanted her to go into a nursing home. After –what happened at lunch. He thought it would be the best thing.'

'How do you know?' That was Flora, of course, her voice sharp.

Thalia met her stare levelly. 'He told me,' she said. 'When I went up to his room with the mineral water for Eloise. In fact,' said Thalia, 'he dictated a letter to me there and then, and signed it. It's here if anyone wants to see it.'

There was a brief silence while everyone absorbed this. Thalia registered with inner irony that every person present was probably dying to see the letter but no one quite liked to ask to do so.

The letter, scrappily written, signed almost blindly, was perfectly in order, and it was a clear and unequivocal indication of Royston's wish. No one had seen Thalia go into Royston's room, and Thalia was not going to tell anyone how she had stood over him and watched his face go greyer and greyer with the heart pain, and listened to him crying with despair and defeat because after all his care Imogen had the taint. She was Lucienne over again, he had said. She was Sybilla reborn. It was unbearable.

He had signed the letter that Thalia had written and put before him, even though he had scarcely known what he was doing. Eloise had certainly not known: she had already been sunk in her sedated stupor, and she was not going to argue against Thalia. Nobody was going to argue against Thalia – she was making very sure of that. It was a good thing that Royston had signed before the pain swamped him

37

and smothered his breathing, and it was even better that he had died so swiftly afterwards. Thalia had been prepared to substitute an ordinary paracetamol tablet for any further drugs that John Shilling might send up, but it had not been necessary.

The letter would reinforce the family's decision. It would endorse it. It was not possible to say that Imogen must be put where she belonged, and the door locked and the key as good as thrown away, but that was what must happen. The bitch who had ousted Edmund, who had stood in his way and might, if Thalia was not careful, even now inherit Ingram's, had to be punished.

'She *must* be put away,' she said aloud. 'Nothing else is thinkable.'

Dilys, who had been crying on and off ever since the appalling thing had been discovered, said, 'But surely . . .' and stopped.

Flora said, 'Are we sure that it was Imogen?'

Thalia was aware of a murmur of agreement. She said at once, 'Who else could it have been? You were all down here in the study. I was in the kitchen—'

'I was in the sitting room,' said John Shilling. 'I heard you all talking. I heard Mrs Foy come down and join you after Mrs Scullion brought in the tray of tea. I think I'd have heard anyone come out and cross the hall to go upstairs.'

'Aren't we overlooking something?' This was Aunt Rosa. 'There were two separate incidents today—'

'I always knew you had a gift for understatement, Rosa,' said Flora. 'I should not, myself, call what happened today *incidents*.'

Rosa said, 'Whatever name you give them, they were both obviously the actions of a sick mind. And I don't know about you, but I find it difficult to believe that two separate members of this family have run mad on the same day.'

'Well, yes,' agreed Flora reluctantly.

'If the Ingram madness – I'm sorry if you don't like the word, Elspeth, but that's what it is – if it's erupted after all this time, it must have been like a – like a simmering volcano finally exploding,' said Aunt Rosa with unconscious eloquence. 'Hurling itself out in several different directions. Doctor?'

'What? Oh yes. Yes, I'm very much afraid you're right. A sudden releasing of restraints. Yes, it would be like a tightly-coiled spring snapping free.' He dredged up a morsel of professionalism and said, 'I gave Imogen a mix of secobarbital. Quite mild. Mrs Foy, you took it up, didn't you?'

'Yes. She drank it, and I left her more or less asleep. Thalia, I'm sorry, but I *can't* believe Imogen is responsible for this.'

Thalia stood up. 'I'd hoped this wouldn't be necessary,' she said to Flora. 'But you'd better come upstairs. John, will you come as well? And George? But the rest of you had better stay here.'

Imogen's room was not quite in darkness, and the curtains had been dragged back from the windows to show the wintry blackness beyond.

Thalia and Flora stood in the doorway with John Shilling just behind them. The bedroom was filled with creeping shadows, and with the dry rustling of the wind in the ivy on the outside wall. It was impossible to avoid thinking that it sounded exactly like dozens of dry, bony hands being rubbed together with evil glee.

The casement window was closed, and the lattice of lead strips that made it rather charming in the daytime cast its silhouette harshly across the bed, like iron bars on a prison floor. Beyond the window, less distinct, was the ghostly outline of an old oak tree, gnarled and twisted, its leafless branches like huge-knuckled hands against the night, lifted, ready to snatch up its prey.

Flora said abruptly, 'I drew the curtains and switched on the bedside lamp. It wasn't really dark outside yet but I thought it would be friendlier for the child. She was tucked into bed and half asleep when I left her.'

John Shilling said, 'Someone's opened the curtains. And someone's switched the light off.'

And someone's lying in bed with blood-dabbled hands and blood-smeared jowls . . .

Imogen was lying amidst the tumbled blankets, sound asleep. Her lashes were dark against her cheeks, and her hair was dishevelled. She looked impossibly young and unbearably innocent. She wore a thin cotton shirt, a rather masculine garment that only emphasised her femininity, and in the shadowy room it was impossible to tell if it was white or cream or pale blue. But across the front were several dark, irregular splashes and the hand that had fallen loosely over the side of the bed was stained with the same dreadful, thick darkness.

Because blood turns black in the moonlight, my dears . . .

Across one cheek was a smear of blood, and John and Flora – the one a slightly drunken and thwarted romantic, the other a practical, shrewd feminist – shared a vivid, sickening picture of Imogen leaning over the drugged bodies of her parents, her hair falling about her face, and pushing it impatiently back with a bloodied hand. Like someone baking and leaving a floury mark without realising, thought Flora.

Thalia said, in a soft voice, 'Do you see there on the floor? Under her hand?'

Just beneath the outflung hand, lying as if it had slipped unnoticed from Imogen's grasp, was a long-bladed kitchen knife – a bread knife or a carving knife. The handle still bore marks of bloodied fingerprints and the blade was covered in blood to the hilt.

Chapter Five

Aunt Dilys could not stop crying. 'She was such a pretty little girl,' she kept saying. 'So lovely. So bright and clever.'

If Dilys – if anyone – was going to become maudlin, it must be nipped in the bud at once. Thalia took the seat behind the desk again, and drew in breath to speak.

She was forestalled. Rosa said briskly, 'Lucienne was beautiful. So, apparently, was Sybilla. She was a Beauty in the days when they gave it a capital B.'

'And,' said a sepulchral voice from the back of the room, 'we all know what *those* two did.'

'Lizzie Borden,' remarked a frivolous cousin who worked in advertising in Bloomsbury, and was told to hush.

'I don't see how you can know about Lucienne when all the photographs were burned,' began Cousin Elspeth querulously.

'Oh, don't latch on to trivialities, Elspeth. The thing is,' said Aunt Rosa, glaring round the room, 'to consider what's to be done. The rest of us don't know the details, and from the look on Flora's face I don't think we want to know, but I take it there's no doubt about the child's guilt?'

'No. Dear God, no. Must have stabbed both of them several times, judging by the amount of blood—'

'The knife lying there in her room, and her own night-gown drenched in gore—'

George and Flora both spoke at once and stopped and begged one another's pardon.

'Didn't either of them struggle?' asked someone. 'Or call out?'

'They were both drugged,' said Thalia. 'Dr Shilling gave them both sedatives.'

John managed to say, 'It's likely that neither of them knew what was happening.'

Aunt Rosa said briskly that this, at least, was one mercy, and looked round the room challengingly. 'I can't speak for everyone,' she said, 'but for myself I don't mind admitting that I think we should consider covering this up if we can. For the sake of everyone here, and for the sake of the child herself.'

Dilys emerged from behind her handkerchief to point out all over again that it would not be the first time they had covered up something dreadful in the family; you could almost say it was history repeating itself, or even nemesis, or the sins of the fathers visiting on the—

'Yes, but look here,' hastily interrupted Cousin Elspeth's husband, who could put up with a good deal but not Aunt Dilys becoming Biblical, 'this is – well, it's murder. We can't connive at murder.'

'Certainly not.'

'Couldn't agree to it for a second.'

'Surprised you even suggested it, Rosa.'

Thalia said, as if the thought had only just occurred to her, 'But you know, it would be the most appalling scandal if the truth ever got out.'

'Oh, I don't think we should let that weigh—'

'Quite right. Duty before inclination.'

'But have you thought,' said Thalia, 'how much damage the truth would do Ingram's? I mean as a business concern? As a *profitable* business concern?'

There was an abrupt silence. This was putting a rather different complexion on matters. All of the aunts had inherited shares in Ingram's from grandfathers or uncles, and all of them enjoyed a modest affluence as a result. Dilys and Rosa were part of several very pleasant little social circles in Battersea, which would not have been possible without their twice-yearly dividends. Elspeth was married to George who was thought to make a reasonably good living out of exporting porcelain, but it was unlikely that he could have run to the very expensive country club in Maidenhead or the delightful cottage in Stratford without his wife's income. The frivolous cousin, whose name was Juliette, dashed around London in an open-top BMW and had a flat near Kensington High Street, both of which were certainly beyond her salary. And even Flora, with the pensions of two dead husbands and the alimony of a third live one, found herself hesitating and remembering such things as season tickets for Glyndebourne and the Royal Ballet, and first-class travel.

She said, rather sharply, 'But even if we agreed, how could we do it? It would mean deceiving undertakers, coroners . . . The – well, the actual wounds would have to be disguised as well. Could we really do all that?'

There was a thoughtful silence. After a moment Thalia said, as if still considering the matter, 'It might be possible. We would have to trust one another absolutely, of course. If we went ahead, there'd have to be no attacks of conscience afterwards.'

'If anyone wants to bow out, they'd better do so now,' said Rosa. 'Just get up and go. No one will think any the worse.'

Juliette murmured, 'Leave now or for ever hold your peace,' and Aunt Dilys said very firmly that they were only *considering* the idea.

Cousin Elspeth's husband, who was as anxious as anyone to avoid a scandal, said, 'But what about all the – well, the practical things? Could they be coped with? It would mean – well, for one thing, it would mean cleaning up the room before the undertakers were let in.'

'They could be taken to another bedroom. Royston and Eloise. And, well, laid out tidily.'

'Could we do that?'

43

'Well, George, we'd have to.'

'So long as nobody expects me to do it.'

As if a signal had been given, everyone stopped talking and stared at one another.

Flora said, in a voice of horror, 'We're talking ourselves into it, aren't we? Listen to us. We aren't asking *if* we're going to do it, we're asking *how*.'

From his slightly removed seat by the window, John Shilling was aware of a remnant of medical integrity nudging him into speech. He said, 'If we do agree to this, and if we can work out a foolproof plan, what about Imogen herself? What would happen to her?'

'She can't be left at large,' said Rosa at once. 'I couldn't agree to that. I hope nobody thought I meant that.'

'I certainly wouldn't agree to it,' said John.

Several people said they could not agree to it either.

'Well, has anyone any suggestions? Flora?'

Flora said, thoughtfully, 'The idea of some kind of private nursing home presents itself. Somewhere discreet and comfortable, but secure.'

'Strict but kind.' This was Aunt Dilys.

'And a longish stay until we are sure – until we have evidence one way or the other as to her state of mind.' Flora looked at them all. 'If necessary, an indefinite stay. I would far rather put her somewhere like that than let the state put her in gaol or Broadmoor.'

'Or somewhere like Thornacre,' whispered Aunt Dilys.

Thornacre. The word dropped into the sudden silence like a deadweight dropping into a black, fathomless pool. Thornacre had never really belonged to the Ingrams but all of them knew its history, both the past and the more immediate. They all knew how the house had been built for Sybilla by the rich mill-owner she had married and how they had eventually been forced to shut her away in one wing of the place with a keeper and bars on the doors. Thornacre had long since passed into the hands of the

Northumbrian authorities, but the name still brought a shiver of horror to most of the family. It was like having a bruise that never quite healed so that it hurt if someone pressed it. It had hurt last month when Thornacre had been on the national news, one of the mental homes investigated by the Rackham Commission.

Rosa was the first to speak. She said, very briskly, 'Look here, wherever we put her, whatever Royston wanted or didn't want, there's still the matter of the death certificates.' She looked challengingly around the room. 'Has anyone thought about that?'

Every eye turned to John Shilling, and as if the words were being scraped out of him, he said, 'Royston had been suffering from angina pectoris. An infarct – that's a coronary thrombosis –wouldn't be unexpected. It might even have been the actual cause. And his medical records would be consistent with that verdict. Yes, I could sign a certificate to that effect, and with reasonable honesty.'

'And Eloise?'

Eloise . . . For the first time, John realised that he was something of a linchpin in this bizarre situation, and the knowledge steadied him slightly. 'That's a bit different,' he said. 'Unless a doctor's been in attendance for the fourteen days immediately prior to death, a certificate can't be given and the coroner has to be informed.' He paused. 'I was treating Eloise for several minor illnesses but none of them were consistent with – with sudden death.'

'Ah. A pity.'

'It would mean tampering with existing medical records, making out a false death certificate. If I was caught, I would unquestionably be struck off. I would probably be imprisoned for several years.' The enormity of it showed briefly in his eyes. 'I oughtn't to be even having this conversation . . .'

'But the very fact that you are . . .' Thalia let the sentence remain unfinished.

'If ever there was talk, if ever an exhumation was called for—'

'Can't that be got around by having them cremated?' asked George.

'Oh no, that's out of the question. For cremation, two signatures are needed on the death certificate.'

'We can't risk that,' said Rosa at once.

'We're asking too much of you,' put in Aunt Dilys. 'Yes, of course we are.'

Asking too much of him . . . John Shilling stared round the room.

After a moment, Thalia said gently, 'It would save Imogen, John. It would save Eloise's daughter from an almost certain life sentence as well, if not in gaol, then in Broadmoor.'

'Or Thornacre,' said Dilys.

'Oh, I don't think we should even consider that as a possibility,' said Rosa. 'And anyway—'

'Lucienne was put in Thornacre, wasn't she?' asked Cousin Elspeth.

'Yes, she was actually,' said Thalia. 'I think it was privately funded in those days. Pre-NHS and welfare state, of course.'

Juliette asked if Thornacre was going to be allowed to continue as an asylum after the findings of the Rackham Commission, and was rather glad that she had thought of a word other than madhouse.

'Yes, I think so,' said Thalia.

'Well, I'm very surprised to hear that,' put in Aunt Dilys, 'after all the scandal. A nightmare place, they called it. The attendants used to lock the troublesome patients into the old outbuildings so that they couldn't hear them screaming. Wash houses and sheds. And there was a really bleak part which was once the workhouse in eighteen fifty-something – they put the really difficult ones in there and left them for days with only a trough of water and no proper sanitation or anything. And to think that Lucienne was once—'

'Dilys, it would have been very different in Lucienne's time,' Thalia pointed out.

'Is it National Health Service now?' asked George, and hoped this did not sound as mercenary as he feared.

'Oh yes.'

It was at this point that John Shilling suddenly saw that although he had never been of much service to Eloise during her life, he could be of service to her now. He could save his untouchable and untouched lady from the prurient curiosity of the world, and in the process he might save her daughter as well. Gaol or Broadmoor. Or Thornacre. Dear God, Aunt Dilys was right about that. Wherever else Imogen went, she must not go to Thornacre. Royston would not have wanted it, and Eloise, so fastidious, so *private*, would not have wanted it either.

Within John Shilling's slightly sottish, slightly self-indulgent soul, an impulse reared up that was almost entirely selfless, and very nearly akin to medieval knight-errantry. He would do it. If he could not risk a bit of discomfort for Eloise, it made his devotion seem a very threadbare emotion indeed. His mind began riffling through acceptable causes of unexpected death. Pericarditis? Viral pneumonia? No, there had been that massive effusion of blood, that ought to be taken into account; it ought almost to be made use of. What about perforation of a stomach ulcer?

Clearing his throat to get their attention, he said, 'I'll do what you want. I think I see a way.'

Every head turned to him. 'You will?' This was Flora.

'What will you do?' asked Rosa.

'How will you do it?' demanded George.

John said, 'If I were to give the cause of death as a perforated stomach ulcer—'

'But Eloise never had a twinge even of indigestion in her life!' exclaimed Rosa.

47

'Do be quiet, Rosa,' said Thalia. 'Let him finish. Go on, Dr Shilling.'

John said, 'It will mean making several fictitious entries on Eloise's medical records.' The word 'fictitious' pleased him; it sounded better than false. He went on more easily, 'There would have to be several entries, some history of pain after eating. Even bouts of vomiting.' He paused, thinking hard. A trial prescription for something like Lo-Sec would have to show on the records as well, and maybe a note to consider a gastroscopy.

'Would you make such entries?' asked Thalia.

'Yes,' said John, surprised to hear his voice sounding so positive.

Cousin Elspeth wanted to know if that in itself mightn't look suspicious to somebody somewhere. 'Things written in or crossed out on a card—'

'Elspeth, darling, everything's on computer these days,' said Juliette. And then, suddenly doubtful, 'Isn't it?'

'Oh yes.' This had been in John's mind while forming the plan. 'Yes, I would only have to call up Eloise's file and key in several extra entries. A couple of consultations, backdated, of course. I don't think anyone could possibly tell that they had been added later.'

'Or if they could, you would only have to say you were updating the disk from a handwritten memo,' said George.

'Exactly.'

'And you're prepared to do that?' asked Rosa.

'Yes. Yes, I am.' And he thought: for you, my lady, my love, I'm prepared to do it.

Rosa said, 'Why a stomach ulcer? Why not a heart attack, like Royston?'

John took a moment to reply, and then said, carefully, as if sorting his own thoughts, 'Because of the blood. Several of you saw it. And it's possible that however scrupulous the cleaning-up process, traces will remain. We should allow for the possibility of an inquiry – a thorough police search that might pick those traces up. Also, if the truth did get out, it would be better if I had given you a credible reason for Eloise's sudden death, taking the haemorrhage into account.' He paused, and then said, 'Supposing I told you here and now that Eloise had a stomach ulcer that perforated and caused the haemorrhage, would you find it believable?'

'Well, yes.'

'There you are then. If the worst happened, you could all appear entirely innocent.'

'You couldn't, though,' Rosa said bluntly.

'No, but I could say I believed that Eloise had committed suicide and that I falsified the certificate to save the family further distress.'

'You could say she stabbed herself?'

'I think so. I could say the knife was found by her bed, and that suicide was the only believable explanation.'

There was a silence while the suggestion was considered.

Rosa said, 'I don't much like the idea of a suicide, but—'

'But that's only if it ever comes out, Rosa,' Thalia pointed out, 'which it won't. We're covering all the pitfalls.'

'But supposing it did come out,' persisted Rosa, 'what reason would Eloise have had for suicide?'

John said, 'Oh, Royston's death.'

'Ah. Yes, of course.' Elspeth's husband George felt it was time that the family took back the reins on this. He said, 'Shilling, I wonder if you'd give us a minute, just to discuss . . .'

'Of course.'

As John went out, the family went into little huddles. George said to Elspeth that it was a credible plan; there was the business of the blood, after all, you could not escape that, and Elspeth shuddered and wished George would not talk about blood when people were still feeling sick. 'The fellow's covering his back, of course,' added George, 'in case the thing goes wrong.'

'You can't blame him for that.'

'And if it does go wrong, he's the one who'll suffer most,' said Juliette sagely. 'I think he's being rather heroic.'

Aunt Dilys did not think a stomach ulcer was the kind of thing Eloise would have wanted to die from. 'Indelicate, you know.'

Aunt Rosa said it could hardly make any difference and the important thing here was protecting Imogen. 'I say we agree to Dr Shilling's proposal,' she said, raising her voice. 'If he'll be good enough to do it, I think we should trust his judgement on the medical details. Thalia? Flora?'

Thalia nodded. 'I agree.'

'Yes,' said Flora after a moment.

'Everyone? Good. Then we'll call him back and tell him—'

'Before we do,' Thalia said, 'there's the question of Imogen. I think we should settle that between ourselves.'

'Quite right, keep it in the family.' This was George.

'Somebody suggested a nursing home,' remembered Aunt Dilys. 'Flora, wasn't it you?'

'Yes, but I haven't got as far as thinking of an actual place.'

'I have,' said Thalia. 'I believe I know someone who might help. Someone I met through one of the committees. He's actually on the Rackham Commission, but I think he has a connection with Briar House.'

The relief at not hearing the terrible name Thornacre again was so great that people relaxed for the first time for several hours, and Aunt Dilys, voluble with relief, leaned forward and asked was that the place on the outskirts of Hampstead to the north. 'A huge grey Victorian building, rather ugly, but with very nice grounds?'

'Yes, that's it. I think it's the kind of place Royston meant.'

'Well, that doesn't sound too bad,' said Dilys, looking round the room for approval, and several people nodded cautiously. Cousin Elspeth knew someone who knew some-one whose brother – or perhaps it had been an uncle . . . Anyway, Briar House had certainly been spoken of with approval. Expressions like 'nervous exhaustion' and 'emotional fatigue' began to be bandied about, and Dilys's voice rose above the rest, insisting that it was important that Imogen was put somewhere *kind*.

Thalia said drily, 'Did you think I meant us to shut the child away in some bleak Victorian institution? Do you think Royston and Eloise would have wanted that?'

'Dear me, *no*,' chorused the aunts, shocked to their toes. Juliette wanted to know how they were to silence Mrs Scullion. Were they simply going to hope for a devoted family retainer, or should something be worked out?

They went into little huddles all over again, working out details of this aspect, reminding one another that Mrs Scullion had left the house before the appalling discovery was made, and Juliette was heard to say it was rather like constructing a country house murder mystery. Flora took the opportunity to ask about Thalia's connection with Briar House.

'I heard of it through someone I met on the fund-raising committee for the Students' Counselling Service,' said Thalia, and several people nodded, because this was the kind of thing that Thalia, dear, hard-working creature, had been involved with for several years. She had met some interesting people through her work and she was kindness itself to the younger people with problems. She had even been known to take one or two of the young men out to dinner at quite expensive places. She could easily afford it, but that was not the point.

Flora asked bluntly, 'Who is the person you know?'

'I don't suppose you've met him, but you might have heard of him.' Thalia paused. 'It's Leo Sterne.'

There was an abrupt silence; even Juliette was halted in her dissertation on how Mrs Scullion could be coped with.

At last Aunt Dilys, stammering a bit, said, 'But . . . Oh, Thalia, you surely aren't suggesting that someone like that would be the right kind of person . . .'

'He was in all the papers last year,' said Aunt Rosa. 'I remember it very well. A patient accused Dr Sterne of – dear me, well, of seduction while under hypnosis. There was a very public case about it.'

A murmur of unease, in which the words 'malpractice' and 'charlatan' were discernible, went through the room. Cousin Elspeth's husband said crossly that it was all nonsense, Sterne had been completely exonerated, and it had plainly been a case of wishful thinking on the part of some silly hysterical female and sensationalism on the part of the tabloid press.

Juliette remembered that Dr Sterne had looked rather intriguing, but nobody paid this much attention because Juliette often considered the most unsuitable people intriguing.

Cousin Elspeth thought there must be a grain of truth in the story; you did not get smoke without fire, and newspapers would not dare print things that were not true (even though George said they were the worst liars out), and several of the papers had related how Dr Sterne had seduced somebody he shouldn't – the *Sun* had said there had been several somebodies and had dubbed Dr Sterne a pirate, not that she read the *Sun*, but George liked it for the gardening notes – 'Well, that's what you always say, George' – and anyhow, there had been a great to-do about it all.

Aunt Dilys, who had been listening to all this in silence, now recovered her equilibrium and with it her voice, and said firmly, 'Well, wherever Imogen goes, it's clear that she can't go to Thornacre. And I think that Briar House sounds all right.' She glared defiantly round the room.

Thalia felt a deep surge of triumph. Right into my hands! Dilys is playing right into my hands!

But her face gave nothing away, and when she spoke her voice was low and tinged with sadness. She said, 'Then if we are all agreed?'

'I suppose we are,' said Flora, slowly.

'With or without the fascinating Dr Sterne?' demanded Juliette.

'Without for preference. But that isn't the issue,' said Aunt Rosa, repressively. 'Don't be frivolous, Juliette.'

'What does everyone else think?' Thalia looked round the room. 'Rosa? Elspeth? George – everyone?'

There was a brief pause while people considered, and then one by one, heads were nodded, and murmurs of, 'best thing in the circumstances', and, 'not really so very bad', were heard.

Thalia said, 'Then Briar House it is.'

As she went from the room, the triumph was surging up afresh. She thought: Briar House, my usurping little bitch! And I'll make very sure that you don't come out for a very long time!

Chapter Six

Thalia waited until everyone had left before going back to the large double bedroom.

Edmund was with her, as he had been almost all along. There had been a brief time just after the crash when she thought he had left her for good, and it had been the blackest, most bitter time imaginable because without Edmund, there was nothing in the world anywhere, ever.

The thing that had lain inside the coffin in the under-takers' Chapel of Rest had not been Edmund, not properly. The undertakers had done what they could with the torn, mutilated body and with the ruined face, and Edmund had looked beautiful and golden and serene when Thalia went in alone for the final viewing. But it had been a sham, a deliberate deceit, like painting over a decaying old house to give it a spurious appearance of soundness. Edmund had been painted over to give his tattered flesh the appearance of health and life, but beneath it he was mutilated and terrible.

She remembered how she had asked the undertakers if they would allow her a final farewell to Edmund before the funeral. The closing of the coffin . . .? she had said. Would they allow it to be her hands that did that? Was that possible – could they indulge her? It would be her final service to her son; afterwards she would not trouble them again. Put like that, who could have refused?

She had not been refused; she had been permitted her half hour in the Chapel of Rest, and she had knelt to ask Edmund's forgiveness for what she was doing, for the gross thing she was doing to his poor dead body . . . But it was for the great punishment for the pampered creature who had lived on instead of dying in Edmund's place; it was the start of their retribution against Imogen – hers and Edmund's.

Bitter anger engulfed Thalia when she remembered how she had prayed later for Edmund's return, railing at the dark forces that ordered such things to reverse death and give back her boy, even if it was only in dreams. She could pinpoint the exact minute when she knew it had happened; there had been a smudge of movement on the edge of her vision and then a deepening awareness. Her heart had skipped a beat, and the blood had begun to sing in her veins, because he had come back to her, her beloved boy had come back, and even though he trailed with him the stench of the graveyard, to Thalia it was sweeter than all the perfumes of the merchant. But as the blurred silhouette came more sharply into focus – a little more each time she saw him – she had gradually seen that those dark forces she had beseeched and besieged had played the cruellest trick of all on her. They had given her the dreams, but they were waking dreams, terrible living nightmares. Edmund had come back, not as his golden self but as he had been at the end: the torn tortured thing who had died in that twisted mass of metal and bone and blood. When he stood before her his flesh hung in bloody tatters, and his face – oh God, Edmund's sweet, beloved face . . .

The simmering hatred of the pampered bitch-creature had boiled over in a huge scalding wave then, burning into Thalia's mind, etching the idea of retribution and punishment into her heart. Punishment for the whey-faced brat who would grow up in Edmund's stead, whole and unflawed, and who might one day have Ingram's, lock, stock and barrel.

Never! thought Thalia grimly. She would turn the tables on Imogen, and she would turn the tables on the cheating forces who had tricked her so viciously. Edmund *would* come back – he would come back and he would come back whole and beautiful and golden! It was then that she had become aware of something lying serpentlike in the darkest, most secret corners of her mind . . . Something that had been there for a very long time, and that was only now slithering and uncoiling into life. To bring Edmund back . . . That would be the sweetest, most comprehensive revenge of all . . .

She went stealthily into the large, first-floor bedroom. She had told the family that she would cope with what was in this room on her own and so she would. She would ask for help presently, she said; in the morning she would be very glad indeed of people to help with the burning of sheets and nightclothes. The family had shuddered as one person, and had reminded one another of Thalia's work on hospital committees; at one time she had even helped in the local Casualty Department – which you now had to call Accident and Emergency – one of several volunteers who helped frightened or bewildered patients to complete forms, or explained about claims for street injuries, or how to find their way to X-ray. She would have seen some extremely unpleasant sights there. Elspeth's husband, George, put forward the theory that some people were less affected than others by these things. Everyone agreed that it was amazingly brave of Thalia to cope on her own.

None of them knew that she was not really on her own. When she entered the shadowed room with its smothering stench of blood, Edmund entered it at her side, pointing out what had to be done.

Thalia threw open the windows, letting in the sweet night air. It was very late; she caught the distant chiming of a church clock. Two a.m. The smallest of the small hours. The time when graveyards yawned and gave forth their wormy dead. When midnight's arch loomed dark and forbidding over the world, and when you could not be sure that eyes did not peer at you from out of the shadows . . .

There was no time to waste on imaginings, and no emotion to spare for being squeamish. The room had to be set to rights before breakfast time and what was in it had to be put into the semblance of normality. And it was important to be very quiet and very quick; Imogen was sleeping her drugged sleep along the landing. It was vital not to alert her. She closed the curtains and switched on the main ceiling lights to chase back the shadows, and then went to work.

She had brought up one of Mrs Scullion's aprons – it went round her thin figure twice, and it could be burned afterwards if necessary – and two pairs of rubber gloves. It was not particularly difficult to strip the bedclothes and bundle them into a large plastic bin liner for the garden bonfire, and it was no more difficult to remove Royston's pyjamas and Eloise's nightgown. She added them to the plastic bag, and then stood looking down at the naked bodies. Royston had become flabby and slightly paunchy of late – that was something the well-cut suits had concealed. Eloise's neck – treacherous area! – was crêpey and dry and her breasts sagged emptily. A pity John Shilling could not see her like this!

Edmund was with her as she sponged the blood painstakingly away, fetching warm water from the bathroom, replacing it several times, and finally tipping it down the lavatory. The sponge and flannels and towels could be burned with the rest of the soiled things.

The blood had been very convincing indeed. Thalia had not been in the least surprised at how thoroughly the family and John Shilling had been fooled by it. They had been fooled because it had all been carefully planned and efficiently worked out, and because Thalia herself had carried every part of it through with panache. It had been absurdly easy – even obtaining the blood had been easy. And it had *worked*! The fools had seen the blood puddling on the bed and they had made the obvious deduction that it was Eloise's blood and Royston's. They had seen the stained knife at the side of Imogen's bed, and they had assumed that Imogen had stabbed her parents. And in the rush to protect Imogen, no one had questioned any farther. Not even that doting fool John Shilling had actually examined the bodies.

Thalia made a final check before locking the door. Everything cleaned that needed cleaning? Everything put out for burning that was blood-stained? Yes. Royston and Eloise were now dressed in fresh night things – blue pyjamas and lace-trimmed nightgown – and at first light John Shilling would come, and between them they would transfer the two bodies to the best spare bedroom and arrange them for the undertaker.

One final thing remained to be done, and that was to remove the cut-glass tumbler that had stayed so innocently on Eloise's bedside table. In view of the way the family had come to a decision – in view of the way that Thalia had nudged them into the decision she had wanted – it was not very likely that any awkward tests would be made. But a thin smear of fluid remained in the bottom of the glass, quite sufficient to reveal that the glass had contained not innocuous mineral water at all, but a hefty mix of chloral hydrate and brandy. Eloise had been so busy with her die-away, I'm-not-strong-enough-for-all-this act, that she had hardly noticed the brandy. She had downed the draught in one go while Thalia watched.

She scooped up the glass. It would be smashed and the fragments consigned to the dustbin. If anyone noticed the set was incomplete, it would be a case of, 'One of the crystal tumblers broken? Oh, what a shame, they are so difficult to match.' But it might be months before it was spotted, and no one would think twice about it, just as Eloise had not thought twice about drinking from it. The poisoned cup.

Thalia turned the light off and at once the shadows pounced forward, blurred and menacing. Edmund was there as well, and there was a moment when she saw him, faint but recognisable, the blurred outline bending greedily over the two still forms on the bed.

It was then that Thalia saw the thing she had been watching for and hoping for ever since she entered the room. From beneath the sheet that covered Eloise came a faint breath and then a tiny flicker of movement. Thalia waited, absolutely motionless, and with heart-stopping slowness Eloise's hand slid from beneath the sheet and dropped to the floor, the fingertips brushing the carpet. For three heartbeats the blueish vein at the wrist fluttered perceptibly, as if somewhere beneath the surface something was still struggling for life.

Deep, strong triumph welled up in Thalia's mind, and for a moment the dressing-table mirror gave back a startling reflection: her own face, but sharper, crueller, thinner. As if a mask had been clapped over her everyday features. Or as if the everyday mask had been removed to show the glaring madness beneath.

Chloral hydrate had not been the ideal drug but she had had to take what she could out of John Shilling's case, and he tended to be a bit old-fashioned. She had measured the dose carefully: enough to plunge Eloise into a coma but not enough to cause death. If John had made a more detailed examination the plan would not have worked, but he had not. He had reacted exactly as Thalia had thought he would react. It was deeply satisfying to know you could gauge people's behaviour so accurately.

She crossed back to the bed and tucked the errant hand beneath the covers. It was flaccid and still now, but for a few seconds there had been a threadlike pulse. Thalia smiled. Exactly and precisely as she had hoped. It seemed she had judged the dose accurately.

The medical textbooks on chloral hydrate had been

largely unclear to a lay mind, but what had been clear was that if it was administered with alcohol, a large enough dose could cause coma or death. Thalia had not wanted death for Eloise; she had wanted coma. And she had wanted the coma to last until Eloise was safely buried.

If things went according to plan, Eloise would come out of the coma for long enough to understand what had happened. She would die knowing she had been buried alive. A bad death. But a just and fitting retribution.

It was rather a pity that Royston had died naturally from that last coronary attack. Thalia would have enjoyed meting out a similar punishment to him.

It was a pity as well that there was no means of knowing how much awareness Eloise would have at the end.

Dan had always known, with a complete absence of vanity, that he had an aptitude for writing. He had been sufficiently successful as a journalist and more recently as a feature writer and biographer to know that he could produce reasonably written, reasonably readable prose. He had not made a fortune out of this aptitude, but he had made a living.

What he had not known was that he would be able to write like this, working deep into the night, oblivious of his surroundings, plunging fathoms down into the strange, slightly surreal world of his own creating, sliding with almost frightening facility inside his characters' minds and into their thoughts, scraping their inner emotions away from their skins, like scraping food from the sides of a pan.

His heroine had been taken, heavily sedated and uncomprehending, to her asylum, and a bleak place it was. Her guardians had been deceived by the manicured gardens and the comfortable public rooms – and by the comfortable public manner of the sister in charge.

Dan had enjoyed himself over the sister: Sairy Gamp in modern-day garb, minus the taste for gin but plus a nicely-judged taste in gentlemen. It amused Dan to provide her with an umbrella —about three-quarters of people reading that would miss the point, but it was worth putting in for the other quarter who would not.

The problem was not so much avoiding the influence of modern-day writers as of steering clear of all those descriptions of nineteenth-century institutions. He had asked Oliver to bring anything he could find about Victorian workhouses or bedlams or even fever hospitals. If Oriel College could not supply the information, the Bodleian should be able to.

'I know you probably won't be allowed to photocopy anything,' Dan said on the phone, 'but you could make notes for me, couldn't you?'

'Oh yes. Yes, I could do that. It sounds rather interesting. You haven't forgotten I'm coming to stay with you for half-term? It is still all right?'

'Yes, it is still all right, and no, I haven't forgotten. I'll meet the train, when you know which one you're catching.'

'Well, as a matter of fact,' said Oliver, rather diffidently, 'I've bought a car. I thought I'd drive up.'

'Heaven preserve us all,' said Dan and went back to his asylum.

Places like Rosamund's mental hospital did not exist any more, of course – at least, it was to be hoped they did not, although Rampton had almost passed into the language as a word in its own right, and there were occasionally cases of abuse in mental homes or orphanages, uncovered by crusading journalists. He had a vague idea that there had been something recently – the Rackham Commission, wasn't it? Something to do with searching out malpractice inside NHS mental homes. He would have to look into that in case there was anything he could use.

Oliver would remember the notes, no matter what else he might forget. Dan could just recall their father being exactly the same: charming, gentle, unworldly almost to the point of exasperation at times, but razor-sharp when it came to his own subject. Oliver was also razor-sharp on his own subject, which was day-to-day life during the Reformation, and he was pretty well honed on other periods of English history as well.

Even without the notes, Dan found himself tumbling more or less involuntarily into the mid-nineteenth century: conjuring up a dark brooding madhouse that was a nightmarish mosaic of every bleak house ever created. Dotheboys Hall and Mr Bumble's workhouse. That stark and pitiless institution in William Horwood's remarkable book *Skallagrig*.

He finished the description of his heroine's prison with relish, and turned with interest to the matter of removing her guardians from the scene for good. It was time for the long, dark sojourn to begin, and it was necessary for the venal Sairy Gamp and the increasingly sinister characters with which he was surrounding his heroine to have complete control over her.

Chapter Seven

Matron Freda Porter was always just a little bit fluttered by a visit from Dr Sterne, and she was fluttered by it this afternoon.

She ordered a pot of tea to be brought to her private office and issued instructions that she was not to be disturbed on any pretext short of fire in the house or raging mayhem among the patients. It was not, of course, that she particularly wanted to be alone with Dr Sterne, but it was as well to keep his visits quiet because, aside from his reputation, which was peculiar, he had a disturbing effect on patients – not just the patients in Briar House, but everywhere.

He fascinated them. Even his detractors admitted this. He fascinated them so much that there had apparently even been occasions when patients had virtually mobbed him, reaching out to him like lepers trying to grasp the hem of Jesus of Nazareth's robe, or fourteenth-century sufferers from scrofula being touched for the King's Evil. Not that you got scrofula these days, of course, any more than you got leprosy, but it was irritating and unprofessional to have Dr Sterne being treated as if he was a cross between the risen Christ and Henry VIII, and Matron Porter was not going to have it in Briar House, never mind what might go on elsewhere. Nor was she going to allow her nurses to cluster about him as they had done on his last visit, batting their eyes hopefully, all giggles and no knickers, most of them, and absolutely shameless. Dr Sterne, to give him his due, had not seemed to accord any of them any particular attention, and it had occurred to Matron Porter more than once that it would not be surprising if Dr Sterne had an eye for the more mature woman. Just in case, she powdered her rather large face before his visit, and sprayed her bosom with scent.

He arrived abruptly, churning up a spray of gravel from the drive beneath the wheels of his ramshackle car, parking it untidily and then erupting through Briar House's front entrance. It was impossible to avoid the thought that he brought with him an aura of exotic brilliance. Freda Porter was not given to fanciful notions, but when she visualised Dr Sterne (which she sometimes did when dropping off to sleep, or during a particularly tedious spell of night duty), she always pictured him permanently silhouetted against a kind of medieval stained-glass window that showered vivid jewel colours over him like a harlequin cloak.

Pouring the tea, she listened to Dr Sterne's request that a place be found in Briar House for the young relative of a business associate of his. It was a straightforward request, although the apparent need for speed was a bit surprising – 'Tomorrow or, at the latest, the day after,' said Dr Sterne offhandedly, as if, thought Freda, half resentful, half complimented, he expected Briar House to be able to supply vacant rooms on demand, never mind the inconvenience to everyone and the staff shortage.

She explained, as she always did, that she did not cater for psychotic cases, nor for the *really* insane, only those who were a little distressed by the world. This having been made clear, she asked the nature of the young lady's problem. It was certainly good to hear that it was neither drink nor drugs this time. Dr Sterne, drinking tea with the brusque manner of one simply intent on refuelling (it could not be dislike for the tea which was grand and strong), said, 'I don't know any details. Teenage hysteria, I expect. Probably breaking her heart over a boyfriend.'

Freda interposed a delicate question.

64

'*Virgo intacta* if the GP's to be believed,' said Leo Sterne.

So it was not a case of an abortion undertaken for convenience and emotionally regretted afterwards. Freda changed tack and asked if a private room would be required. 'That, of course, comes a little more expensive. But we have several double and even triple suites which quite often meet the case—'

'Oh, they'll want a private room,' said Leo. 'The family aren't without money. I wouldn't be here pleading the case if they were.'

Eccentric and distinguished men could be allowed their little jokes. Freda smiled indulgently and lifted the teapot in implicit invitation.

'No, thank you.' The tea was so strong it was barely drinkable. Leo said, 'I'll get them to bring the girl in tomorrow, then.'

'And will you be attending her, Dr Sterne?'

'God, no, I'm only making the contact as a favour for someone. I haven't the time or the inclination to pamper hysterical teenagers, Matron. I don't suppose I shall even see the child. In fact, I'm driving to Northumberland straight from here.'

'Ah yes, we've all heard about your work with the Rackham Commission. What a busy and worthwhile life you lead. We should be grateful you can spare time for Briar House.'

The elephantine coyness of tone grated on Leo like a nail being scraped across slate, but he said, 'I was dragged on to the Rackham thing protesting volubly, Matron. I've no patience with bureaucracy, and no time for it either.'

'Oh, but such worthy work, surely.' It would not do to comment on the extremely public row that Dr Sterne had recently waged with a Government minister about the dreadful things he had found inside Thornacre. Freda permitted herself a small twinge of complacency. There was nothing like that at Briar House and she hoped Dr Sterne knew this. It was not beyond the realms of possibility that he might mention Briar House to Professor Rackham and the commission. 'Excellent place, Briar House,' he might say. 'An example to us all.' Or even, 'My word, Freda Porter does a superb job there; we might consider her for a more responsible post sometime.'

This was a new and promising daydream; Freda tucked it away to be considered later on, smiled her company smile at Dr Sterne who was about to leave, and said they would look forward to receiving the new patient in time for supper.

Even though Dr Sterne had said he would not be attending Imogen Ingram, it would be only courteous to send him a little written report on the girl's progress from time to time. Freda flattered herself that she had something of a way with the written word. She could concoct a few very nice little letters, couched as businesslike reports, of course, but actually drawing Dr Sterne into the care of Imogen Ingram. And thus into the environs of Briar House and Freda herself.

Leo had fought against being part of the Rackham Commission, the body set up to investigate malpractice in mental institutions, but Professor Rackham had been one of his tutors and he had made it a personal request, and in the end Leo had agreed.

'You'll counterbalance the bureaucrats,' Rackham had said. 'Two of us will have more impact than one.'

'Psychiatry isn't about committees and reports and Government White Papers.'

'No, but it's about stamping out cruelty and misman-agement and greed. If you won't do it for any other reason, do it for my sake, Leo. I'm too old to fight them on my own.'

'That's unanswerable,' said Leo. 'You cunning old devil.'

'That's disrespectful,' said Professor Rackham. 'Well? Will you do it?'

'I'll have to after that,' said Leo. 'But don't expect me to be respectful to the mediocrats.'

'I don't want you to be respectful. I want you to be effective.'

He had done it, of course, and he thought that so far he had indeed been effective. There had been grim satisfaction in bringing to light some of the cases of abuse they had found, and there had been mischievous delight in some of the quarrels waged as a result. But the grimmest of all the places they had investigated had been the nightmare mansion they had found in Northumberland. Thornacre.

It had been built by a well-heeled mill-owner for his new young wife, around the time of the Regency. He had reportedly a roving eye, the wealthy industrialist, but also an ambitious disposition and he had married the lady for her society connections. The lady, for her part, had married for love and her disposition was wildly jealous, so that when she discovered the mill-owner *in flagrante delicto* with the be-tween-maid, she attacked her hapless spouse with the nearest thing to hand. The nearest thing to hand had happened to be a meat cleaver and the mill-owner had died messily in the master bedroom, thus providing food for the local gossip for several generations. The lady spent the rest of her days shut away inside Thornacre's east wing with a keeper, eaten up by grief and helplessly insane. According to the local GP, she had died alone and mad, having spent the last thirty years of her life prowling the vast echoing corridors of Thornacre howling frenziedly at creatures who were not there.

There had been no children; if there had been, it was possible that Thornacre would eventually have passed to a normal family, and there would have been no haunted mansion silently growing into the dark legend in England's north-east corner.

'Considering the place's history, I suppose we should have expected a few ghosts,' Leo had said, facing Professor Rackham over the latter's desk.

'Oh yes. Yes, we should have guessed that the legend of that poor insane creature would have lived on.'

They looked at one another, and then Rackham said, 'But it isn't the ghosts, is it, Leo? It's what you – what we – found there. How much are we going to make public?'

'Not everything,' said Leo at once. 'The public would never believe it.'

'Dear God, no. There'll have to be a full report, of course,' said Rackham, after a moment. 'And probably a White Paper.'

'Oh, fuck reports and White Papers,' said Leo, who hardly ever swore and very rarely used obscenities. 'The place was like something out of Dickens. You saw that. We all saw it. We need to focus on the immediate problems – getting some of the staff thrown into windowless prisons for starters, and preferably leaving them to rot.' He sat back in his chair, frowning, and despite himself Professor Rackham smiled.

'That's got a very Biblical ring, Leo.'

'I feel Biblical. I'd like to invoke plagues of boils and curses of pestilence. I'd like to burn Thornacre down and sow the ground with salt.' Oh no, you wouldn't, said a treacherous little voice inside his mind. Oh no, you wouldn't.

'Let's stop thinking about what we found,' said Rackham, 'and think instead about what we're going to do there. Let's think about exorcising the place, driving out the ghosts and laying the dark reputation.'

'Winding up the rough magic,' said Leo, half to himself.

'You always had a lyrical turn of mind. But, yes, if you want to call it that. Not bell, book and candle exorcism, but a purging. And then running the place as it ought to be run. How would you feel about doing that, Leo?'

Leo looked up, startled. 'Me? Why me, for God's sake?'

'Because you're the obvious choice.'

'You're serious, aren't you?' Leo stared at the professor. 'Yes, I can see you are. But I'm not a manager. I'm certainly not a bureaucrat. I'd be appalling.'

'You'd be unusual but you might be what's needed.' Rackham tapped his pen thoughtfully on the desk. 'Let's fold the anger up and put it aside for a moment, Leo,' he said, and Leo smiled inwardly, because this was one of the old boy's positive word imageries. It was the kind of thing Leo himself often used to help patients. Tidy up the anger/ the bitterness/the bereavement. Put it away in a cupboard, throw it to the back of a drawer; we can always come back to it later if necessary.

'Let's look at what could be done in Thornacre,' said Rackham. 'At what good could be done.' He added craftily, 'Supposing, of course, that you agree.'

'Well, all right, supposing I did agree, what about my patients in London?' demanded Leo. 'And the groups – the Students' Counselling Service and the Drug-Watch Centre?'

'Hyatt could take most of the patients. Or Marshall.'

'Yes, that's true.' Marshall had been another of Rackham's students; he and Leo had been good friends in their student days and they were good colleagues now. Yes, he could trust Marshall with them.

'And you could set up similar groups as easily in Northumberland as you could in London. In fact,' said Professor Rackham, tightening his case skilfully, 'it could be argued that a place like that has the greater need. In London help groups are ten a penny.'

'You're a Machiavellian old bastard, aren't you?' Leo thought for a moment. 'I'd need new staff right across the board,' he said abruptly. 'Good registrars and senior house officers. Occupational therapists. And nurses – I'd have to have good nurses, including a matron.'

'You could probably have all of that.'

'Almost all of the present lot would have to go.'

'They are going. They've all had notices served on them. Quite a few have had GMC summonses as well.'

'Well, I hope they're all suspended for life.'

Rackham leaned forward. 'Leo, listen. Nobody seems to have bothered about Thornacre for years. We both saw that. It needs a troubleshooter for a time.'

Leo smiled. 'Now that's one of the few things I've never been called.'

'And there's another thing,' continued Rackham. 'Thornacre's never applied for any research funds. That means you could probably get grants. Even some of the drug companies – I don't mean the ICIs of the world, but some of the smaller firms. That place in Oxford, and there's somewhere in Wales that specialises in the sedative groups of drugs.'

'But would you trust me with it?' Leo asked almost roughly. 'Would anyone trust me with it? After what happened last year?'

Rackham made a dismissive gesture. 'You were unwise and unfortunate last year. That woman was clearly hysterical. Or disappointed,' he added shrewdly, and despite himself Leo grinned. 'Between ourselves, Leo, I suppose you didn't actually seduce her?'

'I didn't.'

'I didn't think you had.' Rackham paused. 'Would you like to think about Thornacre? Perhaps a two-year contract?'

'I don't need to think about it.' He did not. He realised that he wanted Thornacre more than he had ever wanted anything in his life. I could do it, he thought. I could turn that nightmare mansion into something *good*. Somewhere healing.

What would Thornacre be like with the darknesses chased away and the ghosts routed?

The undertaker's assistant thought this was the queerest job he had ever been assigned. Quite a posh house, it was, but an odd set-up all the same.

A double death, it was, and within hours of one another,

70

so they said, on account of some kind of family tragedy. Well, you got queerer things in life, the assistant was bound to admit that you did, but if it hadn't been for the certificates being properly made out and all, old Huxtable might have asked a few questions about this one and reported things to the coroner, like he had done once or twice before. You couldn't be too careful in this business, and Huxtable's were jealous of their reputation. They wouldn't risk being mixed up in anything dubious.

It was unusual these days to be requested to casket the bodies and leave them in the house until the funeral service, but it wasn't altogether unheard of. And Mrs Caudle's instructions had been definite. Two nice oak caskets with brass handles, no expense spared – that was Hampstead for you – and both coffins to remain in this room until the funeral on Friday afternoon. Quite quick, that was; it would mean paying extra time to the grave-diggers who liked to finish early on Fridays. But it could not be helped. Probably the family wanted to clear away all memories of the tragedy, whatever it had been, thought the assistant sagely.

It was quite like the old days to be preparing a laying-out in a house. The assistant was just old enough to remember the time when people kept their loved ones in the house with them until the hearse came to the door. It had been the way things were done. If you were well off you had the body laid out in the billiard room or the library for the family to pay their last respects; if you were poor, you used the front parlour. But people were squeamish about such things now; they could not bear the thought of being in the same house overnight with a corpse, they said, and insisted on it being carted off to the Chapel of Rest there and then. As if the poor dead body of your own husband or mother or gran who had loved you would do you any harm! The assistant agreed with the old ways and could not be doing with such tickle-stomached folk.

There was not a great deal for him to do. The bodies had been washed and their hair combed, and they had been dressed in clean night-clothes, which was apparently how the family wished them to be buried. Huxtable's were used to all kinds of different instructions. People wanted their dead buried with guitars or in leather motorbike jackets, or with a tape or a record of favourite music, or with photographs of children or parents. Old Huxtable always complied short of the downright bizarre. It was an echo, he said, of the ancient Egyptians and he told his staff how the Pharaohs had buried food and drink and familiar objects with them, for comfort on the journey after death – even servants as well. This had been interesting, although it had to be said that you could count on one hand the number of people in Hampstead who held by the burial customs of ancient Egypt, never mind wanting to share a grave with the au pair or the cleaning lady!

Huxtable's had taken measurements yesterday, and the assistant had brought the coffins along now, together with two of the collapsible biers. There was a white linen cloth to go over each, and a small flower display – white carnations and a bit of fern – to stand between the two. All very tasteful and discreet. No candles, of course – Mrs Caudle did not want any Romish observations, which the assistant thought rather a pity; a couple of nice corpse candles gave a properly sombre note to a death chamber. But people had no sense of occasion these days.

He got on with transferring the two bodies into the lined coffins. The man had had a massive coronary, seemingly. He looked a prime candidate for one: well fleshed, and a bit sleek. Too much rich food and drink. Neither of the bodies' jaws had dropped, in fact the man's had been set fast with the rigor. Very good.

There was an odd feeling in this room, almost a feeling of somebody watching him. Peculiar that. You would have thought that by now he'd be used to being alone with the dead, but he found himself continually looking over his shoulder, as if he was no more than a novice, learning his trade, superstitious about the poor empty creatures under his hands. But there was something nasty about this house – something eerie, yes that was the word! An eerie place. He would be very glad indeed to be finished and leave.

There was to be no embalming, which Huxtable's would have preferred, with the bodies remaining in the house, especially since the house was so extremely well heated. People wouldn't believe how easy and hygienic embalming was these days; a simple matter of eliminating the body's contents and injecting a preservative. Still, the instructions here had been specific and would be complied with.

There was no rigor at all in the female, which was probably due to the warmth. The assistant made himself a mental note to turn the central heating radiator off in this room before he left, and open the window. Really it was just as well that the service was being held tomorrow. Good-looking woman, she'd been, if you liked them pale and fair, which the undertaker did not. Perforated stomach ulcer, so the certificate said.

In accordance with his own small private ritual – he was a rather devout man in a quiet way – he murmured a brief prayer over the two bodies.

And then he screwed down the coffin lids.

Chapter Eight

Imogen thought it was going to get pretty boring inside Briar House. There was not very much to do during the day and there was even less in the evenings.

Nobody had actually come out and said so, but it was perfectly obvious that the aunts and everyone else wanted her out of the way for a while. It was possible that this was because of her parents' death, but Imogen did not think it was very likely. Everyone seemed more concerned with Imogen herself than with her father's heart attack or her mother's perforated ulcer. This seemed extremely odd. And had Eloise really suffered from an ulcer for several years and not said anything? There's something here I don't understand, thought Imogen hazily. There's something they're not telling me. Aunt Rosa had referred to nervous strain which had not made very much sense; Aunt Dilys, weeping copiously, had talked about strain and exhaustion, which had made even less. But it made sense if they all thought she was responsible for what had happened at Edmund's funeral. This was an appalling idea, but it had to be faced.

Did the family really think that? Did they believe that she had crept into the mortuary or the Chapel of Rest and opened Edmund's coffin and taken his head and brought it back to the house? How did you carry a human head, for heaven's sake? In a hatbox, like that old film where the murderer kept his victim's head on top of the wardrobe? In a Sainsbury's carrier bag? But a person who would do something like that would be mad.

The word exploded in her mind, sending up clouds of panic, like a depth charge, because that was it, *of course* that was it. They did think she was mad. That was what this was all about. They all thought it: Great-Aunt Flora, Dilys and Rosa, and nice, dizzy Juliette. That was why nobody seemed to be grieving about Royston and Eloise. Had the dark-haired young man at the funeral thought she was mad as well? His face was blurry now – almost everything was blurry now – but he had looked at her in a way she did not think anyone had ever looked at her before. As if she was grown-up. As if she was ordinary and did all the things that ordinary people did. Imogen would most likely never see him again in her life, but it was somehow important that he did not think she had done something so – well, so *grisly*. It was very important indeed that he did not think she was mad.

The regime in Briar House was rather casual. It appeared that no one minded if you missed the occasional meal, providing you did not make a habit of it and providing you were not in Briar House for any kind of eating disorder like anorexia. There was a small kitchen on the floor below Imogen's where tea and coffee could be made, or even scrambled eggs or soup, although you had to ask one of the nurses to bring things in for you and it made problems if you had no actual cash, which Imogen had not. The kitchen was shared between several rooms, and Imogen thought, half enviously, half regretfully, that it was the kind of set-up you had in university halls of residence. It was a sad irony that when she should finally experience the kind of university half-liberation she had wanted and her school had wanted for her, it had to be in a place like this.

The matron was a well-built lady of uncertain age and, from the look of her mouth, even more uncertain temper, and Imogen had disliked her on sight. People talked about the eyes being the windows of the soul, but mouths were a much better indication and Matron Porter's mouth was not

wide and generous to match her build, it was small and
pursed like an old-fashioned drawstring bag. She doesn't
much like me, Imogen had thought on the first day, vaguely
listening as Aunt Thalia explained about the sedatives prescribed by Dr Shilling. 'Diazepam, Matron. Quite a mild
dosage, I understand. But you'll see she takes it?'

'Certainly.'

Imogen thought that Matron looked the kind of person
who would enjoy shovelling repellent medicine down people.

She was given a room of her own, which was a relief
because she had been visualising grim dormitories with iron
beds and lockers. In the really bad moments she had been
visualising iron bars at the windows. But she was shown to a
room on the second floor. It was not very big, but it was clean
and there were chintz curtains and a matching bedspread,
and a small dressing table and wardrobe. The room was by
itself at the end of a corridor, at the foot of a narrow stair that
went up into the attics.

There was still a dreamlike quality to everything. Imogen
felt as if her mind was wrapped in cotton wool. She tried to
think about her parents and how it was appalling that they
were both so abruptly dead but there was only a vague dull
sense of loss. This was terrible. It was terrible to feel so little
about your mother and father. She felt detached and slightly
light-headed, as if her mind had been dislocated and as if it
needed someone to tweak it back into place. Her sight did not
seem to be quite synchronised with the rest of her, either. As
if she was seeing everything through water, or a fraction of a
second after it happened. She thought this might be the
sedatives, and determined that as soon as she was fairly sure
that Matron was not checking on her, she would stop taking
them. There was a washbasin in her room, and it would be
easy to tip the tablets down the plughole and wash them away
with the taps turned on full.

On her second night in Briar House, Imogen met Quincy.

76

It was a curious meeting. Imogen had been taking a shower before going to bed, and she was crossing the landing back to her room, wearing only her dressing gown, when a stealthy movement on the attic stair caught her attention. She stopped, and looked up the shadowy stairway apprehensively. There was a moment of silence, and then a quick indrawn breath and a hesitant step. The slight figure of a girl of around Imogen's own age, or perhaps a little younger – say fifteen or sixteen – came down the stairs. She had short, ragged hair and a triangular face like a cat's, and wide, afraid eyes. She stood on the bottom step, staring fearfully at Imogen.

Imogen smiled at her and said, 'Did I wake you? I'm sorry if I did but I didn't know anyone was up there. I was just going to bed. That's my room over there.'

There was a moment of silence, and then the girl said, 'Yes, I know. Only I thought . . .'

'Yes?'

'I thought you might be Matron.' She stopped and made an urchin gesture of rubbing her nose with the back of her hand and sniffing back tears, or fear. 'She don't – doesn't like me to sit on the stairs. She says it's snooping. But it isn't snooping; I like to watch people.'

'Well, I'm not Matron. I'm just staying here for a while. And I quite like watching people as well. Do you,' Imogen paused, and then went on, 'do you live here?' There was no way of knowing if the urchin girl was a patient or one of the assistants. She looks a bit fey, thought Imogen. As if she might sometimes see things that other people don't. She said carefully, 'I'm sorry, I don't know your name.'

'Quincy.' It was as odd as everything else about her. Imogen wondered if it was some kind of nickname.

She said, 'I'm Imogen Ingram.'

'I know who you are, I saw you arrive yesterday.' Quincy spoke with a London accent; not quite Cockney and certainly not what was these days called Estuary English. It might be one of the older strains of Cockney, one of the vanishing strains.

'I made a drawing of you,' said Quincy, suddenly. 'Last night.'

'Did you really? That's rather flattering. Will you show it to me sometime?' It was not quite like talking to a child, but it was not quite like talking to an adult either. Imogen was curious to know what kind of drawings this odd little creature could produce.

'Now? You could come now while everyone's in bed.' It was as if having confided about the drawing, Quincy had decided to trust Imogen a bit further.

Imogen said, 'Yes, all right.'

The attic room was stuffy and very spartan so that Imogen wondered if Quincy was a helper here after all. But the drawings were astonishing; Imogen had never seen anything quite like them. She really does see things other people don't, she thought, studying them with fascination. She's romanticised me a good deal – all that hair. And my face isn't that exaggerated heart shape either. It's a pretty creepy drawing when you study it a bit closer: the way the curtains are drawn back so that the folds shape into a leery face, and the way the curtain tassels look like a clutching hand with talons . . . But she's amazingly talented. Imogen looked up to meet the frightened-cat eyes. 'Quincy, these are terrific. Have you been to an art school or anything?'

'Oh no.'

'Well, you should,' said Imogen. 'You ought to have proper training so that you could make a real career. Hasn't anyone ever suggested it? Your parents or your school or anyone?'

'I haven't got any parents. I didn't go to school much. Dr Sterne said I should go to an art school, though. When he came to – the place I lived before.'

'Where was that? Where did you live?' Imogen had asked the question without any intention other than that of ordinary friendliness, but to her horror Quincy began to tremble, wrapping her arms about her thin body and rocking to and fro. She's not aware of me any more, thought Imogen, or of this mean little room.

But after a moment Quincy's eyes focused on Imogen again. 'Thornacre,' she said. 'I lived in Thornacre.'

Freda Porter had not wanted to take Quincy into Briar House, but Dr Sterne had been persuasive, and Dr Sterne at his most persuasive was hard to resist.

Quincy was one of his protégées; she was one of the poor souls he had found in Thornacre and brought out with him. He was still uncovering her story, he explained, although this was proving to be a long and difficult task. But it seemed clear that there had been abuse from childhood on, and they were afraid there might have been some ill-treatment in Thornacre as well. She had been there for two or three years, they thought.

'A very pitiful case indeed,' said he, fixing Freda with his remarkable eyes, so that Freda felt really quite peculiar for a minute.

'And what exactly is the problem, Dr Sterne?'

'I'm not sure yet. She's withdrawn from the world a good deal,' said Leo. 'But not quite in the usual way of clinical depression.'

'Ah. Indeed.'

'She seems to have entered some kind of strange twilight world of her own,' said Leo. 'I don't know yet whether it's any safer or kinder to her than the real world's been, and I don't know what nightmares she's lived through either.'

'Well, I am sure you will find out if anyone can, Dr Sterne,' said Freda comfortably. Quite stimulating it was to hear Dr Sterne talk like this. 'A cup of coffee, Doctor?' It was all set ready, with Freda's best flowered cups and saucers.

Leo took the cup of coffee absently. 'I shall find out

eventually, of course,' he said, and Freda thought that any other man saying this would have sounded arrogant. Dr Sterne said it as one simply stating a fact. 'But until I do find out, it would be very cruel indeed to keep her in Thornacre.' Leo paused, and then said, 'I wondered whether you might be able to find a place for her here, Matron. I should be very grateful if you could.'

Freda maintained her smile but said it might be difficult. You did not run a nursing home on fresh air; books had to be balanced and bills paid. Briar House was not a charity.

'I didn't expect there to be any charity in the arrangement,' said Leo, expressionlessly. 'I thought it might be possible for her to work here and earn her keep. I'm sure you find it as hard as the rest of us to get good staff.'

This, of course, put a different complexion on the thing. The idea of gaining an unpaid helper was very appealing, and having one of Dr Sterne's protégées here might mean regular visits from him. Her mind flew ahead, seeing herself and Dr Sterne discussing the case over dainty tea tables, or even cosy little suppers.

And so she said cautiously that it might be possible to find a corner for Quincy. Should they say a trial period? Perhaps six weeks?

'Good idea,' said Leo, standing up. 'I'll arrange for her to come right away. She's an odd-looking little thing,' he said. 'And by the way, she has a really remarkable talent for drawing and painting. I'd like that to be encouraged as much as possible, if you would, Matron. I think it's how we'll eventually reach her mind.'

'We will hope so, of course, Doctor.' It was impossible to resist Dr Sterne when his eyes glowed with enthusiasm like this.

And really, so far it did not seem to be working too badly. Quincy was willing; she would do whatever was asked of her. She helped in the laundry and with the preparation of meals, even though her ideas of hygiene had made Freda throw up her hands in horror.

But she was sly. More than once, Freda had come upon her curled into the deep window seat on the half-landing, or folded into a corner of the nurses' common room, concealed by shadows or long curtains. Listening, said Freda, not best pleased. A sly little thing, creeping unnoticed about the house, picking up gossip and storing it away. A plain little thing as well. Dr Sterne might be concerned with Quincy's mind, or the lack of it, but Freda had to think about character, and what she thought was that Quincy was sly.

As for the famous art talent, as far as Freda could see the drawings were no more than scrappy bits of paper covered with time-wasting scrawls, best thrown in the dustbin. Real drawing was a nice vase of flowers, or a pretty landscape, or a rose-gardened cottage, not queer, warped people with distorted faces or disturbingly out-of-scale backgrounds. She thought, but did not say, that Quincy's peculiar drawings were as likely to be caused by astigmatism as by talent. An eye test and a good pair of glasses would cure that nonsense. She would take the girl to the optician's. It would look well to Dr Sterne; it would look concerned.

She made the appointment herself, and then turned to the matter of the Ingram girl. Unless Freda mistook the matter, this was one who was going to resist the prescribed sedatives. Freda knew all about these sly-boots girls who flushed tablets down the lavatory, and she was going to begin the tried and tested practice of crushing up an extra tablet or two in Imogen's cup of morning coffee. It would not hurt the child, and Freda was not going to risk losing this new and very welcome source of income. All kinds of extras had been suggested to Imogen's family and all had been agreed to without demur. Freda was thinking of having her private sitting room redecorated on the strength of it.

* * *

Having his brother in the flat was as easy and as undemanding as Dan had known it would be.

Oliver arrived just after lunch on Friday, his clothes untidily packed in a suitcase that was already spilling over the back seat of his car, but the notes for Dan's Victorian asylum-cum-workhouse pristinely arranged and slotted into a neat, labelled folder. He had quite enjoyed the drive here, he said. He had had a bit of difficulty finding one or two of the roads, but he had consulted an AA map a few times and in the end had found the way all right.

It was good to see him. It always was. Dan listened with interest to the gentle Oxford news and the unmalicious gossip and bloodless feuds, and wondered, as he always did when he was with Oliver, if he should have followed in his footsteps.

Oliver said he had quite a good set of students at the moment; a surprisingly large number of females were taking his course on national finance during the reign of Henry VIII, which was very gratifying. Of course, females took a much greater interest in finance these days, and old Henry was a colourful personage by anyone's standards.

Dan looked at his brother's ingenuous expression; at the clear grey eyes fringed with thick dark lashes and the lock of soft brown hair that tumbled almost permanently over his brow, and did not find it in the least surprising that Oliver had so many female students. The first time Dan had heard his brother lecture, his mouth had dropped open with astonishment. In everyday life, Oliver was hesitant and unsure; on home ground, talking about his own subject, he was incandescent. The women hung on to his every utterance, and he played them like a violin. The pity was that he did not realise it. Dan suspected the male students realised and privately ground their teeth.

One of the best things about Oliver was that he understood that when you were working, you were *working* and could not always afford to come out of it for very long. Dan, who could hardly bear to leave Rosamund for too long at this stage, seized Oliver's research notes about asylums and plunged back into chapter ten the same afternoon.

Rosamund was now completely isolated from her family and anyone else who might have rescued her – although Dan might allow her a faithful friend who could share some of the ordeals. She was tied up in a careful net of intrigue, starting with Margot who was after Rosamund's inheritance, and who was at the web's centre. She was a very feisty lady indeed, this one; Dan was greatly enjoying her. She had killed Rosamund's parents very satisfactorily, laying her complicated plans, and luring them both down to her country cottage and then into the disused wash house where she first drugged and then stabbed them. Dan became so enrapt with the gore and the stench of spilled blood and the screams for help that went unheard and unheeded that he forgot the time, and it was only when Oliver returned from wherever he had been for the afternoon that Dan discovered it was nearly seven o'clock. He stopped typing and said, vaguely, that they would send out for pizzas presently.

'Certainly not. You've been working and you can go on working. I'll make us omelettes when you're ready. I can't bear those red and yellow rubber pizza things.'

Dan returned to the intriguing problem of how Margot was going to dispose of the two corpses which were still lying in a welter of gore in the wash house. He thought that the phone rang at one stage and he dimly heard Oliver answer it and hold a brief conversation with somebody. There was something about, 'I'll make sure he phones you back as soon as possible – has he the number?'

Dan mentally relegated the telephone to the back of his mind and returned to Margot's dilemma. Was it possible that she could make use of the wash house to get rid of the bodies? Yes, of course she could.

And of course she did and it worked splendidly. She tipped both bodies into the old copper boiler, half-filled it with water, and lit the stove-like contraption underneath. Memories of visits to his grandmother in the country surfaced in Dan's mind: there had been a small stone wash house there, which had provided terrific quarters for hide-and-seek when he and Oliver stayed during school holidays. He remembered exactly how the mechanism had worked; he understood what had to be done, and Margot understood as well.

The stench of the boiling bodies was nauseating but there were no near neighbours so it did not matter. Margot did not mind the smell, in fact she gloried in it. She was an evil, warped bitch, and she exulted in what she had done. The abominable smell mingled with the drifting scents of somebody's autumnal bonfire in a nearby field. It was almost two days before the bodies of Rosamund's parents were boiled down to bones. The chapter ended with Margot standing gloatingly in the evil-smelling wash house, the twilight trickling in through the tiny grimed window and showering her with twisting purple and violet shadows.

Dan reread it critically and thought it was not bad. He thought he had evoked the claustrophobic eeriness of the place when it was deserted and also the nightmarish quality of the huge copper boiler itself. Could any of it be used as the reason for Rosamund's final plummet into real insanity? This had worried Dan quite a lot, because while beleaguered damsels had perforce to be consigned to pitiless stone wings of briar-enclosed castles, and villainesses had to stalk the darkness brandishing dripping knives, manipulating their wards' bank accounts by way of spare-time entertainment, it must all be credible.

Supposing Rosamund accidentally discovered what Margot had done? Supposing she somehow came upon the mutilated remains of her parents – perhaps her mother? Wouldn't that be enough to send a sensitive girl rocketing into hysteria at the very least? And wouldn't that hysteria be sufficient reason to take her from the relatively gentle, more or less humane side of her asylum and lock her away in the grim dark wing reserved for the helplessly insane?

And then Dan thought: what if Margot *makes sure* she comes upon the mutilated remains? Oh, *yes*.

He grinned with delight, jotted this down as the super-structure for the next chapter, and got up from the desk, conscious for the first time of aching back and shoulders. He walked round the sitting room twice to unstiffen his cramped muscles, and then went to see what Oliver had managed by way of supper, and who the phone call had been from.

Oliver was cooking cheese omelettes and the kitchen was pleasantly filled with the scents of melting cheese and garlic. He had found a French loaf that Dan had bought earlier that morning and forgotten about, and had spread it thickly with butter and chopped garlic, and put it in the oven, wrapped in foil. He had managed not to blow the cooker fuse this time, and had remembered how to set the timer as well. He had also opened a bottle of very good red wine which was, it appeared, one of a case given to him by the bursar of his college, three bottles of which he had brought for Dan.

The phone call had been from Dan's agent who had reportedly said that if Dan was not too taken up with writing the Great British Novel, there was a commission for him from a magazine.

'He said it would be light relief and also some income. Dan, you aren't broke, are you?' said Oliver, concerned.

'Not yet,' said Dan, dialling his agent's number.

'Are you ringing him now? Isn't it a bit late?'

'Piers never sleeps if there's money involved,' said Dan caustically.

'It's a profile for *Women in Business*,' said Piers, who answered on the second ring. 'I put you up for it and they're agreeable. Reasonably factual, and not too frivolous – well, you know the kind of thing, you can do it standing on your head. And that new magazine, *Integra*, they're interested in something as well. I've had a word with the features editor. You can be as frivolous as you like for that one, of course.'

'Of course. How much are *Women in Business* paying? Ah. And *Integra*? *How* much? Yes, I thought that was what you said. Yes, I know it's generous. Well, of course I'll accept it.' He made a few quick notes, and then said, 'Who's the subject, Piers?'

Piers laughed. 'The new head of Ingram's Books.'

'D'you mean Royston Ingram?'

There was the sound of papers being shuffled at the other end, and Dan had a swift, vivid image of his agent's office and the serried highly-organised chaos that reigned there.

'Royston Ingram's dead,' said Piers. 'Don't you read the obituary notices?'

'No, I don't. I read the bankruptcy listings, to see if I'm in them yet. When did he die? And how?'

'Heart attack just over a week ago. His wife died at the same time and— Did you say something?'

'No. Go on.'

'She had – what was it? – oh yes, a perforated stomach ulcer. One line of gossip says it was her death that brought on his heart attack, in fact. But no one really knows.'

'I don't suppose they do.' But I think I know, thought Dan. I know why Royston Ingram's heart failed. He said, carefully, 'Where do I come in? And who's the new head of Ingram's?'

'Thalia Caudle,' said his agent.

There was an abrupt silence. Then Dan said, 'Did you say Thalia Caudle? She of the voracious appetite for young men and lip-smacking mien?'

'I did.'

'*Thalia Caudle*'s the new head of Ingram's?'

'In theory. Royston left her control of the lot, or as near

86

to the lot as makes no difference. The house in Hampstead, sixty per cent of the shares in Ingram's. The general opinion is that she'll float a public company like one or two other publishing houses lately, but I wouldn't bet the ranch on that. A press handout's just come through – I'll get a copy to you.'

'How do I get to meet the lady?' demanded Dan. 'Am I expected to climb the dark topless tower of the necromancer? Or ride on a bat's back—'

'I've got her phone number,' interrupted Piers. 'She's expecting a call from you. It's all very interesting, isn't it?'

'That's not the word that springs to my mind.'

'What is?'

'Fortuitous,' said Dan. He wrote the phone number down and rang off.

'In theory she's got the lot,' said Dan, enjoying the omelette and the wine and Oliver's undemanding company. 'At least until Imogen's out of minority. I don't know if that's eighteen or twenty-one in this case – I'd better find that out. But until then, the Caudle's in the driving seat.'

'What's she like, this lady?' Oliver enjoyed stories of the world of business, which he listened to with the absorbed air of one hearing about a distant planet.

'Greedy,' said Dan. 'In all senses. I'll have to take a chastity belt with me to the interview.'

'Oh. But you'll do the profile?'

'Certainly.'

'What about your book? Will you have to put it to one side?'

Dan grinned. This was the academic speaking. Oliver could not visualise how you worked on several projects at the same time, switching between them as finances dictated. 'I couldn't ditch the book. I'll simply work on both.'

'Mortgages and food bills have to be paid?' said Oliver, cautiously, as if trying out alien expressions.

'Exactly,' said Dan. 'And on the subject of food, is there any more garlic bread? Oh good. And let's have another glass of wine to go with it.'

Chapter Nine

For several days after she came to Briar House, Quincy had gone about very quietly and very stealthily in case there were any of the things here that there had been in Thornacre.

Thornacre had been a bad place; it had been the worst place Quincy had ever been. It had been a *haunted* place. Quincy had known without anyone telling her that Thornacre was haunted; she had sometimes glimpsed the poor sad ghosts of the people who had lived there a long long time ago. They all looked alike because they all suffered from the same things: poverty and hopelessness and fear. Quincy recognised these things because she had suffered from them herself. Not having enough to eat. Not having any money to buy things to eat. Hiding in an unlit room if a knock came at the door, in case it was somebody wanting money, or mother's pub friends wanting to do those hurting, shameful things to her with their ugly bodies. They had not done those things to her because she was beautiful, they had done them because they would have done them to anyone who was handy.

Quincy knew quite well that she was not beautiful; she was not even pretty. She was plain and stupid and awkward. Matron Porter said so, making little pin-prick jibes of the words. You're plain, Quincy. You're an ugly street-girl. Ugly little whore. Quincy had watched the words come out of Matron's mouth and turn into evil little barbed things that flew at her and jabbed into her skin.

Quincy always stayed absolutely silent and absolutely still when Matron said things like that, in case Matron decided to send her back to Thornacre. Quincy would do anything in the world to avoid that. Dr Sterne had said that all the bad things had been taken away from Thornacre, but Quincy knew that there was a deep badness in the place called the east wing, and she did not think that it was anything that could be taken away. It was a black place and it would always be black. It was a place where you were locked up if you did not behave, and where the rooms smelled of sick and dirt, and where the people smelled of sick and dirt as well.

The attendants had sometimes hit patients, smacking the bewildered ones for soiling their beds, and sometimes, if the attendants were bored or broke, they had laid bets on who could feed the slops into the barely-conscious ones the quickest, or timed each other at racing the wheelchair-bound patients along the corridors. Quincy would sometimes wake up at night and hear screams coming from the east wing, which was the haunted wing. The screams would go on for a few minutes, and then there would be the sound of running feet and the angry slamming of a door – iron on iron. Someone said the night auxiliaries stopped the screaming by tying the patients' hands to the bedposts and then putting electric light bulbs in their mouths while they were helpless – bulbous side in, so that if they screamed again the glass would break and cut their mouths. It was what the Nazis had done to Jews in the last war. Quincy had once tried to draw all this, but it had come out too frightening, like a nightmare, and so she had torn the paper up.

There had been better things to draw since coming to Briar House, although she had to be very careful because Matron often looked through her things. That was why she had never drawn Matron herself, but if she had she would have drawn her as a fat bloated body with a horrid animal-head. A griffin like the one in the story by Lewis Carroll that she had found in Thornacre's dank-smelling library. Or a bulgy-eyed, lollopy-cheeked pig-lady with little trotter feet and streams of horrid, hurting words coming out of her mouth: 'Ugly little slyboots.' Jab, jab. 'Doing nasty things with men in the street for money. I know all about it, Quincy. Don't think I don't know all about it.'

Matron did not know about it at all, of course, because men had never done the things with Matron that they had done with Quincy. Sometimes nowadays Quincy could not believe she had done them herself. Lying in the bed with Mother's friend from the pub when she was ten, and Mother was out at work. Having to let him touch her all over, while he breathed smelly breath into her face. And then later on, when she was twelve, being made to feel the lumpy bulges in men's trousers when Mother brought them back from the pub. Once one of the men had been sick all over her. There had been a lot of sick and it had smelled of stale beer, and the couch had smelled of it for weeks afterwards as well.

This would never happen in Briar House, where she had her own tiny room at the top of the house. It had been a servant's room in the days when Briar House was a big private house, so it was very small, and there was only just room for a bed and a chair and a chest of drawers. Matron had only let Quincy have it because no one else would sleep there on account of the water tanks being on the other side of the wall, and the room being stiflingly hot, and the tanks making rude gurgling noises when they filled or emptied. But this did not matter because it was Quincy's very own.

It did not matter that she had to work for her keep, either. She liked being shown how to do things; she liked being given polish and dusters and left to polish the mahogany table in the visitors' room, or the table in the main hall that someone said was called a Pembroke table. She enjoyed the scent of the polish and the feel of glossy wood, or the good, fresh smell of newly-washed sheets when you ironed them.

There were a great many very lovely things in this house, but the loveliest of them all was Imogen Ingram. Imogen was the most beautiful person Quincy had ever seen in her whole life. She was so beautiful that the first time Quincy saw her she could not stop staring, and she had drawn her almost without realising.

Imogen had not been given a room with a hot water tank next door; she had a room on the second floor, overlooking the gardens. Just outside was a square landing with a deep window, and in the deep window was a seat with faded covers of something Quincy thought was called chintz – green and blue twining flowers and leaves on a cream background. If you sat on the faded seat and curled into the corner, you were hidden from practically everybody. It was a good place to be, and Quincy took to curling up there, within sight of Imogen's room, pulling a fold of curtain around her and huddling into the tiniest possible space. If Freda Pig caught her she would say, 'Oho, earwigging again, madam?' but Quincy was not here to earwig; she was here to guard Imogen.

Imogen had a lot of visitors. Her family all came to see her, which was what you would expect for somebody so beautiful. They brought flowers and fruit and they drove smart cars. You would expect Imogen to have family like this. Quincy was pleased for her.

And then, just days after Imogen's arrival, Mrs Caudle came just before lunch, and the minute Quincy saw her she stopped being pleased, and began to feel cold and shivery. Mrs Caudle was not here to be nice to Imogen. She hated Imogen.

She did not look like an enemy, not on the outside. She was thin and she had dark hair and expensive clothes. They were casual clothes; the kind that rich people wore for car journeys and holidays, but you could see that they were expensive. She came by herself, driving her own car, and she brought flowers for Imogen and books – not paperbacks or magazines, but real books with glossy covers and photographs.

Quincy knew at once that the books and flowers and the nice clothes were part of a disguise. There were people in the world who wore masks to hide their real selves, and the masks were often very good so that no one knew what was behind them. Mrs Caudle, Imogen's aunt, was the most evil creature Quincy had ever seen and her mask was very good indeed.

The impression that Imogen was being slowly drawn towards something terrible and something threatening began to form.

Quincy was allowed to go out by herself, providing she said where she was going and told somebody when she would be back. Usually when she went out it was just for a walk, to see different faces and different places. She liked watching people in shops; she liked imagining what kind of homes they had and whether the women had husbands or boyfriends, and what they did when they were not shopping. Usually when she went out Porter Pig found an errand for her – 'Oh well, if you're going near the shops, Quincy, you can bring back the fish. And since you'll be passing the Post Office you might as well get the staff's National Insurance stamps this week.' Quincy always did what Porter Pig asked, because of being allowed to stay in Briar House. She could not pay money to be here like the others, so she had to work instead. This was reasonable.

She was going out this afternoon – Porter Pig had said, 'Then you can collect the minced lamb,' which meant it was shepherd's pie for supper tonight – but Quincy was going on an important errand today as well.

The errand was for Imogen; Quincy was very pleased indeed to be able to do something for her even though it was all connected with her parents who had just died, both of them at the same time.

It was very sad. Imogen had told Quincy about it, sitting on the bed in her room, and Quincy had known she was upset. The light was not very good in there, because mean old Freda Pig said no one could have a light, or heating, on in the bedrooms until the evening – all that waste of heating and light when the downstairs rooms were there for everyone to use – but even in the uncertain light of the dark November day, Quincy could see that Imogen's eyes were odd. The little black bits at the centre were so enormous that her whole eyes looked black.

'The funeral was yesterday,' said Imogen. 'A service at three o'clock, and then the burial at four. That's why Thalia didn't come to see me yesterday.'

Imogen's voice was a bit wrong as well as her eyes. She sounded as if she was very tired indeed, as if she was struggling not to fall fast asleep. 'I ought to have gone,' she said, now. 'You don't stay away from your own parents' funeral, do you? I don't know where they're buried or anything. And I know it doesn't make any difference where they're buried or that I wasn't there, but it feels odd not knowing. It feels wrong.'

When Quincy's own mother had died, Quincy had not bothered much about where the grave was. She had not bothered about things like flowers either, partly because she had not got any money, and also because the cemetery had been a long way from where she lived. It was difficult to carry plants or flowers on two lots of trains and then a bus, and anyway the only thing she would have wanted to plant would have been stinging nettles or bindweed or deadly nightshade to punish her mother for making her go to bed with all those men, and nettles and deadly nightshade were not things the cemetery people would have allowed.

But she said, 'I'm allowed to go out. I could go and find the grave for you if you like. So you'd know. I could put some flowers on it if you wanted.' She was not sure if this was the right thing to say because a lot of people these days said it was a waste of money to take flowers out to a graveyard and leave them there to die, and that they would rather give the money to a good charity, but other people saw it as a memorial. It was difficult to know which of these points of view Imogen would take.

Imogen said slowly, 'I don't know if I especially believe in flowers for the dead. But it would be better than doing nothing at all.' She looked at Quincy. 'Would you really do that for me? Go out to the churchyard and find the graves?'

It would not do to say that she would do anything in the world for Imogen, so Quincy just said, 'Oh yes. Shall I go this afternoon?'

It was starting to rain, and most of the light had already drained from the November afternoon as Quincy approached the cemetery gates.

Imogen had said that her parents were to have been buried in the same churchyard as her cousin Edmund – it was vaguely the family church, inasmuch as anyone went to church these days. But it was traditional for christenings and weddings and funerals. And cemeteries were orderly affairs, with new graves added in neat sequence, so it was probable that her parents' grave would be near to Edmund's.

'And I think I can remember where his grave is,' Imogen said. 'If I explain it to you, you could find it and start from there. There's barely a week between the two funerals, so it can't be far away.'

The church was only about a quarter of an hour's walk from Briar House. It was the Church of St Michael, and the cemetery was around the side with its own gates – huge iron-rail gates they were – and there was a bit of wall and a thick hedge. A printed notice said the gates would be locked at five o'clock in winter and half past seven in summer. Quincy had a vague idea that this was something to do with cemeteries always having to be locked before sunset. This was an unexpectedly shivery thought. It might be for all kinds of reasons, but one of the reasons might be that dead people got out of their graves after sunset and walked about. If they saw you, they would do all kinds of terrible things to you, exactly as Sybilla Campbell did at Thornacre. They would bite you and drink all your blood, or they would drag you down into the ground to lie with them for ever. You had to be very careful indeed of these things. Quincy knew they happened: there were books telling about them, and there were stories that people had told as well, on and on for hundreds of years. Quincy had seen some of the books and she had heard some of the stories and so she knew it was true.

But if the gates were locked at five o'clock in winter she had almost an hour before any of these things started to happen, so it was all right.

As Imogen had said, it was not a very big cemetery and Quincy followed the directions carefully, walking on the gravel paths, looking at each grave as she passed it. People did not want to be buried so much these days, they preferred to be cremated. They said it was cleaner and nicer. But walking between the headstones, through the thin autumn rain that was beginning to fall, Quincy thought there was a great sense of peace here. A feeling of people sleeping deeply and satisfyingly after having lived their lives. The cemetery would not feel like this after sunset, of course, because that might be when the bodies would wake up and get out of their graves. But it felt all right at the moment.

The rain was turning into a steady drizzle; it was the kind that seeped through your coat and got into your hair and drenched you all the way through to your skin. Quincy shivered and turned up her collar.

This must be the yew tree that Imogen had described,

with the slight grassy rise behind it. Edmund's grave was almost directly beneath the tree, Imogen had said. Quincy moved forward, warily. It did not really matter if anyone saw her, except that it might look a bit peculiar because people did not visit graveyards at this time of day in November. But it was all right, because there was no one else about.

Edmund's grave was almost directly under the yew tree, exactly as Imogen had said. There was a small wooden cross to mark it, with his name clearly printed, and the date he had died. Quincy looked about her. There were three or four newly-dug graves nearby and she walked over to inspect each one. They all had the same wooden markers with names on: when the grass had grown people would put up headstones and bring little stone urns for flowers, or plant flowering bushes.

Quincy had bought flowers. 'I haven't very much money,' Imogen had said. 'So will you get whatever you can?'

There was a flower-shop in the High Street near Briar House, and the lady in the shop had said why not have chrysanthemums: they would last well, and you got a good, big bunch for your money at this time of year. After careful thought Quincy had chosen the huge mop-headed ones in bronze and yellow. They would make a good splash of colour and Quincy was pleased to think of Imogen's parents having the lovely flowers, and she was pleased to be doing this for Imogen. She had carried the chrysanthemums carefully so that they would not be squashed, enjoying the golden autumn wet-earth scent from them.

The grave was the farthest one and Quincy nearly missed it because it was on the other side of the gravel path and there was a little dip in the ground. But it was a double plot and the marker had the names of Imogen's parents – Royston James Ingram and Eloise Marie Ingram – so Quincy knew it was the right one. She had never heard the name Eloise before. It was very beautiful. She laid the flowers carefully at the foot of the wooden marker cross, and straightened up. That was all she needed to do; she could tell Imogen where her parents were, and she could tell her about the flowers. It would be nice to be back inside Briar House and to get into warm, dry clothes. She would make a pot of tea for Imogen and take it to her room and tell her all about the graves.

She turned to go; it must be getting on for five o'clock and it was important not to get locked in. The rain was turning into a soft smoky mist that rose up from the ground, so that the headstones loomed up blackly and looked ghostly and nearly alive. This might be how they looked when the bodies underneath were getting ready to come out. Whatever it was, it was beginning to be very scary indeed.

And then she heard the footsteps coming along the gravel path towards her.

It was not logical to be frightened, and it was not logical to want to hide.

But Quincy was suddenly very frightened indeed. She looked quickly about her. She was already half-hidden from whoever was approaching, because of the uneven ground, and she ducked behind a large headstone so that she was completely hidden. Crouching there unseen she felt fear – thick scalding fear – begin to start up strongly, like an engine suddenly being revved.

Through the misty rain and the creeping twilight came the thin dark-haired lady who had visited Imogen at Briar House, and who had worn nice clothes and a human mask to hide the evil black hatred of Imogen.

Thalia Caudle.

There was absolutely no reason in the world why Imogen's

aunt should not be here, visiting her son's grave just as Quincy was visiting Imogen's parents' grave. Except that people did not visit graves at five o'clock on dark wet November afternoons, and they did not sit on wooden benches in the rain and stare at graves with such intensity.

Quincy's heart was pounding so agonisingly that she thought it would come up into her throat and choke her at any minute. She stayed where she was, trying not to make a sound, trying to melt into the shadows, her eyes fixed on Imogen's aunt.

Mrs Caudle was leaning forward; her eyes were fixed on the grave at her feet, and her lips were moving as if she was talking to it. Quincy risked glancing over her shoulder. The cemetery looked deserted. If she could inch nearer, she might hear what was being said, not because of what Matron called earwigging, but because this was Imogen's enemy, and it was important to know as much as possible about her.

Thalia had not meant to visit Edmund today, but she had known he would miss her if she did not.

He came to her every night now, not quite a dream but not quite reality either, standing at the foot of her bed and holding out his hands. It was agony for Thalia to see her lovely, golden boy torn and filthy with putrescence, the decay of death a little more advanced each time.

But there were times when the daylight hours until he would be with her stretched out endlessly and emptily, and on those days she would come out here, and sit in the little seat and stare down at the oblong of earth where he lay. Sometimes she could talk to him. There was nothing wrong in it; there was nothing wrong in a bereaved mother seated by her son's grave.

She talked to him today, oblivious of the soft, drenching rain, hardly aware of the encroaching dusk. It was the curious, none-too-comfortable hour when it was neither quite day nor yet quite night; the time when you had the feeling that odd, inexplicable things might happen, that the dead might stir and hear you, that an eerie, purple sorcery might be within your grasp, and if only you knew the right words you might be able to lift it between your hands and spin it into strong enchantment . . . It was a time when the dead might be persuaded to return, not mutilated and hideous, but whole and sweet-fleshed and loving.

Seated by the grave on this darkling afternoon, feeling the strange twilight bewitchment soak into her skin, Thalia knew that Edmund was listening to her. She knew he was pleased at all the things she had done, and at all the things she was able to tell him.

Imogen shut away inside Briar House, and helpless. Royston and Eloise both gone. She, herself, in control of Ingram's. And the marvellous, satisfying punishment for Eloise. When your actions were right and just, the stars in their courses fought for you and with you, and it was very right and very just that Eloise should suffer.

'She's only a few yards away from you, Edmund,' whispered Thalia, and leaned forward. Was he hearing her? Yes, she could feel that something hovered quite close by, listening, absorbing what she was saying. 'She's only a few yards away, but she's not dead, Edmund. Isn't that the best triumph of all? The bitch who would have let her daughter supplant you is buried alive.'

'I don't know if it means anything at all, I might not have even heard properly. But it sounded a bit scary. And it's odd, isn't it?' Quincy had remembered not to say 'ain't it' because she was trying to talk like Imogen.

Imogen was staring at Quincy and her face was so white that Quincy was afraid she might faint.

After a moment, she said, 'But my mother can't be – still alive. That's what you think Thalia meant, isn't it? That she's been buried alive. And Thalia's somehow responsible— But that's – that's like something from an old horror film.'

She frowned again, as if trying to push something away, and Quincy said, 'What are you going to do?'

Chapter Ten

It afforded Dan wry entertainment to discover that the dark tower he had visualised for Thalia Caudle was there for the climbing after all.

He turned his back on the drone of the West End's traffic and craned his neck to look up at the tall modern block where Ingram's carried on its daily work. Top floor, his agent had said. Where else would you expect it to be? Get on with it, Daniel.

Thalia Caudle apologised for receiving him in the large office that had been her cousin's. 'It's sickeningly formal, and it might look like snob-arrogance,' she said. 'But I hope it doesn't. Have you noticed, Mr Tudor, how sudden promotion can sometimes make people appallingly supercilious?'

'And sudden riches can make them disdainful.'

'Well, I hope I'm avoiding both,' she said. 'But the thing is, I don't know much about Ingram's – I mean about the day-to-day running of it – and that's why I'm spending a bit of time here. I'm not going to be making it a full-time job, but I thought I should get to know some of the people here, even if I'm only going to be a kind of sleeping director – I hope that didn't sound suggestive. What I'm actually trying to do is understand the nuts and bolts of the place, and what people's roles are. Do sit down. You'd like some coffee, I expect. Or tea?'

'Coffee. Thank you.' Dan was not exactly thrown off balance by this friendly, prosaic reception, but he was certainly given pause. The black-clad lady he had seen briefly at Edmund's funeral had been superseded by the image of Villainess Supreme. Dan had built his picture of Thalia to his own satisfaction, and to this end had clothed her in swirling black and crimson and given her a paper-white face and blood-red lips. He had allotted to her the disposition of a Lady Macbeth and the appetite of a vampiric Transylvanian countess.

Faced with the real McCoy, he was forced to own that his memory had been selective; the reality was a thin, forty-something lady wearing a modern loose-styled navy jacket and skirt with a plain yellow shirt, and although her hair was admittedly black, it was cut into an up-to-date, just-curling bob, and she looked as if she wore only a light sprinkling of make-up. Only the eyes were the same: dark and penetrating, and the mouth: thin and from some angles faintly greedy. Dan set his portable recorder down and put his notebook next to it.

'It's very good of you to grant the interview,' he said. 'Particularly in view of your bereavements. I'll try not to trespass on anything tender.'

'Will you? But I might rather enjoy it if you did, Mr Tudor.'

Dan had been setting the tape, but at this he looked up sharply and found her gazing at him with sudden intensity. She widened her eyes very slightly, and flicked her glance down over his body. He stared back and incredibly felt a prickle of sexual awareness. Now that would be really crazy, Daniel. That would be absolutely insane. Yes, but it's a damn good lead-in for intimacy, if not full-blown seduction, he thought. It's an effective ploy. Understated, but it's as if she's stroked the inside of my thigh with a velvet-covered hand . . . Oh, hell. Does she know she's struck a chord? Yes, of course she does, they always do. His inner writer's mind wondered briefly if this might do for the seduction scene in chapter six, and the evil Margot, then he folded the whole thing into his subconscious to be dealt with later and focused his mind on leading Thalia Caudle into the interview.

She talked with apparent openness about the family business, and about her cousin's role as its chief executive. She was helpful and interesting, and she did not again say anything that might be taken as double-intentioned. Dan did not trust her an inch.

'Royston was brought up knowing he would one day head the firm, and he went into it when he was twenty-one,' said Thalia. 'He worked his way up and by the time he reached the boardroom he knew the business pretty well inside out. By contrast I've hardly had any involvement at all; I never expected to have any. But when Royston became chief executive the lawyers insisted on certain contingency clauses.'

'In his will?'

'Well, in that of course. But mostly in the company's Articles of Association,' said Thalia. 'Ingram's is a private company, as you probably know, and Royston and Eloise were the major shareholders. I don't suppose it matters telling you that, because you could probably look it up at Companies House. But I hope you won't think it interesting enough to include in the feature.'

Dan thought he probably would not.

Thalia said, 'No one ever thought the clause that gave me this, well, stewardship, would ever have to be invoked.'

'Except the lawyers.'

'Yes. Lawyers always have to guard against every eventuality, don't they? And since someone had to be named, Royston thought I was the closest of his own generation. Which I am.'

'He named you Imogen's guardian?'

Thalia looked at him thoughtfully, and then said, 'Her guardian if he and Eloise should die while Imogen was still a minor, or if . . .'

'Yes?'

'If at any time she should be judged incapable.' She stopped abruptly.

Dan said slowly. 'That's surely a rather unusual provision.'

'Royston wanted Ingram's to remain solely in the family's control for as long as possible,' said Thalia. 'He had a horror of the Court of Protection.' She regarded Dan levelly, and Dan made the discovery that Thalia disliked Imogen very much.

'But why would the Court of Protection ever be involved in Ingram's?' Dan waited, and thought: let's see how you field that one, madam.

'Imogen's health was always precarious,' said Thalia.

'Mentally?' They might as well drag the word out and see what happened.

'Well, physically as well. But Royston knew I would look after her. He knew I would look after everything. Royston and I were – once close.'

She's doing extremely well, thought Dan. She's projecting an image of someone suddenly landed with a huge burden, and shouldering it manfully. Womanfully. She's hinting at some long-ago love affair between herself and poor old cousin Royston – that might be perfectly true, of course – and she's hinting that he named her for auld lang syne. It's all believable, except that I don't think I do believe it.

But the interview turned out to be a good one: *Women in Business* was going to greatly enjoy the account of Thalia's first boardroom skirmish, and *Integra* would lap up the details of the frantic day spent plundering Bond Street for a suitable outfit to wear. Dan led her from there to talk about her plans for Ingram's future, which included developing a line in folklore for older children. He made copious notes to back up the tape recorder.

There was a potentially awkward moment halfway

through. Thalia was pouring a second cup of coffee when she said, apparently apropos of nothing, 'I'm so glad they gave you the commission to do this. It was you, wasn't it? At my boy's funeral that afternoon?'

'I was under false colours that day. But yes, it was me.'

'I thought so. You saw that terrible, terrible business with Imogen?'

It was the 'terrible, terrible' that did it. Over the top, thought Dan, and felt his mind wince with the kind of sudden and sickening pain you get if you turn your ankle while running fast. She's entitled to be bitter and bereaved and emotional, of course, but she's struck a false note.

He said, 'I did see it.'

'But you left almost at once. I noticed that,' said the villainess smiling with open friendliness and calculating eyes. 'I thought it was so sensitive of you.'

Dan said, 'I'm a freelance writer, Mrs Caudle. A journalist for a good part of my working week. And journalists don't normally possess sensitivity.'

'No? But you didn't publish anything. Or if you did, no one in the family has seen it. I don't think you should call yourself insensitive, Dan. I think you're very sensitive indeed.'

Here we go again, said Dan's inner voice. Mental hand on mental thigh. He waited, and after a moment she said, 'D'you know, after that morning, after Edmund's funeral and Imogen's dreadful action, I wanted to contact you. To thank you for being so discreet. Only I wasn't sure . . .'

'Yes?'

'If you would – care to hear from me.' Her voice had slid several octaves lower. Be careful, said one half of Dan's mind. Be very, very careful of this one. She'll eat you for breakfast and spit out the bones. To hell with that, said the other half. Let's go along with it and see what she'll do. Purely for research for chapter six, of course. Oh sure, said his mind sarcastically. All right then, purely to get a line on the girl, Imogen. Yes, there's Imogen. You might never know it, Imogen, thought Dan, and I might never meet you to tell you, but you're inspiring me to write a book that I didn't think I was capable of writing.

Thalia said, 'I didn't want to intrude. If I had phoned you it might have been misread. You might have seen it as an intrusion of your privacy. Perhaps your wife, or girlfriend . . .'

Dan heard himself say, 'I don't think I would have regarded it as an intrusion. Mrs Caudle,' and gave it a count of ten.

At five, she said, 'Do call me Thalia.'

With a feeling of stepping on to a dark, slithery path that might end in catastrophe, but that was by now a path that Margot was certainly going to tread in chapter six, Dan said, 'You know, there's a great deal I still want to ask you. About your charity work – you're quite well known for that, I think – and about how you'll fit it in with this new commitment. Certainly about your ideas for expanding Ingram's Books. This scheme for getting into the folklore areas for older children, for instance. That would make quite an interesting angle.' He paused. Five seconds. Six. 'Are you free for lunch by any chance?'

'I'm afraid not,' she said, and Dan thought, blast! I've misread the signs. Serve me right. But I was so sure—

'But,' said Thalia, and there was no doubt about the sensuous purr this time, 'I am free for dinner.'

Thalia had rather enjoyed the interview with Dan Tudor and she had enjoyed re-living for him that first encounter with Ingram's executive board. She had been wary about what she said, but she thought he had not suspected anything.

It amused her to remember that first meeting in Ingram's small but well-furnished conference room, seated round the oval table, herself pretending to be bewildered by the balance sheets and budgets and extrapolated figures but really laughing secretly at everyone's eagerness to explain things. She had not been bewildered at all; she had not endured all those years of dull charity committee work without learning a little about financial administration, if not in detail, at least in general. And it had been plain from the finance director's report that Ingram's was doing pretty well for itself.

Resolve had hardened then, because Imogen should never have all this. This should all have been Edmund's, and Thalia would burn the building down before she would let Imogen have it. She would fling the other shareholders out of the window one by one.

With Royston and Eloise both out of the reckoning, and with Imogen shut away in Briar House, there should be nothing to stand in her way. No one was going to question anything she did, because no one suspected her of doing anything wrong. The feeling of power was like a one thousand volt electrical current through the brain and the heart and the loins. Probate had not yet been granted, but there was absolutely nothing wrong with Royston's will or with the Articles of Association, both of which gave her stewardship for Imogen's minority, and no one in the family was likely to challenge that. Most of them had known of the provision, and none of them wanted the task of actually running Ingram's. All of them wanted the assurance of continuing dividends, and none of them minded who sat in the chief executive's seat. Thalia was caretaker of the whole shooting match until Imogen reached eighteen. Or in the event of her being judged unfit or incapable.

Thalia thought she had covered every eventuality. She thought she had covered all her tracks and tied up all the loose ends. Except for Dan Tudor. A tiny frown creased her brow. Dan might be a remaining loose end. He had been at Edmund's funeral and he had seen what had happened, and he could not be trusted not to spread it abroad. Thalia had managed to get the family on her side over shutting the bitch-creature away, but Dan was not family. He was no fool, and he was already asking questions. This tale of articles for women's journals might be true, but it might equally be a cover. He would have to be dealt with.

Thalia found herself looking forward to the evening's meeting with a shiver of sexual anticipation.

Freda Porter hoped she was not one of those pitiable, faintly comic females who simpered the minute a man came into their orbit, but it could not be denied that to entertain Dr Sterne to supper was extremely gratifying.

He had phoned in his customary abrupt way to say he would like to call in and spend some time with that odd little creature Quincy; Matron would not be put out if he arrived during the evening?

Matron would not be put out in the least. Dr Sterne was always welcome at Briar House, she said, and perhaps on this occasion they might give him supper after he had seen Quincy. There had been a pause, and then Leo had said, 'Yes, all right. Thank you.'

Probably he would be expecting to sit with the staff and the patients in the dining room. He was in for a surprise, if so; Freda was not going to pass up an opportunity of serving him a nice little supper in the privacy of her own sitting room, or of letting him see her for once in something other than her working uniform. She would wear the navy and maroon silk two-piece which was so slimming, and have her hair done. She might even work the conversation round to the question of the vacant post for a matron at Thornacre. Could she? Well, why not? She thought she could do it tactfully so that Dr Sterne would not realise it was deliberate.

The food was not, naturally, the same food that the patients would be eating, particularly since it was Thursday and therefore corned beef hash with rice pudding to follow.

You could not give a man like Dr Sterne corned beef hash, and Freda had bought two pre-packed gourmet dinners – fish in a cream sauce. If it was served in the blue and white Devonport dish, nobody would be any the wiser. There must, of course, be wine, but by a lucky chance there was a special offer this week in the local supermarket. Wine was wine, and there was no sense in paying eight or nine pounds a bottle when you could get it for a fraction of that.

The fish was really very good indeed, and the Devonport dish set it off a treat. You would never tell that it had not been freshly prepared. The kitchen had sent in a dish of mashed potatoes and Freda had herself bought cheese and biscuits.

It was unfortunate that after the first half-glass of wine Dr Sterne remembered he would be driving later on; Freda was sorry about that, but of course it was sensible of him not to drink. She drank rather a lot of the wine herself as a consequence; it brought quite a flush to her cheeks, but a good many men liked a healthy colour in females. Better than these stick-like, porridge-faced girls people went so silly over.

She listened to Dr Sterne talking about Quincy and how he thought he was starting to uncover some of the child's really appalling early years. People set a lot of store by that kind of thing, although Freda had her private doubts. Bad was bad and sly was sly, and Quincy was plain bad and downright sly. But she listened to Dr Sterne talking, because you could listen to him talk for ever. He told her a little about some of the methods he was trying with his stubbornly unresponsive patients. Most interesting, that was, all to do with stimulation of hidden or buried parts of the mind.

They discussed the situation at Thornacre, of course; Freda was sorrowful over the terrible things that had been discovered there but she was pleased to hear that, as she had thought, the post of matron was available. 'Up for grabs,' said Leo carelessly.

This was very hopeful and Freda made bold to ask a few questions – what qualifications were the commission looking for, and what kind of experience would they be requiring? – when Leo suddenly looked towards the door and said, 'There's someone creeping across the hall.'

The timing, as far as Freda was concerned, could not have been worse. There was nothing in the least wrong about entertaining a distinguished colleague to supper, although Freda was vaguely aware that it would not be an especially good thing for any of the patients, never mind the staff, to see her flushed with wine and dressed in the navy and maroon silk, which had turned out to be a bit tighter across the hips than she remembered. And it was not really so very late, either.

The really annoying thing was that they had been interrupted just as the question of Thornacre's new matron had finally been broached. Freda was quite sure that Dr Sterne had been about to say, 'If you apply, be sure to give my name as reference.' Or, 'I'll have a word with Professor Rackham on your behalf.' He might even have added, 'and if you are interested, I don't think he need bother with interviewing anyone else,' although this was admittedly a bit far-fetched. As it was, the cosy atmosphere was interrupted and Freda had to hide her annoyance and be concerned.

Dr Sterne had opened the door of the sitting room just a chink and was looking out into the shadowy hall beyond. The chequered red and blue glass of the fanlight over the door was casting its subtle harlequin pattern over him. The fanlight had been put in by some long-ago Victorian owner of Briar House and everyone said how ugly it was and how tasteless, but with the light of the moon above it, it showered Leo Sterne with soft, exotic radiance, and it was so like Freda's private fantasy picture that she blinked. This was the trouble with Dr Sterne; every time you saw him he looked different. No wonder his patients said he was a magician. He was a chameleon and the most charismatic man you would ever meet.

Leo was not thinking about being charismatic or chameleon-like; he was more aware of a slight mental irritation induced by the archness of the company, and of a vague physical irritation due to the naivety of the wine. He focused his whole attention forward into the shadowy hall. He caught the faint drift of some strong emotion –fear? – and then of an aching loneliness.

He had been just in time to see the slight figure detach itself from the darkness of the stairwell and slip through the door, and he had been in time to see the pale triangle of face surrounded by hair that seemed to float and melt into the shadows of its own accord. It did not need Freda Porter's slightly bibulous whisper, 'Imogen Ingram,' to identify the fugitive.

He said, very softly, 'Stay here, Matron. I'll follow her and see what she does.'

Chapter Eleven

Imogen had discovered that the more you tried to banish a thought, the more obtrusive it became.

She had gone to her room after supper that evening intending to go to bed early, and to let the cotton-wool feeling take over so that she did not have to think. If that did not work, then she was going to concentrate on ordinary things: the book she had started to read; the supper she was going to cook tomorrow night for herself and Quincy. This had been more or less arranged earlier on. Imogen had gone down to the big square kitchen and found it astonishingly easy to talk to the lady who did the cooking. There was, it appeared, some leftover chicken, and also some mushrooms whose absence from the bottom of the fridge would not grieve the heart of those who paid the food bills. And a half-pint of milk and scraping of Cheddar was neither here nor there either. Imogen negotiated for these modest comestibles with as much care as if they had been the ingredients for a Buckingham Palace banquet. She was going to slice up the chicken and make a cheese and mushroom sauce to serve over it, and invite Quincy to eat it with her. There was discussion about tarragon, of which there turned out to be a small screwtop jar in the back of a cupboard. It had not gone very far past the expiry date.

It was nearly ten o'clock when she finally admitted that she was not thinking about her chicken dish at all, and that what she was really thinking about was what Quincy had overheard. She sat up in bed and switched on the light,

113

because if you faced something nasty with the light on, it was nearly always less frightening than in the dark.

This was not. This, faced head on in the light, was as dreadful as it had been in the dark. It was so comprehensively dreadful that Imogen knew that even with the cotton-wool thing, it was not going to let her go to sleep again tonight. It would claw meanly at her mind and burrow under her skin until it got her full attention.

Eloise was buried and the funeral had been yesterday afternoon. More than twenty-four hours. It was not logical or intelligent to wonder if she was still alive; this was not the eighteenth or nineteenth century where medical science was so inexact – and medical researchers so avid for raw material – that people were buried alive. And it was such a truly bizarre thought that Imogen wondered if whatever Dr Shilling and Matron had been dosing her with had warped her judgement. And then she wondered how far Quincy's judgement could be trusted. Supposing none of it was true outside of Quincy's strange world?

What she really needed was reassurance, but nobody in here was going to give her that. She considered the idea of phoning Aunt Rosa, or Flora, or Juliette, or even of approaching the hard-faced Matron. What would she say? 'You'll think I'm a bit mad, but Quincy overheard something in the graveyard and because of it I've got this wild idea that my mother's been buried alive.' They would think she was a bit mad – they thought she was half mad as it was. If she came out with something like that, they would think she was a hundred and fifty per cent mad, and there was always the chance that they might be right.

It's down to me, thought Imogen in panic. I'll have to do something, I really will. I don't think I'll ever be able to sleep again until I know there's nothing wrong. What time is it now? Ten o'clock. Quite a good time to slip out, really. No one's likely to be about; the others all go to bed at nine thirty and the staff went home ages ago. I could go out to

114

the cemetery and look at the grave and be back here without anyone knowing.

She crossed the room and opened the small wardrobe, reaching for dark trousers and a thick sweater. What else? Well, a torch would be a good idea, only I haven't got one – yes, I have, there's a pencil torch in my night case.

Five minutes later she was stealing down the stairs. Nothing stirred, and the only sound was her own heart thumping as if it might burst out of her chest with pent-up fear. There was the scent of mass cooking lying faintly on the air, underlain with a thin, sick odour. Institution scents. Horrid, thought Imogen. But I suppose it's when I no longer notice them that I need to worry.

There was a faint scrape of sound as she drew back the latches on the huge front doors, and she froze, expecting to be challenged. But nothing moved and no one came, and she slipped out into the night.

As she went stealthily down the drive, keeping on the grassy edges because of crunching the gravel, she thought that the compulsion that was driving her was not coming from within but from without. Her mother telepathically calling for help? Oh, don't be ridiculous! But the sense of urgency was mounting, and the need for haste was thrumming against her mind. Like huge scaly wings beating on the night sky. Like hands flailing uselessly against the underside of a coffin lid . . . Stop it!

With reasonable luck she could be back in Briar House within an hour, and without anyone knowing she had been out. And then she could sleep – she could sleep for about a hundred years with the relief of it.

The night air smelt fresh and good as she walked towards the road where the church was. It seeped into her mind, making it feel cleaner and sharper than it had for some time. I could simply keep walking, thought Imogen suddenly. I could just walk on and on, and maybe at some stage I'd get a lift, and I could be anywhere in the country or anywhere in

115

the world this time tomorrow. She tucked this idea into a corner of her mind to be examined later on.

The cemetery gates were locked, but Imogen had expected this and she thought she could climb over. She looked about her, scanning the darkness. The nearest houses were some way off, and the cemetery was not overlooked. But anyone might drive along the road at any minute, and she would certainly be seen in car headlights. But perhaps if she was very quick . . .

She took a deep breath and swarmed over the gates, using the iron spikes at the top as handholds, and dropped down on the other side quite easily. So far so good.

It was very eerie indeed in the cemetery. Huge old trees rose up at the far end, sharply outlined against the night sky, and behind them was the cold outline of the new moon. I'm grave-robbing by moonlight, thought Imogen in sudden panic. But I won't think too deeply about it; I'll get in and look at the graves and then out again – bam! – and it'll all only brush the topmost layer of my mind.

Edmund's grave was ahead of her. There was the plain cross that Quincy had described, which would mark the grave until the ground had settled sufficiently for a headstone. Aunt Thalia would have something huge and marbly, and order it to be engraved with something mawkish. Had Thalia really sat out here, talking to the dead Edmund in the darkening afternoon? Imogen wondered if Edmund's head had been put back, and instantly wished she had not thought this. In and out – bam! – remember?

A small night wind had whipped up from nowhere. It was whispering to itself in the trees, and ruffling the grass around the edges of the graves. As Imogen approached her parents' grave, there was a scuttering on the ground and something small and clawed darted into the shadows. Rats? If I start imagining rats I'll be lost. I'll think it was a squirrel, except that squirrels aren't nocturnal – or are they? It was probably a mouse. A vole. More frightened of me than I am of it. I'm not frightened of mice, anyway. I'm frightened of headless corpses and I'm very frightened indeed of living people being buried by mistake. Concentrate, Imogen. That's the grave there, I can see the chrysanthemums Quincy said she bought. And I think – oh God, I think there's something following me! No, there isn't, it's the scuttling creature again. Or it's an owl in the trees. Yes, there it goes. Imogen stood for a moment watching the owl soar out of the tree and swoop its way across the night sky. Lovely. In another minute I'll have to look at the graves. All right, deep breath, Imogen, and then aim the torch. On and then straight off again. Here I go.

She flicked on the torch and heard her own indrawn gasp of horror. Ice-water seemed to fill her veins.

The two-second viewing showed Imogen something she had not bargained for. She had thought it would be easy to make sure that there was no disturbance. But she had forgotten, or perhaps had never known, that graves are never left open overnight.

Her mother's grave had been filled in and to see the coffin she would have to dig.

Leo had kept in the shadows well behind Imogen as she padded through the night. He thought she was so intent on whatever she was doing and wherever she was going that she was not aware of his presence.

When he realised she was making for the cemetery he felt a prickle of deep-seated fear. Quench that at once, man of science! The trouble was that however much you thought you had stripped away the primitive beliefs and the ancient superstitions, something always remained to betray you. It was betraying him now, watching Imogen climb over the gates of the cemetery. He waited until the shadows had swallowed her up, and then went after her, feeling muscles and tendons protest as he pulled himself over the portals and dropped down on the other side. The black comedy of the situation struck him forcibly; he thought wryly that he had always been able to beat a hasty exit from a lady's bedroom if her official partner turned up unexpectedly, but that diving out through back doors or conservatories, or even climbing out of windows, had hardly equipped him for breaking into a locked cemetery. As he scanned the shadows, he was uneasily aware that he was following a girl who was probably severely mentally disturbed, and that he was entirely alone with her. Serve you right if she attacks you in a psychotic rage!

He lost her for a while in the thick darkness inside the churchyard, and had to prowl stealthily up and down the grass verges, peering into the shadows and listening. And then he caught a soft scrabbling sound over to his right, and turned sharply. Imogen? Yes, he could see the white triangle of her face and the black hair melting into the night.

For several crowded minutes he could not identify what she was doing, and then he suddenly understood, and his skin crawled. She's digging up a grave. She's trying to get at her parents!

For several seconds the sheer horror of it froze him into immobility, and then he went forward, grabbing Imogen by the arms and pulling her clear of the oblong of newly-turned earth. She struggled and fought him, beating against his chest with clenched fists and drawing breath to scream. There was a moment when she was pressed hard against him, and he felt her heart pounding wildly with terror. He grabbed her hands, and said, 'Imogen, you're safe. I'm a friend! Leo Sterne. Don't you remember me? From Briar House. For pity's sake don't scream!'

His use of her name jerked her out of some of the fear, and she twisted round in his arms, staring at him. Her eyes were huge and fearful, the pupils so wildly dilated that they looked completely black. Drugs? Or just fear? But when Imogen spoke, although her voice was breathless, it was perfectly sensible. 'Dr Sterne . . .'

He said, 'Yes. It's all right, Imogen.'

Imogen made an impatient movement, and Leo tightened his grip in case she tried to attack him. 'It isn't all right,' she said in a low, urgent voice. 'That's the whole point. My mother—'

'She's dead, yes, I know about that. Is this her grave? Listen, Imogen, it's a dreadful tragedy, but you'll come out on the other side, I promise you will. I'll help you.'

Imogen jerked free of his hands angrily. 'No! You don't understand. You *don't*!' she cried, and Leo heard her voice spiral into panic again.

'Listen now, we'll talk about it together.' He took a step towards her. 'Imogen, we can talk about it all night if you want and no one will mind.' He could feel her mind accelerating, not into hysteria but into panic, and he braced himself. Impossible to call up any kind of hypnotic tricks under these conditions and he had no idea what drugs she might have been given, but he had already automatically made a start with the old, proven method of repeating her name as often as possible to create a bridge from his mind to hers.

Imogen shook her head as if to dislodge something that was obscuring her vision. 'No, listen, Dr Sterne, you really *don't* understand! I don't think my mother's dead. There's a – I think there's a chance she's been buried alive! That's why I had to come here.' She stopped, and then said, 'Only I didn't know – I forgot that they'd have filled the grave in straight after the service.'

The forlorn, macabre logic of this scraped painfully against Leo's mind, but he said at once, 'Imogen, it isn't likely. It isn't even possible. Listen, Imogen, listen to me.' Almost without having to think, he scooped up his mental strength as if it was a glittering sphere and projected it forward with such force that he saw her blink. She flinched as if she had been struck, and then he felt her mind leap forward to meet his, and there was a moment of fusion so complete and so dazzling that for a few seconds Leo lost all awareness of his surroundings. Something strong and sweet and light-filled shivered on the air between them, and Leo stared at Imogen and saw that she was staring back at him.

And then awareness returned, and Leo recovered himself and reviewed the situation swiftly. He had no way yet of telling whether Imogen was delusional or whether she was in the grip of a phobia –something connected with dying, with premature burial? Although she was certainly in a state of immense tension, she did not seem actually out of touch with reality. Probably a phobia, then. His mind flew ahead, planning: get her back to Briar House, assess the situation properly. The dilation of her pupils might be from drugs conventionally prescribed, or they might be unconventional and self-administered. Or it might be purely a manifestation of fear; being alone in the middle of a graveyard in the pitch dark was enough to rock the most imperturbable of imaginations. And, of course, said his mind treacherously, it might even be from that remarkable bolt of energy that sizzled between you just now. But you'd better not delve too deeply into your own reactions to *that*, Dr Sterne!

Imogen said in a desperate, despairing whisper, 'Dr Sterne, I'm not mad, I'm truly not. I know I'm supposed to have – done something weird, but this is different. Please, please, will you help me.' She reached out and took his arm, and Leo felt the prickle of electricity again as her hand closed over his coat sleeve. He felt her panic slice into his own mind, but he felt as well the conviction that drove it. Just for a moment, he thought: supposing this isn't a phobia at all? Supposing it's something deeper? Something akin to that strange, ancient instinct that once warned primeval man when danger approached, and that still lingered in the mind's dark corners today, so that you suddenly found yourself turning your head unprompted because you knew absolutely and completely and inexplicably that someone was watching you? *Supposing she's right?* he thought, appalled.

He shook the thought off at once, but lying treacherously beneath it was another. She doesn't just suspect that her mother isn't dead. She *knows*. She knows something she isn't telling me.

He flung his mind forward again, this time with authority, and said, 'There's something you aren't telling me, isn't there, Imogen? *Isn't there?*'

Something I'm not telling him. Something I can't tell him. Quincy stealing out here earlier this afternoon. Thalia talking to her dead son in his grave . . . People don't do that kind of thing, not normal, sane people. He'd either think I was mad or he'd think Thalia was. And I don't know, not absolutely and definitely, that Quincy got it right, or even how normal and sane Quincy is. No, I can't tell him.

The silence was complete, it was closing about them, wrapping them in intimacy. Imogen knew that Dr Sterne could not see, not fully, what she was thinking, but he could sense something. She could feel his mind reaching deep into her own, she could feel it like a thin radiance going back and back, lighting dark corners, illuminating deeply buried things, things you would never admit to anyone, things that you might not even admit to yourself. In a minute she would have to say something, she would have to give her reasons for being out here, and she would have to give a reason why her mother's coffin had to be dug up. And the reasons would have to be *good*.

She said at last, 'Yes. Yes, I do know something.'

'Yes? Something you've heard? Something you've seen? Imogen, tell me.'

'I can't,' said Imogen, her mind working furiously, dodging the insistent arc of awareness. She looked at Dr Sterne very levelly. He was quite old, of course, probably about forty, but he had rather nice eyes. You felt you wanted him to approve of you. Was there a way of getting him to help? Because it had been mad – yes, she would use that word – it

121

had been absolutely insane to think she could do this by herself. If Dr Sterne had really seen those frantic out-of-control minutes when she had flung herself forward and believed she could dig the earth up with her bare hands it was small wonder he had acted as if he was dealing with a full-blown lunatic.

She took a deep breath and said, 'I'm really not mad. I know how it looks, but I've got to uncover my mother's coffin and I've got to do it now. And if you don't help me,' said Imogen, staring up at him, 'I'll start screaming. I'll scream so loudly that somebody will hear and come out to see what's happening. And then,' said Imogen, hating herself, but going on, 'and then I'll say you brought me out here and that you tried to rape me on the grave. If you don't help me, that's what I'll do.'

Dan had spent most of the afternoon working. The story was unfolding with almost frightening rapidity; several times he felt as if he was at the wheel of a car that was accelerating out of his control. He could not decide if this was a good thing or not.

He was starting to tighten the web about his Rosamund and it was tightening very satisfactorily indeed. The hysteria that had gripped her when she discovered the results of Margot's bloodthirsty machinations had sent her spinning into wild hysteria, which was exactly what Margot had been counting on, the bitch.

No one in the family had believed Rosamund's frantic sobbed-out story of human bones in the old wash house, shreds of flesh still clinging to them, and the distinctive wedding ring – 'My mother's wedding ring which she inherited from her own mother!' – glinting amongst a spill of human finger-bones. No one had believed it, but it had to be investigated. A reluctant search was made by torch-light.

And of course by that time there was nothing out of place.

Margot had laid her snare cunningly and well; she had disposed of all the evidence, and the wash house presented a blandly innocent face to the two hapless members of the family detailed to the task. That chapter closed with Margot standing exultantly on the river bank, the greenish water-light rippling across her face as she tipped the bones and the wedding ring into the water and watched the fast current take them downstream.

And so Rosamund was duly shut away for good by her sorrowing family. A very great pity, they all said. The thing they had tried to sidestep for seventeen years and protect her from – the curse, you might even call it – had finally overtaken the child. She was plainly mad, because sane people did not accuse their relations of gruesome murders. Sane people did not go scrabbling around in disused wash houses in the first place, for heaven's sake. What had the child been *doing* there? demanded the family, none of whom had the remotest suspicion of Margot, or of how she had lured Rosamund into the place and locked the door. Rosamund had perforce spent almost a whole night in the dark cobwebby outbuilding, with the boiled-down remains of her parents for sole company. Dan reckoned that this was sufficient to send anyone's reason spinning a bit off course.

Rosamund's asylum was in England's bleak north-east; a nightmare mansion with an appalling reputation, and its very name caused indrawn gasps of horror and blenching cheeks, not dissimilar from the enthusiastic hissings and booings of Victorian audiences at the entrance of the cloak-swirling archvillain. It had been important to avoid descending into melodrama at this point, but Dan thought he had avoided it.

The most recent chapter had seen the appearance on the scene of a somewhat questionable doctor, who was currently the ruling figure at the asylum. Physically he was not unattractive, but his methods were unexpected and his

123

intentions towards Rosamund somewhat ambiguous. Dan had toyed with the idea of making him a leftover from the Nazi concentration camps but had finally decided against it. Don't let's ladle on the gore too thickly and don't let's stretch the credibility of the plot too much either, Daniel. Mind games can be just as scary as blood and guts. And on consideration, he rather liked the idea of Dr Bentinck playing sinister mind games with Rosamund, and probably finding her sexually attractive at the same time. You could not write a book without having a good dash of sex in it; well, you could, but not if you wanted it to sell.

It was unfortunate that this chapter had seen further signs of rebellion on the part of the typewriter, which was developing an amiable habit of creating its own fantasy world by switching unprompted to its in-built foreign print wheel, so that you found you had typed half a page in Cyrillic or Greek script without realising. Dan had made cautious inquiries about the purchase of a new one, which had been greeted with hilarity. Nobody used typewriters these days, it seemed; they all used word processors. In fact, said the salesman, speaking in the indulgent tone of one contemplating a lost culture, he did not know where you might buy a typewriter any more, not for love or money. At this point Dan had said, very crossly, 'Angels and ministers of grace defend me,' and walked out of the shop.

It was seven o'clock when he reluctantly put Rosamund and her attendant villains away. Oliver had listened without comment to the explanation that Dan would be out to dinner tonight, and had gravely said that he would be perfectly all right on his own. He had some work to do on his own account anyway, he said; students' essays to go through, and a lecture for a postgraduate group to prepare.

As Dan was leaving, Oliver said, with the air of one endeavouring to appear immensely worldly, 'I suppose you'll be pretty late getting home, won't you?'

'Pretty late tonight, or pretty early tomorrow morning,' said Dan, and grinned at his brother's disconcerted expression.

Chapter Twelve

Thalia had suggested they meet at Ingram's small company flat just off Great Portland Street. 'I'm half living there for the moment,' she had said. 'And it would be so much more relaxed than a restaurant.' There was the slightest pause, and then her voice slid an octave lower. 'Also we can talk in privacy,' she said, as if, thought Dan, she visualised the Soho bistros as seething with eavesdroppers, all vying for the inside dirt on Ingram's. Which either meant that dirt was there for the uncovering and she was prepared to uncover it or she was setting the scene for a grand seduction. Dan was still trying to decide which would be preferable when he arrived at the flat.

It was just on eight and the sun was setting over Regent's Park when he announced himself over the door intercom and went up to the third floor. The interior had a prosperous air; the stairs and landings were carpeted and there were anonymous but pleasing flower prints on the walls, and tubs of cheese plants and aspidistra.

The flat was a fairly typical company *pied à terre*; clean and modern and comfortable, but a bit characterless. There was a small hall, a surprisingly large sitting room with adjacent kitchen and, Dan presumed, a bedroom. He found himself remembering Margot again, because Margot might very well take a flat like this for her various nefarious activities.

Thalia greeted him normally, asking what he would like to drink and whether he could eat caviare. Dan, who normally opened a tin of whatever came first to hand, said with pleasure that he could eat any amount of caviare. It came rolled inside thin wafers of smoked salmon with lemon wedges and brown bread and butter, and it was followed by cold game pie with three different kinds of salad. There was Montrachet to drink, and fresh fruit and Stilton and Brie to round things off. Thalia appeared to regard it as a semi- business occasion, and seemed to expect the interview to take up where it had left off in Ingram's. That will teach you to read mental thigh-stroking and carnal appetite at every corner, Daniel.

While they ate, Dan asked about the founding of Ingram's. 'Eighteen thirty-five, wasn't it? That has to make it one of the oldest publishing houses in London, surely.'

'It isn't as old as Collins – HarperCollins it is now, of course – or some of the Scottish publishers like John Murray or Blackwood's. But it's quite old.' She ate with a kind of fastidious sensuality that was alarmingly erotic.

'Do go on,' said Dan.

'We started with halfpenny ballads and news-sheets for the Newgate crowds at public hangings and progressed from there to penny dreadfuls.'

'*Hannah's Highwayman* and *The Gambler's Tragedy*.'

'Yes, exactly. Did they really have titles like that?'

'I'm afraid so. But then I've seen books on today's shelves with titles like *Flesh-eaters* and *Decay*,' said Dan. 'The paper splattered with gore and the author committing verbicide on every other page.'

She laughed at that. Her teeth were white and the two front ones were very slightly uneven. It gave her a faintly gamine look. Dan thought it might be this that at times gave her the appearance of being younger than she was. 'We do try to keep up a good standard of English at Ingram's,' she said. 'We publish children's books, up to the age of about twelve or thirteen, but not jolly-hockey-sticks heartiness.'

'Not the *Famous Five* or *Ursula in the Upper Fourth*?'

'No, of course not. Where on earth do you get your ideas of nineties children, Dan?'

Dan grinned, and said, 'Tell me some more about the folklore idea.'

She sipped her wine before replying, and Dan received the impression that she was arranging her thoughts. 'Royston was considering starting a separate in-house imprint dealing solely with English folk legends for children,' she said. 'I expect you know the kind of thing.'

'Robin Hood and Grace Darling and Greyfriars Bobby.'

'Yes. But also the old ballads. He thought there was a wealth of untapped material, and also there'd be a market with the schools. Folk music isn't national curriculum, but most schools quite like it as a sideline for school orchestras and projects and plays. I've suggested to the board that it would be rather nice if Royston's wishes could be carried out, and also,' said Thalia, suddenly sounding very shrewd, 'I've suggested that it might be quite lucrative for Ingram's.'

'And?'

'Well, this isn't for publication yet, Dan, but we think we might do it. At the moment we're considering how viable it is. Availability of the lesser-known ballads, things like provenance, whether there would be enough to fill more than one book, whether too many are simply plagiarised versions of one root. The copyrights would have to be looked at and possibly details about performing rights as well. The board have suggested that I compile a report. It's a tallish order because I've never done anything like it but I'm quite keen to try.'

'It sounds rather a good idea,' said Dan.

'Well, I think I could do it. And there's also the fact,' said Thalia, meeting Dan's eyes levelly, 'that it would be a way of – of blotting out losing Edmund.'

'Yes, of course.'

'More wine?'

'Please.'

As Thalia removed the plates and set out the cheese board

along with Bath Olivers and celery, and a bowl of fruit, Dan said, 'Are you the first Ingram lady who's taken an active part in the business?' He felt her hesitation at once. Damn, she knows what I'm getting at. But he said, as offhandedly as he could manage, 'There are a couple of fairly colourful females in your family's history, aren't there?'

'Yes, but I don't know much about them. They were both causes célèbres in their day, but it's a long time ago.'

She was backing off. She had talked openly and intelligently about Ingram's and about her project for her dead cousin, and Dan could use a great deal of it for his articles. But now she was putting up the barriers. It was polite and courteous but it was unmistakable, and Dan abandoned the subject regretfully. If you had a couple of axe murderers in your family history you were probably entitled to be uncommunicative about them.

And then he asked about Edmund.

With the speaking of the name, Dan was suddenly and inexplicably uneasy. The daylight had almost faded, and Thalia had not yet switched on any lights, so that the small dining table was immersed in pools of shadow. He fought down the compulsion to turn sharply round and scan the dark corners of the room.

Thalia was still seated opposite him, resting her elbows lightly on the table, cupping her half-empty wine glass between both hands, and the uncertain light created the impression that her eyes were sunk in deep, dark pits. Dan had the disquieting feeling that it was no longer Thalia who was seated opposite him but something evil and greedy. Something that had jealously clawed off a brother's masculinity ninety years ago, and something that had hacked a faithless husband's flesh to bloody tatters ninety years before that.

'You asked about Edmund.' Thalia's voice was soft.

'Yes.'

'Edmund is so brilliant, Dan. So perceptive.' Her voice held a blurred, unreal note, and Dan felt as if someone had brushed down his spine with an icy finger. She said 'is', not 'was'.

He chose his next words carefully. 'He would have made a good successor to Royston Ingram?'

'Oh yes.' In the shadowy room her thin face was suddenly alight with haggard radiance. 'Yes, he has knowledge and insight, and even at such a young age—' There was the briefest movement of her head, as if she tilted it to listen, and then she smiled slightly. Her eyes were blank black discs.

And then she set down her glass and deliberately reached out to a small table lamp behind her. Warm light flooded over the table at once, chasing back the crawling shadows. 'Dan, I'm sorry. I'm talking as if he's still alive. I do it sometimes. I am aware that I do it. But it's been so difficult to accept his death, you see. He was such a golden creature.'

'If you would like to talk about it – I mean not as part of the interview . . .' Blast, I'm rotten at this kind of thing, thought Dan. And how genuine is she?

But Thalia said, 'I would far rather talk about something more interesting.'

Dan caught the deepening of her voice. We're off, he thought, and felt a prickle of apprehension, but beneath it the stirring of desire. He met her eyes levelly and said, 'Such as?'

'Whether we might take the rest of the wine to bed?'

Dan was aware that he had been deliberately and calculatedly wined and dined and fêted – not lavishly and not clumsily, but elegantly, and with some subtlety. It was this subtlety that made the issuing of the blatant invitation very nearly jarring. Dan was unable to decide if it denoted extreme sophistication or plain naivety. But there was nothing naive about Thalia. There might be vanity. Yes, there had been a flavour of I-know-you're-going-to-accept about her invitation. And the trouble is, thought Dan, I am going to accept. I'm a bit worried about her motives and I'm very worried indeed about the suggestion that she thinks Edmund is still alive somewhere. I'm not worried about impotence – my God, I'm not! – but that's probably all I'm not worried about. Well, not at the moment. She repels me on the one hand and fascinates me on the other, but as long as I can keep the repulsion at bay and the fascination in the foreground . . . I wonder how old she is. Forty? Forty-two?

Thalia reached across the table and took his hand. Her fingers were cool and silken. She said, softly, 'I am probably fifteen years your senior, Dan. Does that matter?'

'You read thoughts?' It always fascinated and amazed Dan how immensely erotic the stroking of palm with finger could be.

'An educated guess.' She regarded him. '*Does* it matter?'

Dan wondered whether to say, 'Madam, age will not wither you, nor custom stale your infinite variety,' and decided against it. 'It doesn't matter the least bit.'

He was not unaccustomed to being on the receiving end of seduction. He was not unaccustomed to exerting the technique on his own account either. He thought he was pretty much prepared for what was ahead, but what he was not prepared for was for his own character, the dark, greedy Margot, suddenly to claw her way into his mind and from there into the lamp-lit sitting room. When Thalia issued that odd, unsubtle invitation, Dan heard a black echo of Margot luring one of her wretched cat's-paw lovers into bed. For several seconds he could very nearly see Margot, exactly as he had depicted her – tall and thin and faintly haggard – standing just behind Thalia, like a ghost twin or a phantom image seen in the jolting window of a railway carriage or a deserted late-night bus.

It was the most bizarre thing he had ever experienced. He thought he might well doubt his sanity in the morning, but if he was really crossing the line and entering some strange half-world where his characters were not only real but crawling out of the woodwork to seduce him, it was very necessary indeed to put from his mind certain of Margot's grislier techniques. It was absolutely vital not to remember the chapter where she had sucked one of her poor wretched young men dry several times over without respite, using fingers and lips to augment her body, leaving him moaning on the bed, clutching his groin which throbbed with agonising cramp. What they used to call an attack of lovers' balls. Dan had dredged this expression up from the magpie corners of his mind, and he had put the episode in to spice up Margot's character and add the obligatory vein of steamy sex.

By the time they reached the bedroom his tangled emotions were warring with one another and he no longer knew which of the two women he was undressing. Thalia lit candles and set the silver holders on a low dressing table, so that the soft blurred discs of light reflected over and over in the mirror. As Dan parted Thalia's thighs and slid between them, there was a moment when the candle flames flickered and danced, throwing distorted images in the mirror's depths. On the rim of his vision he caught the fleeting glimpse of a figure in the mirror's smoky depths – or maybe emerging out of it. Someone with thin, sexless hips and haggard eyes and a curving, hungry mouth, holding out hands that were dark and dripping . . . There was a faint stirring on the other side of the bed, as if someone had turned back the sheets for a moment and then slipped in beside them.

Margot, straight from that gore-drenched killing of Rosamund's parents.

The sensation sent Dan's body soaring into fierce, helpless passion and when Thalia slid her hands between his thighs and began to caress him to point-of-no-return arousal, he felt Margot's thin, bony fingers twining with

Thalia's, digging her sharp little fingernails into his skin. There was a moment when there were unmistakably two sets of hands exploring his body, and the thought, God Almighty, I'm about to screw them both! skidded across his mind. This is probably most men's major erotic fantasy, he thought incredulously. One in front of me, one behind . . . And then he felt the butterfly touch again, and he thought: if whichever of them is doing *that* keeps on doing it, this is going to be the shortest encounter in history . . . No, it's all right. Here we go, then . . .

He dressed swiftly in the cold, early-morning light, considering whether to wake Thalia before leaving or whether to just leave quietly, putting a note on the table, and phoning her later in the day.

He did not want to see Thalia over breakfast. He admitted it at last, and considered the admission carefully. It had nothing to do with embarrassment and nothing to do with motives of delicacy. It was simply that having dined with a faintly sinister lady by soft, golden lamplight, and having explored her body by candlelight, he did not want the dark romance to melt before a forty-something woman in a dressing gown, frying bacon for breakfast. Half-baked romanticism, Daniel? Or something deeper?

He knew perfectly well that it was something deeper. He was already uneasily aware that Thalia and Margot were becoming inextricably tangled in his mind; he did not like either of them very much, and he certainly did not like the emotions that had been dredged up from his deepest mind earlier on. The trouble was that he might still need Thalia to find out about Imogen and he would certainly still need Margot. But he needed Margot as a cold, merciless bitch who could wind a seductive bewitchment into a man's heart and into his loins, and he did not want that witchery spoiled by seeing her in a dressing gown, or with bad breath in the morning, or looking middle-aged without make-up. He wanted Thalia and Margot both to be mysterious, ageless temptresses; creatures of nightshade deadliness, sable-haired and sloe-eyed . . . *'Come into my parlour, said the villainess to the romantic lead . . .'* – No, that had been Margot, Thalia had made that suggestion about the wine. *'Come into my bedroom, my dear, and see how hungry I can be . . . Bring the wine while you're about it and we'll slake all our thirsts . . . My, what strong thighs you have, my dear . . .'* All the better to ride you, madam . . . *'And my, what splendidly stiff manhood you have . . .'* All the better to screw you, madam . . .

I think, said Dan to himself, very firmly indeed, I really do think that I'd better get out of this particular spider's clutches before I lose my grip on reality entirely. And Margot, you bitch, if you're going to behave in this unruly manner, you might have to be killed off earlier than you expect.

He went out into the odd half-world of the extreme early morning and, after walking for a while, picked up a cruising taxi near Langham Place, which took him home.

His own flat was untidy; the carpet needed vacuuming and the bedroom was strewn with cast-off sweaters and yesterday's shirt and three pairs of socks.

Dan had never been so glad to see any of it. He had never been so grateful for the blessed familiarity and he was even pleased to see the trail of cornflakes on the kitchen worktop where Oliver had taken the packet upside down out of the cupboard. Oliver was still in bed, and Dan moved quietly about his own bedroom. His brother might later ask if he had had a good evening, but he was more likely to avoid the subject altogether, partly from tact and partly from embarrassment.

At half past six Dan gave up the fight to sleep, got up, brewed a pot of coffee, made a sketchy attempt to tidy the worst of the chaos and sat down at his desk with a sense of relief. He had sometimes heard writers – or maybe they were only would-be writers – wax complaining about their work and their characters, cursing their heroes and denouncing their heroines as irritating. This was completely incomprehensible; Dan loved every one of his characters with consuming passion. He embarked on a new chapter with a feeling of safety and homecoming. While he was here, the world and its problems could go hang for a while.

Rosamund was by this time nicely incarcerated in the old Victorian madhouse. Dan had unashamedly used Oliver's notes, which had been so vivid and so graphic that they would probably give him nightmares. Oliver had turned up several primary-source references to Victorian workhouses, and also to the original Bedlam sited first at Bishopsgate and later at Lambeth. These conjured up an appalling image of people discarded by society and forgotten: orphaned children and elderly, impoverished men and women flung into workhouses to sew sackcloth aprons or mailbags; long windowless dormitories and wards where the stench of human excrement and human sweat was like a thick wall, and where the reek of sadness and loneliness and neglect was just as strong. There were horrific descriptions of what was called a commode bench: a wooden structure like a multi-seated earth closet, to which the incontinent and the paraplegic and the severely retarded were strapped for months on end. Dan read the descriptions feeling a bit sick, and was grateful to hear Oliver making coffee and toast in the kitchen. There was the smell of burning, and then determined sounds of a second onslaught on the toaster. Presently Oliver appeared with a cup of coffee which he set down at Dan's elbow along with a plate of buttered toast, and went off to shower. Dan ate and drank with enjoyment and felt as if he was back in his own skin again.

It was time now for Rosamund to go into the long sleep that was the kingpin of the book and the heartwood of the ancient legend. This dramatic plummet into unconsciousness had been steadily drawing closer ever since she had discovered the mutilated remains of her parents and spun into hysteria, and Dan had considered several methods for creating the actual sleep. It would have been nice to have somehow introduced a spinning wheel, or at the very least some kind of spindle mechanism, but he had abandoned the idea in favour of a straightforward drugged slumber – perhaps even a full-blown coma – which was something that modern readers would more easily identify with.

With this in mind, he had earlier in the week borrowed an armful of medical books from the nearest library. He tumbled them on to his desk and inspected his booty. Some of the books were long-winded and some were technical and most were multi-syllabic. One proved to be a kind of Lambs' Tales From Psychiatry, which explained hypnotism in terms of bright swinging pocket watches and started off by saying, 'Sigmund Freud believed that dreams tell us a lot about our lives.' Two turned out to be written wholly in German and would therefore have to be returned unopened, which was a nuisance because they were heavy to carry.

Dan stacked them crossly in the hall to await his next forage in the library, and returned to his desk to pick his way through the maze presented by the rest. He started with the hallucinogenic drugs, and read solemnly about mescaline and marijuana and lysergic acid diethylamide, only realising after ten minutes that this last was, of course, the LSD of the flower children of the sixties and seventies. He cast the book irritably aside. Beleaguered on all sides she might be, but Dan was blowed if he was going to let his heroine be felled by a plot device that was twenty-five years out of date. He turned hopefully to the chapters on barbiturates and psycho-active drugs, and considered whether Rosamund might be sent into her death-like coma by a deliberate overdose of chloral hydrate or methaqualone, both of which were apparently sedative-hypnotic and either of which could be administered by the manipulative doctor with satisfyingly spectacular consequences. Or maybe it would be better for her to be subjected to psycho-active substances, which could modify the biochemical or physiological processes of the brain.

He reread this last section three times, got up to pour another cup of coffee from the pot Oliver had made, and read it again. No better. Even with the help of a large dose of caffeine he could only make minimal sense out of brain neurons and the artificial ways of bridging the gaps between them, which could, it appeared, have any number of startling results. Even if he had fathomed it, he doubted his ability to inject much entertainment into it. It would admittedly provide terrific medical verisimilitude, but Dan did not think many readers would really want to read about electrical and chemical transmission between nerve cells, unless of course they happened to be biophysicists or neurosurgeons in which case they were not very likely to be reading this kind of book in the first place. He abandoned the psycho-active substances and hoped he was not dishonestly ducking out of essential research.

It was now ten o'clock, an hour when most people might be expected to be about their lawful occasions, and he reached for the phone and dialled Interflora. Flowers might not be original, but they were an honourable tradition on these occasions. He thought out an appropriate note to go with the flowers, and dictated it to the helpful florist.

'Thank you for a memorable evening, Thalia' – would she guess at the irony that had guided his pen on that, and smile the curving cat smile? 'May we meet again soon? My work commitments are cluttering up the next few days, but I will try to telephone you towards the weekend. Dan.'

He asked for it to be read back, gave his credit card number, and rang off, wondering if florists ever questioned the stories that lay behind messages accompanying flower deliveries. There was surely a huge potential for blackmail in floristry. Perhaps they all had to sign a Florists' Official Secrets Act.

But he felt better for having sent the flowers and the note, because honour had been satisfied on both sides, and without insincerity.

Chapter Thirteen

Perversely it was Imogen's defiant threat to cry 'rape' that convinced Leo.

He stared down at her and felt the fear raying out from her mind, but he felt the determination as well. He thought again that she knew something she was not admitting to. And she's no more mad than I am, thought Leo suddenly. Or if she is, it's time I retired from psychiatry.

After a moment, he said softly, 'You're blackmailing me.'

Her head came up and she stared at him. 'Yes. If you don't help me, I'll swear you tried to rape me. I really will.' She held his gaze and Leo's conviction that she was sane strengthened. 'Well?' said Imogen. 'Will you do it?'

Beneath the hardness, Leo caught a flicker of something frightened and something vulnerable, but something that was fiercely sure of itself. He thought quickly. It was impossible to leave her here while he went for help, and it was equally impossible to get hold of any kind of medication to subdue her. Physical force was unthinkable; Leo did not stop to examine why. In any case, she seemed quite calm and sensible.

He said, slowly, 'You're very sure about this, aren't you?'

Those words that Quincy had overheard, repeated in Quincy's immature voice but still conveying a deep, deep hatred . . . *'She's not dead, Edmund . . . The bitch who would have let her daughter supplant you is buried alive . . .'* My mother is buried alive, thought Imogen. And Thalia is somehow responsible. None of it could be spoken. She simply said, 'Yes, I'm very sure.'

Leo thought quickly. If I stick my neck out on this one, will I be branded as a greater charlatan than I already am? Oh, what the hell. He said abruptly, 'All right. Come with me. There's a phone box outside the cemetery.'

'A phone box?'

'The first thing to do is ring the coroner,' said Leo. 'It's lucky for you I know him.' He looked down at her. 'If we're going to do it at all, we've got to do it properly, Imogen. Even I can't go digging up a grave in the middle of the night. You'd better be prepared for a bit of company.'

The coroner, whose name was Frisby, took some persuading. In the end, Leo, who was reasonably familiar with the law on exhumations, put forward the most unanswerable argument of all. Disturbance of the grave, he said into the phone. There was clear evidence that something was wrong. He stopped, as if fearful of being overheard, and when Frisby spoke again his voice had sharpened. 'Disturbance?'

Leo looked at Imogen, who was listening closely. I'm risking a hell of a lot for you, Imogen. I don't give a damn what you accuse me of, but I'm going out on a very thin limb indeed here.

He said into the phone, 'Yes, disturbance. No, I can't be more specific. All right then, I won't be more specific. Will you come out right away? Can you set it up for us to take a look at once?'

'Oh, blast you, Leo, why do you have to get mixed up in these freakish things?' said the annoyed voice on the other end of the line. 'Yes, all right, I will set it up. You know perfectly well that I'll have to. No, it's all right, I can do it, but you'll have to give me about half an hour. Say three-quarters to be on the safe side. Listen, while you're waiting, get on to the local police. Ask for Inspector Mackenzie if he's available, and mention my name. That'll save us a bit of time. Do you know who the undertaker was? No, of course you can't be expected to . . . No, it's all right, I'll ring the cemetery manager from here. He'll know.'

Frisby arrived more or less at the same time as the cemetery manager; Frisby was resigned and the cemetery manager was irritable. The small brick building that comprised the office was unlocked, and heaters were switched on. Somebody set a kettle to boil for instant coffee.

The cemetery manager telephoned the rector, and Leo, watching Imogen and only half listening, heard phrases like 'faculty from the diocese' and 'Home Office licence'. My God, he thought suddenly, I'm going to look the worst fool in Christendom if I've misjudged this. Yes, but I'd rather look a fool than risk ignoring it and finding out afterwards that Imogen was right and the rest of us were wrong. But I don't think that's going to happen; I think she is right, I think she's found something out, and because of it she knows her mother was alive when they buried her yesterday. Nearly thirty-six hours ago. And if I am made to look a fool at the end of it, it won't be the first time. He did not much mind whether he looked a fool anyway.

Dr John Shilling was in a pitiable condition. He sat docilely enough in the car speeding from Hampstead police station to the cemetery, but Inspector Mackenzie, who sat next to him and who had not been best pleased at being dragged out of bed at midnight on a cold November morning, saw how his hands were restless and how twitchy he was.

The entire thing was enough to make anyone twitchy, of course; it was as bizarre a tale as Mackenzie had ever encountered. You came across odd things in life – fifteen years in the police and ten of those in the Met taught you that – but on balance he had yet to come across anything odder than this. He did not believe it, but the call had apparently come from a medical gentleman and therefore could not be ignored. It would not have been ignored whoever it had come from but the inspector was bound to say that on an occasion like this you'd take a bit more notice of a doctor than of anyone else.

It was unfortunate that there had been some delay before setting out, but it had been unavoidable. Several people had had to be traced and routed out, and it had all taken time. Mr Frisby, who was the coroner, was apparently on his way to the cemetery with the necessary authority, but there had been Huxtable the undertaker, who would be needed for identification of the coffin, and also Dr Shilling who was the family GP. Huxtable had been reached easily enough, and after a slight altercation had agreed to meet Mackenzie and Frisby at the cemetery, but Dr Shilling, instead of behaving like a normal GP who should be accustomed to being woken in the middle of the night, had apparently gone to pieces and would not believe what was being suggested. In the end Mackenzie had solved the matter by simply driving out to Shilling's house and collecting him.

The inspector thought it sad and rather shaming to see someone in John Shilling's state. The man's eyes were bloodshot and his face was grey. He did not look as if he had slept for several nights, and there was a frowsty smell about him. It was the smell Mackenzie associated with alcoholics; their breath became tainted with stale alcohol in the way that habitual garlic-eaters' breath became tainted with garlic, and they either forgot or could not be bothered to wash and put on clean clothes. He was familiar with it, but he still thought it sad, and he thought it particularly sad to see a medical man in that condition, although it would be his guess that Shilling had only just got going on that particular path. But if Dr Sterne was right, John Shilling might well be setting off on an even worse journey than alcoholism.

Inspector Mackenzie had automatically cursed at being summarily hauled out on what would almost certainly prove to be a wild goose chase, but as they approached the cemetery he felt a chill hand close about his guts. Wild goose chase or not, this was going to be nasty. He noticed that it was coming on to rain.

PC Porling was standing guard outside the cemetery gates, and quite right too. They did not want anyone to get hold of this story before they knew what was what, and before they had worked out what they were going to say about it. They most emphatically did not want the press getting hold of it. Mackenzie had a lively mind and it conjured up with ease the kind of headlines that might splash the pages of tomorrow morning's papers.

He slowed the car and wound down the window. 'Anyone else here yet, Porling?'

'Mr Frisby's here, sir, and also the cemetery manager, along with Mr Huxtable, the undertaker.'

'Quite a party. Is there someone else who can stand guard here, Porling? Right, then you'd better go along to the grave and wait for us there.'

'Yes, sir,' said PC Porling stolidly.

'Good man.'

Frisby was waiting in the porch of the small brick office on the outskirts of the cemetery itself. He had the air of one who has crammed a sweater and jacket over his pyjamas, and the cemetery manager, whom Mackenzie knew by sight, was with him, looking irritable. Mackenzie did not blame him. He said, 'Good evening, gentlemen. Sorry you've been called out. Nasty situation this, but it couldn't be ignored. It's probably just a mare's nest.'

'I very much hope so,' said the cemetery manager frostily.

Frisby said, 'If it had been anyone other than Leo Sterne who rang me, I think it probably would have been ignored, Inspector.'

Mackenzie supposed that there was a bit of the old-boy network at work here, or possibly the Masonic brotherhood. He said, 'Where's Huxtable? Oh, there you are, sir. Good of you to come out so quickly.'

143

Huxtable, who was thin and dour, said something about waiting for first light. 'Usual, you know.'

'I know, but I don't think we dare wait in this case,' said Frisby. 'If there's been disturbance to the grave . . .'

'Quite.' Mackenzie thought the use of the word 'disturbance' had a chill ring to it. He said, 'Has anyone told the rector what's afoot? Oh, you have. Good. Is he coming out? Ah. Well, I can't say I altogether blame him. We'd better go into the office first.'

Imogen had accepted a mug of coffee and was huddling over it in the office, cupping the mug between her hands as if to draw warmth and strength and comfort from it. Warmth and light and food, thought Leo, sitting in the other chair, watching her. Three of man's most basic needs. She's a bit withdrawn. Is she panicking at what she's set in motion? Did she expect all this? Coroners and emergency Home Office licences and people dragged out of bed in the middle of the night? She's certainly not retracting anything. She's being reasonable and logical. She believes this is what has to be done, and she's staying with it. Good for you, Imogen.

The entrance of Inspector Mackenzie and Dr Shilling, with Huxtable and Frisby behind them lent an even deeper note of unreality to the situation. They're actors assembling for a play, thought Leo, and his heart gave a lurch of panic at what was ahead.

Subdued introductions were made, and there was a discreet request that Dr Sterne accompany them to the grave. They want help with the digging, thought Leo, and although he had more or less expected this he felt his heart begin to thump erratically again. But he said at once, 'Yes, certainly I'll come with you. But Imogen must stay here. In fact she ought really to be given a sedative.'

'Dr Shilling is her GP.' Mackenzie gestured to the blotch-faced man at his side.

Leo frowned. 'Dear God preserve us.' John Shilling was shaking so badly now that he looked very nearly palsied. Leo looked him up and down, and then said dismissively, 'This man couldn't prescribe an aspirin. I'll take responsibility for Imogen tonight.' And then, impatiently, 'Shall we get on with it? I don't imagine any of us wants to delay this. Is everything all right in your department, Frisby?'

'It is. Mr Huxtable and I have conferred. We don't like it,' said Frisby. 'Well, you know that. But we agree to your request.'

'Because of who you are,' said Huxtable frostily.

'Because you found evidence of disturbance,' said Frisby softly, casting a wary glance at Imogen.

Leo nodded brusquely and turned back to Imogen. When he spoke again, Mackenzie and Frisby both looked up, startled at the change in his voice. 'Imogen, you will stay here,' said Leo, not particularly quietly but with an unmistakable undercurrent of authority. 'You understand that? You must stay here, and we'll be back with you very quickly indeed. Everything is all right.' He glanced round. 'One of you had better stay with her.' His glance fell on the cemetery manager. 'It had better be you,' he said. 'I'm sorry, I don't know your name.'

'Arthur Williams.'

'Well, Arthur Williams, you stay here with Imogen. She's all right, but call me at once if she isn't. You understand? At once.'

Arrogant, thought Inspector Mackenzie. I daresay it works well enough with his patients, however, particularly the females, although it doesn't look as if this one's reacting too well. Unusual looking girl. 'Better leave us to decide who does what, if you please, Dr Sterne,' he said with an edge to his voice.

'Then bloody get on with it.'

Frisby said, 'We are getting on with it, Leo. We'll need Mr Huxtable to identify the coffin, and we'll need Dr

145

Shilling as the doctor concerned in the actual death. Well, I'm sorry about it, Doctor. Yes, I know how you must feel, but it's unavoidable.'

'That does in fact leave Mr Williams to stay here,' put in Mackenzie. 'Is that all right with you, Mr Williams?'

'Oh yes,' said the cemetery manager with evident relief.

'Exactly as I said in the first place,' said Leo impatiently. 'We'll need spades and a toolbox as well. I suppose you've got such things here, have you, Williams? Good. Well, gentlemen? Are you coming with me, or have I got to do this on my own?'

As they set off, the inspector said to Frisby, 'Would he really have done it on his own?'

'I'm only surprised he bothered to contact us in the first place,' rejoined Frisby drily.

The grave was exactly as it had been left, and PC Porling was standing guard at one end.

'Is someone on the gates, Constable?' asked Frisby.

'Yes, sir.'

'And you've got your torch?'

'Sir,' affirmed Porling.

'Then I think that first of all we need to take a photograph of the grave as it is. Have you the camera, Mackenzie? Only a couple of shots, I think. Here and here.' Frisby looked across at Leo. 'Is this the disturbance you referred to?'

'Yes.'

'And this is how you found it when you and Imogen Ingram arrived?'

'Yes,' said Leo, perjuring himself unhesitatingly.

'But look here, that's not evidence of any movement from beneath,' protested Mackenzie.

'Do you want to take a chance on that, Inspector?' demanded Leo. 'For goodness' sake, let's make a start. Shine the torch, Porling, and hand out the spades – that's unless the inspector wants to come up with any more

146

unnecessary police procedure to delay us, or Mr Frisby feels like reciting the last act of *Hamlet* to provide atmosphere.'

'All in good time, sir. And there's plenty of atmosphere without any recitations.'

'So there is, Inspector.' Leo looked across at Mackenzie. 'Well, shall we make a start? Will you take shovel or spade, Inspector?'

Chapter Fourteen

The rain had stopped, but as they began to dig, a thin mist drifted over the graveyard, spangling the trees and dripping from the branches. The air was clammy and dank on their faces, and there was a stench of wet earth.

Leo had entered into a half-world where time no longer had any meaning, where the only reality was the crunch of the soil beneath the spades and the only people in the world the other men with him. None of them spoke much but there was an air of grim doggedness about them. Once Mackenzie swore as his spade hit a large stone, and once Leo sent Porling back to the little office to check on Imogen. The constable returned within a few minutes, carefully balancing six mugs of coffee on a biscuit-tin lid. All was well, he reported. Mr Williams had said not to worry and to send for him if he could help, and in the meantime here was a hot drink for everyone.

They stopped briefly, grateful for the coffee and the respite, and then returned to work, taking turns to dig, even old Huxtable taking a brief spell. To begin with John Shilling worked with them, but after only a few minutes he broke off, sick and shaking, wiping his face with the back of one trembling hand. 'Can't do it. The thought of what's down there, what we might find . . . Sorry, Mackenzie, Sterne, don't think I'm up to it.'

Leo looked at him contemptuously. 'You'd better stand watch instead of Porling then. Porling, take Dr Shilling's spade and lend a hand, will you?'

As Porling grasped the spade, Mackenzie said softly, 'Aren't you being a bit hard on Shilling, Doctor? Don't forget he knew the lady.'

'Don't forget he signed her death certificate,' said Leo.

As the soil level went down it was necessary to go down with it, so that within a short time they were waist deep and then chest deep in the open grave. There was a black, sour stench, and a damp clinging miasma of mould. The noisome breath of the grave, thought Leo. The stink of decay and putrefaction. He knew this was absurd; the coffins had only been in the ground for a day and a half, but the impression persisted. They were neck deep in the grave now, and it felt as if they were sinking inexorably lower and lower into a black, yawning maw. This is the stuff that nightmares are made of, Imogen, thought Leo grimly. I'm right out on that limb for you now, and a dangerous and precarious limb it is.

He was beginning to think they must be nearing the bottom when Huxtable leaned over and said, 'Keep well to that side from now on if possible. Royston Ingram's side.'

'Why?'

'To cause as little disturbance as possible to the – to Eloise Ingram's coffin. So that we get as true a picture as possible.'

'Oh yes, I see. I hadn't thought of that.'

Leo thought he was prepared for the scrape of the spade on the coffin lid, but when it came it jolted his heart into a painful too-fast beating once more, betraying the raw state of his nerves.

Mackenzie, who had gone up to take a breather on the grave edge, slithered back down to help clear away the soil. 'And Porling, if you and Mr Frisby will wedge the torches in the ground just there – yes, that's it – we should be able to see what we're up against.'

'D'you want us down there with you, Leo?' This was Frisby.

'I don't think there's room.'

'Where's Huxtable? Oh, there you are. I think we'll need your formal identification of the coffin in a minute.'

Leo straightened up for a moment, suddenly aware of a monstrously aching back from bending over for so long, and of mounting apprehension. The inside of the grave smelt of fear and despair. In a very few minutes they would know.

As the torches were directed into the grave, the two beams met and joined, giving the eerie impression of miniature spotlights aimed on to a small stage set, with black swirling darkness beyond. Leo was perched awkwardly on the foot of Royston Ingram's coffin, and he stayed where he was. But the horror was scudding across his skin again and he felt as if a huge weight was pressing down on his lungs.

At his side, Inspector Mackenzie drew in his breath sharply, and then said, 'Move that torch to the left a bit, Porling. Dr Sterne, can you see just there?' He leaned forward, pointing, and as Leo followed the line of his finger, he felt a surge of dread.

Huxtable and Frisby were leaning forward, both of them still outside the torchlight. 'What is it?' called Frisby softly. 'Leo, what have you found?'

Leo said, in a voice devoid of all emotion, 'I think the coffin's moved,' and felt the recoil of the others. He indicated the left-hand corner and Frisby adjusted the torch again. 'Can you see? Just there? There's a mark in the wet earth. Like the rut you get in wet ground when a car's been parked.'

'Are you sure you didn't dislodge it in the digging?'

'No, the coffins are lying quite tightly together and anyway we kept to the other side. But there's a definite depression in the wall of the grave surrounding Eloise. We haven't made that.' And even if we have, he thought, I'm not admitting to it. I'm not letting them give up now. If I can use anything to force them on, I will. He leaned forward cautiously. 'It's as if the corner made a deep gouge in the earth and then shifted. And I don't think,' said Leo, infusing his voice with conviction, 'that it could have been done by anything other than the coffin moving after it was lowered.'

Huxtable was kneeling on the edge of the grave, peering down. 'But it's quite impossible, Dr Sterne. The weight of the earth alone would preclude any movement.'

Frisby said, 'And there shouldn't be any movement at all. Not unless—'

'Unless what's inside the coffin caused it. Quite,' said Leo. And then, 'Shilling, if you're about to throw up, go and do it somewhere else.'

There was the sound of somebody blundering into the darkness, and then of being wetly sick on the ground.

Mackenzie was staring down at the coffin. When he spoke again, the others heard the extreme reluctance in his voice. 'We'll have to get it open, won't we?'

'Oh yes. Right away. Are we in order for that, Frisby?'

Frisby said, with an edge to his voice, 'Even if we weren't, I don't think any jury would convict us for opening up a coffin that looks as if there's been movement from inside.'

'You agree with me, then?'

'I agree that we should investigate. Inspector, what's your opinion?'

Mackenzie was still examining the area around Eloise's coffin. After a moment he said, 'I couldn't be sure about it, and I couldn't say that – that there's anything untoward, but . . .'

Leo sent him a look compounded of irony and grim amusement. 'You're a master of understatement, aren't you, Inspector?'

'I think the marks are suggestive,' said Mackenzie. 'But I don't think they're conclusive.'

'But we'll have to make sure.'

'Oh yes.'

There was an appalled silence, and then Frisby said, 'But look here, wouldn't it – I mean surely she would have called for help?'

'Would anyone have heard if she did?' This was Huxtable.

'I don't see how they could, not from – not from down there,' said Frisby, frowning. 'Good God, she was under six feet of earth!'

Leo looked about him. 'And it's pretty deserted here as well,' he said. 'The nearest houses are easily a mile off. I remember noticing that on the way.'

'There's the office,' began Mackenzie. 'No, that's on the other side. But there'd be people coming and going a bit, surely.'

Porling cleared his throat. 'Begging pardon, sir, but the cemetery manager said the funeral was late yesterday afternoon. If it was their last one for the day—'

'It was their last one,' said Huxtable. 'They fitted it in at short notice because the family wanted a quick interment.'

'And so the office probably closed shortly afterwards,' said Mackenzie, thoughtfully. 'What time do they lock the gates, Mr Huxtable?'

'Five o'clock at this time of year.'

'And,' said Porling, determinedly, 'if you remember, sir, it rained for most of yesterday, which means you wouldn't get many relatives visiting graves either.'

'Yes. Thirty-six hours. My God, Eloise Ingram could have screamed until her throat burst and no one would have heard her.'

In the harsh torchlight they looked at one another. 'We'd better get on with it,' said Leo at last.

'Yes. Wait a bit though, Doctor, I'll need to get a couple more shots first. Porling, pass down the camera again, will you? Huxtable, while we're doing that, I suppose you have to formally identify the coffin, don't you?'

'I – yes. I – identify it,' said Huxtable. 'Mr Frisby? Is that sufficient? Is there anything you need me to do?'

'If there is, I'll worry about it afterwards,' said Frisby. 'Let's get it over with.'

The sudden white flash of the camera lit the scene to vivid and bizarre life. Inspector Mackenzie took several shots, and then passed the camera back to Porling.

'Hold on to that as you value your promotion, Porling. Ready, Dr Sterne?'

'Yes. And Porling?'

'Sir?'

'Concentrate on keeping a watch up there. We're about to break open a coffin to get at a corpse, and the fact that we're doing it with the blessing of Her Majesty's coroner doesn't make it any more acceptable to the average night prowler weirdo.'

'And we don't want any tasteless jokes about body snatchers or Burke and Hare either,' said Mackenzie, suddenly grateful for Dr Sterne's abrasive mood, and attempting to match it.

'The only Burke in the party is over there being sick on somebody's headstone.' Leo took the small metal toolbox from Frisby and surveyed its contents. 'It looks as if we have quite an embarrassment of riches in the way of implements, Inspector. Which do you fancy? Screwdriver or chisel?'

'Screwdriver,' said Mackenzie, pointing to the coffin's edges. 'See there? Brass screws. Driven into the lid and then down into the coffin sides. The wood's pretty thick. Huxtable, your people do a good job, don't they? I'll bet those screws are all of three inches long.'

'And there are at least twenty of them,' said Leo, peering to look more closely.

'Would we do better to lift the thing up on the ground to work on it, d'you reckon?'

'If the guy ropes were still around we might. But I think it would be a harder job than it looks,' said Leo, frowning at the coffin. 'Huxtable, what's the expert opinion?'

'I'm afraid you'll be better in situ, Doctor. I can fetch guy ropes but it will take some time.'

'I was afraid you'd say that. All right, Inspector, it looks as if we're stuck down here.'

'Right you are.'

It was an appalling situation. The grave was a double plot, but it was only sufficiently wide to take the two coffins lying side by side. Leo and the inspector jockeyed for position, and in the end Mackenzie half knelt on Royston's coffin, with Leo astride Eloise's. Mackenzie glanced at him and said, 'I hope you aren't subject to nightmares, Doctor.'

'If I wasn't before, I will be after this. Ready, Inspector?'

'No. But here we go anyway.'

Together they began to unscrew the coffin lid.

For a long time the only sound was the faint drip of moisture from the trees and the thin, barely perceptible squeaking of the disengaging screws. Once Leo caught a movement from above, and realised it was Porling keeping John Shilling back from the grave, and once an owl flew out of a tree behind them and sent its low, whooping cry into the night. Both men jumped and Mackenzie's hand shook so badly he had to pause before going on. Leo brought up the back of his hand to wipe the sweat from his forehead. Mackenzie glanced at him, and thought, so he's not as detached as he's been making out after all.

Neither of them could have said how long it took them to remove the brass screws. They were in a strange and unreal world where time seemed to have run down and stopped, or to be grinding itself into reverse. At length Leo said softly, 'That's the last one, I think. If we both take this edge and push it across on to the other coffin . . .'

There was the scraping of wood against wood, and then the lid slid free. Something gusted dry, sour breath upwards, and both men flinched. And then the light from Porling's torch fell across the thing inside the coffin.

* * *

154

The face that Dan Tudor had compared to a fair, pale *Morte d'Arthur* heroine and that John Shilling had guiltily and lubriciously fantasised over was suffused with purple where the veins had swollen with the frenzied efforts to escape and the panic-filled struggle for air. The eyes were staring and bulging from their sockets, the whites stained crimson where the tiny capillaries had haemorrhaged, and the lips were stretched wide in a silent scream, with blood-specked froth staining the corners.

The coffin was quite shallow, but she had managed to draw her knees up a little to push against the lid, and her hands were curled into helpless, frantic claws, most of the nails broken and the fingertips crusted with blood. Leo glanced at the underside of the coffin lid and saw that the lining was stained with blood and ripped. He drew in a shaking breath and forced himself to look back at the dreadful thing in the coffin.

Examination under these circumstances was unthinkable, and he did not attempt it. But he forced his mind to clinical observation. She was plainly dead and he thought that rigor mortis was still present in most of the body. If it had not started to wear off – and he did not think it had – she might have been dead for just under twenty-four hours. Sometime during last night, then, or maybe the early hours of the morning. If the funeral had taken place in the late afternoon, and depending when she had come out of whatever cataleptic state she had been in, she might have had twelve hours of horror before she died. Or had she suffocated almost at once? It did not really matter whether she had had twelve hours or twelve minutes of it; two minutes at full consciousness, fighting to breathe, dreadfully aware of what had happened, would have been sufficient to send her mad.

He looked more closely at the neck and jaws, which was where the relaxing of rigor usually started, and for the first time saw several crimson weals. He bent closer, puzzled, and then understanding flooded his mind. The small wounds had been made by her own fingernails, and Leo had a vivid and dreadful image of Eloise Ingram despairing but still appallingly conscious, attempting to claw open her own jugular vein in a pitiful bid to die quickly and cleanly. He looked hopefully at the inside of the coffin, but there were no stains to indicate a sudden effusion of blood. Then if she didn't die of asphyxiation, she died of exhaustion and fear, thought Leo in horror. And someone's got to deal with this unbelievable situation. Someone's got to tell Imogen.

As if in response to this last thought, he caught a quick movement above. He straightened up, aware that Inspector Mackenzie was straightening up as well, and saw backing away from the grave's edge, just outside of the torch's beam, Imogen.

Her eyes were on the terrible thing inside the open coffin.

Porling just managed to catch her before she fainted.

Leo straightened up in the narrow hospital cubicle and regarded the A and E registrar levelly.

'No change at all?'

'Not yet, I'm afraid. The lady's staying determinedly out of the world. We've checked for the usual things – drugs overdose, diabetic coma.'

'It's stupor rather than coma though, isn't it? There are still some responses.'

'Yes. Oh yes. The swallowing reflexes and so on are all still there. She's breathing normally, and the limbs are flaccid. Well, you can see all that for yourself.'

'And her eyes are open,' said Leo, half to himself, looking down at the still, remote figure on the bed.

'Yes. We've checked to see if they're following deliberate movements and there is some response at times. I thought you said she was on only a mild dosage of diazepam, by the way.'

'So she was, according to Briar House.'

'H'm. The tests don't show it as mild at all,' said the registrar caustically. 'Either she was supplementing it with her own private supply – and you know as well as I do that they *will* do it, these teenagers – or someone's been trying to keep her more or less permanently doped.' He glanced at Leo. 'Is that a possibility?'

'I wouldn't put anything past her GP,' said Leo.

'Could he have made a mistake?'

'Any amount from what I've seen of him.' Leo paused, and then said, 'Listen, I don't want to trespass on your territory—'

'Oh, trespass away.'

'But in view of what happened, isn't the likeliest diagnosis hysterical stupor? She simply couldn't face what she saw and withdrew?'

'If we're talking about territories, that one's yours rather than mine,' said the registrar. 'But I wouldn't be surprised if you're right. We'll have to wait for the CT scan, and we've still got to do a lumbar puncture to eliminate meningitis. We can't rule that out yet, or subdural haematoma or a subarachnoid haemorrhage either.'

'Tumour?' said Leo. 'No, that wouldn't present in such a sudden way, would it?'

'Well, it's unlikely. Unless there's any history of epileptic fits.'

'Not as far as I know. Her GP should be able to tell you, if he can stay sober long enough to tell you anything at all,' said Leo.

'We'll check it with him. What about clinical depression? Is there any history of that, do you know? I mean prior to what happened tonight?'

'I don't know. I don't think so.'

'What about a blow? When she fainted, did she hit her head?'

'Almost certainly not.' Leo remembered vividly how

157

Imogen had tumbled forward, and how the young police constable had caught her.

'Well, we're getting an X-ray of the skull as well just to be sure there aren't any fractures. It shouldn't take too long at this time of night,' said the registrar with the instinctive and defensive vagueness of one constantly working under interruptions. 'But in view of what you've told me . . .'

'You agree with me.'

'Well, yes, I do.'

'Hysterical or depressive stupor.'

'Yes. Appalling thing for her to witness,' said the registrar, glancing at the bed. 'Enough to make anyone shut down for a while. All that diazepam wouldn't have helped either.'

'I know,' said Leo, suddenly understanding why people occasionally ground their teeth with sheer anger.

'We'll probably have to admit her, or hand over to your people. We've started a chart measuring the time she's unconscious, counting this as day one. D'you want to stay with her until we get the X-ray done?'

'Please.'

'OK, I'll get someone to bring you a cup of tea.' A buzzer bleeped imperatively in the registrar's pocket, and he made a resigned gesture. 'I'll have to leave you to it. But sing out for someone if she looks like coming out of it.' He paused, and sent Leo a quizzical look. 'You'd take the case yourself, I suppose, Dr Sterne?'

'Oh yes.'

'I thought you would.'

The thin curtain twitched as he went out, and Leo was alone with Imogen.

Chapter Fifteen

The powers that ordered life and death and ordained judgement were still with Thalia. Even if she had not known it before, she knew it now. And once that was accepted, it was no longer surprising that matters had played so neatly into her hands.

Thalia had not planned that the bitch should find out what had happened to Eloise – she had not even thought about it – but it had been like the last coruscating piece of a cosmic jigsaw fitting into its appointed place. Imogen was sunk deep in what the doctors were calling hysterical stupor, she was four days into it now, and there was no way of telling how many more days she might remain like that. Everyone agreed that it was very sad even while they were all shuddering and stunned over what had happened to Eloise. George reported that Elspeth had taken to her bed for three days, and Dilys had had hysterics all over Battersea. Juliette was believed to have got most enviably drunk at some nightclub or other, and Rosa had told Great-Aunt Flora that it was anybody's guess whose bed the naughty girl had ended up sharing.

It was not sad at all, of course; it was the creature's punishment and judgement, just as Eloise's fate had been her punishment and judgement. Thalia had experienced once more the deep, secret pleasure when she had heard just how successful the plan against Eloise had been.

Wearing the falsest of all her false faces, she listened to the various suggestions put forward by the family who were beginning to recover a bit from the shock and were turning their attention to what ought now to be done regarding Imogen. As Great-Aunt Flora pointed out, it was at least something positive to think about.

Thalia pretended to agree with everyone. She made notes and nodded when stupid old Dilys made ridiculous suggestions about private nursing homes and long-term care, with the cost shared between the family. She held a serious discussion with Flora who wanted to buy an annuity which would pay for Imogen's care indefinitely, and said this was a very intelligent idea. It might be possible to do just that; Thalia would consult with Matron Porter and Dr Sterne and report back. They could then approach Royston's bankers for advice on how best to go about it. What did Flora think?

What Flora thought was that she had misjudged Thalia Caudle who, in the present appalling situation, was proving a tower of strength. She said so in her forthright way, and Thalia smiled faintly and looked at her nails.

Coercing Freda Porter proved to be the easiest thing of all. The secret with coercion was to find out the weakness in your victim's armour, and use it.

Freda Porter's weakness had been obvious. The creature had applied for the matron's post at Thornacre, and she was waiting to hear whether it was successful. It was instantly plain to Thalia that Leo Sterne had something – probably everything – to do with it. It looked as if the Porter woman was suffering from a bad case of middle-aged infatuation for Dr Sterne. Very good; it should be used against her. Thalia, wearing the most guileless of all her guileless masks, explained to Freda that *of course* there was no question of anyone blaming Briar House, or Freda herself, for Imogen's having slipped out so easily, and *of course* no one was going to ask for an investigation. As to the fact that Imogen had apparently been systematically fed a far heftier dosage of sedatives than was necessary, or even prescribed, oh, that was a mere nothing, said Thalia. These things happened, and it was not something that need blight Matron's future.

Especially since that future looked so promising just now. Especially with the Thornacre post on the horizon. It would be a very great pity if that was affected, said Thalia, slyly.

The shaft went home. The creature turned an unbecoming crimson and began to bluster, and Thalia felt a faint contempt for her. But she said coolly, 'I believe it is not an unusual practice to increase a prescribed sedative dose with, shall we say, *difficult* patients. I don't blame you in the least, Matron, and we should not dream of making trouble for you.' A pause. 'Of course, if Imogen should wake, if she should *talk* about how easy it was to get out of Briar House that night, and about all those sedatives she was given,' a brief gesture of helplessness, 'it might be difficult to keep it quiet. On all counts, it might be less dangerous if she could be got out of London.'

Freda said, thoughtfully, 'Well, I have to say, Mrs Caudle, that we haven't really the facilities or the staff to look after her at Briar House. Not in her present condition.'

'You haven't really, have you?' Thalia slid into her softest, most coaxing voice. 'Tell me, Matron, if you were to get this post at Thornacre, how easy would it be for you to have Imogen transferred there?'

'Permanently?'

'Oh yes.'

'It would probably be quite easy,' said Freda, slowly. 'Dr Sterne has an interest in the case, you know.'

'Really?'

'Oh yes. He believes that Imogen will come out of the stupor more or less naturally, although he can't tell yet how long it might take. But I think he would like to study her, which would mean transferring her to Thornacre anyway. Although it would probably have to be approved by the girl's family.'

Thalia said, 'But if I, as Imogen's guardian, did approve it, it would place her directly under your care?'

'If I were given the post, certainly it would.'

'Yes,' said Thalia, thoughtfully. 'If you were given the post.' She studied the other woman for a moment, and then said, 'Let's suppose for a minute you were given it. Let's suppose we could get you into Thornacre as matron. I'm sure you would be excellent at the job, by the way.'

Freda permitted herself a small smile.

'Would you be able to ensure that Imogen stayed there indefinitely?' said Thalia.

They looked at one another. 'Well, do you know,' said Freda, at last, 'I believe I might be able to do that. As matron I should have considerable authority.' This had such a good ring to it that she repeated it. 'Yes, *considerable* authority. I should have to be consulted about the cases there. Of course, Dr Sterne discusses a great deal with me already.' This also sounded well. It sounded as if Dr Sterne reposed great confidence in her.

Thalia said, 'Yes, I have realised for myself that you have quite a lot of influence with Dr Sterne.' She registered the woman's smirk, and the way she put up one hand to give her hair a little complacent pat. 'And, of course, once Imogen was under your care, you could make sure that she didn't talk about the sedative overdosing, couldn't you? That's a side issue, but we ought not to forget it. We ought not to minimise the possible danger there, ought we?'

Freda, white rather than red now, said, 'Oh no,' and gave a mad little laugh.

'What concerns me most is protecting the rest of the family,' said Thalia. 'And that means protecting the reputation of Ingram's –the company, I mean.' She paused, frowning, as if selecting her next words with care. 'I believe I can be open with you,' she said, leaning forward. 'You know what happened at my son's funeral?'

Freda shuddered delicately and said, 'Dear me, yes. Very nasty for you all.'

'Imogen will inherit Ingram's eventually,' said Thalia. 'But if it became known that she was, shall we say, *dis-*

162

turbed, it might harm the company severely. People are so hidebound by the conventions, don't you agree?'

'Oh, quite.'

Thalia, satisfied that she had got the point across, changed tack. 'I have met Professor Rackham,' she said, as if she had only just remembered this. 'In the course of some of my charity work. I wonder, supposing I were to send him a personal reference about you.'

Freda said, carefully, 'And in return for that, you would want . . .'

Dear God, did it have to be spelled out in single-syllable words for the woman? Thalia said, 'I would want you to make sure that once inside Thornacre, Imogen stays there.'

The two women looked at one another. Eventually, Freda said, 'For how long? And asleep or awake?'

'I don't care which,' said Thalia. 'But I don't want her to come out of Thornacre for a very long time.'

Quincy had been given the especial task of watching Imogen in case she woke up.

This was an extremely important job, and Quincy had stared with wide, scared eyes when Matron Porter and Dr Sterne had explained it to her, and then had said a bit breathlessly that she would do it; she would do anything in the world for Imogen. She would sit up all night and not go to sleep in order to watch, she said earnestly. Dr Sterne had smiled at that – he had a nice smile but at the moment it was very tired – and had said that would not be necessary; they would have an extra nurse on duty by tonight, and in any case Imogen would have woken up by then. Quincy had not liked to ask what would happen if Imogen did not wake up.

Porter-Pig had not been pleased about any of it; Quincy had known that at once on account of the little jagged spikes all round Porter-Pig's head, like angry buzzing hornets. Hornets were like wasps only a lot bigger and a whole lot more dangerous. Drawing Matron with the hornet-crossness around her head would make a good new picture.

Dr Sterne would make a good picture as well. Quincy had not drawn him yet, but when she did, she would make him a dark, faintly mysterious figure against a background of light, like the coloured windows you saw in church. She had never been to church until she came to Briar House; people in Bolt Place had spent Sundays sleeping off Saturday night's drinking, or dodging the rent man. Quincy had once, greatly daring, ventured into St Thomas's and crept into one of the seats, fascinated by the marvellous rich colours in the windows, and by the faint drift of polish and old wood and the enormous feeling of peace. She went several times after that, until Mother and the men in the pub found out and sneered, and told coarse stories about vicars, and Mother dug the men in the ribs and shrieked with mirth at the things they said.

Quincy did not go to church again after that, and she did not go when she came to Briar House, either. It was not part of what you did here; Freda said her staff had better things to do than trail people all the way to church, particularly with Sunday being a visiting day for so many. Visitors to Briar House expected to smell the good scents of beef roasting for a traditional Sunday dinner and to go away feeling comfortable about leaving their relatives in such a pleasant, homelike place where such nice meals were cooked. A few favoured guests were sometimes invited to stay to share the roast beef and Yorkshire pudding or the pork with apple sauce, and it all meant extra work and the staff demanded bonuses for working on Sundays.

Imogen might stay asleep like this for a very long time. She might not wake up for months and months and she might not wake up at all. Quincy had heard Matron say this to Dr Sterne; they had been crossing the hall and Quincy had been on the half-landing. She had huddled behind the curtains at the long windows, and she had heard Matron say something about comas and something else about vegetables, which was bewildering, and then about brain death which sounded appalling.

Normally Quincy would have gone away then, but she wanted to hear more about what was going to happen to Imogen. Matron and Dr Sterne were going into Matron's sitting room – the light from the front door was just falling across Dr Sterne so that it looked as if he was wearing a crimson and sapphire cloak of light, and Porter-Pig was poking and pecking her head forward like a long-beaked, bulgy-breasted animal.

Dr Sterne said, very sharply, 'It's not a coma, Matron.'

'Whatever name we give it, Dr Sterne, she can't stay here. We haven't the facilities.'

'Have you talked to her family yet? There are some very good private places that specialise in that kind of care.'

There was a sudden pause, and then Freda said, 'I've talked to Mrs Caudle, of course. She is the girl's guardian.'

'Why on earth – oh, she's still under age, of course. Sixteen?'

'Almost eighteen. And it seems,' said Freda, still in the same careful voice, 'that the family are not prepared to finance an indefinite stay in Briar House. Even if we had the resources.'

Quincy, still curled into her hidey-hole, could no longer see Porter-Pig's face, but she could hear that there was something very odd in her voice when she said this about Imogen's family. Dr Sterne seemed to have heard it as well, because there was a moment of silence, as if he might be looking at Matron very carefully.

But after a moment he seemed to accept it. 'I see,' he said. 'I wonder if it's "can't" rather than "won't". Maybe Ingram's is suffering from the recession like everyone else.'

'Well, that isn't for me to say, Dr Sterne.' And then, as if she might have taken a deep breath beforehand, she said, 'And so if you are to continue to treat her, I am very much afraid there is only one place for her, isn't there?' She did not say 'I' when she talked to Dr Sterne: she said 'Ai', in the way people did when they were trying to sound expensive and well educated. Porter-Pig was neither of these things and she only made Dr Sterne wince when she put on this pretend-posh voice. The words came out as, 'Ai am very much afraid there is only one place for her,' and Quincy knew that Dr Sterne would have liked her much better if she had been ordinary and natural.

But he said, half to himself, 'Thornacre,' and Quincy felt a wash of cold horror engulf her. 'I'll ring them up straight away and make the arrangements. If the guardian is agreeable—'

'Oh, most definitely.'

'Then she'd better go at once.'

And Matron Pig said, in her silly, simpering voice, 'And did you know Ai shall be going to Thornacre as well, Dr Sterne? Yes, confirmed this morning. Professor Rackham telephoned me himself. Mai word, what a charmer he is. Ai almost think Ai made a conquest there. And you and me working together. It almost seems meant, doesn't it?'

Imogen's room smelt of nice things, expensive things like the good soap she had brought with her and the box of powder that went with it, which Quincy thought was like floaty pink icing sugar. There was the scent of clean hair as well, and of thin, soft underthings. On the little table under the window was a bowl of what was called potpourri. Quincy knew about potpourri; you saw it in shops and it smelt delicious. But Imogen had said it differently to the way Quincy had thought it was said. Quincy had pronounced it silently when she was on her own, trying to make her voice sound the same, and then she wondered if she was only being like silly old pretend Porter-Pig, trying to be something she was not. It was not very nice to think of old Freda being at Thornacre with Imogen. Quincy was unhappy about that.

Somebody had undressed Imogen and put one of the silky nightdresses on her, and Quincy had been allowed to brush the long dark hair and arrange it neatly on the pillows. Imogen had not moved the whole time and although her eyes were a bit open, she looked as if she was seeing things a long way away from Briar House. Quincy knew it was because of what she had seen in her mother's coffin; she had heard two of the assistants talking about it and she knew that Imogen had crept out to the graveyard when it was dark.

Imogen's mother had been alive when they put her in the ground, just as Thalia Caudle had said. The lady with the beautiful name, Eloise, had been alive, and she had tried to get out and she had died screaming for help, and nobody had heard her.

Quincy had dreamed about Imogen's mother several times and woken up frightened. Once she had tried to draw it, because Dr Sterne said that drawing frightening things was a good thing to do. There was a long word for it which Quincy could not remember, but it meant that it helped you to stop being frightened of things. But the drawing of Imogen's mother had been so terrible that she had had to stop. It had started out as a good-looking lady, a bit like Imogen, but then it had changed on the page into a red, raw screaming thing, all twisted and writhing and blood-spattered, with torn-off fingernails where it had tried to claw its way out of the ground.

Quincy had not been able to stop thinking about it. She had not been able to stop thinking that it was all her fault. If she had gone to the cemetery earlier that day she might have saved Imogen's mother. If she had not gone at all, nobody would have known anything about it, and Imogen would not have fallen into this faraway sleep. Quincy did not know which would have been better.

She sat down in a chair at the foot of Imogen's bed. Dr Sterne had made a chart so that they could keep a count of how long Imogen was asleep like this. He was crossing off the days, one at a time, and six had been crossed off already. Quincy stared at the chart, not seeing it.

Imogen was going to Thornacre, and Thornacre was the worst place in the world. It was a place that made people evil; they looked ordinary on the outside, but underneath they were evil and cruel. They wore masks, just as Thalia Caudle had worn a mask.

There had been a doctor in Thornacre who had looked quite ordinary and who had pretended to be kind. He had talked to Quincy in a special voice, and listened to her telling about how after her mother's funeral the man who owned the house was going to throw her into the street because she had no money and how she had had to lie on the bed and let him poke himself inside her. The man had said it was what her mother had always done when there was no rent money, and a young slag was as good as an old one, and one pair of open legs the same as another.

The Thornacre doctor had listened to everything, and then he had locked the door and told her to undress, beause they were going to act out what had happened with the rent man and all the other men, and then afterwards Quincy would be able to forget all about it. He had used a word Quincy had never heard – something beginning with cat, something that sounded like cattersis – and his eyes had been cold and glittery. He had said she must tell him exactly what each man had done to her, and then he had unfastened his trousers and pushed her over the desk. She had felt the hard poking part thrusting against her.

He had not done it to her at the front like the other men; he had done it from behind and it had been the most painful thing she had ever known. It had gone on for what had seemed to be a very long time, but then right at the end the doctor who was the Cattersis-beast had jerked her round to

168

face him and forced her to kneel down, pushing into her face and making her open her mouth. He had panted smelly breath on to her, and his body had been sour in her mouth. There was a word she had heard – rancid. People said butter was rancid when it went off in the hot weather. The doctor's body and the wet stickiness spurting into her mouth were rancid.

Quincy had wanted to get into a bath and scrub her skin and scour out her mouth until it was raw to get rid of the feel and the taste, but you could not have baths when you felt like it at Thornacre, and she had had to go about with the tainted Cattersis-breath in her nostrils and with his sour taste in her mouth.

He had said she must not talk about it because keeping it a secret was part of the treatment. It was part of the cat-word. He said that if she ever broke the secret, she would be punished. Even if it took years and years, there would be a punishment waiting for her. She would be locked inside Thornacre for ever, he said; perhaps she would be locked in the old east wing, with the black iron door. He had thrust his face close to her, his eyes glittery like dead fish eyes. Did she know about the black iron door? he had asked. Ah, but did she know what was *on the other side of it*? If she told what had happened in this room today, she would find out because he would throw her into that room and lock the door.

Quincy sat in a miserable little huddle in the chair in the corner of Imogen's room, staring at the still figure in the bed, and then without warning an idea began to form in her mind. As it grew and got stronger and more definite, she began to feel very frightened indeed, because it was a truly terrible idea. She squeezed her eyes tight shut to pretend it was not there, but this was cheating, because once ideas were born, you could never send them away.

Quincy took a deep breath and opened her eyes. She was going to look the terrible idea full in the face, because if she

169

could not have courage for Imogen, she could not have courage for anything.

She would have to go with Imogen to Thornacre. To look after her and to protect her. The Cattersis-beast would not be there. Dr Sterne had told her that once people had found out what had been going on, they had taken him away, and probably he was going to prison for a very long time, which meant that Quincy could feel entirely safe.

The only person Quincy really felt safe with was Dr Sterne himself, but she couldn't say this. She trusted him completely and she would die for him – not pretend die, not like when people said, 'Oh, I'd *die* if such and such happened,' but really truly die.

It was not the Cattersis-beast that worried her about Thornacre. It was the haunted east wing, and it was what was inside the east wing, behind the black iron door.

Chapter Sixteen

None of the Ingrams wanted to attend the inquest on Eloise, but somebody had to go.

Somebody had to be there to represent the family, and somebody certainly had to hold a watching brief for Imogen. Juliette said that somebody had better hold a watching brief on Dr Shilling as well, which caused a considerable stir because everyone had tried very strenuously to forget that bizarre little conference on the day of Edmund's funeral. Several people tried to say they had important appointments in foreign countries the very day of the inquest but were not believed.

Cousin Elspeth created an unpleasant stir by wanting to know had anyone thought to ask where Edmund's *head* was, for goodness' sake? You could not get away from the fact that there was a *head* lying around somewhere, said Cousin Elspeth shrilly, and what were people doing about it? It was all very well to say in that quelling voice that Thalia had dealt with it, but were they sure that she had?

'Of course she has,' said Rosa sharply. 'I remember her telling me that she had a meeting with Huxtable's. It'll have been re-interred, Elspeth.'

It was generally agreed that Dr Shilling ought to shoulder the blame at the inquest, although not, as Juliette pointed out, if it meant blowing the gaff. Aunt Dilys voiced most people's unspoken fears by pointing out that if John Shilling could get it wrong about Eloise, he could get it wrong about Royston as well, and wondered if it had occurred to anyone to ask about this? But Inspector Mackenzie, to whom it had occurred very forcibly indeed, rang them up to reassure them. There had been a discreet second exhumation almost straight away, he said, and Royston Ingram had been peaceful and perfectly serene. There was no doubt that he had died from a massive coronary thrombosis, and it was probably not going to be necessary even to refer to it at the inquest.

Flora, descending on Battersea, agreed with Rosa and Dilys that it had been kind of the inspector to reassure them about Royston, but unfortunately added that while it was a tragedy to have one relative buried alive, it would be a farce to have two, which had the effect of upsetting Dilys all over again. Rosa remembered that Flora had always had a flippant streak and was not surprised she had never managed to keep a husband.

'At least I *got* a husband,' retorted Flora. 'I got three, in fact.'

'Yes, but did you keep th—'

'Oh, *please* don't let's fall out,' wept Dilys. 'We should be thinking about Imogen inside Thornacre. I can't bear it. I keep remembering those pictures on the television news, those photographs of the east wing. It looked absolutely terrible, black and cold. They said it was known as the haunted wing. Not the BBC, of course. And Elspeth said George had read an article in his paper about it.'

Flora remarked that George had always had a taste for sensational literature of the worst kind.

'Yes, but every time I saw those photographs I felt an icy shudder all down my spine, because if there is a ghost there, it's Sybilla. Yes it is, Rosa, you said so yourself.'

'What I said was that a ghost never hurt anyone,' said Rosa tartly.

'Prowling the east wing, that was what one reporter said. You remember, Rosa, because you said it was a disgraceful thing to put on the evening news, and he should be reported to somebody. Oh, *isn't* there any alternative?'

'Apparently not, as things are at present,' said Flora. 'That Porter woman's making the arrangements. In fact she's been appointed as Thornacre's new matron, so she'll be going with Imogen. That ought to be a help, oughtn't it? With her knowing the case and the family and everything. And Dilys, Thornacre's all right now, it really is. The commission – Dr Sterne and Professor Rackham – they made a clean sweep.'

'I don't care. It's still an evil place, I can feel that it's evil. It's malignant. That can happen in houses, you know. Evil can stay in the walls and infect the people who live there.'

'Don't be hysterical, Dilys.'

'I'm not being hysterical, and even if I am I don't care. Sybilla lived there – she died there. And Lucienne. And they were both mad. Sybilla was *evil*, you've said so yourself, Rosa. And now Imogen's going there as well.'

Rosa said, 'I must admit I don't much care for the idea myself, Flora. Couldn't she go to an ordinary hospital? Or a private clinic? I suppose all the possibilities have been explored, have they?'

'Oh yes. Thalia seems to have been extremely thorough.'

'What if we paid? We could pay,' said Dilys eagerly. 'I don't understand all these dividends we get, although Thalia tried to explain it to me. But we all have an income from Ingram's; if we all contributed something, it wouldn't cost anyone very much. Rosa, you and I could afford it. Mother's shares – you know we always put the interest away and we hardly ever touch it. And Flora, you could afford it as well, couldn't you? I don't mean that to sound rude—'

'I'd gladly contribute whatever's necessary,' said Flora. 'In fact I've already told Thalia so. I offered to help with the arrangements as well.'

'What did she say?' Rosa and Dilys had been quite worried about this, because it had seemed as if Thalia was shouldering everything, which was surely not fair.

'She said as Imogen's guardian it was her duty to do it.'

Dilys said, 'Oh, but—'

'And that coping with it was helping her forget about Eloise and Royston. And also Edmund,' said Flora. 'I couldn't force it. Not in the face of that.'

Rosa and Dilys, shocked, said, well, of course not.

'In any case, it doesn't seem to be a question of money,' said Flora. 'The only solution at the moment is apparently Thornacre. Dilys, if you cry for much longer I'm going to buy shares in Kleenex.'

In the end, the family was represented at the inquest by Flora who insisted on being present; by Thalia, who had to give evidence anyway, and by Elspeth's husband George because it was important to have a Man there.

Dilys could not stop crying, and Rosa could not leave her, and everybody else managed to find a good reason for being somewhere else on the day. It was probably better not to create any suspicions by all turning up in a crowd anyway. Not that there was anything to be suspicious about, of course.

Flora had telephoned Dr Shilling and demanded to know precisely what he intended to say, and it appeared that he would stand by the original plan. There was an air of relief, although Cousin Elspeth wanted to know whether they could really *trust* a person who had let Eloise be buried alive, and said George had never liked him.

Thalia was shown into the witnesses' waiting room, and Flora sat unobtrusively in the public gallery with George who was praying to escape prominence at this appalling inquest. He was disappointed in this when Juliette arrived at the last minute and bounced into the courtroom wearing a cherry red suit with an extremely short skirt and sheer black tights. She caused quite a flurry in the public gallery by trampling over people's feet in order to sit next to Flora, who did not in the least mind people turning round to stare at them and was pleased at the defiant red outfit.

'I'm flying the flag for us all,' said Juliette. 'I suppose we're going to be stared at, so I thought we might as well give them something worth staring at. Oh, do budge up a bit, George, of course there's room for me.'

George turned up his coat collar and slid down in his seat in an effort to escape the worst of these Ingram flippancies, and wished himself elsewhere.

'Here we go,' said Juliette, as the coroner entered and everyone obediently stood up. 'The coroner's rather nice looking, isn't he?'

'He looks a bit like my first husband,' said Flora.

'The one who ran amok with half the typists' pool?'

'That was the second. George, is that the jury in that loosebox thing? Looking as if they've had to be locked in for the duration? Oh, it is. Poor dears, they look as if they're here under duress. I suppose you can't blame them.'

'I didn't know you had a jury at a coroner's inquest,' put in Juliette. 'I was wondering if I should vamp the coroner to get a verdict in our favour, but it looks as if I'd have to take on the entire jury as well.'

'Rather extravagant, my dear.'

'Well, you can hardly talk, Aunt Flo. What's the matter with George now? Oh, don't be so glum, George, it won't help poor Eloise. We'll all go across to the pub afterwards.'

'John Shilling looks as if he's been there for the past week nonstop,' remarked Flora. 'He looks pretty sick in fact.'

'So he should. He'd look sick on the end of a rope if I had anything to do with it.'

'George, they don't hang people any more.'

'I don't know about hanging him, I'd flog the bastard,' said George.

As John Shilling took the stand, he was visibly trembling and he saw the courtroom through a blur. He did not think he had slept since that terrible night in the cemetery; he did not really want to sleep, because every time he closed his eyes he saw Eloise's face, twisted and frozen in that final terrible agony. His lady, his shining, beautiful goddess whom he had been prepared to die for . . . whom he had condemned to that dreadful, lonely death. Terror and remorse gripped him, not romantically by the heart, but embarrassingly, in the bowels, and he had had to make several hasty visits to the bathroom already that morning. He had drunk large draughts of white digestive mixture, but he was uneasily aware that viscerally speaking he trod a thin line.

He told the court how he had been called to examine the bodies of Eloise and Royston Ingram on the afternoon of Edmund Caudle's funeral; Mrs Caudle, Royston Ingram's cousin, had found them and had called to him at once.

The coroner knew all about this case; he knew about the appalling night when Jim Frisby and Leo Sterne had discovered that Eloise Ingram had been buried alive, and he had agreed with Frisby that while nobody wanted to distort the cause of justice, if the impromptu exhumation and its outcome could be kept private, they should be. Frisby had said, with some truth, that if once a story about a premature burial came to the public's notice, there would be a nationwide panic. An inquest there must of course be, but if it could be treated as an ordinary case of suspicious circumstances, so much the better. They had consulted very carefully over this, including Inspector Mackenzie and his superiors in the discussions, and even Inspector Mackenzie, a good, honest officer, and the Chief Constable (with whom Frisby played golf), had agreed. Frisby could hardly, in the circumstances, head the inquest himself, but if he had to give evidence he would be discreet, and the police would be discreet, and John Shilling, who stood to lose more than any of them over this, would be discreet as well. It was true that discretion did not figure very highly in Leo Sterne's list of priorities, but on this occasion he could probably be trusted; in fact there was not really any need for him to give evidence at all, said the Chief Constable firmly. To some extent they could control this inquest and they would do just that.

And so the coroner, who wanted to get this horrific matter over with as soon as possible, and who did not like the way the reporters were taking down every word, eyed Dr Shilling firmly, and said, 'Will you tell the court what examinations you made on that afternoon?'

John Shilling felt rather than saw the ruffle of unease from the public gallery. He said, very firmly, 'I made virtually no examination at all.'

'None?'

'I checked for pulse and respiration, of course. But there was none. Royston Ingram had certainly died from myocardial infarction – in layman's terms a heart attack. He had a history of angina pectoris, exacerbated – possibly caused – by arteriosclerosis.'

'You had treated him for it?'

'Yes, he had been taking beta-blockers – propranolol – and an angiotensin-converting enzyme.'

The coroner made a note. 'And Eloise Ingram?'

John Shilling paused, and thought: this is for you, Eloise. And for Imogen. With a feeling of crossing a private and very dark Rubicon, he said, 'I believed Eloise Ingram to have committed suicide.' A murmur of surprise went through the press bench, and John, staring determinedly into the middle distance, said, 'I gave a fictitious cause of death on the certificate because I wanted to spare the family further pain.'

This was not quite according to the plan mapped out by the coroner and Inspector Mackenzie, but there was a rough and ready formula on these occasions, and so the coroner said, 'Was Mrs Ingram suicidally inclined?'

John hesitated, and then said, 'Both Royston and Eloise had found the funeral extremely distressing. It was almost

177

certainly the stress of it that gave Royston Ingram his final heart attack. And Eloise relied on him very much.'

'You think his death might have caused her to take her life?' said the coroner.

'She was a very sensitive and delicately balanced lady,' said John, and several people caught the wistful note. 'If she perhaps woke from a sedated sleep and found him dead, lying next to her in the bed – it would have been enough to tip her into an unbalanced condition for a time. There could have been deep despair and acute depression.'

'Suicide whilst of unsound mind,' said the coroner, thoughtfully.

'Exactly.'

'I hope,' said the coroner, suddenly glaring at the press bench, 'that there are no reports of any harassing of the family after these proceedings.'

One of the older journalists whispered to his neighbour that the coroner was a close friend of somebody on the Press Complaints Commission, and a respectable air of decorum instantly descended on the entire press bench.

'There had been a massive haemorrhage,' said John after a moment. 'The body was covered in blood, and in places it had soaked into the bed. It was – I found it extremely distressing. I had known the lady, the whole family, very well for many years. That was why I did not make a full examination.'

'You were personally involved?'

'Yes.'

'I believe I must ask if you were emotionally involved as well, Dr Shilling.'

'No,' said John Shilling loudly. 'No, I was not.' He saw the embarrassment on most of the jury's faces, and realised they all thought he had been Eloise's lover. What a sad irony. He said, 'There was no involvement between us, other than that of friends.'

'Very well. Please go on.'

'The blood – the quantity of blood on the bed was consistent with self-mutilation.'

'Such as cutting the wrists?'

'No, more like stabbing.' Another deep breath. 'I found a knife under her hand,' he said, firmly. 'It was smeared with blood.'

'Ah. But you did not examine for wounds?'

'No. I . . .' Shilling paused, and wet his lips. 'I thought it was fairly plain what she had done,' he said. 'And so I made fictitious entries on the medical records consistent with symptoms of a stomach ulcer. And I gave the cause of death as a perforated stomach ulcer. In order to explain the blood. Several of the family had come into the room, you see.'

The coroner gave John Shilling a very level stare. 'You do realise what you're admitting to?'

'Yes.' Across the Rubicon and into the River of Jordan now, thought John Shilling. In fact neck deep. But the structure of the plan was holding so far.

'Well, it isn't my concern,' said the coroner, rather testily. 'But you'll have to answer to the GMC, you know. And probably the police, as well.'

'I'm aware of that.'

'All right, stand down, Dr Shilling. For the moment, anyway.'

Thalia came next, and gave her evidence briefly and concisely. Flora had the impression that Thalia was shutting her eyes so that nobody would see her, in the manner of a child.

Thalia said she had looked in on her cousin and his wife just before the funeral guests left, and explained that they had all been concerned about both Royston and Eloise.

'Royston had had some kind of heart spasm. Dr Shilling had given him something for it.'

'Propranolol,' said the coroner, flipping his notes back.

'Yes, I think it was that.'

'Because of the funeral presumably?'

179

'Yes. We had all been very upset.'

'Of course. Go on if you will, Mrs Caudle.'

Thalia said there had been a great deal of blood on the bed, and that Dr Shilling had told them that both Eloise and Royston were dead, Royston from a heart attack, Eloise from haemorrhage following the perforation of a stomach ulcer. They had all accepted this, and the funeral had taken place two days later. They had wanted to get it over with as quickly as possible. 'All the anguish in one lump,' said Thalia.

'Did you know Dr Shilling had falsified the cause of death?'

'No, of course not.'

'You didn't – forgive me, Mrs Caudle, this must be very distressing for you – but did none of you question the abruptness of Eloise Ingram's death? Or ask Dr Shilling questions about it?'

Thalia looked at the coroner and then said, with a faint air of reproach, 'With respect, you have to remember that we were all stunned. My son had just been killed in a car crash. He was nineteen. This all took place on the afternoon of his funeral. We were none of us in a fit state to reason or to think very clearly, other than to be profoundly grateful for Dr Shilling's help. He dealt with the formalities for us. We were punch-drunk with misery.' Flora noted that this was an extremely effective line, and then was cross with herself for suspecting Thalia of deliberately trying to create an effect. I might do it, thought Flora. And I daresay Juliette might do it as well. But it simply wouldn't occur to Thalia. Or would it? She's an odd creature at times. Secretive. Concentrate, old girl, here's the inspector.

Inspector Mackenzie had the air of an old hand at these affairs, and gave dry and deliberate evidence of the exhuming of the body 'because of certain suspicious circumstances'. He said this with an air of finality, and was succeeded so swiftly by the forensic pathologist that the reporters barely had a chance to register the brevity of the policeman's explanation.

As the pathologist took the stand, the coroner and Inspector Mackenzie exchanged looks, because this was the part of the proceedings over which they had no control at all. The coroner thought that so far things had gone amazingly well, and that even Dr Shilling's unexpected admission had not really thrown things off course. Providing there were no other revelations to come from the pathologist, he could wind things up and direct the jury. At the moment it was touch and go whether the verdict would be death by misadventure or manslaughter against John Shilling. But the cause of death was still to be established.

The first really awkward moment came when the pathologist reported the presence of a near-lethal dose of chloral hydrate in the subject's stomach, which appeared to have been administered in brandy. This produced a stir of uneasy interest, and Juliette and Flora stared at one another in bewilderment.

Flora said, 'But Eloise never drank brandy. She hated it.'

'Then somebody must have given it to her.'

'She wouldn't have drunk it.'

'She might if she was heavily sedated.'

Two people from the back row, who, having managed to get into this exceedingly promising inquest, did not want to miss any denouement that might be going, both said 'Shush' very sharply indeed, and George shunted further down the bench to disassociate himself as much as possible from his wife's embarrassing relatives.

The pathologist was explaining that alcohol together with chloral hydrate could produce extremely deep levels of coma, and then death. 'There was the characteristic irritation of mucous membranes and skin,' he said. 'It's impossible to know how long the coma state lasted, but it's probable that she passed from that into death.'

Juliette said, softly, 'Oh, the old pet,' and George, who

181

had been about to denounce the pathologist as a prattling old creeper, suspended judgement.

There had been no marks on the body indicative of suicide, said the pathologist, and Eloise Ingram had been in quite good health. He gave details of his findings, some of which were graphic and some of which were vaguely embarrassing, lost himself amid a welter of bone density and degeneration of fatty tissues, dwelled briefly on liver weight and kidney function, and confused several of his listeners by reference to an old appendicectomy scar.

Juliette remarked, not quite *sotto voce*, that one apparently got a far more thorough examination when one was dead than ever one did when alive.

'And,' said the pathologist, emerging from a flurry of notes, 'although I have heard the evidence of Mrs Caudle and Dr Shilling, I have to say that my examination showed that the cadaver had not suffered any significant blood loss.'

The journalists' pencils skidded across their notebooks all over again, and the coroner, with the feeling of seeing a hitherto unsuspected abyss open up at his feet, said, 'None at all?'

'No. I understand,' said the pathologist, whose name was Simcox, 'that Dr Shilling believed massive haemorrhage from stab wounds to be the actual cause of death.'

'But it was not?'

'No. There were no wounds on the body,' said Simcox.

'Then the cause of Eloise Ingram's death was the chloral hydrate?'

'Almost certainly. Chloral hydrate isn't as strong as some of the more recent drugs in the narcotic or opiate range, but administered with alcohol and in sufficiently large quantity, it can be fatal. The analysis showed a sufficiently large presence of the drug to have caused death in this case.' He began to explain about dosages and quantitative analysis, and Juliette whispered to Flora, 'But what about the blood?'

182

'What about the blood?' said the coroner, as if in faithful echo of this.

'Well,' said Mr Simcox, regarding the court solemnly, 'I made a close examination of Eloise and Royston Ingram's bedroom.'

'Yes?'

'It had been very thoroughly cleaned up, but we did find traces of blood, minute but sufficient for analysis.'

'But you've said she didn't die from loss of blood. And there were no wounds.'

'That's correct. The blood wasn't human blood,' said Simcox. And then, with timing and delivery that would not have shamed Olivier, 'It was beast blood,' he said.

There was a silence. The coroner took off his glasses and regarded Mr Simcox. 'Could you repeat that, please. I don't think I can have heard properly.'

'To be precise, it was sheep's blood,' said Simcox. 'Not very fresh – it had been subjected to a freezing process.'

'Let me get this clear,' said the coroner. 'You're saying that the blood that Dr Shilling and Mrs Caudle saw on Eloise Ingram's body and on the bed was that of a sheep?'

'Yes.'

'And that it had been frozen?'

'Yes. The picture that presents itself,' said Simcox, 'is of a quantity of beast blood being obtained and—'

'Mr Simcox, I wonder if you would mind not using that expression.'

'What expression?'

'Beast blood,' said the coroner, with force. 'I don't doubt it is correct usage in pathology and forensic circles, but it conjures up the more gruesome types of horror fiction. And the gentlemen of the press are already devouring this tragedy with their customary tastelessness.'

'Oh, I see. I'm sorry. Well, the – the blood was probably obtained from an abattoir under some pretext or other and stored in an ordinary domestic deep freeze.'

183

'And then smeared on the body to make it appear that Eloise Ingram had slashed her wrists or been stabbed?'

'That was our conclusion. Perhaps with the aim of implicating someone, or perhaps with the idea of covering up the real cause of death. Either of those or perhaps both of them. That's what it looked like. But it's not for me to say.'

'No, but considering all the evidence, which we can now do—' The coroner broke off as the jury foreman held a hastily whispered colloquy with his fellows, and then hesitantly raised a hand. 'Yes, Mr Foreman?'

'I hope it's in order to interrupt at this stage, sir, but several of us would like to ask a question before you go any further.'

'By all means.'

'Does Mr Simcox have any suggestions as to what kind of reason you could give to get blood from an abattoir? Because nobody over here can think of a single one.'

'A good question,' said the coroner. 'Well, Mr Simcox?'

'Oh, it isn't very difficult. You could say you were teaching a sixth-form class about analysing the properties of blood. Or you could say you were an amateur dramatic society putting on a play. Or even giving a first aid demonstration. It's quite difficult to fake blood convincingly, and it can be dreadfully messy to use ketchup or paint. It's far better to use beast— to use animal blood. I believe there's actually an abattoir near Covent Garden that supplies several of the theatres. *Grand Guignol* and Greek tragedy, you know,' added Simcox chattily.

Juliette was heard to murmur, 'Just like we've got in front of us now.'

'All right, Mr Foreman? That seems reasonable to me. Does it to you?'

'Oh yes, thank you very much, sir. We hadn't thought of any of those.'

The helpful Mr Simcox was dismissed, and the coroner looked at the jury.

'I expect,' he said, 'that most of you were thinking this would be a case of death by misadventure. I thought so myself. But Mr Simcox's evidence makes a vast difference. There's no reason to doubt any of it, or indeed to doubt the ability of Mr Simcox or his team.' He paused, and then said, 'Taking into acccount the bizarre fact of the animal blood on Eloise Ingram's bed and the presence of chloral hydrate in her body, there was certainly murderous intent, although as to the murderer's identity we can't say. That's a job for the police, and if you return a verdict of murder or manslaughter, they will begin their own investigations. Your job now is to weigh the evidence you have heard very carefully indeed and give us your verdict.' He paused, and then said, 'But I do most strongly recommend that you cannot, in justice, return any other verdict than that of murder by person or persons unknown.'

Thalia, leaving the court with Flora and George and Juliette, thought that on balance things had not gone too badly. It was a wretched nuisance that the business with the blood and the chloral hydrate had come out, but she had been prepared for that. She was not in the least worried that suspicion would fall on her. She had obtained the blood anonymously – it had been ridiculously easy to get it from the large impersonal abattoir. She remembered how she had laughed in secret over her cleverness, and how satisfying it had been to set the scene in Eloise and Royston's bedroom that day. She had sprinkled the sheep's blood on to the bed, and the scent of it had mingled with the scent of triumph. It had been deeply and fiercely exciting.

She had been clever and cunning and she had covered her tracks completely. She would not be found out because everything she had done had been guided.

John Shilling would probably be charged with murder or manslaughter – Thalia was unclear as to the difference and it did not much matter – and it would be assumed that he had administered the chloral hydrate. Thalia did not think he would drag in the family, and even if he did, it would not do them much harm. They had not done anything criminal, Shilling had done the criminal part.

Really, she was managing everything very well indeed. She had had a fair amount of luck, of course, but on the whole it was all by her own efforts. The thought was a good thought, it was very nearly sexual in quality.

Sexual.

The thought of Dan Tudor surfaced again, and with it all the memories, some of them good, some of them outstanding, every one of them linked to Edmund.

Chapter Seventeen

It had never been possible to find Edmund's exact replica, of course; Thalia had known that, and she had never tried.

He had been the most beautiful child. Even Royston had said this once, and the aunts had always made a great fuss over him and said, oh, *what* a lovely boy, and wouldn't his poor dear father have been proud? It was only natural that Edmund should like being the centre of attention; it was kind of him to let the aunts fuss over him. The aunts enjoyed fussing and it did not hurt anyone.

It had been much later that Royston had turned against Edmund, saying the boy was lazy and selfish and a parasite and that if he carried on like this there might not be a place for him in Ingram's. This was spite and jealousy on Royston's part, and in the early years it could be disregarded. It was only when Royston began trying to persuade the rest of the family to his side that it became dangerous and it was then that the schemes and the plans for making Royston and the rest pay for their treachery began to uncoil in Thalia's brain.

And Edmund was not lazy or selfish; it was just that different rules applied to him. You did not apply the rules of a carthorse to a thoroughbred. Edmund was at odds with the harsh, jarring twentieth century; he would have been more at home in an earlier age, one of the golden Renaissance ages, a time of music and poetry and love, because he had been filled with all those things. But it was no good expecting Royston and Eloise or the aunts to understand any of this.

Thalia's discovery that there existed in the world a few young men (and one or two girls) who possessed a spark of Edmund's own golden quality happened without warning, shortly before his fifteenth birthday. He had changed by then, of course, and he had grown up. The golden-haired seraph had grown into a wand-slim young boy; a mischievous Apollo, with secrets in his eyes. He was charming and irresistible and it was small wonder that annoyed or embarrassed fathers – once or twice mothers – came to the house to complain. Trying out his wings, Thalia had said. Acting like a dirty little pervert, rejoined Royston. The aunts had twittered anxiously, because fourteen was surely *far* too young for, well, for that kind of thing. Elspeth's husband George said severely that he himself had been a *great* deal older than Edmund before embarking on his first physical relationship with a girl, and added that he wouldn't have dreamed of attempting anything of the kind with Elspeth until after they were married. '*Well* after,' said Elspeth.

'It isn't just that,' said Royston curtly, and called George into the small study at Hampstead. They were closeted together for a very long time, and Elspeth said afterwards that George had emerged shocked to his toes but had refused to tell what had been said.

The trouble was that none of them had understood that Edmund would want to experience all the pleasures available to him and that those silly girls had been utterly bewitched. It was unfair and unkind of Royston and George to say that Edmund was behaving like a pervert. Even Juliette once remarked that Edmund was precociously immoral and acted like some half-fledged Arabian princeling, draped on a silken divan and disdainfully inspecting females as if they were a new consignment of Circassian slaves brought for his consideration. There was nothing callow or half-fledged about Edmund, and anyway Juliette was the last person to talk about immorality.

It had been the oddest of coincidences that after the first of these episodes Thalia should begin seeing similarities in one or two of the young men who came her way through her charity work, but so it was.

The work itself was tedious beyond words – Thalia had got into it without realising how boring it would be – but once involved it was difficult to get out. The first time she saw this pallid likeness to Edmund was shortly after the first of the incidents with the bewitched girls, and the similarity struck her with such force that for a moment it blotted out everything else.

She had tried to dismiss it; it was surely only the bloom of youth, or a likeness of colouring and type. But it would not be dismissed. The young man was helping with a student counselling service that some boring Hampstead women's group were setting up, and Thalia had been asked to help as well. He was reading psychology at London University and he had what people called a social conscience. Helping with the new group was part of what he said was field work. Edmund had been away at school then, and the days were occasionally empty and there had been a fierce satisfaction in seducing the student. Seeing the spill of golden hair on her pillow, feeling the firm, supple thighs and strong jutting manhood had brought such violent satisfaction that Thalia had begun to look for others: strong, attractive young men who possessed bright, darting reflections of Edmund. It was astonishing how many there were. It might only be colouring or the slant of a cheekbone or the curving smile. Or it might be a shard of intelligence, or an interest in the things that interested Edmund. They were all golden and special, of course – Thalia was not going to associate with monosyllabic yobs.

The gratifying thing was that when she beckoned to them, they came to her bed without hesitation. They were not monosyllabic, although occasionally they were genuinely inarticulate. Once or twice she miscalculated and they turned out to be impotent and therefore had to be discarded. But the strong, virile ones, the ones who had been made in Edmund's likeness, could be used several times over. After Edmund died it became even more necessary to continue the search.

Dan Tudor was the exception. He had not been made in Edmund's likeness at all but there was the sharp, bright mind that Edmund would have developed if he had lived; the impression that he would not suffer fools gladly, too slight to be called arrogance but too definite to be missed.

And Dan was neither inarticulate nor impotent.

Yes, it would be a pity to let Dan get away.

Dan had gone back to Sleeping Beauty's origins, back beyond the Grimm brothers' emasculated version, beyond the nineteenth-century Covent Garden actor-managers with their pantomimic extravaganzas, and certainly back beyond Disney and the film-makers, to the story's core.

He had begun with Charles Perrault's startling tale, and had found it so very much grislier than he had realised that his imagination had been fired and he had worked backwards to uncover other sources. There was an Italian writer called Giambattista Basile who had published an even earlier version than Perrault's, around 1636. Dan half-bullied, half-coaxed his local library into tracking down a translation, promising any number of author's acknowledgements and credits by way of reward. It occurred to him as well that Perrault and Basile and one or two others might provide good subjects for biographies sometime, and he jotted a few notes down. When he finally got Basile's translation, he was so pleased that, without thinking, he took it to bed to read that night, only to discover that it was so strong and so macabre it would probably give him a fresh batch of nightmares to put alongside the ones already engendered by Oliver's material on Victorian madhouses. Dan had to get up and check that all the doors in the flat were locked before he could read any more of Signor Basile.

Perrault and Basile both presented the villainess not as the cross fairy godmother who had sulked at not being invited to the christening and thrown out a bad-tempered curse as a result but as a fierce, blood-guzzling, child-eating creature who, in Perrault's picturesque prose, 'had come of a race of *Ogres*, and that it was whispered about the court that she had *Ogreish* inclinations, and when she saw little children passing by, she had all the difficulty in the world to refrain from falling upon them . . .'

Monsieur Perrault, clearly anxious that none of the horror should be lost on his readers, added a rider which further informed his audiences: 'Now an Ogre is a giant that has long teeth and claws, and with a raw head and bloody bones, that runs away with naughty little boys and girls and eats them up . . .' Which was all a very long way indeed from Tchaikovsky and Walt Disney.

Basile portrayed the villainess as the prince's mother, but Perrault portrayed her as the prince's wife. Adultery as opposed to mother-in-law problems, then. There was a black irony in regarding the fairy princess as the prince's bit on the side, but whichever way you viewed it, the prince had not been nearly as eligible as Jacob and Wilhelm Grimm, and certainly Walt Disney, had made him out. As for the ogreish lady herself, Dan felt a cold prickle on the back of his neck at the resemblance to Margot. He felt a clutch of fear in his stomach at the resemblance between Margot and Thalia Caudle.

He burrowed deeper in, finding echoes in the unlikeliest of places, like a bloody thread running through scores of gentle romances. Yes, there was unquestionably material for a half-scholarly, half-entertaining non-fiction book here. Dan carefully noted source references as he went.

The legend surfaced in English lore as well as French and Neapolitan; Dan thought it was even possible that Shakespeare had tipped his Elizabethan bonnet to it in the writing of *Titus Andronicus*. There were resonances in Norse legends as well, most notably in the *Volsunga Saga* where Brynhild was placed in a deserted castle by Odin and surrounded by a massive barrier of flame in order to escape the curse of being mated to a coward, and a human coward to boot. Dan supposed that this was something any self-respecting immortal might go a long way to avoid.

But it was amazing how strongly the menace of the prince's mamma came across.

It was amazing how strongly the sensuality came across when Dan heard Thalia's voice on the phone. There was a purring resonance, and there was certainly no hint of the strange and arousing ferocity of last time.

The supper invitation was proffered with a kind of amused cap-doffing to the conventions. I'm really inviting you to bed again, Thalia Caudle was saying. I know it, and you know it. But it's polite to pretend for a while, isn't it?

Dan thought he could be forgiven for feeling a quickening of his heartbeat as he went up the stairs of the Great Portland Street block. Well, all right, it was more than just a quickening, and it was not his heart that was most affected either. But, for heaven's sake, he was surely allowed a scudding of lust-ridden apprehension. Of apprehension-ridden lust.

Thalia, on the phone, had said something about leaving the door on the latch for him – 'Just push it open and come inside' – and it was ridiculous in the extreme to hear the dark echo: *Lift the latch and step inside, my dear . . .* But Dan did hear it, and the scales tipped over to apprehension because this was surely the timeless invitation by all dark ladies of chill and hungry intent, and by all icy-hearted snow queens of sorcerous lineage. *Come inside, my dear . . .*

But here I go again anyway. Straight into the land of the greenwood shade where sinisterly beautiful sorceresses offer the poisoned chalice and the tainted apple. You'd think I'd know better.

But Margot and Thalia were still inextricably tangled in his mind, and Margot, his own dark, sensuous Margot, had slid under his skin and fastened her claws, if not about his heart then around his loins. He disliked and distrusted Margot, but he could not deny her sensual pull. And it had been almost impossible to forget the feeling that Margot's phantom had come into the bed with them that night, raking her nails across his skin, sliding her hands between his legs . . . As Dan went warily into the flat, he thought that Margot was at his side. Down into the greenwood shade together then.

Thalia was lying on the smooth-sheeted bed, only her bare shoulders and arms visible. There was candlelight again, just as there had been last time, only tonight there were dozens upon dozens of tiny glowing flames, reflecting over and over in the mirrors. There was a strong scent of expensive perfume and candle warmth, and Dan could almost hear the heady, sensuous thrumming of the air.

Thalia said softly, 'The wine is in the cooler over there, Dan. Will you pour us both a glass?'

So it was not only the greenwood shade, it was the poisoned chalice as well. But she does it with style, thought Dan, pausing transfixed in the doorway. You have to admit she does it with tremendous style.

'And when you've poured the wine, come to bed, Dan,' said Thalia.

For the second time Dan fell fathoms down into the surreal world of his own creating.

There was virtually no conversation after that soft invitation; it was as if Thalia had created a flame-lit cave, a glowing secret world for them both; a land singing with sexual stirrings and erotic rustlings. To have made polite small talk would have splintered the atmosphere. Never let it be said I killed an atmosphere, thought Dan, shedding his clothes at speed and turning back the sheets.

This time it started off by being easier, and by being very nearly companionable because they were a little more familiar with one another's bodies. Dan was managing to keep Margot at bay, and Thalia's hands were insistent and exciting, her fingers flicking at nerve endings, her tongue probing. She pushed him flat on the bed, and bent over him. Dan drew in his breath sharply as he felt the silken brush of her hair between his thighs. Her lips closed over him, working expertly, and for a time that could have been five minutes or five hours he was totally lost in voluptuous eroticism.

Without warning, something began to seep into the warm sensuous room; something jarring and faintly disturbing. It reached Dan through a warm sea of pure pleasure and rasped lightly on his mind. Something to do with Thalia? Was she about to suggest something outrageous? Something that would probably be erotic but that might verge on the perverted? Wild visions of throbbing sex toys –the empty wine bottle, even? – of animals introduced into the bedroom or whips and chains and near-strangulation to heighten orgasm spun through his mind. He had absolutely no idea how he would react if any of these were proposed.

Thalia lifted her head and said, very softly, 'And now, Dan, I'm going to blindfold you.'

It was not precisely what Dan had been imagining, but it was unexpected for all that. He blinked and stared at her. She reached across the bed and took a silk scarf from the bedside table. Their eyes met. 'All right?' said Thalia, still in the same purring voice. Her tongue came out to lick her lips and Dan stared, caught in fascination.

Blindfold. He said, 'I've heard of it, although I've never actually done it.'

'It concentrates the senses, Dan.'

'I don't think mine could be any more concentrated than they are at the moment. But let's find out.' He took the silk blindfold from her hands and twisted it round his head, tying it in a loose knot at the back.

The silk did not quite blot out the candlelight. Dan could still make out tiny specks of flames, but nothing more. When Thalia's tongue flicked him again, and then when he felt her mouth go round him once more, he half-closed his eyes and gave in to the swelling waves of arousal a second time. Every fibre of his body was focused on what she was doing to him; there was nothing in the world save this warm, candle-scented, female-scented bower, and there was nothing save the silken mouth of the woman bending over him.

He felt her move slightly, and he thought one hand went out to the bedside table. She had done this last time; not making a fuss, not even referring to it, simply sliding the condom over him without comment. It had been a smooth, practised movement, but it had also been unexpectedly exciting. In another minute she would do it again, and then Dan would push her on to her back and go in—

There was a faint scrape of something that had nothing to do with condoms waiting discreetly and conveniently in bedside tables. Dan half turned his head. Something on the bedside table. She had put something on the bedside table. She was enclosing him again, moving up and down, her hair swinging across his legs which was arousing by itself. In another minute he would be beyond the point of control . . . There was something different about the angle of her head. She was lying more to one side and for some reason this broke into the mood of heady passion. Dan reached up to pull the blindfold away.

Thalia was still crouching between his thighs, her mouth and her lips working with that deadly expertise. But she was facing the small bedside cabinet, and her eyes were on the silver-framed photograph that was angled towards her. It had not been there earlier on; Dan knew it had not.

The photograph showed a young man with Imogen Ingram's eyes but with a cruel mouth and fair hair. Edmund. *Edmund*.

Thalia had been watching the photograph with unblinking worshipping eyes all the time she was licking Dan into orgasm.

Sickness welled up in his throat; at the same instant he felt his body spin out of control and spasm in climax.

They did not leave the bedroom to eat; Thalia brought food in, and Dan saw with a sinking heart that it was the kind of sensuous, tactile food that they could feed to one another, in an extension of the earlier passion. Cold duck with cherries and triangles of brown bread spread with rich pâté. There were *petits-beurre* spread with almonds and melted chocolate, and small ripe grapes which had been dipped in sweet dessert wine and then in sugar. She'll certainly expect me to feed her with the grapes, he thought, torn between revulsion and a sudden treacherous stab of fresh arousal. This is either immensely sexual or it's farcically old hat. Hell and the devil, I really *don't* want to screw her again! But it looks as if I'll have to. *Noblesse oblige*. I only hope I can *oblige* after what I saw earlier. Thank God she's brought in another bottle of wine at any rate. That ought to settle matters. One way or another.

Thalia was still asleep in the tumbled bed when Dan finally slipped out and dressed with silent swiftness in the bathroom.

He used the loo and scowled at his reflection in the mirror. He was not really in hangover territory, but there was the suspicion of a skewering headache above one eye and his mouth felt intolerably dry. Too much wine, drunk too quickly. Too much sex with somebody who was mentally having her sex with someone else? And that someone her dead son? But this was too convoluted and too potentially worrying a thought to consider yet. Dan concentrated on the immediate and the tangible, which was getting a cold drink before leaving.

He padded through to the kitchen. There was a carton of milk on one of the worktops, and he flipped the top open and poured it into a tumbler. It was fresh but it was at room temperature, and he opened the fridge for an ice cube, only to find that the tray was empty. That was the trouble with service flats, small details got missed by cleaners. He glanced round the kitchen, and his eye fell on the chest freezer in the far corner.

He did not stop to think that freezers are usually kept solely for food rather than for neat little trays of ice cubes; he did not think, either, about invading anyone's privacy – people do not normally keep their bank statements or unit trust account numbers in the deep freeze.

It held the usual jumble of stand-by food. Bread and bags of frozen vegetables and ice cream and packs of steaks and chops. Dan propped the lid up and moved a pack of chicken portions aside, exposing the lower section of the cabinet.

Exposing what was lying on the freezer bottom.

The kitchen tilted and spun sickeningly, and jagged tag ends of memory splintered his mind. Imogen bringing in the covered dish that was supposed to be a baked ham but that had not been a baked ham at all. The bloodied fragments of legend about Sybilla and Lucienne Ingram, prowling those grim pages of Ingram history. Even, incredibly, snippets of half-understood information about human transplants and human embryos, about kidneys and livers and eyes that were kept at sub-zero temperatures and severed limbs packed in ice until they could be grafted on or sewn in or joined. And the nineteenth-century anatomists plundering fresh graves for the raw material of their groping research. But the anatomists had had to use formaldehyde

197

or formalin; they had not had the advantages of modern freezing processes.

They would not have been able to put a human head in a modern freezer and pack it with ice so that it was glazed and hoar-rimmed, so that its once-golden hair was matted and stringy, and so that it stared with clouded ice-poached eyes at whoever lifted the lid.

Chapter Eighteen

By the time he let himself into the blessed normality of his own flat, Dan had passed through a dozen different emotions, ranging through repulsion to perplexity and then finally to downright disbelief.

What he had seen must have a perfectly innocuous explanation, and the likeliest was that he had misinterpreted. Almost certainly it had been an animal, and something to do with cooking. But people didn't eat the heads of animals, did they? At least not any more. Vague notions of chitterlings and sweetbreads crossed his mind, along with memories of his grandmother telling how people made brawn during the war because you had to use what food you could get. Dan thought there might conceivably still be enthusiasts who hoarded pig's faces in freezers and then boiled them up to make brawn and it was probably very good indeed, but homemade brawn and Thalia Caudle were not two things that occurred to you in the same breath.

What he had found was not credible at all. Margot might with impunity stalk Lady-Macbeth fashion through the pages of his book, dealing out death and mutilation and boiling away troublesome corpses, but Thalia would not. This was the twentieth century, for goodness' sake; people in London and respectable suburbia did not do things like that.

People in London and respectable suburbia did do it. Women did it as much as men, more often than men sometimes. They lived in ordinary places like Gloucester and they had light, feminine names like Rosemary West, or they prowled the moors of northern England in the 1960s and were called Myra Hindley. Or they lived in America and stored chopped-up bodies under the floor and then boiled them up in a cauldron to eat . . . Oh God, yes. Nothing left remarkable beneath the visiting moon, Daniel.

Yes, but they were surely all mad, those people. Then was Thalia mad? Not raving mad, not schizophrenic or depressive or melancholic. But fee-fi-fo-fum mad. Mad as in, 'Let me strip the flesh from your bones, my dear.' Mad as in, 'Let me store the head of my mutilated son and croon over it by the dead vast midnight.' But this was so bizarre an image that he refused to consider it.

And then another fact struck him.

He had been trying to persuade himself that it had been the carcass of an animal he had seen, but if he could not tell the difference between a pig's head and a human's, even after the better part of two bottles of Chablis, he had a severe problem.

He *had* been able to tell the difference. The head *had* been human. It had frosted golden hair, and a crushed-in mouth and splintered cheekbones. Edmund Caudle, carefully preserved. You should recognise him if anyone should, Daniel, you were the one who saw the photograph tonight while Thalia thought you were still blindfold. Yes, and you were the one who clanged the lid down on the appalling thing while all the mourners stood around in mute, helpless horror that afternoon. And if the thing was real then, it was real tonight. Because if you were hallucinating on the day of Edmund's funeral, then so were about twenty other people.

He considered this. Everyone had believed that Imogen was responsible for that gruesome episode; everyone thought it was the Ingram taint erupting and boiling over in a huge insane froth, and they had put Imogen in a clinic somewhere as a result. Dan did not know where the place was, but it did not matter because if Imogen was in a clinic somewhere she could not have put her cousin's head in the freezer of the Great Portland Street flat.

Only one person could have done that, and it followed, therefore, that the same person had caused the thing to appear at the lunch. Someone who had wanted it to seem that Imogen was mad. Someone who wanted to get Imogen out of the way and get her hands on the Ingram empire and the Ingram money. Someone who had been named as Imogen's guardian, and who perforce had the control of Royston Ingram's publishing empire.

Thalia Caudle.

But Thalia was not Margot – it was vital to keep remembering that. Yes, but that did not mean she was not capable of doing something monstrous. People performed all manner of monstrous actions to get their hands on fortunes. Imogen had been very neatly put out of the way, and was presumably reasonably safe until she was ready to pass out of Thalia's guardianship. This was most likely at the age of eighteen, but Royston Ingram's will might overrule the law and as far as the company was concerned Imogen might be a minor until she was twenty-one.

This was one of the times when Dan would have been grateful for Oliver's sharp, analytical mind, but Oliver had returned to Oxford and his breathless, wide-eyed students, and Dan was on his own. How would Oliver have viewed this problem?

Dan thought about it a bit more, and eventually came to the conclusion that he needed two separate pieces of information. One was the exact provisions of Royston's will regarding Imogen's inheritance. If Thalia's guardianship ended when Imogen was eighteen (in six months? a year?), Imogen could well stand in imminent danger. If it ended when she was twenty-one, Thalia might be satisfied to keep the girl in a nursing home for the next three years.

The other thing to find out was Imogen's present

whereabouts, so that he could make sure that she was safe from any further assaults on her sanity.

Getting a copy of the will should be easy enough; Dan thought it was possible to request a sight of anyone's will, and he thought there was somewhere in the Strand where you put in a formal application.

Finding Imogen might be more difficult.

Juliette Ingram was charmed to be phoned by the mysterious young man who had been at Hampstead on that *grisly* afternoon, and delighted to accept his invitation to dinner. With the idea of testing the financial waters, so to speak, she suggested Langan's – 'So *convenient* for my office.'

I'm spending money like a drunken sailor, thought Dan, but said, 'Eight o'clock?'

'Perfect.' Juliette rang off in order to phone Great-Aunt Flora and tell her that she had the most *intriguing* dinner date with the unknown gentleman who had clanged the lid down on the you-know-what at Edmund's funeral while the rest of them had stood around wringing their hands and keening and being sick on the Sheraton.

'If he's a writer he must be successful to afford Langan's,' said Flora, repressing an unworthy wish that she was Juliette's age again and being asked out to expensive restaurants by intriguing young men.

'Do you suppose he's going to *pump* me about the family scandal?'

'I shouldn't be surprised,' said Flora rather grimly.

'I'd rather be asked out for my *beaux yeux*,' observed Juliette. 'But I don't mind, really. I remember thinking he was rather Heathcliff – all dark and damn-your-eyes.'

'Well don't be beguiled by damn-your-eyes seducers, Juliette, and don't give away anything about the family.'

'Of course not,' said Juliette, shocked. 'But Aunt Flo, darling, it won't matter, not really. Dan Tudor can read all about it for himself when Friday's papers come out – that's always supposing he can find it without a magnifying glass, because it was played down to an amazing degree, wasn't it? The premature burial and so on. I don't suppose it'll get more than a tiny paragraph on page five. And after all, it wasn't actually any of *us* who did it, which is such a comfort, don't you think?'

'Rosa thinks it was John Shilling,' said Flora. 'She thinks he gave Eloise an overdose by mistake.'

'Well, I shouldn't think it was intentional, should you?' said Juliette. 'We all knew he'd harboured a grand passion for her for years, poor old Shilling. I daresay he was pickled at the time – in fact I remember thinking at the funeral that he was knocking it back a bit. I'll bet he mixed his doses up and poured a triple down her without realising.'

'And realised when it was too late and panicked,' said Flora, thoughtfully.

'Yes, and put up that elaborate plot to make it look like murder. Is he going to plead guilty to the manslaughter charge, d'you know?'

'Oh yes. He's apparently prepared to go to gaol,' said Flora. 'I think he actually wants to, in fact.'

'How very peculiar of him.'

'It's something to do with restitution,' said Flora. 'Or do I mean penance – no, that's the Catholics, isn't it? Purgatory and absolution. Anyway, he thinks he needs to be punished for what happened.'

'So he does,' said Juliette. 'Although I expect they'll find him mad as a hatter, poor old thing.'

'You think he was mad, do you?' said Flora.

'Flo, dear, it isn't sane to slosh sheep's blood all over the place and pretend to cook up plots about perforating ulcers,' said Juliette. 'And I bet if we delved a bit deeper, we'd find he was responsible for the head-thing on the dish as well. Did I say elaborate? I should have said tortuous. Poor old Shilling.'

'I hope,' said Flora repressively, 'that you won't talk about all this to Dan Tudor, Juliette. Heads on dishes and tortuous mad doctors.'

'Of course I shan't,' said Juliette. '*Wild horses* wouldn't drag it out of me.'

One would not, of course, talk in any detail about the inquest, and one would most definitely not spill any details about Imogen, poor darling. Juliette could not begin to think what would happen to Imogen now. Being mad and in a coma was one thing, but being sane and in a coma was very different indeed. One rather felt that it was wrong for Imogen to be sent off to Thornacre in view of all the things that were coming to light now. But it was too exhausting to consider what the alternatives were, and so Juliette shelved the problem for the moment and concentrated on deciding between the Jacques Vert two-piece and the Zandra Rhodes mulberry velvet for her date with Dan Tudor.

Having expected Dan to quiz her and having gone to the trouble of preparing a number of polite and evasive answers, it was a bit miffing to discover that what he really appeared to be interested in was the gruesome Ingram ancestresses. Still, anybody was welcome to Sybilla and Lucienne, and Juliette did not in the least mind being seen at Langan's (wearing the mulberry velvet), dining with somebody as good-looking as Dan Tudor.

She enlarged enthusiastically on the subject of the blot on the Ingram escutcheon – 'Although it's a whacking great gargoyle rather than a blot, of course. They were both mad as March hares, you know. My grandmother used to tell the torridest tales about Lucienne – you do know what she actually did, do you? Oh, you do. And of course everybody's gone about on tiptoe for at least the last ten years waiting for something to happen again.'

'Why? I mean, why for the last ten years?'

'Well, because – oh, this is *very* good wine, Dan –because of it being due to surface again. It's all frightfully

Galsworthy and Brontë, but somebody counted it up, and about every ninety years there's been a female born in the family who was a bit *peculiar*, although to use the word peculiar about somebody who chops off her brother's—'

'Couldn't it be coincidence?' said Dan hastily, mindful of the hovering waiter.

'Whatever it was, they were all waiting for it to happen again, and in fact they all thought it was *me* at one time,' said Juliette, and managed to make an all-embracing, can-you-imagine-it? gesture without going over the top. Dan mentally calculated how much his credit card was good for, and ordered another bottle of wine anyway. He thought Juliette was not exactly drunk, but she had reached the confiding stage. Juliette registered with approval that the waiters did not ignore him. It was very gratifying to dine with a man who could summon waiters and taxis without thinking about it. Integral authority. Authority was immensely sexy. This was a very good evening. Juliette mentally wriggled her toes in delight, and allowed Dan to refill her glass.

'Do go on, Juliette.'

Juliette rested her elbows lightly on the table and curled her hands round the wine glass, regarding Dan across the rim. 'I wouldn't normally breathe a word to a *soul*,' she said; 'but you were there at Edmund's funeral, weren't you? And you saw it all. Well, you covered the thing up, didn't you? So courageous, I thought, because it was really too blood-curdling.'

Dan said, 'What happened afterwards?'

'Well, for a long time people scurried about and got into little huddles and whispered anxiously about what ought to be done. Elspeth had to be given sal volatile – she was the one who was sick into the eighteenth-century whatnot – and George – that's Elspeth's husband, pink and jowly and a bit grumbly, but a pussycat really, although Aunt Flora says he's got a woman in Maida Vale, and all I can say to that is

205

that if *I* was a man and married to Elspeth, *I'd* have a woman in Maida V—'

'What happened to Imogen?' said Dan.

Juliette sent him a sudden unexpectedly shrewd look. 'I suppose this is on the level, is it? I mean, you aren't some squalid little tabloid reporter, trying to get an inside story?'

'I'm a writer and I have done work for newspapers,' said Dan. 'But they've mostly been Sunday colour supplements because I mostly write biographies and profiles. I promise you I'm not a tabloid reporter trying to dig up an unpleasant story, Juliette.' He paused, and then said, 'But I do admit that your family interests me very much, although not from the point of view of gutter-press sensationalism.'

'Lucienne and Sybilla,' said Juliette, nodding. 'I often thought there might be a book in it. I don't suppose you'd do anything without consulting us?'

'No, of course not.' Dan paused. 'Juliette, what happened to Imogen?'

'I think,' said Juliette, glancing round, 'that we need a tad more privacy than we've got here. Just a tad.' They looked at one another. Dan waited, and after a moment Juliette said, 'Suppose we adjourn to my flat.' Dan heard the unmistakable invitation in her voice, and felt, with a feeling of wry despair, the mental hand caressing the mental thigh.

As he paid the bill he wondered how many more Ingram females he would have to take to bed to find out the truth about his beleaguered heroine.

Juliette curled up in a corner of the chesterfield in her sitting room, tucking her feet under her. She had kicked off her shoes and the short mulberry velvet skirt had ridden up rather a lot. Her legs were very good indeed and Dan caught himself wondering if she was wearing tights or black stockings.

They had a pot of coffee, and Juliette set out a bottle of

brandy and two glasses and switched on the electric fire. The red glow reflected in the half-full bottle and in Juliette's short glossy hair, and the room was warm and intimate. She embarked on the story of how Imogen had crept out to the cemetery – 'although what took her there we'll probably never know' – and on to the exhumation. 'And the trouble is, Dan, that we all thought she was raving mad and responsible for serving up the head-thing at the funeral, and so when she fell into this profound sleep they arranged to cart her off to Thornacre.'

Dan felt as if he had been plunged into black, icy water. He said, 'Imogen's in Thornacre?'

'Yes. And really, it's utterly tragic, Dan, because Royston and Eloise – oh dear, poorest Eloise – never let her have any kind of life at all, and now it doesn't look as if she ever will have any.'

'Really?'

'They always insisted she was delicate,' said Juliette. 'She wasn't, of course.'

'No?' said Dan, and Juliette waved a hand dismissively.

'My dear, strong as a horse. But Eloise used to throw these ghastly attacks of migraine or something to keep Imogen at her bedside. Sofa-side. *Malade imaginaire*, or,' added Juliette with another flash of acumen, '*malade à la convenance*.'

'Didn't Imogen need to work? What about a job or a career?'

'She left school when she was seventeen at Easter,' said Juliette. 'I think the school wanted her to go on and try for university, but Royston blocked that at once. Great-Aunt Flora thought she could take some kind of business course and go into Ingram's – she's an absolute darling, Great-Aunt Flo – and even old George said he would be very happy to take her into his own office as a secretary or trainee buyer. He's something to do with china exporting, and he said there was a genuine opening, not just a nepotism one.

They blocked all that as well: "No, it would be far too much for the child, she gets so exhausted after even the slightest exertion . . . None of you has the least idea . . ." And Eloise lay back on one of her couches, put her hand to her head and said she would *try* to manage if Imogen left them, but it would be so very difficult, and all this bickering was giving her such a headache.'

Dan smiled. The mimicry of Eloise Ingram was extremely good.

'So then I had a go,' said Juliette. 'I suggested Imogen helped some friends I have who run one of those home dinner party set-ups – you know the kind of thing, *haute cuisine* brought to the door and you serve it up on your own plates so your guests think you're Elizabeth David or Peter Stringfellow. Now that she really would have liked, and she could have done it on a part-time basis as well. She enjoyed cooking, poor child. It was probably the only thing they let her do.'

'It didn't take her out of the house,' said Dan, thoughtfully.

'Yes.' Juliette was pleased to find him so perceptive.

'And now she's in a coma.'

'That's what Thalia says. Stupor, the doctors are calling it, although I can't see that it makes any *difference* to the poor darling.'

'And Sterne's treating her?'

'Yes.'

Dan reached for the coffee pot again.

'It's empty,' said Juliette. 'But I can make some more if you want.'

'Actually I'd quite like another cup if it's no trouble.' Hot coffee might chase away the cold dread that the word Thornacre had induced.

'None in the world. Come and help me.' She went out to the kitchen and Dan followed her.

He made the first physical approach over the coffee

grinder, partly because she clearly expected it and partly because the kitchen was so small that avoiding physical contact was impossible, but also because he suddenly found himself wanting to dispel the tainted memories of lovemaking with that other Ingram female. Being in bed with someone different, someone *normal*, might do that.

Juliette was blessedly normal, and her response was immediate and gratifying. Her mouth opened under Dan's and she moved forward at once, so that they were pressed hard together. She was taller than most girls, nearly as tall as Dan, and for several minutes they stood locked thigh to thigh in an increasingly passionate clinch. Dan began to slide his hands beneath the sensuous mulberry velvet, and Juliette gasped with delight and then reached down to pull at her skirt. There was the snapping open of buttons, and a rustle of sound as the skirt slid to the floor. She stepped out of it and kicked it out of the way, and Dan registered that it was black stockings rather than tights after all. They were held up by garters and she was wearing silk underwear.

Juliette freed her lips from his for a moment to say in a voice husky with amusement and passion, 'The coffee grinder's still running.'

'Well, turn it off. And then come back into the sitting room. The sofa—'

'Screw the sofa,' Juliette said. 'Let's do it here.'

Dan supposed they could always drink instant coffee afterwards anyway.

It meant another silent exit from another unfamiliar flat in the small hours, and it meant another phone call to Interflora. Dan used a different branch this time. He did not really mind the Belsize Park florists viewing him as a lecher, but two lots of flowers to two different ladies in as many days might look boastful.

He sat brooding over a late breakfast. If Oliver had still been here he would have been convinced that his younger brother was an irreclaimable lecher. It was as well he was not here. Dan poured another cup of tea and carried on thinking.

Imogen, his inspirational heroine, Rosamund's role model, was in Thornacre – or if she was not, she was on the way there. Dan had read the stories about the place and he had seen the photographs, and listened to the rumours. One newspaper had called Thornacre the site of the most outrageous ill-treatment in any English institution for nearly a quarter of a century. Another had hinted at sexual abuse of patients. There had been rumours of corruption as well – blatant and consistent stealing of patients' belongings, and falsifying of records as well as concealing deaths so that pensions and allowances could be drawn by the unscrupulous nurses and auxiliaries. One of the doctors – Dan could not recall his name – had just committed suicide, to a fresh blaze of publicity and speculation.

And now Imogen was there, just as Rosamund was. It was nature imitating art. Or it was art imitating nature. Dan was unable to decide which way round it was; he was unable to decide if he had been influenced by the recent publicity about Thornacre and used it, or whether there was some other, more supernatural explanation.

At length, he pushed the thing to the back of his mind and sat down at his desk to deal with the current chapter. Rosamund's consciousness was now satisfactorily shrouded so that she could not argue against Margot's machinations, and Margot was beginning the systematic transfer of Rosamund's fortune to her own bank account. Dan had finally managed to fathom a shred or two of the medical tomes, and had chosen the drug methaqualone, which the evil and lascivious Dr Bentinck had administered for its sedative and hypnotic qualities, and which had sent Rosamund into a death-like coma and thus entangled her in the complex strands of Margot's plot. But neither Margot nor Bentinck knew that the dashing and heroic Adam

Cadence had discovered what was afoot, and was even now poised to drive hell for leather to the remote Northumberland village where Rosamund's grim asylum was situated.

It was at this point that Dan found himself thinking not about Rosamund, who was going to be rescued in chapter twenty anyway, but about Imogen, who might never be rescued at all. But it was one thing for Adam Cadence to go haring off on rescue missions without evidence or back-up or authority, and quite another for Dan to do it. Imogen would presumably be perfectly safe in Thornacre. Leo Sterne was unconventional and his methods were reportedly unorthodox – the tabloids had called him the 'pirate of modern medicine' over some slightly questionable case of hypnotism last year – but there was every reason to suppose that he genuinely searched for cures for the people in his care. He was not the evil, flawed Bentinck, just as Thalia Caudle was not Margot and just as Dan himself was not the dazzling young Adam Cadence.

Imogen was quite safe until it was time for Thalia to acccount for her stewardship. Dan had diligently made application for a sight of Royston Ingram's will, but he had no idea what he would do when he received it. He was not going to rush fruitlessly up to Northumberland – of course he was not.

Still, it could not hurt to just look out the route and jot down the names of likely pubs or small hotels where he could stay. He found a couple of likely sounding pubs in Thornacre village itself, and marked one of them. The journey was a long one, even taking into account the motorway stretches and the A1. It was unlikely that his beaten-up Ford Escort would manage it, even with carefully planned breaks.

There was absolutely no reason to be concerned. Thalia could not possibly do anything to Imogen while she was inside Thornacre, and while Imogen was in this coma-sleep she would not need to do anything. As for Thornacre itself, it had certainly been the subject of a nationwide scandal, but for that reason alone it was probably the most strictly run place in the entire country at the moment. It might be on probation, so to speak, for a time, but the real evildoers had been routed out and hauled to justice

It was ridiculous to think that Imogen was becoming surrounded by enemies.

Chapter Nineteen

Imogen was becoming surrounded by enemies.

Quincy had known this ever since Imogen fell into the terrible dark sleep and she had known that she could not leave her, although for some time she had not known how this could be prevented. In the end she had simply asked point-blank to return to Thornacre, knocking on Matron Porter's door, and standing in front of Matron's desk to make the request. It had taken every shred of courage she possessed, but she had managed it. 'Please let me go with Imogen to Thornacre,' she had said, and had stared at Matron and refused to look away, and she had seen Porter-Pig's mean little eyes narrow. Porter-Pig did not like her, but she was weighing up the advantages of having her as unpaid servant in Thornacre.

Quincy had said, very loudly, 'If you don't let me go, I'll simply walk out. I'll beg lifts on the road until I get there.'

And then Matron had said, slowly, 'Why of course you shall come with us to Thornacre if you want to,' and Quincy had seen the gleam of calculation in her eyes, and known she was doing the right thing. The Pig was not quite an enemy to Imogen, but she was definitely not a friend.

And so here they were in an ambulance with all the windows blacked out and Imogen lying on the stretcher-bed, remote and still. The chart numbering the days she had been asleep was tucked into a cardboard folder beside her.

Porter-Pig was driving ahead of them in her horrid fat

little car with the snout-like headlights; Quincy could probably have travelled with her, but the ambulance men had seemed to think it a good idea for her to be in the ambulance with Imogen and Quincy thought it a good idea as well.

One of the men travelled inside the ambulance with them. He talked to Quincy on the journey, and they played word games to pass the time. 'I Spy', and Twenty Questions, where you had to think up a name or a place or a TV programme, and the other one had to ask questions to guess it. The ambulance man had three children and they often drove to the coast at weekends and holidays, and these were two of the games they played so that the children would not get bored. If the ambulance had had windows they could have collected pub names and scored points; you only got one point for animals' names like the Fox and Hounds, but you could get two for people's names, like the Green Man, and four or five if the pub was named after royalty like the King's Head. You could not do this very well on motorways, of course.

It had never occurred to Quincy that people thought up games to keep children from getting bored. In Bolt Place children were left to find their own entertainments, and when Quincy was there they had formed gangs and taken it in turns to sneak sweets and comics out of shops. When videos started to be popular, a lot of parents had had sets installed, and there had been films to watch all through the school holidays. But then some of the sets had to go back to the shops because of people falling behind with payments, and others were taken by the police because of forbidden videos being in circulation, and quite a lot were broken in Saturday-night fights.

When they were eleven or twelve, most of the Bolt Place children graduated to one of the teenage street gangs. In Quincy's time there had been the Scrum and the Clan. The Scrum – which most people called the Scum – had mostly been for boys who took cigarettes from off-licences and purses out of shopping bags in supermarkets. The Clan was headier stuff and the people in it were older; they smashed jewellers' windows and forged Social Security cheques and beat up cashiers if they would not hand over the contents of the till. Some of them had dealt in drugs.

Getting into the Scum was easy, but you had to steal two cars and not be caught before you could be accepted as a member of the Clan, and even then you had to be male. There were no females in the Clan, because the only things females were good for were screwing and cooking. When Quincy first went to Briar House she had been astonished at the way the kitchen helpers and the nursing staff talked about their husbands and boyfriends. They shared shopping trips and cooking and choosing new bedroom curtains. No one from the Scum or the Clan would have been seen dead shopping or choosing bedroom curtains.

Two Clan boys had once dragged Quincy into the back room of Farley's Bar because they thought she had seen them breaking into an off-licence. One of them had smashed a beer bottle and brought the jagged end up to her face. If she grassed on them they would carve her face up with it, they said. Grassing meant telling, and Quincy would not have told even without the broken bottle, but the trouble was that somebody else might do it, and the Clan would think she was responsible and come after her. She had been so frightened that she had shut herself in her room for a very long time, crouching behind the door and keeping the curtains drawn and not switching the light on because the dark was safer.

It had been then that people had come; they had broken the lock on the door and somebody had fetched a doctor because of Quincy not having eaten for so long and being weak and muzzy-headed. There had been no food in the house and she could not go out to get any because of the Clan lying in wait. She had tried to explain this, but she had found it difficult because of not having spoken for such a long time and not having eaten much, and also because of being frightened. A doctor had said she was confused, and he had used the word withdrawn. When he found out that she was only fifteen he had said she should go to a place where she could be helped to be less afraid of the world. He had sent her to Thornacre and he had meant it kindly, but he had not known about the Cattersis or being shut in the haunted part if you were a nuisance or made a noise.

The journey to Thornacre took quite a long time, but it was not as bad as Quincy had feared because of the ambulance men being so friendly. They stopped at a motorway place for a cup of tea and sausages and chips and to go to the lavatory. Quincy had been worried that Matron Porter might be there, but the snouty car was nowhere to be seen. Probably she was well ahead of them. The ambulance men took it in turns to come in to eat because of not leaving Imogen on her own, and swapped over the driving afterwards. The second man did not play 'I Spy', but he produced a writing pad and biro and showed Quincy how to play noughts and crosses and crossword games.

It was late afternoon when they reached the outskirts of Thornacre village and drove up to the house. There was no chance of missing it; it stood on a hillside overlooking the small village that had rooted itself in a fold of the Northumbrian landscape, and huge iron gates guarded the way. The ambulance driver annnounced himself into a small tinny intercom and the gates swung open. As they drove through, Quincy looked back through the ambulance's small rear windows and saw them swing shut with a horrid hoarse grating sound.

They drove slowly up the steep incline, with the raggedy overgrown gardens on each side, and then the house was suddenly there ahead, like a huge, crouching monster, rearing up against the darkling sky. Quincy shivered.

Somebody had built Thornacre a very long time ago – more than a hundred years ago – and that somebody had used harsh black stone, the kind that grazed your skin if you touched it. The house had a distorted look as well, as if whoever had built it had not worked out the space for walls and windows and chimneys properly. If you stared up at it for too long you would start to feel dizzy and get a headache.

It was not completely dark when Quincy got out of the ambulance, but it nearly was. Twilight. Twilight was a lovely word as a rule; it was purple and violet and it was brimful of soft scents and subdued stirrings. It made you think of fairy story things: mysterious forests and prowling creatures with three-cornered faces and cloven hoofs. Magical spells and secrets.

But the twilight that surrounded Thornacre was a different twilight entirely; it was a creeping, oozing darkness, it was black goblin-juice bleeding into the sunshine, and it had ugly hungering creatures at its heart. It had Cattersis-beasts who leapt on your back and dug their claws into your flesh, and poked their bodies into you until you were bleeding, and who said, you know what will happen to you if you ever tell, my dear . . . Quincy stood staring up at the house, wrapping her arms about her to stop from trembling.

Behind her the ambulance men were starting to carry Imogen's stretcher out, and one of them called cheerfully to Quincy to ring the bell and let people know they had arrived.

Quincy went obediently into the deep porch at the centre of the main wing. On the left was the low wing that was Thornacre's haunted part. It was covered with ivy and the ivy would tap at the windows at night and you would think it was the ghost coming to get you, dragging its rotting body through the shadowy passages, dribbling its juices as it came. Dr Sterne had said that the Cattersis-doctor had gone, and Quincy believed him because Dr Sterne would never tell a lie. But there were still the ghosts to worry about. There was still the black iron door in the old east wing.

There was a huge old-fashioned bell pull attached to the door, and Quincy pulled it and heard it jangle somewhere deep in the bowels of the house. At once there was the sound of footsteps crossing the stone-flagged hall on the other side, and there was a pause as somebody fumbled with a bolt. The door swung open and there was nothing for it but to cross Thornacre's threshold once more.

As Quincy did so, she felt the darkness descend about her shoulders, and she felt the black despair and the sick hopelessness of all those other people who had lived here.

And beneath all of that, she caught the thick, curdled whisper, which was the house's voice. It said in its gobbling, chuckling voice, *you're back* . . .

Freda Porter had quite enjoyed her journey to Northumberland although unfortunately it had been rather a long way, and the motorways were shocking things to negotiate these days; she had almost forgotten how loud and how fast they could be. And, of course, Araminta was not one of your fast, showy cars, although Freda kept her nicely polished, and there was an amusing nodding dog on the back window shelf, and flowered cushions on the back seat.

It was really rather interesting to stop at the motorway service stations. A lady travelling alone was always intriguing and she had dressed carefully for the occasion. She had no time for these scrawny girls who seemed to think it acceptable to wear jeans and sweaters and the kind of shoes that were called trainers today but which Freda had known as plimsolls. Quite scruffy they looked.

It was a pity that the only men who had taken any real notice of her had been a couple of lorry drivers who had tailed her all the way from the turn-off at Newcastle-on-Tyne, flashing their lights and making vulgar gestures in the driving mirror. Anyone would think she had done something silly, or even dangerous, when she had in fact been driving in a most responsible fashion. All she had done was to take a little time over choosing the lane at the bypass, which was something that anyone might need to do. And she had signalled properly and clearly when she changed lanes because of getting the wrong one to start with, so there was really no call for people to hoot and flash their lights.

Freda did not really like the odd, wordless compact she had entered into with Thalia Caudle, but there had been no other course of action. Do what I want or I'll make sure everyone knows you were overdosing Imogen with sedatives. Not that the dosage had been so very large, in fact now that she came to think it over, it had been only marginally over the amount prescribed by Dr Shilling.

Still, the carrot held out had been a good one: a personal reference to Professor Rackham and his commission, not that Freda thought it had actually been necessary in the end. She had given a very good account of herself at the interview, which would have counted for a good deal. Four gentlemen, there had been, and my word they had asked some stiff questions, all about methods of care and the kind of work she had done at Briar House. One of them had asked her opinion of what was being called holistic medicine. It had been unfortunate that she had misheard the word, but they had had quite a laugh about it in the end.

Freda was greatly looking forward to working at Thornacre alongside Leo Sterne. She had already begun to weave a whole new daydream, in which they were comrades by day and something a little more intimate by night. Well, why not? Her mind flew ahead and she saw herself and Dr Sterne side by side, discussing patients, happy and absorbed, working into the night, hardly aware of the time. Sometimes she would work with him on these occasions; at others she would go back to her own room where she would doze in a chair until he came, when she would serve a relaxing little supper.

This was a very promising scenario indeed; Freda dwelled with glandular pleasure on it. She had bought a new dressing gown in pink quilted satin and had had her hair permed before leaving Briar House so that she would not need to wear rollers in bed. As she turned off the A1 she developed the theme to allow Leo to discover some marvellous new treatment which he would not have found without her own quiet support and encouragement and the late-night suppers.

She found the turning to Thornacre without any difficulty, although the condition of the driveway was a scandal, all rutted and cracked, with weeds growing up everywhere. The rhododendron bushes and the dripping laurels shut out the light and made the place shockingly gloomy. Freda would see about having them all torn up and some nice neat lobelia beds and marigolds planted instead. Quite melancholy it was at the moment.

The house was much bigger than she had expected, but it showed the same disgraceful signs of neglect. It was built of black stone or even granite, and there was a central portion, which had probably once been the main living area, with two jutting wings, both covered with ivy. They would have that removed as soon as possible; Freda could not be doing with ivy which everyone knew weakened brickwork and darkened rooms. And seen at closer quarters, everywhere was dirty and shabby. Freda felt momentarily quite depressed. But all that was needed was a good session of cleaning and plenty of elbow grease.

Driving up to the house, Freda began to visualise the outfit she would wear to Buckingham Palace when Dr Sterne was given the long-deserved recognition for his services to his profession. She would have to find out whether an OBE was higher than an MBE. She would be at his side, of course; she rather thought there was an area specially set aside for relatives to watch the ceremony on these occasions. She would wear navy silk with white polka-dots and white gloves and a daring hat.

She drove happily on up the drive.

Chapter Twenty

Leo Sterne alighted from Tottenham Court Road Tube station and walked down Charing Cross Road.

It was that curious hour when Soho was just crossing over the line that separated its daylight identity from the dark and frequently sleazy face it wore at night.

Leo found this part of London endlessly fascinating. She was a hypocritical old tart, Soho. By day she catered primly for ordinary business people and workers and shoppers, and twitched her lace curtains aside to admit them into the bistros and trattorias and restaurants for their blameless lunches. But when night fell, the lace curtains were dragged back to display the red lights, and the short skirts came out and the high heels and black stockings. The tart painted her face and rummaged into her tatter-demalion ragbag of whips and chains and black leather, and, suitably accoutred, went padding off to peddle sex and vice.

Crossing into Old Compton Street, Leo went deeper in, glancing into the window of one of the bars as he passed. Pulsating crimson light washed endlessly over the walls like a rippling river, and the pounding of hard rock music assaulted his senses. At the far end was a tiny stage with two marginal nudes, dancing. Their faces were blank and their eyes were glazed and bored, and a sudden image of the street markets and the flesh traders of ancient Rome flicked across his mind. The main difference was that the music was louder, and that now you could read the book and you could see the film of the book if you wanted to. You could even play the lead in the film. Films . . .

He paused before a dimly-lit door, where a bluish light showed and where the legend 'Original Videos' was set over the entrance. Somebody had tried to smudge the first letters so that it would read 'Vaginal Videos', which was probably quite a good description of much of the merchandise. The sour smell of stale cigarettes and spilled beer gusted out, and the yeasty reek of raw sex. If anyone recognised him now they would probably think it unexpected of the eminent Dr Sterne to frequent such a place, but it was not very likely that anyone would see him. He did not much care anyway, but from force of habit he glanced up and down the street, and then took a deep breath and went in.

The man who was both owner and manager of the cinema was at first incredulous and then suspicious. This looked as if it might be one of those potentially awkward situations where the customer wanted to poach the settings and use other actors, and then flog the whole thing under a different packaging. He embarked on his customary explanation-cum-apology, which was liberally sprinkled with the words 'copyright' and 'performing rights'.

Leo said impatiently, 'God Almighty, man, I'm not interested in how many laws you're breaking. And I certainly don't want to buy pornographic films. Or steal your ideas and flog them on the black market in Amsterdam. All I'm interested in is the backgrounds you use. Those whirling kaleidoscopes and all that violent raw colour. I want them to try to jolt coma patients back into life. I'll pay the going rate, whatever it is, and you can put in as many write-protect gadgets as you like.'

'And you don't want the actors?'

'I don't want the actors. Oh, and that music that went with the first one you showed me, the one with the females dressed as cats –yes, that's it. Yes, that I do want.'

222

'You like the music?'

'It's dreadful,' said Leo. 'It's like a throbbing migraine. But I want it. Was it chosen for its erotic qualities?'

The manager was understood to say that it had been shown that certain types of music reached the erogenous zones of people's minds.

'Yes, you've only got to walk into a disco these days to know that,' said Leo.

'We do have others that are not so . . .'

'Abrasive? Arousing? Erectile?'

'Exactly. Slower, more sensual. Voluptuous rather than actually lusty. Would you wish to see one of the romantic sequences?'

'No, I want it abrasive. I want the whole thing as violent and as raw as possible. Well? Can you do it?'

The manager did not say that in this business people would do anything if they were paid enough. He said, 'Certainly. In view of the unusual nature there would need to be an extra charge, of course.'

'Of course,' said Leo coldly.

He was aware that he was treading an unconventional path with the videos, but he knew it was not really much more than unconventional. It was common enough practice these days to try to reach even persistent vegetative patients with favourite pop music or videos of football matches. New methods had to be tried and uncharted areas had to be explored. Physicians had to experiment. What about Dr Knox sending Burke and Hare to disinter fresh corpses for dissecting rooms? What about Freud delving yeastily into the dreams and sexual repressions of disturbed minds? Or even the Old Testament Joseph donning his dream cloak and sitting at Pharaoh's feet to interpret visions? Spiking into the erogenous zones with framework pornography was small stuff by comparison.

Six hours later, the videos in his briefcase on the seat beside him, Leo drove through the rose and gold dawn that was painting the eastern skies, and turned off the dual carriageway.

He had driven through the night after leaving London, and although he was not conscious of fatigue he knew he would need to sleep for a time. He would have argued that fatigue was something he had long since learned to overcome, but he was stiff from the long drive and if he was to make any impression on the unyielding blackness of Imogen's mind, he would have to rest and re-charge his mental strength.

Imogen . . . It suddenly seemed entirely right that he should be driving through this mistily beautiful autumn morning towards Imogen. Leo felt his heart quicken. He had believed himself to have long since grown the physician's necessary armour, but he knew that Imogen had slid under it, almost from the start. He had not been able to forget the sight of her backing away from her mother's grave on that terrible night, holding her hands out in front of her as if to push away what she had seen. It was the classic retreat, rare but unmistakable. An abrupt hysterical withdrawal into a stupor state. An interesting case, the A and E registrar had called it.

As he took the narrow turning that led to Thornacre, Leo remembered that the Porter woman would probably be in residence by now, and that common courtesy would require him to spend a little time with her during the next few days. This was a nuisance, because he wanted to concentrate on Imogen's treatment.

He considered Freda's appointment. 'Have you any strong objections?' Professor Rackham had asked before making it.

'I don't think so. She's not the world's finest nurse, but as far as I know she's ruled Briar House efficiently enough. She's a bit long in the tooth, although that sometimes works to advantage, of course. She's rather vulgar although she tries not to be.'

'I didn't know you were a snob, Leo,' said Rackham, amused.

'Neither did I.' Leo frowned, and then said, 'I don't think I am, in fact. But she's false. One voice – one face come to that – for people she thinks are important and something quite different for the rest of the world.'

'Aren't most of us guilty of that to one degree or another?'

'Yes, but not to excess. She's – there used to be a word, *genteel*.'

'Well, can you work with her or can't you?' demanded Rackham. 'We'll keep interviewing if necessary. I have to say we thought her methods were a bit old-fashioned when we interviewed her, and her qualifications aren't very good by some of today's reckoning.'

'That isn't necessarily a bad thing,' said Leo. 'Some of the best psychiatric nurses I've known never passed an exam in their lives. And I do want to start with a clean slate.'

'True. The reference from Thalia Caudle was very good indeed,' said Rackham.

'Oh, appoint her,' said Leo. 'Providing she does what I tell her when she's on duty and keeps out of my way when she's not I don't care whether she's the Grand Cham of Tartary or a Piccadilly hooker. In fact on balance I'd prefer the hooker – they're more in touch with ordinary people's problems. I don't suppose I'll need to see much of her anyway. We really only want an overseer for the nurses.'

'They call them managers these days,' said Rackham, rather drily, and Leo had grinned.

The marvellous dawn was giving way to a grey-streaked November morning when he drew up before the huge iron gates and wound the window down to punch his number into the electronic intercom. The company who had helped tighten up and modernise the security arrangements had issued most of the senior staff with individual numbers, so that the small intercom system only needed to be manned during office hours. Leo waited for the gates to open and drove through, engaging second gear for the steep rutted drive that had been the old carriageway.

He liked this part of Thornacre. He liked it for the ghosts that lingered here, the imprints of things that had happened before Sybilla Campbell had bequeathed her dark legacy of murder and madness –the carriages that would have driven up here, and the sound of the horses' hooves on frost-hardened ground. Box lanterns would have cast a warm light across the snow in winter, and the house would have been lit by dozens of candles, the long windows welcoming and bright. In spring the garth would have been starred with bluebells and primroses and windflowers, and in summer the lilac would have scented the air for miles and the liquid notes of wood pigeons would have poured softly into the long, drowsy afternoons. The lilac was long since dead, the garth was overgrown and forlorn, and the house had lost any grandeur and any attraction it might once have possessed. But driving towards it, Leo felt, as he always did, Thornacre's romance. It was a dark romance, a cobwebby Gothic thing of midnight shadows and tangle-wood gardens with crumbling old stone archways and lichen-crusted ruins . . .

He frowned and shook his head to chase away the ghosts, and parked his car in the old stable block which had been sketchily converted to garages. But as he entered Thornacre's central hall, the ghosts entered it with him. Leo could feel them clustering around him, and he thought they would never quite go from Thornacre; their sad presence would linger on, just as other sad presences lingered, for there were parts of Thornacre and secrets inside the place that Leo and Professor Rackham had agreed they would never dare to make public . . .

Even with Thornacre beginning to emerge from its grim years, too much of the darkness was still here.

* * *

226

The news that Thalia was leaving London for a while created a mild stir within the family but no one was very surprised because everyone had known, in a vague way, about the plan to collect folk songs and old ballads for the proposed new Ingram imprint. Everyone had known that Thalia was taking on the project as a kind of memorial to Royston and Eloise.

The aunts thought it was very nice indeed that Thalia was finding solace in work. A roving commission, she had called it, and she had told Rosa that she thought of starting off in Warwickshire – all those associations with Elizabethan England: the ballads of Shakespeare and his troupe of players; Richard of Warwick and Charles Stuart's armies fighting at Edgehill. All very interesting. From there she would work gradually northwards. The Midlands: Abbots Bromley in Staffordshire where the thousand-year-old Horn Dance originated. She would delve in the old bookshops and she would talk to historical societies and librarians, and even old residents of villages.

After that she might go north. She might even drive up to the border; there were dozens of border legends and folk songs and she would see what could be garnered. She might cross the border into Scotland and go across to Skye. Over the sea to Skye . . . Didn't everyone want to visit Skye at some time in their lives? But she was going to look on this project as a working holiday; they were not to expect too much contact with her. She would phone in from time to time, but she would have a little time by herself as well.

The aunts thought it all sounded very interesting indeed, although Dilys maintained that what Thalia was really doing was leaving London to escape the memories, and Rosa talked about delayed reaction and said mark her words, this was the reckoning. Cousin Elspeth said the mercy was that Thalia had held up as long as she had. 'But thankfully for long enough to see us through that terrible time. Yes, I *know* we said we would never refer to it again, and I haven't, truly I haven't, Rosa. George will tell you that. But now with poor Dr Shilling's trial – well, who knows what might come out? I think it's very sensible of Thalia to leave London, in fact I think we all ought to do the same. I mean, if one's in the Grand Canaries or somewhere, one can't be reached by Scotland Yard. Or can one?'

'Yes, one can,' said Rosa grimly. 'Stay put, Elspeth, unless you want to stir up Inspector Mackenzie's suspicions. No, it isn't wicked of us, none of us has actually committed any crime. Shilling was the one who did that.' She put the phone down and went off to tell Dilys that they should have put Elspeth out of the room when all this started. She was only annoyed with herself for not thinking of it at the time, said Rosa, and repeated this to Flora who had been invited to Battersea for Sunday lunch.

'Elspeth won't let us down,' said Flora, eating the very good roast beef that Dilys had cooked because dearest Flora always enjoyed her food. 'George will see to that. He'll be thinking about the scandal for Ingram's – he won't want any publicity there, I'll be bound. He likes his creature comforts too much, does George. Did you know he's got a woman in Maida Vale?'

'So would I have in George's place,' observed Rosa.

'That's what Juliette says. But he's quite discreet, which is more than you can say for Juliette. She's been dining at Langan's with that good-looking writer who was at Edmund's funeral, in fact I think she did more than dine with him, because Diana Lorrimer saw them going off in a taxi to Juliette's flat afterwards.'

'How did she know where they were going?'

'She heard Juliette give the address.'

'Naughty girl,' said Dilys indulgently. She and Rosa loved hearing about Juliette's adventures. Juliette would tell them all about this new development when next she visited Battersea.

'John Shilling won't stir up any scandal either,' said Flora. 'He's definitely going to plead guilty to the manslaughter charge, you know.'

'So I should hope,' rejoined Rosa. 'No one else would have given Eloise chloral hydrate – well, I don't imagine anyone else could have got hold of the stuff. Even if we knew what it was, which I don't suppose we do.'

'I've never even heard of it,' said Dilys.

'Of course it was Shilling,' said Rosa, firmly. 'The tragedy is that Imogen's been so damaged because of it.'

'Oh yes, but she'll recover, Rosa. You know we agreed that she'd recover. And you quite took to Dr Sterne when we went along to meet him that afternoon.'

Rosa said tartly that Dilys had always been gullibility itself when a handsome face was involved. 'Handsome is as handsome does, Mother always said.'

'But you said yourself you thought we could trust him to look after Imogen,' responded Dilys with spirit.

Flora said, 'Never mind Leo Sterne. Listen, if Shilling's the villain of the piece how did he stage the fake blood?'

'They said at the inquest it was sheep's blood.' Dilys shuddered, because this was not a nice thing to discuss while people were eating their lunch.

'That's precisely my point,' said Flora at once. 'Sheep's blood – any kind of blood – surely isn't something you just happen to have lying in your medical bag in case it might come in handy. Anyway, what was his motive?'

'Revenge? Because Eloise – hum – turned him down?' suggested the romantically inclined Dilys.

'Don't talk rubbish, Dilys. And carve Flora some more beef.'

Flora accepted the beef and then said, 'I've been wondering—'

'Yes?'

'You don't suppose Imogen really did kill Eloise after all, and John Shilling's been trying to protect her?'

The three ladies considered this, and Dilys said doubtfully that Dr Shilling was going to rather extreme lengths if so.

'Yes, but he might be doing it for Eloise's sake. You know how dotty he was about Eloise.'

'Oh, I see.'

Dilys helped everyone to more potatoes, and Rosa said, 'Then why didn't he hide the knife we found in Imogen's room?'

'Perhaps he didn't see it,' said Dilys. 'If he thought Imogen had stolen his chloral hydrate and poisoned Eloise with it, he wouldn't be looking for knives at all. He wouldn't be thinking about knives.'

'Juliette thinks he's mad – I mean clinically mad,' said Flora. 'She thinks that explains the whole thing. But I'm not so sure it's as simple as that.'

'Why not?'

'I'm not so sure that it was Shilling. There's a – a *calculated* feel about all this. As if someone's plotting in secret somewhere. The knife planted by Imogen's bed, and the false blood – that was premeditated.'

There was a silence. 'That's rather an unpleasant idea,' said Rosa at last.

'I don't believe it,' put in Dilys. 'Flora, I really don't believe anyone's plotting in secret or premeditating murders. It was Dr Shilling who did it – either because he was mad or because he was drinking too much. And it's all dreadful and tragic, but Imogen will recover – I refuse to think anything else – and Shilling will go to prison, or be rehabilitated or something, and everything will be all right.'

'George says Shilling ought to be strung up,' remarked Rosa.

'Yes, but then he offered to help with the legal fees when Shilling was arrested,' said Flora. 'And he stood bail. He's as soft as butter really, George.'

'Did Shilling accept?' Rosa wanted to know.

'He accepted the bail but he said he'd better pay his own legal fees, and anyway they wouldn't be very high because he wasn't offering any defence. But he said it mustn't appear as if there'd been any jiggery-pokery. Collusion, that's the word I want.'

Dilys opened her mouth to say that there had been quite a lot of jiggery-pokery, and then thought better of it.

Rosa asked if anyone knew where Thalia was going. 'And Dilys, pass Flora the horseradish sauce.'

'She thought of starting in the Midlands, I think,' said Flora. 'Somebody said something about Warwickshire. But I daresay she'll move about a good deal. Is that some of your homemade horseradish sauce, Dilys? In that case I'll certainly have some.'

'If Thalia's going to Warwickshire, she could have borrowed George and Elspeth's house in Stratford,' said Dilys. 'Couldn't she, Rosa? It's in a very nice part, and she could have used it as a base. I'm sure George and Elspeth wouldn't have minded.'

'George probably said it wasn't available because he wanted to take his floozie there.'

'Where *do* you get your expressions, Flora?'

'Don't they call them floozies any more?'

'Not since about nineteen twenty, I shouldn't think.'

'What a pity,' said Dilys. 'Such a lovely word. Treacle pudding, everyone?'

It had amused Thalia to lay a false trail and it had pleased her to see them all accept what she told them without question.

They had all nodded solemnly, their sheep faces heavy and serious with sympathy, and Thalia had wanted to laugh aloud because it was so easy to fool them.

She had laid her plans with infinite care and everything was working out as if she was being given divine guidance.

She was not going to Thornacre itself, but she was going

231

very near to it. There were a number of corollary villages spidering out from Thornacre, and it had been simplicity itself to phone the two or three house agents listed in the directory and inquire about the leasing of a house for a while. Perhaps six months, was that possible? she had asked. She was not familiar with these procedures. Her husband had always dealt with business matters, and since he and her son had died . . . But she had in mind somewhere secluded and peaceful, and somewhere with a garden where she could enjoy pottering. She liked to dabble a little in photography, so if there could be some kind of outbuilding, or even better a good, dry cellar that might be used as a studio and dark-room? She gave the impression of a bewildered widow, rather charmingly helpless, bravely trying to piece together a shattered life.

The agents were instantly responsive and immediately sympathetic, and several sets of details describing suitable properties were sent to her. She used her real name for the arrangements, because there would be a tenancy agreement to be signed and a cheque to be written for the rent, but all the correspondence went to the service flat. It was not very likely that some small office in Northumberland would connect her with Ingram's or the Hampstead manslaughter case when eventually it came to court, and it did not really matter if they did. It did not really matter if the family found out where she was either, because they would assume that it was part of her roving commission. But it would be preferable to preserve as much anonymity as possible.

From the sheaf of holiday houses available on long autumn and winter lets, she chose the four-square, greystone October House in Blackmere, a village five or six miles from Thornacre. It had been built around the turn of the century, and the rooms were described as spacious. Thalia thought estate agents had to comply with a fairly stringent code of practice nowadays, so spacious probably meant exactly what it suggested. So far so good. There was a large garden and no other properties nearby. The village centre was a couple of miles down the road, where there was a small general store, a pub and a garage. A church, doctor and dentist and a small supermarket were in Thornacre village.

October House was fully furnished down to bed linen and crockery. There was a modern cooker, freezer, fridge and washing machine, and the agent had added a note explaining that there was someone in the village who would come up twice a week if required, for cleaning and some cooking. The charge for this was amazingly low in comparison with London charges. Best of all, the house was owned by a man who baked pots and ceramics for tourists and designed original china for the pottery manufacturers in the Midlands. He had recently left for America on a six-month lecture tour, which was why the house was available. The old coach house at the rear had been converted to a pottery where the man normally worked, and there was a kiln and a couple of firing ovens; providing certain safeguards and restrictions were agreed to, the tenant could have the use of the coach house. The agent knew the house fairly well – they had let it a couple of times before under similar circumstances – and he thought that the coach house would do very well for a photographic studio.

Thalia signed a six-month lease by post and left for Blackmere village and October House ten days later. It sounded a remote district, but in the later stages of her plan remoteness would be very necessary indeed.

The house was absolutely right.

It stood in grounds of about an acre and it was shielded from the road by tall old trees. There was a long drive, fringed with laurel and laburnum, and a gravel turning circle in front of the house. Even though there was probably a fair bit of traffic, the house was so far back from the road that you would never hear it. You wouldn't see cars or passers-by, and they would not see you.

233

There were two large, high-ceilinged sitting rooms, one on each side of the hall, both with deep bay windows overlooking the front gardens. At the back of the house was a small breakfast room and a kitchen. The kitchen still had the original stone flags and a built-in range and ceiling rafters, but the potter had brought it up to date with modern cooking facilities and a central work counter with a cool ceramic surface. There was a microwave cooker as well, and a large fridge. In one corner stood a large deepfreeze, switched on and purring. Thalia smiled and stood for a moment with her eyes on it.

The potter's studio was at the rear; the drive led all the way round, and it was on the left, partly hidden by more laburnum bushes: a long low building, not built of grey-stone like the house, but of old red brick, mellow with age. It was possible to see the ghost shape of the old coach-house door and make out where it had been bricked up to make a conventional door.

She saw at once the room that would be Edmund's, and she spent a great many hours there. It was the largest bedroom, and it would have been the master bedroom in the days when October House had a master. The potter probably used it when he was at home, and he, or someone else, had papered it in cool blue and green, with chintz curtains and a matching, chintz-covered window seat. There was a huge oak wardrobe and chest of drawers, fragrant with the scent of old, well-polished wood. The windows were latticed and there was a pear tree outside. In autumn the ripening pears would perfume the room, and in spring there would be a froth of blossom. Edmund should sleep in here, with the scent of the pears and the rose-perfumed sheets. There would be a bowl of dried lavender on the rosewood table beneath the window, and the morning sun would slant through the panes, showing up the spill of melted honey on the pillow that was Edmund's hair. This room would be the shrine, and the coach house would be the temple that would see his renaissance. Renaissance meant the rebirth and resurgence of art and literature and learning under the influence of classical models. The use of the word like this, in connection with Edmund, pleased her.

There was a series of small attic rooms, one leading out of the other, mostly windowless. At some stage in the house's history someone had fitted a stout lock and a bolt to them. Thalia smiled again. Yes, the house was exactly and completely right.

She would do all she could to become part of the scenery here. Unremarkable and unremarked. A recently bereaved lady, staying in this part of England to recuperate from a tragedy, here to collate research for a project for Ingram's Books, and to be near a favourite niece who tragically had been consigned to Thornacre. She would give herself a month, two at the outside.

And then she would begin her real work.

Chapter Twenty-one

Dan was immersed in work when he was jerked back to reality by the sound of the letter box clattering and something largeish dropping on the mat. It would be a circular or a trial size of shampoo or washing powder. It might be a seed catalogue for the ground floor flat, delivered to the wrong number. Likeliest of all was that it was a bill, in which case it could wait. He carried on working.

His original idea had been to end the book with Rosamund waking. He had thought this was how the story did end: the awakening of the princess to the prince's embrace, preferably within that marvellous frame of Tchaikovsky's inspired ballet music, and a general epithalamium with all the characters clasping hands and good triumphing over evil. Even the Wicked Godmother and the Good Fairy usually took their bows together.

But according to both Perrault and Basile, the real trials of Sleeping Beauty – Perrault's *La Belle au Bois Dormant* – did not start until *after* she was woken, when she was confronted with the villainess of the piece. Dan worked steadily on, mesmerised by the swelling horror of the legend.

The prince's mother had set herself to seek the princess out and, upon finding her, to kill her. Several of the sources made much of her bloodthirsty nature, and most referred to her scouring the countryside to find the princess. All described her bitter fury at losing her beloved son to the whey-faced little cat who had done nothing for the last hundred years but sleep.

Perrault described the villainess's luring of the princess to a house deep in the woods 'that she might with greater ease put in execution her horrible desires', and referred to the house's lonely situation. According to Basile, when the ogreish-inclined lady found the princess, she channelled her anger on to the whey-faced cat's twins, born to her and the prince exactly nine months after the famous kiss.

Twins. Dan stared at this on the page. The princess had given birth to twins. Which means that I was right all along about her being woken by a prick.

It was all to the good. Adam Cadence could buckle swash with the best, and when it came to hacking his way through thorns and briars he was unrivalled. But Dan had never thought he was of the calibre to be satisfied with a chaste peck on the lips when finally he reached fair Rosamund's virginal couch.

Dan leaned back, stretching his arms to ease his protesting neck and shoulder muscles, and considered the next twist of the plot. It was becoming increasingly plain that Rosamund was going to have to emerge from her drugged unconsciousness and face any number of tribulations before she could go hand in hand into the sunset with her prince, and this was something that would have to be carefully thought out. The overly melodramatic would have to be diligently avoided, never mind the downright comic. Dan's mind instantly went to all those other heroines who had opened their eyes from entranced slumbers and been faced not with the swashbuckling hero but with the villain of the piece, or even – heaven forfend! – the jester. Rosamund might still have a few trials to face that Dan had not bargained for, but she was certainly not going to be confronted with an ass-headed Bottom, or a frog prince or some freakish hunchback dwarf. In fact if Rosamund's creator was going to remain faithful to the original version, it looked as if Margot would have to travel in extreme secrecy to Rosamund's bleak asylum and encamp at the gates, there to make plans for what Perrault called the execution of her horrible desires.

Dan glanced at the clock. Two p.m. No wonder he felt hungry. It would be easier to cope with Margot's horrible desires on a full stomach. He wandered into the kitchen, and absent-mindedly heated a tin of soup and cut a hefty cheese sandwich. The post might as well be investigated at the same time.

On the mat lay a large manila envelope, probably a circular, and a preview copy of *Women in Business* with his article about Thalia Caudle on page five. The features editor had scribbled a note on a compliment slip, saying how good they thought it looked, and how they hoped to use him for future work. The cheque had been sent to his agent in the same post. This was all very satisfactory.

Dan boiled the kettle for coffee and propped himself on the kitchen table to drink it while he read the article through. It did not sound at all bad. There had not been too much mangling by the sub-editor, and somebody had got hold of a decent photograph of Thalia, seated at her desk with a smudgy view of Regent's Park just discernible through the window behind her. She looked exactly how the readers of *Women in Business* liked people to look, and she sounded exactly how they liked career women to sound. Intelligent and understated and well dressed, but with a recognisable vein of ordinariness, so that readers could think: that might be me. I could do that.

At the end of the article was a brief paragraph inserted by the features editor, explaining that since the interview with Ms Caudle, she had left London for a time to gather material for Ingram's planned new imprint dealing with ballads and folk songs. She had undertaken a roving commission and she might be gone for as long as six months.

Dan laid the magazine down, his mind tumbling. It was important to keep a sense of proportion about this, and it was vital not to leap to any conclusions. Dan was not, he absolutely was *not* going to assume that Thalia had gone to Northumberland to put into execution her horrible desires with greater ease. Remember that Thalia isn't Margot, Daniel. Keep remembering it.

In any case, short of breaking into the Great Portland Street flat and ransacking it for clues, there was no way of finding out where Thalia really was. And whatever else Dan was going to do, he was not going to start house breaking.

He opened the second letter, and found that it was not a circular or a bill after all; it was the response to his request for a sight of Royston Ingram's will. It contained a neatly stapled photocopy of what appeared to be the whole document. Dan carried it back to his desk and spread it out.

It was a relatively brief document, considering the position Royston had held, and assuming that by today's standards – by Dan's standards anyway – he had been fairly well off. Dan read it as he ate the cheese sandwich, skimming the paragraphs dealing with disposal of real estate, sums left to various charities and the small legacies for various long-serving staff at Ingram's. Real estate appeared to refer to immovable property, and could be buildings or just land.

Several times the phrase 'as laid down in the Articles of Association of Ingram's Books' occurred, usually in relation to the disposal of Royston's financial interests in the company. The term 'settled estates' was used as well, and Dan took this to indicate a kind of entail; in other words, Royston had been free to dispose of his personal property more or less as he liked, but the Ingram shares were controlled by the Articles. There was something called net personalty, which appeared to be anything other than land and property that was not freehold, and which Dan supposed could amount to anything from a thousand pounds to a few hundred thousand. The term 'valuation as at date of death' was also spattered liberally throughout the document. He read on, his heart beating fast. At any minute he was going to find out how near the danger was to Imogen.

And then it was there. Towards the end of the final page was the paragraph he had been searching for. It was wrapped up in legal jargon but the intention was perfectly plain.

In the event of Royston and Eloise Ingram dying before Imogen reached the age of eighteen, Thalia was appointed as Imogen's guardian, to administer her interests in Ingram's and act as the governing board's chairman. *Eighteen.* Dan stared at this, and only then realised how strongly he had assumed that the period of guardianship would be until Imogen was twenty-one, which would have meant she was safe for two or three years yet.

He read on and discovered that if Imogen died or was declared unfit to manage her own affairs, Thalia Caudle continued to rule Ingram's.

He broke into Thalia's flat the next day. He chose the middle of the afternoon, which was a time when people might be thought to be safely about their own lawful occasions and not thinking about catching housebreakers. He wore gloves and an anonymous dark jacket, and he took the underground to Oxford Circus and walked up Regent Street. A taxi, or even a bus, might be traceable, but if you could not go unnoticed on the Central Line you could not go unnoticed anywhere.

Getting past the door intercom had bothered him quite a lot; it was the kind where you pressed a particular button for an individual flat, and the individual flat-owner then opened the door electronically from within. This meant that pretending to sell double glazing or being a spurious man-to-check-the-meters was out. Double-glazing salesmen were a joke anyway nowadays. But he had thought up a couple of fairly credible reasons for requesting entry.

He pressed the first of the three buttons for the floor below the Ingram flat. No response. He pressed the second button and a voice answered. Dan announced himself as having a delivery of flowers for the first. 'Only there's no one in.'

'Flowers!' said a pleased-sounding female voice. 'Oh, how nice for her.'

If there had not been a 'her' in the picture, Dan had been ready to enter into arguments about wrong addresses, or to go on to other flats. But it was all right. 'Who are they from?' asked the unknown voice.

'No idea. Just to deliver to Number Four this afternoon. P'raps she's got a secret admirer. I could leave them in the lobby.'

'Oh yes, do that, will you?' said the voice. 'She'll be home about seven. I'll make sure she knows. I'll open the main doors for you now.'

'Right you are.'

Dan felt so guilty about raising the hopes of the unknown Number Four that as he crossed the lobby, he almost wondered whether to send flowers to her on his own account. But half a dozen trip-wires stretched across his path at once, one of these being that flower orders could be traced, and another that Number Four might have a jealous lover or husband. And when it was eventually discovered that the Ingram flat had been broken into, searching inquiries would be made. Sorry, Number Four.

Getting inside had been so easy that Dan began to feel suspicious. Probably there was a hidden security camera or an electronic eye somewhere, and at any minute he would be caught and hauled off to justice. But he was unchallenged as he went up to the flat where Thalia Caudle had dined him, seduced him, and left the grisly contents of the freezer for him to discover.

The door to the Ingram flat had several small panes of glass let into the frame. Dan had remembered this and had reasoned that they could be broken with minimum disruption. He had brought a small but heavy-headed hammer. He studied the door and the lock carefully. The glass was

241

the swirly, bottle-bottomed kind and fairly thick. Dan eyed it doubtfully, wondering now whether it really would break sufficiently to let him reach inside and release the lock. He had no idea what he would do if the lock was some kind of double-treble security arrangement or something needing a code, or if he came up against a thread of thin wire woven into the glass which needed wire-cutters to get through. He also had no idea whether there was an interior burglar alarm. He glanced up and down the corridor. There was a fire escape at the far end of the hall. If he unwittingly set off an alarm system, could he be down the fire escape and into the street before anyone came running? He thought he could.

In films people picked locks with credit cards, but Dan had never been able to understand how they did it. He could not see how this one could possibly be opened other than with its designated key. It would have to be the glass. He looked about him again. There was a silent, deserted air about the entire floor, and the chances were that most of these flats were not occupied during the day. But there had been the female voice on the floor below and she might hear him. There were three other flats on this floor, and for all Dan knew there were any number of people inside them who might hear him as well.

None of it could be helped. He had got this far, and he was blowed if he was going to duck out now. He took a deep breath and brought the hammer smashing down on the pane of glass surrounding the lock. The sound was appallingly loud in the enclosed space and Dan's heart came up into his mouth. But nobody came running to find out what was happening, and no ear-splitting alarm bells rang.

The glass had crazed, but it had not quite shattered. Dan took another deep breath and raised the hammer a second time. This time the glass broke more thoroughly and he managed to push out several jagged splinters so that he could reach inside and release the lock. It sprang back and the door swung open.

Dan hesitated, wondering if it could really be this easy. But it was possible that the electronic intercom arrangement was thought sufficient to keep out prowlers. He remembered that this was a company apartment, and generally used only for odd nights here and there. Probably the more permanent residents had stouter front doors and better security.

The minute he stepped inside he knew that the flat was empty, in the way that you always do know if places are empty. But it was still an eerie experience. The apartment was shadowy and still, and the sky outside was grey and already sliding down into the early November night. A single glance around the rather characterless sitting room showed that the desk under the window was the likeliest place for information. But Dan found himself crossing to the kitchen and, with a feeling of helpless compulsion, reaching for the freezer lid. There would be nothing inside, of course, but . . .

But if I don't open it I shall keep wondering.

The freezer was innocent of anything except the packs of food Dan had seen last time. He propped up the lid and stood looking into it for a moment. Did I imagine it then? Was it Margot clawing her way out of fantasy into reality again? Because if I really did imagine it, then I'm committing the most appalling intrusion here. But then he remembered that macabre scene at the funeral in Hampstead, and he knew it had not been imagination. And there was a rounded depression at the freezer's centre, the ghost of something that had lain there for a time and left its imprint. Something that was roughly the size and shape of a large melon.

Dan closed the freezer and went back into the sitting room. He had to force himself to open the desk and rifle through the small drawers. Pillaging, hadn't this once been called? It conjured up mad visions of marauding Vikings bouncing lustily across the North Sea.

There was not very much to pillage. A copy of the lease of this flat – the ground rent was astronomical. A neat list of plumbers and electricians and a number to ring for exterior maintenance. The name of somebody who apparently came in to clean, and a couple of phone numbers of fast-food delivery services. Dan tried to imagine his villainess eating pizza out of a cardboard delivery box and failed entirely.

At the bottom of the drawer was a large manila envelope, postmarked Berwick-on-Tweed. Berwick-on-Tweed. Northumberland. Dan's heart began to beat faster. She's there, he thought. I was right, and she's there; she's going to enter Rosamund's castle and she's going to kill her . . . No, you fool, this is Thalia, this is real.

He slid the envelope's contents out. There were four or five sets of property details sent by an estate agent from Berwick, and there was a brief letter attached, referring to Mrs Caudle's request for properties on long-term lets in the area. Her requirements had apparently been a little difficult to meet, but the agent hoped one of the enclosed would be suitable. All were available immediately for periods of between six months and a year.

Dan scanned the details quickly. They were all for rather up-market houses, and they all looked as if they were in isolated areas, although that might merely have been the agent's photographic skill. Cooking and cleaning services were available for most of the properties. The location of each property was carefully described, and all of them were within five – at the most seven – miles of Thornacre.

The ogress was at the gates of Rosamund's enchanted castle after all.

Safely back in his own flat, Dan sat down at his desk to consider this new twist.

He was still no nearer to finding out Thalia's real motives. Margot had followed Rosamund to her east-coast asylum in order to kill her but Margot's motives would not be

Thalia's. At least Dan hoped they would not, because that would mean he really was tapping into some strange, invisible world, brimful of portents and harbingers, and he refused flatly and absolutely to believe in such things. He refused flatly and absolutely to become any more involved than he already was. He would get on with what he was doing, which was writing a book.

But the plot was stuck fast and Dan could not unstick it. Adam Cadence was due to travel north to rescue the imprisoned Rosamund, and Dan wanted him to go helter-skelter through the night, hurling his sleek, showy Jaguar XJ effortlessly across the country, sizzling with acceleration (the car) and testosterone (Adam). Rosamund was going to get quite an awakening when Adam finally reached her scented bower.

But Adam could not summon up enough energy to set off tonight and Dan could not summon it up for him either. He moved on to the calculation of how long Adam and Rosamund could be given before they were finally allowed to go to bed. Rosamund would presumably have to recover from the lingering effects of Bentinck's drugging, and it would not do for Adam to pounce on her the minute she opened her eyes. Apart from it being inconsiderate on Adam's part (and therefore alienating to a good many female readers), it would not make very good dramatic sense. Dan did not in the least mind Rosamund losing her virginity, in fact she was going to lose it very thoroughly indeed before the finale, but she was not going to lose it in a hospital bed, hooked up to a battery of intravenous drips and gastro-feeds. He would defy even Shakespeare to squeeze romance out of such a setting.

His mind returned yet again to the house details he had found in Thalia's flat, and he tried to think what he ought to do about them, and whether he ought to do anything.

It was then that there was a soft footfall on the stair outside, and a light tap on the door. Dan got up to answer it, and there on the doorstep was the villainess herself. Thalia Caudle.

She was at her most charming and her most hesitant. If she was not disturbing him, she said, she would like to talk to him if he could spare the time. A little proposition, she said, indicating the large briefcase she carried. She had taken the chance of finding him in, and also of finding him alone.

'Come inside,' said Dan, with the feeling that he was saying someone else's lines. To dispel this, he said, 'Do sit down.'

Whatever else Thalia was, she was not obvious. She did not gush over his flat, and say, oh, what a very nice room, or even, so this is where you work. She sat on the deep sofa that needed re-covering, looked about her and gave a little satisfied nod, as if she liked what she saw. In a minute common courtesy would force Dan to offer her a drink, or at the very least a cup of tea or coffee. The thought of her hands curled round one of his wine glasses or cups, after they had been curled round the obscene thing he had seen in the freezer, sent prickles of revulsion scudding across his skin. He said, 'You mentioned a proposition,' and hoped he was giving the impression of someone who was very busy but politely snatching ten minutes' break. She looked so utterly normal, and so attractive in a scarlet wool jacket with a calf-length black skirt and black leather boots, that he began to wonder if he had dreamed all those bizarre events in her flat. He offered her wine, and uncorked it while he listened to her talking.

Thalia seemed perfectly at home and entirely relaxed. She said that what she was about to propose might be asking too much. Also, of course, she might have misread his feelings towards her. 'I don't mean that in any committed sense, Dan; I'm just referring to friendship and companionship. I did think we had shared that.'

246

This was where older women scored over younger ones, of course. A 22-year-old would have found it difficult or embarrassing to refer to the couple of nights they had spent together; Thalia appeared to think it perfectly acceptable to do so, and to use it as a springboard for claiming friendship. Dan could not decide if this was extremely clever or unusually honest.

She accepted the wine, which fortunately was the claret Oliver had brought, and explained that what she wanted was to offer him a commission for the work she was doing for Ingram's. He would remember perhaps. They had discussed it when they first met.

Dan said warily, 'I do remember. A new imprint focusing on folklore and ballads and legends, wasn't it?' Something prompted him to add, 'It sounded interesting.'

Thalia said, 'I'm so glad you thought that, because frankly, Dan, I need your help. I can do many things but I can't write acceptable prose.'

Dan drank his wine and waited.

'I would,' said Thalia, 'pay whatever you thought a suitable fee. Of course I would. I expect you're quite expensive, aren't you?'

The faint, self-deprecatory irony that Dan had once found so attractive was there, and he heard himself say, 'I expect you could afford me.'

'The thing is that it would mean you coming to Northumberland with me. Just for a short while.'

'Northumberland?' Dan felt as if he was treading on brittle ice. At any minute it would crack and drop him neck deep into black freezing water.

'Yes, a place called Blackmere. I'm using it as my base. Would that be a problem?'

'Not necessarily.'

'A few days only, of course. We could say a week.'

'Fair enough.'

'You could stay with me,' she said. 'I've taken a house up

there. Quite large. You could have your own study.'

There was silence. I will not, said Dan silently, I absolutely will *not* ask if I can have my own bedroom.

'I see you're working on something at the moment,' said Thalia, her eyes going to the cluttered desk. 'You could bring that with you, of course. I wouldn't want you to break off anything that was current.'

'No,' said Dan, almost too quickly. 'No, I can leave that to one side for a few days.' The thought of his characters coming into Thalia's sphere of influence, of Thalia even reading parts of the manuscript, was deeply distasteful. The manuscript could stay here for a week. He said, 'Why Northumberland?'

Thalia looked at him thoughtfully. 'Why not Northumberland?' she said. 'It's very rich indeed in border legends and ballads and folk stories. Let me show you what I've done so far.' She reached into the briefcase and handed him a thick folder.

Dan got up to refill the wine glasses before sitting down to study Thalia's notes. It was possible that she was using this as a ploy to get near to Imogen, or even as a ploy to lure Dan himself into her clutches once more, but it had to be admitted that she was providing herself with a very comprehensive alibi. The folder was marked 'Northumberland and the Border Counties', and there was a file reference number on the front, suggesting that it was one of a series. It was filled with cuttings about folklore and photographs of old castles, and there were several pages of notes, some handwritten, some typed.

Dan saw almost straight away that Thalia – or whoever had compiled the file – had only skimmed the surface. The obvious legends and characters were faithfully listed: the Hermit of Warkworth and Grace Darling, and the better-known folk songs were noted as well. Dan's interest was caught, and he found himself itching to dig deeper: to Harry Hotspur hunting in the Cheviots and falling into the famous Hell Hole; to the sources of Walter Scott and Robert Surtees; to the Lambton Worm and the Jarrow Marches. The old Northumberland fortresses would yield a wealth of material as well: Bamburgh, reputed to be the Arthurian Joyous Gard, and Lindisfarne and Alnwick. Whatever the motive and whatever the outcome, this would be a very interesting commission.

'I don't want you to actually write the book,' said Thalia, and Dan looked up to find her eyes on him with what he could have sworn was nothing more than interested friendship. 'We'd use specialist freelances for that. It's more a question of arranging the material. Deciding what could be used and perhaps delving a bit deeper into sources in the different areas. Simplifying some of the old newspaper archive stuff and translating all that florid Victorian prose from privately printed diaries and memoirs into twentieth-century language.'

'Yes, I understand that.' Dan turned over several more pages, frowning. 'If I agree,' he said, slowly, 'I couldn't give you more than five days or so. A week at the outside. I've got commitments here – deadlines.'

He was not sure whether he was giving himself a safety net by saying this, but Thalia said at once, 'Yes, of course. Five days should be more than sufficient.'

There was a silence. Then Dan said, carefully, 'When would you want to leave?'

'You'll do it?'

'Yes,' said Dan slowly. 'Yes, I'll do it. We'll talk about the fee when I see how much work's involved.'

'Ought I to contact your agent?'

Their eyes met. Dan said, 'I think we'll keep this one just between the two of us, shall we, Thalia?' and was rewarded by the sudden satisfaction in her eyes.

She said, 'Do you think you can work with me, Dan?'

Dan smiled at her. 'Oh, Thalia,' he said, and forced his voice to take on a note of intimacy, 'we'll work together and we'll keep together as two yoke-devils sworn to each other's purpose.'

She smiled the satisfied smile again, and Dan saw she did not know that the yoke-devils Shakespeare had been referring to when he wrote that speech had been treason and murder.

The villainess had presented him with the perfect vehicle for keeping a watch on her and for finding out about Imogen and Thornacre. Because if he could not find out her intentions by breaking into her flat, then he would do so by living in her house and, if necessary, sleeping in her bed.

Dan Tudor's interference had nearly thrown things out of kilter, but as Thalia drove away, she thought she had dealt with it very well indeed. She had meant to contact the family on this brief visit to London, but now she would not. The fewer people who knew she had been in London the better. It might be necessary for Dan to discreetly vanish quite soon, and the fewer trace lines there were from him back to her, the better.

The thought of having him with her in October House was exciting. The arrangement was that they would set off tomorrow, and they would use Thalia's car. There was no point in taking two cars, she had said, and they could share the driving. When the work was completed, she would drive him to the nearest railway station for the return.

Thalia was not absolutely sure that it had been Dan who had broken into the Great Portland Street flat, but she was nearly sure. She had considered turning him over to the police but, after thought, had decided against it because she had no idea how much he knew.

Today's visit had not been the impulse she had pretended, of course, but it had worked brilliantly. She had set herself out to be her most charmingly helpless, and she had succeeded. He had been dazzled, just as all the young men were dazzled. He had seen it as another episode in their affair – just the two of them in a secret hideaway, remote and romantic. And, of course, he was a very good writer; he would be of considerable use in this tiresome smokescreen she had put up of the folk legends for Ingram's. Thalia had seen at once that his interest had been fired by the preliminary notes, and she was pleased. The new eager young editor at Ingram's who had been so delighted to take on the research for Mrs Caudle's pet project had done an excellent job.

And if Dan became troublesome, or if he ceased to be of use, there were ways of dealing with that.

Chapter Twenty-two

Quincy knew that Thornacre's ghosts were the ghosts of the children who had once been kept here. They had not been the ill-mannered jeering children you saw today and the kind of children who had lived in Bolt Place, but pale, silent, thin creatures, hollow-eyed and lank-haired. Men sometimes came to the house to look at them. They were towering brutish men with coarse black hair on the backs of their hands and greedy, snatching fingers. They were ogres really, only they were wearing human-face disguises so that people would not know. They gave the mothers money and took the children away. They said the children would be put to work, they would work in coal mines and sweeping chimneys in rich houses. It was hard work, but at least they would be fed and housed and later on they could be apprenticed and learn a proper trade. But Quincy knew that really the men wanted to lie in bed with the little girls and stroke them with their hairy hands and jab their thick fingers into the little girls' bodies. When they had had enough, they would sell them to other men who wanted to do the same things.

The children had been very frightened of the ogre-men. When they were locked into the east wing, they had known what was going to happen, and they had knelt down and prayed, which was something people did in those days more than they did now. They had said things like, gentle Jesus meek and mild, look on me a little child, and they had held hands and sung hymns so that they would not hear the ogres coming to get them.

The prayers and the hymns had not saved them. When the moon was beginning to change – sickle moon the children had called it, which was an old country word for new moon – the ogres had come, with their huge meaty hands and little mean pig-eyes and brutish red faces. They had come through the forest surrounding Thornacre, so that the ground had shaken with their heavy footsteps, and they had come right into the house and shouted for the children with their terrible deep-chested roars. 'Four little girls to be taken tonight,' they had bellowed. Or, 'A nice plump little boy for a change. Bring up the sacks and unlock the doors!'

It had all happened a very long time ago. But Quincy was afraid that they might somehow still be inside Thornacre.

Imogen had been taken to a room of her own, which Quincy thought was very good. There was a ward here called Campbell Ward – Quincy had seen it last time – and it would have been dreadful if Imogen had been put there. It was a terrible place, a long, hopeless room with sad hopeless people in rows of beds and bad smells all the time. It had been so filled up with despair and defeat that it was difficult to breathe. The people had all been senile or so zonked out on the drugs they had been given that they could not do much more than lie in bed and wait for whatever was going to happen to them. Quincy had not known if the drugs had been to help the people get better or if it was simply the attendants' way of keeping them quiet. Most of them had to be fed, and the attendants had been a bit slapdash so that the food was quite often spilled or got dribbled, and was not always properly wiped away.

Quincy would not be able to bear it if Imogen was treated like that, or if she stopped being able to swallow and dribbled everything. She thought she might kill Imogen rather than let that happen. At Briar House she had been allowed to feed Imogen with soup or milk pudding, or something called Complan, and she had done it neatly and

253

carefully, using a small spoon. Dr Sterne said the fact that Imogen was awake enough to take the food when it was spooned into her mouth was a very promising sign; it showed that she was not very far away from them. Quincy had been pleased about this, but after he had gone, Porter-Pig spoiled it by saying, 'Oh, we'll probably put a naso-gastro tube down her. I can't have my nurses wasting time feeding one patient.' The nurses were not doing the feeding, and if Quincy could not have fitted in her other jobs, she would have stayed up all night just to go on looking after Imogen, but it would not have done to say so.

Quincy's own bed was in the long narrow room which was the women's dormitory. It was cold and stuffy, and there were rows of narrow, black iron beds. Each bed had its own locker where you were supposed to put your things – your sponge and toothbrush and soap, and any money you had. You could lock the little door and wear the key round your neck, but most keys fitted most locks, and last time somebody had stolen the ten pounds that Quincy had painstakingly saved up to buy shoes. No money was going in there this time! Imogen had a locker by her bed as well, and her things were so nice – the beautiful scented soap and powder and the lovely underclothes and lawn nightshirts – that somebody was sure to take them within forty-eight hours if Quincy was not very watchful.

The dormitory looked a bit better than last time but not much. But it did not really matter because Quincy was not going to be sleeping here; she was going to be guarding Imogen. That was why she had come back to Thornacre.

Supper was served in the room that was now the dining room, which the assistants had called the canteen last time. This, also, looked a bit better. The walls had been painted and there was still the nice fresh smell of new paint instead of sickness and stale bodies, and there was a different arrangement for serving the food. At one end was a long display of all the different things you could have to eat, with everything kept warm on electric plates, like the motorway place where the ambulance men had taken her. You went up to the counter and took a tray and asked for what you wanted. The food was better as well. There was lamb stew or a fluffy fish pie with creamed potatoes on top. Tonight Quincy had a plateful of stew with cauliflower and a roast potato. There was apple crumble for afterwards or jam sponge with custard.

Last time there had been one long narrow table with benches fastened down to the floor so that they could not be drawn comfortably up to the table and you got backache after a while. Dr Sterne or somebody had got rid of these, and there were lots of small tables like a cafe, so that six or eight people could sit together.

At one of the tables was an older woman with wild hair and eyes and the most bedraggled assortment of clothes Quincy had ever seen, even in the Bolt Place years. She sat by herself, and there was a pile of plastic carrier bags at her feet, most of them spilling out filthy rags and rubbish. From time to time she looked furtively around the room and then snatched one of the bags on to her lap and rummaged through it crooningly, shielding the pitiful contents from everyone's view. The bags smelt sour and stale, and the woman smelt of the bags. Quincy remembered her from last time.

She thought some of the others were familiar as well. There was a woman who talked incessantly to an invisible companion in a moaning whine, and another who prowled suspiciously around the tables, peering into people's faces. The attendants kept taking her back to her place, but she would not stay put. At the next table was an ugly hunchbacked man with horrid mean eyes that swivelled in different directions. He might have been any age from twenty-five to sixty-five. He had been in Thornacre for years and his name was Llewellyn Harris, but everyone called him Snatcher Harris because he was always snatching at the groins of the women and sometimes the men and making ugly and obscene gestures at them. He was grotesque and squat, and his mouth was crusted with scabs that did not heal because he was always picking them. No one had ever heard him speak, and he communicated by grunts. Quincy did not know if this was because whatever had deformed his spine had deformed his mouth as well, or if he was too stupid to know how to speak, or even if he was just being sly and pretending.

Porter-Pig was there, of course, patrolling the tables, pausing occasionally to exchange a word with a patient like the royal family did on TV when they walked through a crowd of cheering people. When one of the women near to Quincy's table stood up and started to cry and take her clothes off, Porter-Pig made a puckered, disgusted mouth. While she was telling the woman to sit down and behave herself, Snatcher Harris banged down his plastic knife and fork and scuttled across the floor, lunging at the moaning woman with the invisible companion and thrusting his hand under her skirt, gibbering with glee, and then grunting with a horrid nasal sound when she pushed him off.

Porter-Pig gestured impatiently to the attendants and they ran down the room, dragging Snatcher Harris away and ignoring his threatening fists. One of them said, a bit jeeringly, that Harris would not hit anyone because he was a coward, and the other said that if the Snatcher did not mend his ways they would tie a piece of string round his dick and pull it tight, and then wait for it to wither and drop off. Quincy did not think Snatcher Harris could understand much of this. Porter-Pig understood it, but she made a big thing of showing she was not shocked, folding her chins into her neck and nodding slowly several times.

Things were a bit better than Quincy remembered them but not much. She would not have minded anyway, or at least not for herself. She would have put up with much, much worse because it was all for Imogen.

★ ★ ★

Leo set up Imogen's first treatment very carefully. He was conscious that several layers below his ordered thoughts there was a strong current of anticipation. This one's different. This one's special.

It afforded him a faint, ironic amusement to discover that he was going about the preparations like a priest preparing the high temple for some elevated act of worship, or a medieval squire undergoing fasting and purification on the evening before his knighting. The hypodermic syringes lay ready, and near to them was the remote control device for the video player. Medical science and media science hand in hand. Well, all right, not quite hand in hand, but on the same table, at any rate.

He was going to play the videos to her, but first there would be a single preliminary dose of methidrine for stimulation. I can just trigger an abreaction and release the suppressed terror, he thought, if I can once get her to hear me . . .

Leo admitted that what he really wanted to do was deliberately summon the strange lodestar power and call Imogen out of her dark sleep unaided. And play Pygmalion, breathing life into the statue? jeered his mind. Once you cross that line, you really will be entering the shadowlands of improper conduct.

He had to make a strenuous effort to remain calm while the attendants wheeled in Imogen's bed and set it to face the small television screen. He was conscious of rising excitement, and the sudden need to be alone with Imogen was so strong that it was almost a physical pain; it was nearly sexual arousal, which was a very dangerous way to feel indeed. When the attendants went out, he drew down the window blinds and turned back into the room.

This is it, Imogen. I'm about to try to bring your mind up out of its silent ocean of nothingness. Here we go. Stay with me, Imogen.

The silence in the room was so complete that the

preliminary whirring of the video tape sounded unnaturally loud. And then the jagged, splintering patterns began to whirl across the screen, casting crimson and purple and violet light across Imogen's face, and the pounding of the raw, abrasively sexual music filled the room.

Leo sat back as the video whirred forward. After a moment he took Imogen's hand in his.

Quincy waited until Imogen was with Dr Sterne, and then slipped away from the dining room and across the huge shadowy hall to the east wing.

There was not really a good time to do this, but when Imogen was with Dr Sterne there was no need for Quincy to be on guard and so it was as good a time as she would get. She would be quick and quiet and she would be back in the dayroom before anyone knew she was gone.

It was not logical to be afraid that the ogres were still here. Quincy knew this. But she knew that there was something in Thornacre, something in the air surrounding it, something in the dark clouds that massed behind it as night fell, and she knew that it was something evil. It might not be inside the house at all, of course; it might be outside, crouching in the dark grounds, watching its chance to creep inside and pounce on Imogen. It most probably was outside.

But supposing it was not. Supposing it was in the east wing, hiding itself behind the black iron door. There was a saying, 'Know your enemy', which meant finding out who your enemy was so that you knew how to fight. Quincy would find out who Imogen's enemies were and fight them.

The east wing was a rambling, echoing place, with long, soulless passages and the smell of pain and fear. Dr Sterne had changed quite a lot of things in Thornacre but it did not look as if he had done anything here yet. This might be because none of the patients lived in here, or it might be for some other reason altogether. Quincy understood that Dr

Sterne was trying to make everywhere different but she knew it would take a long time, because you could not rub out years and years of unhappiness and pain like you could rub out a pencilled line in a drawing. You had to put layers of very good things over the bad and even then the bad things would linger.

She paused at the foot of a wide, shallow staircase. The wood was dull and scarred, but it was made from solid oak, beautifully grained, and there was a banister decorated with lovely carved fir cones and oak leaves. Quincy reached out to stroke the surface. It felt harsh and dead, like a cat's fur when the cat was ill. Probably they would do something about that when they began work here; she would ask if she could help with the polishing, because it would be nice to feel the poor dry wood become satiny and warm under her hands.

Beneath the stairs, facing the door leading to the east wing, was the remains of a printed notice fixed to the wall, its surface pitted and dimmed by time but much of it still readable.

> . . . no attempts should be made to touch the Lunaticks, for although the Diet is extraordinary Good and Proper, yet they may be subject to Scurvy and Other Disease . . . the Lunaticks may not be viewed on Sundays . . .

Viewed, thought Quincy, staring at the notice, huge-eyed with horror. People used to view lunatics. Like today they went out for a day to the seaside or the zoo, or to garden centres or to look round stately homes. Once upon a time, when this house had been young, mad people had lived here, and it had been a day's outing to come and view them.

She went up the stairs, careful not to make any noise, hearing, very faintly, the ordinary sounds coming from the central part of Thornacre. There was the cheerful clatter of crockery and a door being closed and someone calling out something about going off duty.

The sticky spider's web of darkness that crouched at the house's heart stirred, and Quincy shuddered. It knows I'm here. It knows I'm coming, and it's lifted its head and it's listening and waiting . . .

She reached the corridor with the black iron door, and stopped. This was the worst part, this was the core of all the nightmares and all the frightening stories. If you don't behave we'll put you in the east wing, the nurses had said last time. The Cattersis-beast had said, if you tell what I've done to you, my dear, you'll find out what's behind the black door.

There was a bad moment when she heard someone open the door from the main part of the house and cross the hall below, and her heart beat so fast she thought it would burst out of her chest. She ran silently back to the head of the stairs where she could see down into the hall, but it was only poor old Mad Meg McCann, the bag woman. She had got hold of a trolley again today – probably she had given the attendants the slip and walked into the village and stolen it – and she was trundling it along the corridors, counting the bags of rubbish as she went, darting furtive, fearful glances from side to side. She was not in the least afraid of the east wing because she had no room for anything in her scatty old brain except her bags of rubbish. In a minute she would run off down the corridor with them, hugging the dirtiest to her withered chest. Quincy waited, and sure enough Meg grabbed the bags up and went scuttling and limping away.

Quincy went back along the corridor. This was the door; she could see the black iron bands and the huge steel hinges. She could feel the strangeness that breathed outwards. This was the black core and the evil heart of Thornacre.

She took her courage in both hands and went right up to

the door and pressed her ear against the panels. Nothing. Absolute silence. Or was there? Quincy listened again. Her heart was beating so furiously that it was difficult to hear anything else, but she thought that something moved on the other side. Something that had come to stand against the door, pressing against it in exactly the way Quincy was doing. Something that sniffed the air for human blood, and that snatched up children to cook them for supper . . . The ogres still here? But this was the most ridiculous idea in the world.

Quincy sank to the floor, huddling in a tight little ball and wrapping her arms about her bent knees. The door would certainly be locked.

But I have to know, thought Quincy with helpless despair. I have to be sure. Know your enemy. She took a huge gulping breath and stood up.

The door had a latch and a lever, and Quincy saw, with horror, that her hand seemed to have developed a life of its own; it reached out to the lever, depressed it and turned the latch. Both clicked down easily, as if they had recently been oiled. The door swung open and Quincy's heart came up into her mouth.

A sour, faintly greasy smell wafted out of the black room. It was the kind of fat-laden smell that brought all the nightmare things rushing back again. Quincy took a cautious step forward. It was fairly dark in here, and there was a bluish flickering light. Television?

Her eyes were adjusting now, and she could make out things in the room. Objects. Chairs and a table and a rug on the floor. There was a window high up in one wall, and a muddy, uncertain dusk trickled into the room and lay across the floor, showing up the drab furnishings. And beneath the window, huge squatting things. Quincy frowned, and waited for her eyes to adjust a bit more.

She was dimly aware that she had thrust a fist into her mouth to stop herself screaming, because what she was seeing was dreadful, it was the most dreadful thing she had ever seen. It was not believable, it was a nightmare, and in a minute she would wake up.

In the corner of the drab room, positioned just far enough from the small window to escape most of the light, was a plain, heavy-looking table, the kind you saw in large, old-fashioned sculleries. The remains of a meal was set out on it. Quincy could make out bowls of soup and a bread board with bread and a crock of butter or cheese, along with a dish of the stew that had been served in the dining room earlier on. The greasy scent of cooling meat lay on the air, mingling with a faint, stale odour.

Drawn up to the table were four or five chairs, and seated on each of the chairs—

The badly-lit room with the flickering bluish light that looked like television but could not possibly be television spun dizzily before her eyes and she gasped.

Seated on each of the chairs was a grotesque figure, squat, repulsive, *immense*. Giant bodies and giant faces. Giant hands resting on giant knees, all sitting back after eating their dreadful meal.

Supposing the meal had not been lamb at all, but something far grislier? *Giants like their bread made from human bones, Quincy . . . They like their dinner made from human meat . . .*

Confused, fragmented shreds of knowledge whirled through Quincy's mind. All those poor children cooped up in here, waiting for the ogre men to come stamping and shouting out of the forest to snatch them up. But the ogre men were still here; it was exactly as she had feared, they had got into the house and they had made a horrid lair in the deserted wing, and they were sitting here feasting and drinking.

As Quincy stood there, frozen into the most appalled horror she had ever known, the monstrous things turned to look at her. The repulsive heads with the overhanging brows nodded and smiled.

262

'Hello, little girl . . .'

Quincy gave a strangled scream and tumbled back down the dark corridor.

Imogen was fathoms down in the violet and turquoise mists; she was at the silent secret heart of an old, old forest where nothing moved and no one came and where frightened crying did not reach.

At times there were sounds, splinters that came jaggedly through the thick undergrowth. The rasp of a voice calling her name, the brief jangle of music. Once – perhaps two or three times – there had been tiny pinpoints of light flaring somewhere out beyond the trees; darting will o' the wisp specks, glow-worms or fireflies or perhaps dancing cressets borne by mischievous spirits, like the elusive creature in the old Irish play who was bent on seducing the humans into the land of heart's desire. *Come away, human child . . . Come away to the land of faery . . . Where nobody gets old and godly and grave . . .*

It was important to remain very silent and very still so that no one could see her and no one could hear her, and so that she did not have to go back, up and up through the mists and the twilit undergrowth. So that she could remain here. *In the land of faery, where nobody gets old and bitter of tongue . . . Stay with us here, Imogen . . . Where it is safe . . . Where nobody gets old and crafty and wise . . .*

Where it was safe.

PART TWO

'And now, as the enchantment drew to an end . . .'

Charles Perrault, *The Sleeping Beauty in the Wood*

Chapter Twenty-three

Oliver Tudor stood indecisively on his brother's door-step. It was nine o'clock on the evening prior to Christmas Eve, and he had rung the bell of Dan's flat and knocked loudly on the door several times. There were four or five pints of milk on the step, and a box of eggs. Some of the milk looked as if it had gone off.

Oliver was not especially concerned. It was possible that Dan had forgotten he was joining him to spend Christmas in London, or that he had been called away and was due back soon. It was entirely possible that Oliver himself had got the arrangements wrong.

But Oliver knew quite definitely that he had phoned Dan because the answerphone had been on, and he had left a careful message. He did not entirely trust the answerphone, because it was amazing how often machines went wrong, and so he had posted a quick letter as well, confirming the date he would arrive and the approximate time. He was actually a bit later than he had said because he had missed a turning which had taken him quite a long way off his route, but Dan would surely have allowed for something like that.

Oliver had driven to London on Thursday afternoon, straight after what had been a really very good party in the rooms of a fellow don. It had been nice of her to include him; in fact it was very nice the way so many people did invite him to things.

He fished in his pocket to find the key which Dan had given him when first moving in here. Always useful to have a spare somewhere, he had said. And there might be occasions when Oliver would turn up in London and Dan could not be here to let him in. This looked like one of those occasions.

There was a large pile of post on the mat and a film of dust everywhere. Oliver switched lights on, which made the flat feel friendlier, deposited his suitcase in the tiny spare bedroom, and came back into the living room. The first thing to meet his eyes was Dan's manuscript, stacked in two piles, one on each side of the typewriter. Oliver had a swift, vivid image of Dan working, the finished pages on the right, the draft pages on the left. The cover was off the typewriter, although this did not necessarily mean anything; Dan tended to be erratic about things like that. Oliver understood this because he was erratic himself.

There was food in the fridge – cheese and bacon – and bread in a bin. The bacon had unpleasant whitish spots, and the cheese and bread were both white and furry and in a disgusting condition. Oliver threw everything away, and tipped the sour milk down the sink.

This was beginning to be very worrying, because it looked as if Dan had not been in the flat for some time. Oliver scooped up the pile of letters and studied the postmarks under the light of the desk lamp. Some were blurred, but many were readable. With a feeling of mounting concern, he saw that several were dated the end of November.

Dan had not been in the flat for a month.

It was no longer a case of respecting his brother's privacy; it was a case of searching for clues as to where he might be. Oliver considered phoning the police but decided to leave this as a last resort. In any case, as Dan's nearest relative, he would have been notified of accident or illness. Dan kept the Oxford address and phone number in his wallet and diary, under the 'In case of accident, please inform' section.

The answerphone was flashing, which presumably meant there were messages on it. Oliver eyed it nervously;

machines were so unpredictable. But it would have to be dealt with in case any of the messages provided the answer, and so he rummaged in the desk and eventually found the instruction leaflet. It took quite a long time to understand, and he was worried about wiping off messages that might be important, but in the end he understood which button did what. He found pen and paper from the motley collection on the desk, and scribbled everything down as it came.

There were three calls from Piers, Dan's agent, each one sounding more exasperated than the last, and ending with an exhortation for Dan to ring pronto, or find himself another bloody agent. And there were a couple of invitations from friends to join them for drinks or a meal over Christmas. One added that Dan must be sure to bring his brother if he was spending Christmas in London, which pleased Oliver.

One was from a lady with a feline-sounding voice, who announced herself as Juliette Ingram, and who was apparently ringing to thank Dan for taking her out to dinner, and also for a delivery of flowers. So he's at it with somebody new, thought Oliver, torn between vague embarrassment and envy. Juliette sounded rather attractive.

There was his own message as well, explaining about arriving today, and hoping this would be all right. Oliver had had no idea that he sounded so apprehensive on the phone. He hoped he did not sound like that when he lectured.

Certain things had to be given priority. The phone calls had better be returned and, if possible, dates when they had been made established. Oliver rang Dan's agent first, and then the friends who had issued the drinks invitations. He explained to them all that Dan seemed to have vanished; agreed that there would certainly be a logical and ordinary explanation in the end, and promised to report progress. The dates of the calls confirmed his original suspicions: Dan had not been in the flat for at least a month.

He left Juliette Ingram until last.

'Goodness, I don't know *where* he could be,' said the breathless, slightly husky voice on the phone. 'He certainly isn't here, in fact I haven't heard from him since we dined together four or five weeks ago. But it all sounds very intriguing. Shall I dash over to discuss it? I'm expecting people for drinks shortly, but I could—'

'No, no, I wouldn't dream of troubling you,' said Oliver, terrified. 'But – would you by any chance know what Dan was working on at the moment? It's possible that he had to go off somewhere in connection with a – a commission, and forgot to leave a message.'

'He did the article on Thalia,' said Juliette, thoughtfully. 'That's Thalia Caudle, my aunt.'

Oliver said he knew about this.

'As a matter of fact, it was very good,' said Juliette. 'But I don't know what else. Doesn't his agent know?'

'No.'

'Oh. Well, I can tell you one thing, Oliver – you did say Oliver, didn't you?'

'Yes.'

'I've *always* wanted to meet someone called Oliver.'

'You said you could tell me—'

'Oh yes. Well, I do know that Dan was interested in my family,' said Juliette. 'I mean interested as a writer. The two mad Ingram ladies who went wild with meat axes and butchered people, you know.'

Oliver began to wonder if this husky-voiced lady was mad herself, or only a bit drunk. This was the party season, after all. He said, 'I'm sorry, I don't think—'

'It's *ancient* history,' said Juliette. 'But I suspect that Dan was planning a book about it. In fact he half admitted it, now I come to think back.'

'Ah.'

'It's quite a good story,' said Juliette, cheerfully. 'And so long ago that it wouldn't hurt anyone if it was resurrected.

Sybilla was the Regency one, you know, and they shut her away in an attic for chopping up her husband with a meat axe. I daresay it was what they did in those days. Shut mad people in attics, that is, not chop them up. She lived until she was eighty-five, but of course her husband died there and then.'

'Well, yes.'

'And then Lucienne, the Edwardian one, was locked up in Thornacre too. Dan was fascinated by that.'

'Fascinated by Thornacre?'

'My dear, riveted by it.'

'The Thornacre that was in the news a couple of months ago?'

'Yes. Too dreadful for words, wasn't it? And now, d'you know, there's my cousin Imogen there as well. It really seems as if—'

'You've got a cousin in Thornacre?'

'Yes, poor darling, she—' Juliette broke off abruptly and Oliver caught the sound of a door bell being rung peremptorily at the other end. 'Oh, bother,' said Juliette, crossly. 'Oh, *isn't* it infuriating when people arrive early! *Frightfully* bad etiquette. Listen, Oliver, are you sure I can't scoot across to you? Or you could come here. There'll be dozens of people wandering in, and you'd be very w—'

Oliver said firmly that he had a great deal to do, and rang off before he could get dragged into any alarming situations. It was only then that he saw two things amongst the jumble of papers on his brother's desk.

One was the *Women in Business* article on Thalia Caudle. He glanced at it briefly, saw the photograph and registered that Thalia had left London.

The other was the AA guide, which was lying on the desk, with slips of paper marking two of the pages. Oliver hunted in his battered briefcase for his glasses because the AA print was very small. The first marker was in the listings of towns, under the Ts, and the entry for a place called

Thornacre in Northumberland was circled in pencil. A pencil mark also indicated the Black Boar Inn in Thornacre, and in the margin the approximate mileage from London, 350/375 miles, and next to it '7 hours? 8?'. What looked like stopping-off places had been underlined: Leicester Forest East and Woodall on the M1, and Scotch Corner on the A1. Oliver pushed his glasses back on the bridge of his nose thoughtfully. These were exactly the kind of notes you would make if you were contemplating an unfamiliar journey, and earmarking somewhere to stay when you got there. He turned to the other marked page, which was the map for Northumberland, and saw that the route out of London all along the motorway and the A1 had been lightly traced, right up to the tiny village near England's bleak north-eastern edge. Thornacre.

That was circled in pencil as well.

It was almost eleven o'clock when Oliver put the phone down. There was no record of Dan having booked into either of the two inns in Thornacre, and no record of him at any of the adjacent villages either.

This had taken an hour to discover, and after that Oliver had phoned several of the hospitals, and then the police. No, they said; no accidents involving anyone of Dan's description had been reported over the last four weeks. Yes, they could be absolutely sure; these things were all stored on computer now, sir, and it was just a question of calling up the information.

Oliver, who distrusted computers as much as he distrusted most machines, thanked the duty sergeant and said he did not think he wanted to make an official report of a missing person yet. Very likely his brother had been called away and he would hear from him shortly. The duty sergeant said this happened all the time and wished Oliver a happy Christmas. At least he had not said have a nice day.

Oliver assembled some kind of meal from the tins in the kitchen cupboards, made black coffee and reviewed what he knew.

Dan had left his flat at least a month ago, although from the look of the things Oliver had found, he had not intended to be away for very long. Toothbrush, flannel and sponge and shaving things had gone, and Oliver thought a couple of jackets were missing as well. As to shirts and underthings, he had no idea, but the weekend case Dan used when he came to Oxford was nowhere to be found. The food in the fridge was the kind that would have kept for several days – say a week at least. The bacon had been a vacuum pack and the cheese was in an airtight container. Milk and eggs had been delivered. Oliver began to form a picture of Dan going away, perhaps for a weekend or three or four days, intending to come back to food and fresh milk. He had not bothered to let his agent know, and he had not done things like turning off the water which Oliver thought he would have done for a longer absence.

What else?

He had not gone in his car. Oliver had checked the mews garage earlier on, and Dan's old Escort had been there. This might not mean anything because the car was so ramshackle it might be out of commission. Dan could have gone somewhere by train or plane or boat, or he could have gone off in someone else's car. He could have hired a car – the AA book suggested that he had been planning a road journey. But that, and Juliette Ingram's reference to Thornacre and the Ingram family, were the only clues so far. Was the fact that Thalia Caudle had recently left London connected? Oliver re-read Dan's article with more attention, and saw this time that the magazine was dated the end of November, which fitted, more or less, with the date when the post had begun to pile up. He remembered how Dan had gone to Thalia's flat for dinner and not returned until the next morning.

It was possible that Dan had gone to Northumberland and Thornacre to research a book, quite possibly the one about the Ingram ladies. Oliver could accept this, and he could also accept that his brother might have gone off with Thalia, although she did not look to Oliver like someone Dan would have forsaken the world for. What he did not believe and could not accept was that Dan would go away for longer than a week without taking his manuscript. He might have done it if the book was finished and submitted to a publisher, but it was plainly not finished.

With a feeling that he was committing the worst intrusion yet, Oliver hunted about for his glasses all over again, picked up the thick wad of manuscript, poured a large measure of Dan's whisky, and sat down in the armchair to read.

He saw at once what Dan had tried to do, and he thought on balance that he had brought it off. There was the right flavour of Gothic darkness about the writing, and the peppering of clues on the original legend. There was the dark romance of crumbling old castles as well, and of wicked stepmothers and helpless heroines and swelling menace. Dan had romanticised his Rosamund a little – Oliver thought that like most writers Dan had been a bit in love with her – but there was nothing seriously wrong with that.

It was the depiction of the evil Margot that disturbed him most. Oliver read on, his critical faculties to the fore, hardly aware of the house settling into silence all around him. Twice he got up to refill his whisky glass, and once he made another mug of coffee. Each time he did this, he passed the desk with the magazine article on Thalia Caudle. It was not a face for which you would count the world well lost, but it was a face that might well tempt you to a brief madness.

It was not until he came to the chapter where Rosamund was carried with grim ceremony into the haunted lunatic wing of the old asylum that Oliver felt the strands and the clues mesh. Dan had called the place Thornycroft Hill. It did not take much of a leap to link Thornycroft with Thornacre.

He picked up the AA book again.

Oliver spent what was left of the night wrestling with the warring logic of what he had pieced together, and when he drove out of London at first light, he still had no idea whether logic or panic or some other emotion altogether had dictated his journey.

The length of the journey would have been daunting at any season but it was a nightmare prospect on Christmas Eve. Dan or somebody had calculated it to be seven or eight hours, and Oliver thought he could not possibly reach Thornacre before nightfall. Even following the sketched-out route which Dan might or might not have followed, Oliver knew perfectly well he would get lost several times. The notion of a train on Christmas Eve had only to be briefly examined to be discarded, and in any case he would need a car at the other end. It would have to be attempted. He had no idea what he would do if his car broke down halfway there.

In the event, the car behaved properly, and Oliver did not go too far out of his way too many times. This was largely due to the greater part of the journey being on the motorway. He stopped at the places that Dan had jotted down, which were quite well spaced out, and gave thanks that although the skies were leaden and menacing, no snow was falling.

He booked into the Black Boar as the church clock was chiming six o'clock that evening. He was stiff from the long drive, and he felt grubby and crumpled, but there was a sense of achievement at having reached his destination.

The Black Boar appeared to be the traditional oak-beamed, inglenook-fireplaced inn. Charles II had hidden here, Elizabeth I had slept here, and Walter Scott had written something here.

'At separate times, of course,' said mine host with the automatic geniality of one who produces this epigrammatical gem for all newcomers.

'Of course.' Oliver signed the book and was shown to a chintz-curtained, flower-papered room on the first floor.

Dan's hero, Adam Cadence, had stayed at a similar place in one of the later chapters, when he was trying to find the captured Rosamund. Dan had described it in detail and it had a good deal in common with the Black Boar, although there was no decadently luxurious four-poster here as there had been for Adam, and there had not been an Egon Ronay recommended sign outside either. But the room he was shown to was clean, the bed was comfortable and the sheets were lavender-scented, with a white honeycomb quilt. There was a pleasing scent of old timbers and wood smoke, and a printed notice on the dressing table informed Oliver that dinner was served in the dining room between seven and eight thirty each evening; bar meals were available in the Oak Bar, breakfast was between eight and nine, and please not to use all the hot water when bathing because they were not on mains out here and hot water sometimes ran a bit low.

Oliver washed, pulled on a clean shirt and sweater, and went down to the bar. Seven o'clock. He would have a drink and something to eat, and mingle with the locals in the hope of finding out a bit about Thornacre. From there he would lead up to questions about lone visitors to the area. In such a small place, a single man would surely not have gone unremarked.

He had the curious sensation that Dan was quite close to him.

Chapter Twenty-four

The Black Boar's meals fell a long way short of those enjoyed by Dan's hero. Oliver, dining off something called Chicken à la King, which was served in a peculiar brown dish, and which, as far as he could see, was glorified chicken soup out of a tin, remembered with regret Dan's description of the candle-lit dining room where Adam Cadence had partaken of a gourmet meal washed down with a very good vintage Bordeaux. Afterwards he had talked the manager's daughter into joining him in the four-poster by way of diversion until it was time to set off for the castle keep and fair Rosamund. Dan had been quite graphic over the sexual athletics in the four-poster; Oliver felt he was learning a good deal about Dan that he had never suspected.

After the chicken, he went through to the public bar. The local beer was so fierce it would have peeled varnish from wood, but the locals were amiably disposed and apparently perfectly ready to discuss Thornacre. This slightly disconcerted Oliver who had expected them to be evasive after all the publicity.

But whatever else Thornacre might be it was certainly not an embarrassment, in fact the drinkers in the bar vied with one another to tell the quiet, rather shy young man about Thornacre's history. Of course, there was a good deal as hadn't come out in the investigation by Professor Rackham, they said.

'What kind of things?'

Things that had happened in the past, said the drinkers. How in Victorian times the place had been the official workhouse, serving about seven parishes in its heyday – and the treatment the poor inmates were given a shame and a disgrace by all accounts, what with the beatings and the starvings and all manner of cruelties.

Somebody said sagely that the workhouse side had been a cover-up; his grandfather always used to tell how *his* grandfather said that the real purpose of the place was to supply little children for prostitution. 'Used to come up from London and walk through the wards – paupers' wards they called them – and pick out the prettiest of the little girls and carry them back to London.'

'Stews,' said Oliver without thinking.

'Beg pardon?'

'Stews. It's a Victorian word for sleazy back-street brothels. So Thornacre acted as a supply-house for that trade, did it? Do have another drink, by the way.'

Everyone had another drink, the young man clearly being able to afford it despite his rather worn corduroy jacket, and as the decibel level increased and the beer went round again, the tales grew wilder.

It had been a place for those blokes who dug up corpses and experimented on them – anatomists, that was what they'd been called. Burke and Hare and them. Edinburgh was only an hour or so's drive away, after all. No, said someone else, that was all wrong; the real truth was that Thornacre had been run by a Nazi spy gang during the war. Oh yes, they did have spies over here in the war, ain't you ever heard of the fifth column? The speaker glared truculently at his audience, most of whom had received his remarks with raucous and derisory hoots. He stuck to his guns and said belligerently that it was all very well to laugh but on dark nights you could still hear the screams of the poor tortured victims who had been imprisoned there, always supposing you were inclined to be sensitive to that kind of thing, and always supposing you actually ventured up the hill at night in the first place.

This was not quite what Oliver had been expecting to hear, but clearly it was going to be difficult to stop these people once they were in full flow. He listened patiently, and presently the conversation touched on Thornacre's origins. You mustn't forget the original owner of the place, said somebody, old Jeremiah Campbell who had built it for his young wife Sybilla, and then cleared off with another woman – or disappeared, anyway – and left Sybilla to go raving mad. Now old man Campbell really had left a black lot of memories behind him, say what you liked.

There was general agreement on this. Old man Campbell's wife had spent thirty years of her life shut up inside the house, screeching her mad curses against the spouse who had long since left her. Prowled around the great empty house at midnight, howling at the full moon like a she-wolf, said one of the drinkers, with unconscious poetry.

'I heard,' said the speaker who had proffered the Nazi spy theory, 'as how she lay dead for a month before she was found.' He took a long pull at his beer. 'Heaving mass of maggots, she was, when they finally found her.'

'Heaving mass of nothing!' scoffed his auditors. 'You been at the beer again! Or you been watching those horror videos. Nightmare of the Bone Crunchers and Resurrection of the Walking Dead!'

The conversation showed signs of drifting. Oliver, wondering whether this could possibly have been Juliette's ancestress and unable to remember which of the two had done what, said, 'But isn't Thornacre a mental home now?'

The drinkers said it was, that was very true. Properly run National Health Service now it was. But all the National Healths in the world couldn't stop ghosts, and there were some odd tales still told about the place. How people saw things there, and how, on certain nights, the ghost of old Jeremiah's lady was said to walk.

'Maggots an' curses an' all.'

'Oh, shut up.'

'My cousin over at Blackmere's doing a job on the heating,' said the drinker who had told about the workhouse side and the supply of children to brothels. 'Whole new central heating system they're having.'

'They're being very particular about tarting the place up because of all the stuff on the TV about it being unfit and all the rest,' put in somebody.

'That'll be that Dr Sterne,' said someone else. 'They say he's spent no end of money.'

'Spent no end of *somebody*'s money, at any rate.'

'Well, anyhow, my cousin said it was a revelation what he saw in the east wing,' said the first drinker, determinedly retrieving his share of the limelight. 'A revelation, so he said.'

'What kind of revelation?'

'Well, he had to go into the east wing, see, on account of the old piping. Miles upon miles of old piping there is, and all of it lead. He said you wouldn't believe—'

'Get to the point,' somebody grumbled.

'Well, he said in that east wing there's one room where they got people who're hardly human.'

Derisory noises greeted this and doubt was cast on the cousin's reliability as a witness to anything. 'Pissed as a fart most of the time, he is.'

'Nothing wrong with his eyes, though. He knew what he saw. They try to keep 'em hidden away, so my cousin said, but he saw them all right.'

'Your cousin couldn't trace a pig in a poke!'

'I don't know about seeing inhuman beings,' said somebody else. 'The tales you hear about Dr Sterne are enough to make your hair curl!'

'What kind of tales?' asked Oliver.

The conversation, which had earlier shown signs of drifting towards pulp videos, now took a turn in the direction of the lascivious. Women, said the drinkers nudgingly. A *lot* of women. You wouldn't believe the women Dr Sterne was believed to get through in the course of a year. There had been that court case ten, twelve months ago: female accusing him of shagging her while she was under sedation. *And* she'd described in open court what he'd done as well. Right down to the last—

'I remember the case,' said Oliver hastily. 'But wasn't it proved that the woman was hallucinating? Sterne was acquitted.'

'Tied her up and gave it to her four times without stopping, so it was said, and if that's research then I'm the King of China.'

'Balls! Nobody can do it four times without stopping.'

'My cousin over to Blackmere once did. When he was eighteen, it was.'

'Your cousin over to Blackmere can't remember what he did last week, never mind when he was eighteen!'

It was the second time Blackmere had been referred to, and Oliver thought it might be used to turn the conversation. He said, 'You mentioned Blackmere before. Where exactly is it? I'm looking around for somewhere to rent for a couple of months. Any one of the villages hereabouts would do. What's Blackmere like?'

It appeared that Blackmere was quite pretty if you liked that kind of thing. Picturesque, some people called it. It had a few houses that got let, although not generally at this time of year. Several possible addresses were offered for Oliver's consideration. Oh, and there was October House, of course, although that might be a bit large for a single gentleman. Opinions on this were divided. The owner of the place, it appeared, held weekend courses during the summer for people wanting to try their hand at firing pots, him being a potter with a proper studio and kilns and all. He made a good thing out of it if all you heard was right. But he was off lecturing at the moment, and somebody had said the house was available.

Damn, thought Oliver, ready to start again.

'No, that's not right,' put in the drinker with the cousin. 'October House was taken a month ago. I know that for a fact.'

'Ah.' Oliver waited.

'Somebody from London took it. Woman on her own – a widow with a son just died. Come up here to get over it. She's something to do with publishing in London, they say. Children's books, it is.'

Oliver said in an expressionless voice, 'It sounds an interesting village anyway. I might drive out there after the Christmas break. Same again all round?'

To begin with, Dan had found the work for Thalia Caudle absorbing.

The first few days in October House had not been so very remarkable. Dan had been watchful and guarded; he had searched the house as far as he dared on the few occasions when Thalia had been out, but he had found nothing. Thalia had made no reference to Imogen or to Thornacre; Dan wondered if this in itself was suspicious. But he thought that while he was here, Thalia was not very likely to put in motion any evil plot against Imogen. And with the framing of this thought, Dan at once began to doubt whether Thalia had any evil plot in mind at all. Would anyone with villainous intent invite a co-writer-cum-lover to the house? Did that mean that Thalia had no villainous intent after all? Yes, but what about the head? demanded Dan's inner voice. Don't forget the head in the deep freeze. I'm not forgetting it, said Dan, crossly.

Whether Thalia had any malevolent intent or not, the first priority was to gain her trust. Dan thought he probably had that already, but it would not hurt to make sure. After that he might go out to Thornacre himself and assess the situation there. And see Imogen again, remarked the sneaky inner voice. Well, all right, it would not be a hardship to see Imogen again.

First things first, then. He drew up a strict work schedule. For the first couple of days he would collate and arrange what Thalia had done. After that he would compile a report recommending different forms in which the legends could be presented: in book-form or anthology, as straight fiction, or as educational books. There could be subdivisions relating to links with genuine historical events and persons, and also suggestions as to which legends lent themselves best to illustrations. That would probably take two or three days, and he would end by mapping out areas for future research. They would probably not actually travel anywhere which would be time-consuming, but they could note down villages and towns of interest, and list local historical societies Thalia might approach, or National Trust centres which should be visited. Locally written leaflets about little-known fragments of lore could often be found in such places. They could use the local phone directory and various tourist guides to help them, said Dan, becoming more and more interested.

But if the work was absorbing, the nights were alarming. Dan had known that this was the unspoken part of their agreement, and he had been prepared for it. He did not like Thalia very much; he was even slightly afraid of her and he was sickened every time he remembered what he had found in the Great Portland Street flat. But she was attractive and companionable and easy to be with; he had actually felt rather pleased to walk into a motorway restaurant for a break during the journey here, and then later into a pub where they had lunch. She was no raving beauty, but she was unusual-looking, and most people, having looked once, looked a second time at her. And feeling sickened at what he had found in London did not seem to be affecting his physical responses. He tried to analyse this and thought it was because he was identifying Thalia so strongly with Margot, and the opportunity to explore Margot's dark seductive mind, to talk to the person he had created and to share her bed, was irresistible. He would defy any writer confronted with one of his characters in the flesh *not* to succumb to that lure! Imagine Tolstoy talking to Anna, or Shakespeare to Lady Mac, or Miss Austen drinking sherry with Mr Darcy. Dan jotted the idea down to be used for something or other sometime or other, and returned to *The Lay of the Last Minstrel* which, considering his own situation up here, struck him as apt.

Each night, with the work finished and a meal eaten and wine drunk; with the curtains drawn against the bleak northern nights and a single muted light illuminating the room, he was drawn helplessly down into a sensuous shadowland place where nothing existed save the whisper of skin on skin, and where little silk-mittened, velvet cat-claws travelled across his body, sometimes scratching and drawing blood, and where tongues and teeth licked and bit, and bodies jerked into helpless and frequently exhausted climaxes.

But even while his body was reacting with such violent arousal, even while his mind was drinking in Margot's strong invisible aura, he was aware that Thalia or Margot – or perhaps both of them – were edging him nearer and nearer to the line that divided intimacy and perversion. It was so far so good, thought Dan, but if there should be any attempt to drag him over that line he would baulk and then the spell would shatter. It would no longer be a question of, 'Then exercise your craft and your sullen art in the still night, Lady,' or even, 'Down, wanton, down.' It would be more a case of, Let me get the hell out of here.

But nobody tried to drag anybody anywhere. Nobody crossed any Rubicons and nobody forded any rivers – Jordan or otherwise. The allotted week slid into ten days almost without him minding.

And then, on the night before he was intending to leave, with his case packed in the hall, and a farewell supper eaten, she caught him with a ruse so ridiculously simple that Dan did not see through it until it was too late. Something caught in one of the attics, she had said, coming into the kitchen where Dan was pouring the coffee to drink after their meal. Something fluttering about up there. A bird, probably. Poor thing. She had sounded indifferent.

'We ought to let it out,' Dan said, looking up. 'If it's trapped it'll die.'

'All right. Will you do it or shall I?'

She had known, the bitch, that he would offer to do it. She had known he would go up to the dark gusty attic in the dark, taking a strong torch, treading warily and softly up the narrow creaking stair, trying not to alarm the bird or the squirrel or the baby owl that might be trapped and flapping about.

She had followed him, and as he stood in the attic doorway she had given him a sudden hard push – her hands had been strong and he had been taken off guard and off balance. He had fallen forward, and before he could right himself, she had slammed the attic door hard.

There was a grating sound as the lock turned and then there was the sound of a bolt sliding home. As Thalia went back down the narrow stairs, her mad laughter filled the dark attic.

Manipulating Dan Tudor, and finally trapping him, had been immensely exciting.

Thalia had been drugging him ever since his arrival in order to take the edge off his awareness and quench any suspicions he might have. She had done it carefully and subtly and he had not guessed. John Shilling had prescribed the sedatives when Edmund died to help her sleep, and Thalia had given Dan a double measure each night, crushing the pills in soup or in their after-supper coffee. Once or twice he had looked vaguely disoriented, and once or twice he had appeared to lose the thread of a conversation, but that was all. It had certainly not blunted his sexual awareness.

The work he had done on the folk legends was brilliant; after he was dead it could be presented as Thalia's own, which would give authenticity to her excuse for being in Northumberland.

With Dan safely locked up, she would sleep in the bed that would be Edmund's now; in the large room where the pear tree cast its latticed shadow on the walls. She felt nearer to him there than anywhere else now.

As she drifted towards sleep, she began to plan her next move, which was to find what would probably be her last accomplice. The Porter woman had served as an accomplice of sorts, she had been useful, but she was another whose usefulness was ending. Someone different was needed now; there were things that had to be done that required more physical strength than Thalia possessed and which required less squeamishness than Dan possessed. There had been a time when she had considered involving Dan but he was too fastidious. Once or twice during their times together Thalia had sensed a mental flinching.

What was needed now was a jackal, a stooge. Ideally it should be someone who could be dominated, or who could be bribed or coerced or just plain terrorised into doing what she wanted. Someone whose actions might seem a little mad to the rest of the world but who would actually have a very serious purpose indeed. And if you wanted someone whose actions would seem a little mad, where else did you look but inside a madhouse?

The best place to find her accomplice was undoubtedly Thornacre itself.

Leo was surprised to receive a phone call from Thalia Caudle, and even more surprised to learn that she was in Northumberland for a time.

'I'm travelling about and working on a project for Ingram's,' said her voice over the phone. 'A new imprint we hope to launch – I'm collecting material and conducting some research.'

'Interesting.'

'Yes, it is. But also,' said Thalia, purringly, 'I felt the need for a rest.' Leo felt the hairs on the back of his neck prickle. A carnivorous lady, this one. But he remembered that she had been active on one or two fund-raising committees, and that she had given a great deal of help to the student counselling group attached to one of the London universities. He remembered Thornacre's many needs, some of which the Health Service might supply, others which it would not. Was Thalia Caudle likely to be of some use here?

And so although the instinctive response was to get rid of the wretched woman as quickly as possible, he forced his tone into the soft, blurred note that most females apparently found intriguing, and said, 'I recall that you've had some tragedy in your life recently, Mrs Caudle, and I'm sorry for it. But work and play combined is a good recipe for forgetting.'

'You think so, Dr Sterne?'

'Certainly. The only thing to do with tragedy is to overlay it with other things. To build a bridge away from it. Several bridges, if possible. And work – especially if it's interesting work – is always a very good bridge.' Leo waited. Thalia Caudle was not ringing him up to ask his advice about coping with bereavement.

'I've taken a house in Blackmere,' said Thalia. 'It seemed as good a base as any, and also . . .' A slight hesitation. 'Also,' said Thalia, 'I hoped I could see Imogen. I've been concerned – we all have. Has there been any improvement?'

'Not yet.'

'She's still – asleep?'

'Yes.'

'I wondered,' said Thalia, 'whether I could – could I visit Imogen over Christmas? It seems dreadful not to when I'm near, even though she won't be aware.'

Leo thought quickly. There was no real reason why Imogen's family should not visit her; in fact there was every reason why they should. He quenched the faint, unreasonable flicker of distrust, and said, 'Yes, of course you can visit her, Mrs Caudle. The patients are having a Christmas lunch at one o'clock. You would be very welcome to come along and join that.'

'Thank you.'

'We'll expect you at around twelve thirty then.' Leo forced himself to add, 'I shall look forward to meeting you again.' He waited for her to say, 'Oh, and so shall I, Dr Sterne,' which was usually what these ladies said.

Thalia said, crisply, 'Thank you, I will see you then.' And rang off.

There was no point in speculating about Thalia Caudle or the effect she might have on Imogen. Leo put the phone call from his mind and reached for the file of patients' notes. As he began to read and review treatments, he became absorbed, as he always did, and for a while he was able to forget Imogen and concentrate on the others: on the odd fey child Quincy, haunted by God alone knew what horrors from her early life. On scatty old Meg McCann, and how he was trying to enter her crazed world, painfully and pitifully made up of little collections of rubbish, and peopled with acquisitive monsters who wanted to take everything away from her.

There was Llewellyn Harris as well, poor, pathetic Snatcher, warped and deformed by the syphilis his mother had contracted before his birth and ignored, and which Harris had ignored as well because he had not understood. Leo was finding Harris increasingly interesting. The ugly little creature presented most of the classic signs of tertiary syphilis; he had the sore eyes and the typical outward-turning nostrils – 'opera glass' nose. Leo thought that the brain lesions had probably destroyed Harris's speech centres, but what fascinated him were the occasional glimpses of a bright, logical mind somewhere under the grunting randiness. It was glib and probably trite to conclude that Harris was being revenged on his mother by plunging his own diseased body into every female under sixty, but Leo thought it might be quite near the truth. He suspected that the Snatcher would be impotent if he was ever faced with a willing female, and several times lately he had actually toyed with the idea of an experiment, of hiring a prostitute and making Harris face his anger. Playing God again, said his mind. And what would it tell you that would be of any value?

He did not care that these poor, driftwood creatures were rough and unattractive, or that their problems were squalid, or even that sometimes they had caused their own problems. He did not mind when they were aggressive or whining or disgusting, and occasionally dangerous, and he did not mind about the vomit, the seizures, the blood-flecked foam or voided urine, or the dry white patches of stale semen on Snatcher Harris's trousers. Ten minutes in a hot shower sluiced it all away in any case.

The clean private-home patients with families and friends had never attracted him; it was the homeless and the friendless and the drop-outs whose cracked and disturbed minds he wanted to heal. The Snatcher Harrises and the Mad Megs and Quincys of the world. He wanted to find out why they were like they were and what had happened to flaw them. He wanted to enter their warped worlds and help them fight their nightmares and slay their dragons.

And when their blind need of him fell about his shoulders like Dante's cloak of lead, and when there was not enough money to do all the things he knew ought to be done – at Thornacre and everywhere else – he still had the sudden energy, the unpredictable sunbursts of magnetic radiance that could make up for hours and weeks of profitless study or discouraging work. When that happened it was as heady as pure oxygen and so violently satisfying it was like a mental orgasm.

Mental orgasm. Imogen. Full circle once more.

He got up to put the files away and, leaving his office, crossed the deserted hall and went up to Imogen's room. As long as his feelings for her did not cross the line into real sexual awareness, as long as the mental orgasm did not become physical and Svengali did not turn into Baron Frankenstein, it would be all right.

Svengali . . . An idea began to form in Leo's mind.

Chapter Twenty-five

Quincy had never gone back to the east wing, and she had never told anyone what she had seen there.

She had not even told Dr Sterne when he found her later that day, huddled in a frightened little ball in a corner of Imogen's room. He was so kind that she had wanted to cry, only she had not dared because if she had started she might never have stopped.

The words *ogre* and *giant* could never be said aloud, not under any circumstances. If you said things out loud it could make them real, and if she was not very careful the creatures she had seen beyond the black iron door would break loose; they would come stamping and shouting out, snatching people up as they came and carrying them off to do bad things to them.

Once upon a time, there had been a lot of ogres and giants in the world; they had walked about openly and everybody had known who they were and been able to keep out of their way. But they had become secretive over the years and they had gone into hiding. Probably there were hundreds of hiding places all over England and all over the world, and she had found one of them by mistake.

Dr Sterne had not forced her to tell him what had frightened her, not then and not since. He had smiled the nice smile and said he understood that some things were better not said aloud. But whatever it was, she might try drawing it sometime, he said. Drawing did not count in the way telling counted, did she remember about that? And he would rather like to see her pictures of whatever had upset her so much.

This was a good idea. Quincy had drawn the Cattersis-beast several times and nothing bad had happened; in fact Dr Sterne had been interested in the drawings. He had studied them and talked about them as if they were important. He had said she had a very great gift; perhaps quite soon they might talk about her having proper lessons and learning about techniques and the draughtsmanship of drawing, and about all the famous people in history who had painted beautiful pictures. And there was what was called commercial art as well: book illustrations and record sleeves, and posters and advertisements. People could make a living from such things, did she know that?

Quincy did know it, of course, but she also knew that it was not the kind of thing that anyone from Bolt Place ever did. In Bolt Place drawing and painting had been silly time-wasting, not work at all. Why don't you do something useful? Mother had said. Quincy could not explain this to Dr Sterne, but the idea of learning about painting and drawing was the most entrancing thing in the world.

It was while Quincy was sitting by Imogen's bed that Dr Sterne came in to talk to her. He sat on the other side of Imogen – Quincy felt as if they were both guarding Imogen which was a very good thought – and he explained that he had had an idea for a new treatment. It was something that might help him to reach down into Imogen's mind and wake her, he said. It might not work but it was worth trying. The thing was that he needed Quincy's help.

Quincy would have done anything in the world to help Imogen wake up. She said so at once and waited to hear what Dr Sterne's idea might be.

'I want you to take Imogen's hand, and try to see the world she's in,' said Leo, and he looked at her so intently that Quincy had the oddest idea that he was seeing into her mind. 'And then I want you to draw it for me.'

They stayed in Imogen's room to try out the idea. Dr Sterne put some very gentle music on. Quincy did not know the name of it, but he said it was the kind of music that would make her think of drowsy summer afternoons with bees humming over scented roses, and of winter nights by the fireside, with frost outside and the stars sharp and clear against a black black sky, and a series of footsteps all neatly printed in the crispy snow, one after the other, going on and on. She would see all these things just listening to the music, he said, but most of all she would see the footsteps, and they would go on and on and on. She must concentrate on them, crisp, even footprints that went forward and forward and on and on and up and up . . .

He gave her an injection of something as well – a long word that Quincy did not know. The injection did not hurt and the music was lovely, like rippling silk being drawn across your mind. Quincy took Imogen's hand, and felt herself tumbling down and down.

There was a moment of black velvet nothingness, an overwhelming absence of sight and sound and feeling, and a tiny shred of panic uncurled in Quincy's mind. I'm failing. And then there was the faintest ripple of something, and a tug of response – Imogen? – and then she was there.

She was at the centre of an ancient forest where it was never quite day and never quite night. To begin with, the pouring blue and purple shadows were blurred, but after a few minutes they grew clearer. That might be the injection or the music, or it might just be that she was getting used to the dimness. The secret forest was an old, old place, it might be a hundred years old, or even a thousand. You could feel the oldness and you could smell it. On the ground were pools of misty green light, like the dark cloudy water you saw in old stone-edged ponds, and scattered about were broken marble statues with moss growing over them and the faces worn away. There were jumbly bits of ruined stones as well, as if once upon a time there had been a house or even a castle here, only it had crumbled away little by little over the hundreds of years, and then the forest had grown up.

The trees were very tall and in places the branches were thickly twined together so that it would be difficult to get through unless you had a hacksaw or an axe. The branches were a bit frightening; they were like long poking fingers that would reach down and brush your face and tangle in your hair as you walked under them. The tree trunks were knobbly and twisted and harsh – Quincy thought the word was *gnarled*, and the gnarling looked like faces, and some of the faces were solemn and wise but others were leery and sly.

Imogen was at the very heart of the forest. Quincy could see her, half hidden in the soft, slanting rays of purple twilight pouring in from above. She was lying on the ground with thick moss under her head and trailing ivy tendrils all about her like a curtain. She was very quiet and very still. There were tiny pinpoints of light dancing directly over her head – Quincy thought they might be glow-worms or fireflies. As they darted to and fro they left little sprinklings of light everywhere. Beautiful. Quincy was just trying to see the patterns the firefly creatures made as they danced when someone took her hand and Dr Sterne's voice said, 'Quincy. Quincy, I think that's enough. Can you hear me? Open your eyes now, Quincy. We've done enough for today. Open your eyes and come back.'

Coming back from that enchanted forest was like being wrenched out of a wonderful dream, but Dr Sterne's voice could not be ignored, and so Quincy opened her eyes and blinked and looked around her. There was the narrow room in Thornacre, and the high, black iron bed with Imogen lying under the sheet, and the chart at the foot of the bed that told how long she had been asleep. Quincy could not read it from here, but she had heard one of the nurses say that at this rate there would soon be a hundred days on the chart.

* * *

There was no telephone listing for October House, and nothing under the name of Caudle. Oliver supposed that the phone, assuming there was one, would be registered in the name of the actual owner, and he had no idea what that was.

He looked around his small bedroom. Rain was lashing against the window panes but in here it was warm and safe. It was nearly the shortest day of the year; a day when you wanted to draw the curtains, curl up in front of a warm fire, and shut out the cold and the encroaching dark. He remembered that it was Christmas Day.

It could not be helped. Oliver shrugged himself into a duffel coat, wound a scarf round his neck, found his glasses for driving, and went down the stairs. From the bar came the sounds of revelry, and in the small oak-beamed dining room several family parties were assembling. The entire ground floor was redolent with the scent of cooking. Roast turkey and all its accompaniments.

His car had been standing outside in the rain for a good eighteen hours and it took a bit of starting. Oliver blew on his hands for warmth, banged the accelerator down hopefully a few times, and at length the engine chugged into life.

A thin, icy rain was falling as he drove out of Thornacre, and every house he passed had lights burning at the windows. Each one was a tiny lit stage, with families in varying stages of Christmas celebrations: tables were being set for meals, and there were trees with winking lights and paper decorations inside, and holly wreaths outside on front doors. The pundits said that Christmas was a fraught time for many people, a time of tension, what with so many families being awkwardly split these days, what with single parent families and unemployment. Not everyone enjoyed spending time with relations and not everyone could afford to buy presents, or extra food. Not everyone wanted to be cooped up in the kitchen, cooking.

But driving past the houses, Oliver had only the impression of happiness and warmth and normality in each one.

He and Dan had almost always been together at Christmas, either in London, meeting Dan's friends, some of whom Oliver knew, most of whom he liked; or in Oxford, where Oliver's colleagues would include him and Dan in family meals. It suddenly felt vastly and painfully wrong to be out here like this, completely alone. However much you enjoyed solitude and your own company, if you were alone on Christmas Day you felt wrong. You felt isolated. Oliver liked his own company; he was used to being on his own and comfortable about it, but now he felt appallingly lonely. He should have turned this whole thing over to the police at the beginning. He was mad to be out here on Christmas Day, chasing a wild goose or a mare's nest through a driving rainstorm.

He nearly missed October House, but Blackmere was even tinier than Thornacre village and there were only a very few houses that met the description. Oliver eliminated them carefully as he drove. But when he finally found the wrought-iron gates with the stone pillars and the carved sign that said October House, the place looked deserted. Oliver parked on the grass verge and walked back to the gates. The rain was edged with ice now as if it was turning to sleet, and he hunched his shoulders against it and dug his hands into his coat pockets.

The gates were uncompromisingly locked and they were high and strong. There was a high brick wall and a thick hedge. Oliver contemplated climbing over the gates and decided against it. There was no legitimate reason for committing trespass; there were any number of reasons why Thalia Caudle should have taken a house up here, the most obvious and innocent being to visit the girl who was in Thornacre. If that was the case, Thalia had almost certainly gone to Thornacre itself to spend Christmas Day there. Oliver tried to remember if Juliette had said how old the girl was, and thought she had not.

The only thing to do was to return to the Black Boar and

296

get through the rest of Christmas Day. He would come back here tomorrow or the day after. Perhaps he could leave a note, asking Thalia Caudle to contact him at the Black Boar. Yes, that was a good idea. There was a postbox set into the gate. He could say quite openly that he was looking for his brother who seemed to have vanished, and that the trail had led him up here. In the meantime, he would have to make sure that it really was Thalia Caudle who was living up here. The local post office or village shop might tell him.

The visibility on the way back was even worse. Oliver hunched over the wheel, peering through the dark afternoon and the lashing rain. His glasses wouldn't stay put and he had to keep pushing them back up, which was a nuisance. What with that and continually having to wipe condensation off the windscreen it would be easy to miss a turning here, in fact he was beginning to think he had missed it. Yes, he had come too far along this road, which meant he had to turn round somehow and go back. Damn.

It was as he was reversing cautiously into a side road that the car's headlights picked out the sign on the grass verge. 'Thornacre House. Private road.'

Dan's nightmare mansion.

Oliver looked at it for a moment, and then swung the steering wheel across and turned towards it.

The malevolent ugliness of the real thing was like a sharp, jabbing blow under his ribs. Oliver stopped the car abruptly and sat staring up at the house. A cold darkness eeled around his mind.

Thornacre House was a grim place, even viewed from the road through a silver beaded curtain of rain and through the old trees that had grown up around it. Oliver stared at it and thought: how did Dan describe it so accurately? There were the ill-proportioned wings, the eastern one larger than the west, and there was the humped roofline, giving the place a lumpish, grotesque appearance, as if a hunchbacked giant was crawling across the landscape on all fours. It was an ogre's castle, it was Macbeth's ruinous Dunsinane or Bram Stoker's Carfax Abbey.

And it was Rosamund's sea fortress on the jutting rock face. There to one side was the haunted west wing which Dan had used for chapter fifteen, in which Rosamund, with the companion who had determinedly and faithfully accompanied her, had hidden from the blood-hungering Margot. Dan appeared to have created this companion as a kind of female second lead, a back-up heroine to keep the reader's interest during Rosamund's long inactivity; he had made her a distant cousin of the family, a girl who had been callously abandoned by her husband and who was therefore broke and glad of a bit of practical help. Oliver thought she was rather an interesting character. He suspected that Dan was quite fond of her.

Dan had described his house's history in the same chapter: how its origins went back and back like twisted black roots into the ancient Anglo-Saxon kingdom that had once been called Bernicia. Thornycroft Hill had been a sea fortress, and of course Thornacre was miles from the North Sea and there was no rock face within view. No, but the barren wastes of the Northumberland landscape were here, said Oliver's mind. And the desolate, rolling moors of Bernicia, where the ancient beasts of paganism and myth once prowled and from the look of this place might still do so.

He switched the ignition on again and reversed erratically down the narrow road, back to the Black Boar.

He shied away from going into the inn's crowded dining room or the bar, even though the landlord was encouraging about the degree of conviviality that he would find if he did so.

'You'd be made welcome at any of the tables, Dr Tudor, that I do know.'

'It's very kind, but I'd rather not.'

'A few games laid on after everyone's eaten, and a bit of a sing-song – good fun it'll be.'

Dan would probably have entered into the spirit of the celebrations with enthusiasm and discovered a few kindred spirits among the people in the dining room – he might have discovered a female companion to spend the night with as well. In any event, he would have enjoyed the motley group of people. But to Oliver the prospect was terrifying. He thanked the landlord but said he would prefer to go up to his room, and asked if it would be possible to have a tray of food sent up. 'Anything will do – I don't want to put your kitchen staff to trouble. An omelette, or even soup and sandwiches . . .

But the landlord was genuinely horrified at the idea of anyone dining off sandwiches on Christmas Day. Oliver had barely had time to don a dry shirt and was still towelling his hair from the rain when there was a knock on the door and a tray appeared, laden with a plateful of sliced turkey which was flanked with roast and creamed potatoes, Brussels sprouts, cranberry sauce, and buttered carrots. A generous helping of plum pudding lay under a lidded dish, with brandy sauce, and whoever had set the tray had dug out a bottle of claret which was apparently presented with the landlord's compliments.

'Thank you very much,' said Oliver, helplessly.

The little waitress asked if there was anything else she could do. Did he need any help to dry his hair – shockingly wet he'd got, hadn't he?

'No, truly, I can manage perfectly well.'

'I've got a hair dryer – my room's only up the stair. My name's Michelle, by the way.'

'It's very kind of you, Michelle, but I really won't trouble you.'

It was nice of the little waitress to offer the loan of a hair dryer. Oliver remembered that northern people were supposed to be famous for their hospitality. Here was proof.

He finished towelling his hair dry, and set the pages of manuscript on the small table under the window. He found his glasses, and while he ate the very good Christmas food, he went on reading Dan's book. He thought it was good. He thought this was a publishable, potentially successful book. If Dan never reappeared – this was a truly appalling idea, but it had better be faced – if Dan never reappeared, Oliver would try to get the book published for him. He had himself written and had published a couple of academic textbooks, one about Lady Jane Grey and one about the early years of Elizabeth Tudor. They had been scholarly and there had been much cross-referencing and considerable listings of various primary sources. The indexing had taken nearly as long to sort out as the actual writing, and Oliver had enjoyed it all immensely. But he had absolutely no idea how you went about getting fiction published. Dan's agent would be the person to ask, of course. He read on, increasingly absorbed.

A second waitress collected the tray midway through the afternoon. She seemed inclined to linger, smoothing down the bed, which as far as Oliver could tell did not need smoothing down, and perching on it while she asked if he was having a nice time and whether he would maybe like a bit of company for an hour or so.

The staff here really were enormously friendly, although the fact of it being Christmas Day might have something to do with it. Even so, he must remember to express his appreciation to the landlord when he checked out. But for the moment he did not want any company; he wanted to get through this wretched Christmas Day as quickly as possible and reach a time when he could investigate October House. In the meantime, he wanted to finish reading Dan's manuscript. He said, as politely as possible, that he had a great deal of work to do. The waitress seemed to find this a matter for regret. If he should want anything, she said, anything at all, he must ring the bell and ask. He might like to ask for her personally; her name was Sharon.

'I'll remember,' said Oliver firmly, and held the door open so that she could manipulate the tray.

Dan's Rosamund and the companion-cum-friend, Anne-Marie, were being drawn deeper into the web of intrigue. Anne-Marie had been enticed away by the evil Margot and her fate was still uncertain, although if Margot's track record was anything to go by, it would be unpleasant. She was locked up in a dank wash house adjoining Margot's house which, in the best tradition of these things, was a rather isolated place, surrounded by trees. October House, thought Oliver, with the familiar chill. This was reporting before the event, not after it.

He paused, and glanced towards the uncurtained window. Rain was driving against the glass again, and even at four o'clock in the afternoon it was necessary to have the lights on. He shivered and got up to draw the curtains. The radiator could apparently be turned up or down, but Oliver knew from experience that the minute you touched a radiator something fell off or started to leak or even rendered the entire system out of order, and so he left it alone. There was a small two-bar electric fire which he switched on, and there was also a drain of claret left in the bottle. He poured this out, and with the room filling up with warmth now, stepped back into Dan's remarkable story.

Anne-Marie was safely hidden and Margot was intending to wait for the hue and cry surrounding the girl's disappearance to die down before going for Rosamund. In the meantime, she was considering the idea of an accomplice.

Oliver paused before turning the page. What kind of accomplice would Dan have given his archvillainess? That traditional witch's familiar, a dwarf? Or maybe a deaf mute so that he could not betray her if things went wrong. Assuming that things did go wrong. Dan would undoubtedly give this contemporary fairy story the correct, moral ending, which meant that Margot could not be allowed to get away with any of her evil. It was remarkable how strongly Margot came off the page and took shape in the small bedroom. Oliver thought Dan might have had a bit of trouble controlling her, and then pushed this rather sinister thought firmly away.

While Margot was weighing ways and means and considering who to inveigle to her side, the venal Dr Bentinck moved centre stage. Dan had written a scene where Bentinck sat at Rosamund's bedside, projecting his rather warped lusts on to her, turning back the sheets with slow, sensuous anticipation, and feasting his eyes on her near naked form. It was curiously distasteful to read about Bentinck slavering over the unconscious Rosamund, but Oliver recognised this for an obligatory passage of raunchy sex. He was pleased to find there was no rape, although Dan had allowed the man a few caresses, dwelling chastely on tip-tilted breasts and slender thighs seen through transparent silk, all of which twisted Bentinck's face with agonised desire and then sent him stumbling from Rosamund's room in a state that Dan described as 'perpendicular with lust'. Bentinck, whom Oliver heartily disliked by this time, went hotfoot and steaming-loined into the nearest town to seek out a wine bar where girls were to be had for the asking. He found the wine bar all right, it was a kind of poor man's Soho strip joint, pulsating with throbbing rock music and leather-jacketed, mini-skirted girls on the prowl. It sounded a bit sordid; Oliver would not have been seen dead in such a place and hoped Dan would not either, but it suited Bentinck very well. He downed several large brandies before approaching a female with a passing resemblance to Rosamund and persuading her into the back seat of his car. Oliver was very glad indeed that when it came to the crunch Bentinck had drunk too much to give a good account of himself (in fact to give any account of himself at all), and was beginning to feel sick from the brandy. The girl was raucously insulting about his stubbornly soft manhood but at least she got out of the car before Bentinck was sick over himself. Oliver was pleased that Dan had given the slimy doctor such a humiliating experience.

Chapter Twenty-six

On Christmas Day Mrs Caudle came to visit Imogen. Quincy had not known she was coming, and the first she knew about it was when Porter-Pig said in a false, bright, won't-that-be-nice voice that they would be having a visitor at their Christmas dinner.

Mrs Caudle was very friendly and Quincy began to wonder if she could have dreamed seeing her in the graveyard that day, talking to her dead son and gloating because Imogen's mother had been buried alive and because Imogen had been shut away in Briar House. Mrs Caudle talked to all the people at her table while they ate, and said she enjoyed her lunch very much indeed. She had never tasted such good plum pudding, she said. She had brought presents as well: the most beautiful cream silk dressing gown for Imogen, and boxes of biscuits and chocolates for the other patients. There were bottles of sherry for the nurses. For Quincy, whom Mrs Caudle said she remembered from Briar House, she had brought a thick drawing block, a really good one, with what Mrs Caudle said was hand-milled paper. With it was a box of watercolour crayons – aquarelle crayons, they were called, said Mrs Caudle; professional artists often used them for outdoor work. She had heard all about how Quincy had come to Thornacre with Imogen – Matron Porter had told her – and she thought it was very kind and loyal. Mrs Caudle had heard from Dr Sterne that Quincy was something of an artist and the Christmas present was a small thank you from Imogen's family.

But later on, when Mrs Caudle leaned over Imogen's bed and took her hand, Quincy knew that nothing was really any different. Mrs Caudle hated Imogen, just as she had done in London. And then quite suddenly Quincy understood.

Mrs Caudle was one of the giants, she was a female ogre. As soon as Quincy saw it, she did not know why she had not seen it before, because although her disguise was very good, she was unmistakably an ogress, exactly like the ones in the east wing. She had put on a human mask and human clothes and crept up out of her own world into Thornacre.

The invitation for Quincy to go out to tea with Mrs Caudle came as a surprise. At first Quincy was not quite sure what was meant; tea in Bolt Place had meant your evening meal – beefburgers and chips, or fishcakes or sausages. In Briar House and Thornacre it was called supper and you ate it later, so that tea happened at five o'clock and was a cup of tea and a biscuit, or bread and jam or honey. Quincy listened carefully to find out, and it appeared that Mrs Caudle meant this second kind. There was a rather nice tea shop in the village where she was staying; they had very good homemade scones and jam, and there was a small art gallery attached. On the day after Boxing Day there was to be an exhibition of paintings by local artists, and perhaps Quincy would like to go to the gallery to see the paintings. It would be a way of repaying some of Quincy's kindness to Imogen, what did Quincy think?

What Quincy thought was that this was exactly what giants and ogresses did. They pretended to be kind and they promised you treats, and then, when they had got you in their houses, they locked all the doors and leapt on you and did bad things to you. She did not want to go out to tea with Mrs Caudle at all because she was Imogen's enemy – Quincy knew this definitely, and she was frightened. But it might be a way of finding out what Mrs Caudle was plotting.

There was that thing about knowing your enemy and if she could find out what was going on she might be able to explain it to Dr Sterne. She would not tell him yet; she would wait until she had something definite. Evidence, it was called. She would go out to tea and she would try to get evidence so that everyone knew about Mrs Caudle, and then Imogen would be safe.

The mention of paintings was intriguing; it might be a big pretence or it might be real. Quincy had never been to a place where you could look at paintings, and she wanted to very much. And probably she would be safe in a tea shop and painting place because there would be other people there. She looked at Dr Sterne for guidance and saw him smile and nod slightly. So she said to Mrs Caudle that she would like to go out to tea and she would like to see the paintings, and thank you very much. She tried to say it how Imogen would have said it but it did not really sound right.

Mrs Caudle said she would look forward to their little expedition. Would half past two be a convenient time? Half past two the day after tomorrow.

Mrs Caudle turned back to Dr Sterne then and Quincy had the feeling of being dismissed. This was perfectly all right; she would do some more drawings of Imogen's secret forest, which was the next best thing to being there herself. Dr Sterne would look at them later on.

Leo thought he had managed to hide his impatience with Thalia Caudle. To do the woman justice she seemed genuinely interested in Thornacre's work; she had asked if it might be possible to see more of the place after lunch. She had done a little work among the mentally sick in London, she said, only a very little, and mostly it had been to do with fund-raising. But she would be interested to see some of the methods used here and it might be that she could be of some help. She supposed, she said, with a slightly ironic glance at Leo, that Thornacre was not averse to accepting donations.

305

'Good God, we'll take anything anyone offers,' said Leo at once. 'I'll give you a list of Thornacre's most pressing needs here and now, if you like.' He smiled at her. 'If you've really got time to spare, we could have a potted tour now.'

They started in the dayroom, which Leo had tried to brighten up but which was still furnished with cast-off chairs and tables, and curtains that did not draw properly, and a rattling old radiator that did not give out very much heat. The new heating system was still being installed. A plumbing firm from Blackmere had been given the job, but they were not very efficient and they were taking a long time over it.

Some of the patients were sitting vacantly in front of the television where they had been put, which infuriated Leo and was a painful reminder of his first sight of Thornacre's patients: most of them systematically drugged into stupors, almost all of them dumped, sacklike, in unheated rooms or left in bleak corridors. He switched the television off angrily. But at least some of the patients were seated at one of the large tables, drawing or making plasticine models or playing draughts.

The wretched Porter woman came steaming in within minutes, of course. She switched the television on again, saying it was a shame to turn it off, it was nice for the patients to watch, it perked them up no end, and it was really quite a tonic to see them laugh at some of the comedy programmes or the cartoons.

Leo had told her that the set was to be kept off, except for the designated programmes, mostly during the evening. He had explained that when the patients laughed, they were almost always copying someone laughing on the television, and that he wanted to stimulate their minds and make them think for themselves, but she had either not understood or forgotten. He was losing patience with her fast; the nurses did not like her much – Leo had heard them making up

306

rude limericks about her when she was out of hearing – and he had almost decided that she would have to go. She would not be any loss to anyone.

Thalia Caudle seemed genuinely interested in everything. She asked to see the work that was going on at the large table: messy painting with thick, primary-colour pots of poster paint on acrylic boards, and the making of scrapbooks and flower montages. Leo was trying to get some of the more withdrawn ones to illustrate their fears, in the way that Quincy could sometimes do, although none of the others had a hundredth part of Quincy's talent. But some of them were responding to using colours or fabrics or even dried flowers, which was encouraging. Sometimes he made them join in loud sing-songs – one of the nurses played the piano – and held little talent competitions at which the patients could sing or recite. Two of the therapists had even started a small writers' group, encouraging patients to read aloud stories they had written and persuading the others to listen and comment. Leo had been very pleased, both with the modest success of this and with the therapists' initiative in setting it up.

Thalia listened – really listened, Leo admitted – and made a few comments. Her attention seemed particularly taken by Mad Meg McCann and Snatcher Harris. 'Our two longest inmates,' said Porter, as proudly as if this was a geriatric home where longevity was praiseworthy.

'Really?' said Thalia, politely. 'What about Meg's foraging expeditions? Are they official?'

'Well, we probably aren't as strict about Meg as we should be,' said Leo. 'But she doesn't do any harm when she wanders off and she always comes back.'

'Loaded with new bags of rubbish?'

'Yes, I'm afraid so. We're trying to ration her to a few possessions at a time – she derives security from them. We're trying to find other ways to make her feel secure, but it's a long job.'

307

'Dr Sterne is so patient,' said Matron Porter. 'I tell my nurses we're lucky to be working with him.'

'I'm sure you are.' Thalia looked thoughtfully at Snatcher Harris who was leering at her. 'I find that an interesting case as well, Dr Sterne. Has he always been like this?'

'Probably,' said Leo. 'We're working on him but I suspect the speech centres of his brain were damaged, or simply weren't developed fully, before birth. I think that he actually understands more than he lets on, the old rogue.'

Freda Porter said archly, 'I think we underestimate our Llewellyn. We shall have him reading Shakespeare before long, shan't we, Dr Sterne?'

Leo ignored this and said to Thalia, 'By rights Harris oughtn't to be here at all. He's more handicapped than mentally ill but we inherited him and we'll do what we can. I don't think he's ever known another home, so it would be cruel to uproot him.'

'An unusual case,' said Thalia, and then looked at Leo. 'But then I believe you have several extremely unusual patients here.'

Leo felt the hackles rise on the back of his neck, and the expression 'freak hunter' slid into his mind. He said, 'We have many different cases here, Mrs Caudle. They all have their stories. But I daresay there are some greatly exaggerated tales told about some of them in the village.' He looked at her carefully. 'There are certain slightly freakish conditions that most people would deny exist any longer.'

'But they do exist?'

'Oh yes. Any doctor or nurse will tell you that they see some very strange things from time to time.' Choosing his words very carefully, Leo said, 'Some pitiful and very ancient diseases, which have plagued mankind over the centuries, occasionally do still recur. In remote country areas like this one, where old-fashioned beliefs still hold, or where there's ignorance, that can lead to some colourful stories.' A pause. 'Have you ever heard of acromegaly, Mrs Caudle?'

'I don't believe so. What is it?'

'A rather grotesque condition that produces excessive symmetrical growth of the bones, particularly the limbs and the face. In children it's called gigantism.'

'It sounds appalling.'

'It's usually due to over-functioning of the pituitary gland – to exorbitant production of a growth-stimulating hormone, often from a benign tumour within the pituitary. There's sometimes an imbalance of the secondary sex characteristics as well, so you get coarsened features. There might be some bearding of the females, and sometimes there's what's known as masking. That's a kind of blank, stony stare – unnerving unless you know what it is, and sometimes unnerving even when you do.'

Thalia said in a soft voice, 'The explanation of every monstrous fairy story.'

'Possibly.'

'Is there any cure?'

'It's curable providing it's diagnosed,' said Leo. 'Sometimes micro-surgery can remove the hyper-functioning tissue. The real tragedies are if diagnosis is made late, when the effects might be difficult to reverse. Once bones are enlarged, reducing them is a problem. And once there's beard growth on the skin—'

'It's very rare?'

'Not as rare as all that,' said Leo, 'but it's rarer for it to go untreated these days, so it's not often encountered in its full-blown state. It's an ancient disease,' he said. 'I've often thought that's what was meant in the famous bit in Genesis – "There were giants in the earth in those days." There probably were.'

'And there are giants inside Thornacre today?'

A pause. Leo said lightly, 'I never break the oath of confidentiality to my patients, Mrs Caudle. And sometimes Nature's freakish tricks can be distressing to an untrained eye. Would you like to come and see our therapy wing now?

It's in what used to be the stable block. We haven't got very far with it yet but we're hoping to convert it so that the patients can learn carpentry and wood-turning. We've been promised some benches and a wood-turning lathe, and we're hoping for photographic equipment next month as well. Do come and see. I think you'll find it interesting.'

It was four o'clock when Leo managed to get free. Matron Porter was making twittering noises about afternoon tea, which was ridiculous when everyone had eaten an enormous Christmas dinner at half past one. But he was glad to leave them to it because his thoughts were already moving forward to the evening's session with Imogen.

He went quickly along to her room, his heart beating fast with anticipation, and seated himself at the head of her bed. After a moment he took her hand and, half closing his eyes, reached down into his mind until he brushed against the thin silver and gold light lying like a coiled serpent in the deepest recesses. It shivered through his mind, instantly and fiercely responsive, and Leo felt a lurch of panic. Here we go, he thought, his mind spiralling with excitement.

He grasped the thin silken coil and sent it spinning into the still, silent darkness surrounding Imogen. Come up, Imogen, and come back. Come up and up and up. Come up and out of the misty twilight woodland that that remarkable child Quincy saw and drew, come up and come back to me.

Quincy's images were printed on his mind, and he kept them firmly fixed on his inner vision. The dusk-laden forest, the lichen-crusted archways and the tangling mats of bracken and briar.

I see it! thought Leo suddenly. I see the twilit forest and the glimmering dusk! I see the ancient trees with their wise faces, and the elusive outlines of the naiads and dryads. And between the trees, darting in and out of the light, cloven-footed beings with three-cornered faces and pointed ears and gentle, sly magic . . .

Fierce excitement blazed through him in an immense charge of power, and with it a sense of awe, because it was so complete, so perfect, this secluded hiding place that Imogen had created for herself.

Confidence poured into him. He could see and he could hear and he could feel. But could he reach deep enough in to brush her mind? She's lying at the heart of it all, thought Leo. She's protected by wild woodland magic, but it's magic of her own spinning, and if only I believe, if only I can keep believing, I can enter it. And if I can enter it, I can reach her and I can wake her . . .

He gathered his entire strength and threw it forward and down. There was a sense of tremendous anticipation as if something invisible was stirring and drawing nearer, and there was a low thrumming on the air as well, as if cobweb wings were beating overhead, and then a sweet, plangent singing, as if someone was drawing a finger round and round the rim of an immense glass bowl.

Nearly there, thought Leo. I'm nearly there. Down the silver threads of his own mind, strong now and shivering with life as if they were electrically charged. Down into the heart of the uncharted amethyst dusk.

Come up out of the forest, Imogen . . .

There was a moment when the soft, sweet humming was louder and that was when Leo thought the trees parted to let him through. Imogen's eyelashes fluttered and a soft wind stirred her hair. I'm there! thought Leo. I've reached her! Come up and come out, Imogen . . .

The magical woodland shivered all about him, and the violet-edged shadows closed over Imogen's head once more.

Shutting Leo out.

Imogen knew that the ancient forest was no longer as safe as it had been. She knew that someone was coming towards her. Someone was coming through the twilight, creeping stealthily between the trees, snapping twigs with a sharp, cracking noise, shocking in that soundless twilight. Some-one was trying to reach her, to take her hand and pull her up into the light, and panic rippled through the safe, secret dusk. *Be careful, Imogen. Be careful, because something evil this way comes . . .*

The darting jack o' lanterns and the flickering marsh lights were spinning with panic, and the friendly glow-worm specks were zigzagging in alarm.

Because something's out there, something's watching and waiting and biding its evil time and rubbing its hungry hands together in anticipation . . .

Supposing that the secret forest that had hidden her was not a forest after all? Supposing it never had been a forest? Supposing it was a trick, an illusion, a cobweb make-believe?

The smoky dusk was beginning to dissolve; it was melt-ing shred by shred, like thin, gauzy fabric held over a candle flame. Quite soon she would catch glimpses of the unknown country that lay on the other side. Quite soon it might not be possible to crouch down here in the safe, warm, scented gloaming.

Quite soon now the cobwebs would be so thin that she would be able to see the glaring evil thing that was hiding on the other side.

And the glaring evil thing would be able to see her.

Chapter Twenty-seven

Quincy's outing was at a time of the day when Imogen was usually with Dr Sterne, which meant it would be safe to go. Also, she would be with Mrs Caudle, who was Imogen's enemy, and it was not possible for Mrs Caudle to hurt Imogen while she was taking Quincy to tea and to look at paintings.

She washed her hair in the morning. One of the nurses had given her a sachet of shampoo called Chestnut Glow, and helped her to use it. It had been quite easy; you just rubbed it all in and then rinsed it out and it left reddish lights. The nurse said it looked pretty – grand was the word she used, which was what people in the north sometimes said. She said why didn't Quincy let her hair grow a bit, because you could do all kinds of nice things with long hair; you could scoop it up on top of your head if you were going out somewhere special, or you could tie it back with a velvet ribbon. That was worth thinking about.

Freda Pig did not say Quincy looked grand. She said it was very odd of Mrs Caudle to be taking her out like this, upsetting all the nurses' routines, and what a shame Quincy had not anything better to wear than that blue jumper, and dear goodness what on *earth* had she done to her hair? But then that was always the trouble with cheap hair dyes, they always went wrong. Quincy was to remember her manners with Mrs Caudle and to be sure to be back for supper.

Quincy kept the blue jumper on because she had nothing else that would do, and went down to wait in the hall so as to be ready when Mrs Caudle arrived. The nurse who had helped wash her hair said this was a good thing to do, and to take no notice of Matron who was an old sourpuss; Quincy's hair looked terrific and there was nothing in the least wrong with the jumper. She was to be sure to have a nice time and eat lots of scones, and they would want to hear all about it when she got back.

Mrs Caudle came at half past two and Quincy saw at once that she was wearing her most human disguise. It was important to remember that behind it she was evil and that she was bloated with hating Imogen. It was necessary to listen and watch carefully, and get evidence to tell Dr Sterne.

But she was very kind; she made sure that Quincy was belted into the front seat of the car, and she pointed out bits of the countryside as they went. It was warm in the car because the heaters were turned on full which made Quincy feel a bit sick. It was a bit worrying to be driving through strange countryside like this.

Quincy had thought they would drive straight to the tea and painting place, but it appeared that something had to be collected from the house where Mrs Caudle was living. It would only take a minute to stop off, it was on the way, and it was important. In fact they might even have their cup of tea at the house if Quincy liked.

Quincy was beginning to feel very frightened now, and being frightened was making her feel even more sick. Mrs Caudle seemed to think the question of going to her house had been settled, and she was concentrating on driving the too-hot car; she was slightly hunched over the wheel, and you could see that the human mask had slipped a bit. You could see the slavering lips and the too-long teeth, and you could see that underneath the leather driving gloves she wore, her hands would have huge knuckles and reaching, clutching fingers.

When Mrs Caudle said, 'So we'll have our cup of tea at

the house, shall we, Quincy?' Quincy heard the slurry ogress voice and saw the grinning ogress mouth. She was very frightened indeed of going into the Caudle giant's house. In the days when the ogres had walked openly about the countryside, their houses had been littered with human hearts and livers and bones, and they sometimes hung up their victims by their hair until they were ready to gobble them up. It was in all the stories, the ones Quincy had not really believed, not until she opened the black iron door, and not until she met Thalia Caudle. But now she knew it was all true. And she was being taken to the ogress's house, which meant that Imogen would be left in Thornacre on her own.

Quincy had only ever seen houses like October House on television, and there was a moment when she was so intrigued that she nearly forgot about being frightened and about getting evidence, and stared up at it.

They had to drive up a long drive with whispering trees on each side, and the trees bent over in the wind as they went past. It would be silly to imagine that the trees were bending over to whisper to her, to tell her to run away because terrible things happened to people who went inside this house, but it was what she did imagine. *Run away as fast as you can, Quincy, run away and hide where she can't find you. Because once you're inside, once you're in the ogress's house, she'll lock you up in the dungeon and fatten you for the oven . . .*

In Bolt Place, when you went out of the house you switched off all the lights as a matter of course and returned to a darkened house, but here lights had been left burning at the windows. It ought to have been a friendly thing to see as you came up the drive, but it was not friendly at all.

Mrs Caudle smiled as she unlocked the door. There was a light over the front door as well – Quincy thought it might be what people called a carriage lamp – and it cast a reddish glow so that when Mrs Caudle smiled, her eyes shone with a red light, and Quincy could see that the human mask had gone completely. When Mrs Caudle stepped back and said, 'Come inside, my dear,' Quincy shivered, because this was what all the stories told you happened; the evil ogress lured you to a warm, welcoming house, and got you inside by pretending you were going to be given nice things. Sometimes she was already inside, waiting for you, and you had to knock on the door yourself, *toc-toc*, and then the ogress said, 'Pull the bobbin and lift the latch and step inside, my dear . . .'

Quincy drew a deep breath, ready to turn and run back down the drive with the whispering trees, but just as she was summoning up her courage, a hand came down on her arm, the fingers curling about it like steel, and a voice hissed, 'Running away, my dear? Surely not?' And the next minute the latch was lifted and the door was open, and Quincy was inside.

To begin with it was not too bad. There was the promised tea, served in china cups with the milk in a jug to match, and little squares of embroidered cotton to catch the crumbs while you ate. There were warm scones and jam, and slices of shortbread, and delicious chocolate cake. They ate and drank in a large room overlooking the drive; it had beautiful things in it. Later there was wine to drink. Quincy was not very used to wine, but she was afraid to refuse in case the Caudle giant became angry. The last thing you wanted to do was anger a giant. So she drank half a glass as slowly as possible, and Mrs Caudle knelt down in front of the hearth where a fire had been laid, and set a match to it, and said, there, wasn't this cosy.

It was not cosy at all, it was terrifying. As the flames leapt up, the room seemed to change, so that it was not a nice sitting room with ordinary chairs and tables and carpets any more, it was an ogress's lair, smelling not of the smouldering logs in the hearth and the wine but of evil magic and of old, dark enchantments. Quincy leaned back in her chair, gripping the sides.

The fire was burning up strongly, and the Caudle giant stayed there on the hearth rug for a moment, watching the flames. And then she turned her head slowly and smiled at Quincy, and Quincy felt icy terror run all over her. Yes, you could see her now for what she was; you could see that she was just like the monstrous squatting creatures behind the black iron door at Thornacre. The firelight showed up the cold glittery eyes and the slick of saliva on the ogress teeth which were large because of being all the better to gobble you up, my dear. Her voice had changed as well; it was blurred and there was a wet clottedness in it, so that you wanted to clear your throat and swallow hard.

But she only said, 'More wine, Quincy?'

'No, thank you. I don't want—'

'Just half a glass.' The wine was poured before she realised it, and it was then that the Caudle giant said, 'And now, my dear, I think it's time for you to take off your clothes.'

Quincy stared at her, thrown off balance. For the first time the fear receded a very little, and she thought, so *that's* what you want! Although it would be extremely horrid to take her clothes off and do the things that Mrs Caudle would probably want her to do, it would not be anywhere near as bad as being strung up by her hair or put into a cage and eaten. Quincy thought she would not mind so very much about going to bed like this, because it could not be any worse than Mother's pub friends with their sick-smelling breath, or the Cattersis, or the Clan.

It was a bit strange to be undressing in the living room because it was normally something you did in a bedroom or a bathroom. Quincy felt exposed and vulnerable; she had the feeling that she was being watched, and this was so strong that she looked around, almost expecting to see someone standing in the doorway. But there was no one and there was nothing, and after a moment she took a deep breath and stood up.

317

It was not very nice to be stroked all over, but it was not really too dreadful so far. Quincy had the idea that females used things on one another – Mother and her pub friends had sometimes made jokes about them, mostly to do with size and staying power – but there did not seem to be anything like this here, or if there was it was not being used yet. It seemed simply to be a question of stroking and touching, and of having her hands taken and looked at.

When Mrs Caudle said, softly, 'Come with me, my dear,' Quincy thought she meant to the bedroom, and she thought that the real business of the evening was about to begin. This would probably be when the objects would be brought out and used.

But they did not go up the stairs to the bedroom; they went down a little back stair tucked away behind the kitchen. There was a smeary light and it was hot because of being below ground. There was a dreadful smell on the air as well, like bad meat, like when you had forgotten to throw out a piece of meat and were afraid to open the cupboard or the fridge where it was, because you knew it would be a mass of weaving maggots. It was just how a giant's lair would smell.

The stairs were immensely steep; Quincy had to take huge strides to get down them, but the Caudle giant did not seem to notice. She seemed taller down here; she seemed ten feet tall and impossibly thin and she went down the huge steps with ease. Giant steps.

She led Quincy through a cellar filled with jumble – broken furniture and rusting mangles and an old copper boiler – and unlocked a little door at the far end. The bad meat stench was so thick now that Quincy felt dizzy with it, and the wine was making her head ache.

The room beyond the locked door was small and dark and filled with thick badness. Quincy stopped, trying to see what was in here, and then there was a sharp push between her shoulder blades and a torrent of mad, evil laughter. The door was slammed shut, cutting off the light, and there was the sound of the key turning. There was another peal of the mad laughter – Quincy did not know the word jubilant, but she knew the word triumphant and she knew it meant you had scored over an enemy. The Caudle giant was screeching with triumph and the sounds were cascading into the darkness. Quincy flinched and cowered back. And then above the laughter was the sound of light, quick footsteps going back through the outer cellar and up the kitchen stairs.

Quincy was locked in. She was by herself in the pitch dark with the evil stench.

Freda Porter was not especially worried when Quincy did not appear for supper, in fact she was not worried at all. It would cause her no heartache if the scrubby little creature never came back, because in her opinion far too much attention was given to Quincy, and most of it by Dr Sterne.

It had to be admitted that things with Dr Sterne were not working quite as she had hoped, although it was early days yet, of course. There was plenty of time for the cosy discussions she had visualised and the even cosier suppers afterwards. She was furnishing her sitting room with an eye to this; she had brought some of the Briar House furniture with her because no one was likely to remark its absence, and there was a nice moquette settee and a folding table which you really could not tell was not a proper antique. It was just right for an intimate little meal for two, and it was a pity that pressure of work had so far prevented Dr Sterne from accepting any of her invitations.

But what with one thing and what with another, Freda had other things to worry about than the truancy of a dirty little tramp with no consideration for anyone and no morals either. She was in fact more worried about Imogen.

It had been disconcerting to see Mrs Caudle turn up at Thornacre on Christmas Day, but Freda flattered herself that she had been equal to the situation. She had been graciously welcoming, and she had naturally gone along to join in the tour they had taken because she had known that Dr Sterne would wish her to be there.

After the tour she had invited Mrs Caudle to afternoon tea in her own rooms, because she knew what was correct on these occasions. Proper afternoon tea they'd had (one of the nurses who had nothing better to do had been told to bring in cakes and scones and be sure that the tea was freshly made and hot), and Mrs Caudle had talked with interest about everything she had seen. And if she was *checking up* on their arrangement (a nasty, sneaky thing to do, but not improbable), she would have seen for herself that their bargain was being kept, the Ingram girl was still soundly and safely unconscious. Freda thought the visit had really gone off quite well, and Dr Sterne had even said afterwards that they might hope for a donation to Thornacre's funds. His eyes had glowed with fervour when he said this, and it had made Freda feel quite hot.

The problem with Imogen was that the signs of emergence were beginning to present. The girl was coming out of the long sleep very slowly indeed, but that she was coming out was something only a half-baked trainee would have missed. Freda was very worried indeed; she was occupied with trying to think up a suspicion-free way of retarding Imogen's recovery, and it was too bad of Quincy to draw attention to herself like this.

But it was necessary to give an appearance of concern, and so Freda took the trouble to question the nurses. One of them – a bold little hussy, she was, Freda had heard nasty stories about what she did with the male orderlies in the laundry room – said it was something that occasionally happened. Despite all your care, patients gave you the slip and wandered off, she said. Mad Meg did it on average once a fortnight, and Snatcher Harris sometimes took himself out into the grounds even though he was not supposed to go out without an attendant. As far as they all knew, he had never actually got beyond the gates, said the nurse, but he always leered evilly when he came back, to make everyone think he had been having his disgusting way with a woman somewhere, the sinful old reprobate. She said this almost as if she had an affection for the revolting Harris creature, and added that Dr Sterne was considering stronger restraints for him.

Freda listened to this impassively, and did not say that if she had her way it would be the locked cell with the cardboard table and chair and sheetless bed for Master Harris before long! It was galling to think that Dr Sterne might actually have discussed a patient's treatment with such a brass-faced piece of impudence.

Sipping coffee with the off-duty nurses, which was a little ritual she had introduced because you had to fraternise occasionally and she could not be doing with nonsense like going off to cinemas and wine bars, she said they would not start to worry about Quincy quite yet. The likeliest explanation was that Mrs Caudle had kept the girl out a bit longer than had originally been planned and if that was the case it was slightly thoughtless of Mrs Caudle, but nothing worse.

The nurse who had washed Quincy's hair that morning and helped her choose the blue sweater said, but supposing it was a bit more than just thoughtlessness? She did not think Quincy would have stayed out to supper without letting somebody know, and wondered if they ought to tell Dr Sterne.

'Dear goodness, of course not.' Freda was not going to say that Dr Sterne was with Imogen and that it was more than anyone's life was worth to disturb him. But since Thornacre's supper was over, she telephoned Mrs Caudle, apologising for bothering her but explaining that there seemed to be some confusion about whether Quincy was staying out to supper. Mrs Caudle would understand that they had to keep a careful check on patients' visits outside Thornacre.

Thalia said, in a perplexed voice, 'Yes, of course I

understand. But, Matron, I dropped Quincy at Thornacre's gates more than two hours ago.'

Really? As long ago as that?

'Certainly. We had tea here – I mean at the house here. Quincy seemed to prefer it. I wanted to take her into the tea rooms in Blackmere and to look at the exhibition of paintings, I thought she would enjoy it, but when we got there she took fright. I didn't know if it was typical behaviour but I thought I shouldn't force the issue. So I played safe and brought her here. We had tea and buttered toast and scones and chocolate gateau, if you want the details, and then I drove her back. Why? Is there a problem?'

'Oh no, no problem. No, indeed there is not. Thank you so much.'

Over two hours. This looked like developing into a bit of a nuisance. Dr Sterne could be humiliatingly scathing if he thought a patient had been neglected. Quite tingly it made you feel to see him in a blazing temper, unless you were on the receiving end which Freda did not intend to be. It might be as well to be very responsible and efficient about this and so she rang the local police, explaining what had happened. It was nothing to fuss over too much; there was no need to start sending out tracker dogs or helicopters or anything like that. The child was vague and a bit out of tune with the world, but she was a lot more sensible than some of Thornacre's inmates and she would almost surely come back soon. 'But I feel quite cold, Constable, when I think of all the things that can happen to these unwary innocents,' said Freda.

The officer who took the call, and who happened to be a newly-promoted detective sergeant and therefore a bit touchy about his rank, said temperately that it was likely that the girl had simply wanted an hour or two's freedom. 'In which case she'll find her own way back, or we'll find her for you.' He made a few notes and wanted to know if

Quincy was sufficiently sensible to ask for directions or make a phone call if she should have got herself a bit lost.

'Oh yes,' said Freda. 'All our people have a little card with our address and phone number, and *quayte* sufficient money for emergencies. We are *very* careful about that, Constable.'

'Well, we'll get the various patrol cars to keep a weather eye out,' said the sergeant, and asked for a description. Small and thin and pale, medium-brown hair and grey eyes. What was she wearing?

'Does anyone know what Quincy was wearing when she went out? Nurse Carr, you know, don't you? Well, I should have thought you would have that all ready for me, you might have known I would need— Ah, a navy sweater and skirt, with a dark raincoat. Have you got that, Constable? No, a *dark* raincoat. Well, if you would circulate the description. And you'll ask about a bit in the villages? Thank you so very much.'

It was still more than Freda's life was worth to disturb Dr Sterne.

Light was pouring into Imogen's secret forest, raying out and out into the violet mists like a glittering gossamer cobweb. It was as if the portcullis to a light-filled fortress was being slowly raised, and as if soft, gentle light – like molten gold, like melted silver – was leaking and running out in little rivulets into the shadows.

For a moment Imogen could almost see it: shards of pure, clean sunlight and spikes of luminous moonlight cascading through the ancient trees, leaving little scatterings of radiance everywhere. She could feel her mind spanning the two worlds as well: one half still deep within the magic-laden enchantment where there was only the sick twilight, the other half going forward, going up, into the warm light.

There was a sudden feeling of panic and the impression of something dark and heavy hovering over her head, blotting out all the light. Something was happening. Something good? Or something bad? The evil, slavering thing creeping towards her? It was still there – Imogen could smell that it was still here, like a whiff of old evil tainting the darkness.

It was at this precise moment, with the waves of pouring sunshine lighting up the forest, that the forest itself began to crumble. The ancient enchanted wood where she thought she could hide was suddenly no longer safe. It might never have been safe in the first place. But now it was abruptly and dreadfully a sham, a pretend-place, and as soon as Imogen saw this, she knew it could no longer hide her. And as soon as she knew that, she understood it was necessary to leave it.

It was as if she had been engrossed in a marvellous play or a film, and was jerked abruptly into the realisation that the marvellous castles and the mist-wreathed isles and the cloud-capp'd towers and gorgeous palaces were plaster and timber, and that there were men behind them creating an illusion. The insubstantial pageant was fading; it was not made up of hundred-year-old bramble hedges or lichen-crusted stone archways or moss-covered paths. After all it was not a deep greenwood or a hidden thicket; it was tawdry pinchbeck and flimsy cardboard. It was a fake.

As soon as Imogen saw it for what it was, she felt the real world start to trickle in. Remembered fear and panic came with it. There were things she had run from: appalling things. Somebody trying to prove she was mad. Edmund's head at the funeral. And Quincy seeing Thalia in the graveyard, and Imogen's own nightmare journey out to the cemetery. Men digging up the grave, by torchlight. And the red raw screaming thing in the coffin, and finally, the dizzy tumble down and down into the deep purple twilight, into the enchanted bewitchment where nothing could touch you and nothing could get near enough to harm you.

The fragments whirled crazily for a moment, like too-bright jigsaw pieces that would not fit together. Imogen made a huge effort and pushed back the last clinging shreds of melting cobwebs and opened her eyes. She did not know where she was precisely; the room was unfamiliar, and there was a too-strong light in it, that hurt her eyes. There was someone in here with her, and it was someone she ought to know. In just a minute she would remember.

A soft voice was telling her she was safe and repeating her name. It was a voice you could believe – it was strong and reassuring.

Imogen said, 'Safe.' Her voice sounded dry and husky because of not having spoken for such a long time and the person with the soft reassuring voice held a cup of water to her lips. Imogen discovered she was so weak it had to be held there for her. The voice said, 'Just a few tiny sips.' There was a good scent of soap and clean skin. 'Don't try to remember yet, Imogen,' he said. 'Just think that you're safe. I'm with you, and everything's all right.'

Safe. Yes, she was safe. Or was she?

Because something had followed her down and down into the pretence-forest, and that something had hunted her there, exuding its hungry evil.

And supposing it had followed her? Supposing it was in the real world up here?

Chapter Twenty-eight

As Thalia made the now-familiar round of October House, locking doors and checking window latches, she was aware of a strong, sensuous pleasure at what she had accomplished.

The odd fey Quincy was exactly and precisely what she had been looking for. To start with she had been surprised at the ease with which she had found the child, and then not surprised at all. She had been guided to Quincy, just as she had been guided in everything else.

There had been a titillating piquancy about the brief abortive episode before the fire, the child obediently naked and apparently prepared to acquiesce in whatever was asked of her. The feeling of you-are-entirely-at-my-mercy had been amazing. Thalia had felt as if she was surrounded by an immense force-field, entirely of her own creating. I am invincible. I can do anything.

And it had been intriguing to explore this new source of sensuality. There was a piquancy in allowing her senses to be raked into arousal by the child's immature body, and the feel of Quincy's hands on her skin. A smile curved her lips. She would do it again – perhaps she would do it tomorrow night before the final glorious culmination of her plan. It would add an edge of remarkable sensuality. She would bring the girl up from the cellars, and she would force her to undress again, by the light of the fire in October House's large sitting room. She would make Quincy caress her and she would relish the child's fear and repulsion.

It was a curious sensation to be made love to by another female. It was something Thalia had never before experienced, but it was something she might want to explore more thoroughly when all this was over. Under certain conditions it could be considered inconclusive, of course, and even frustrating. But it was not frustrating to Thalia; not while she was keeping the creature in the attic alive.

Yes, tomorrow night again, for sure. She would bring Quincy up from the cellar again. It pleased her to think of the two creatures serving her sensuality: the male in the attic, the female in the cellars. Her mind spiralled with delight and anticipation.

Every time Thalia went up the attic stair she experienced a fierce surge of power. She went up tonight, her mind spiralling with delighted anticipation.

There was electricity in the attic room, but it was a single naked light bulb suspended from one of the main ceiling joists and the light it gave was harsh. Thalia did not switch it on; instead she set candles in silver holders around the room – one on the small deal table and another on the washstand where it would reflect in the small mirror. As the candles flared up soft light fell across the attic, blurring its ugliness, casting a glow over Dan's supine body. There was a dark growth of beard on his face, and his hair, badly in need of cutting, tumbled over his brow and on to the pillow. He looked like a drop-out, but it was a drop-out from the eighteenth or nineteenth century: the planes of his face were a little sharper than they had been, and he looked like one of the romantic poets – Keats dying of consumption in his garret, or Coleridge deep in an opium-sleep.

Thalia discarded the thin robe she had been wearing, turned back the blanket and slid into the bed. There was the scent of warm masculinity. She ran her hands over Dan's thighs and then slid one hand in between them. Was he aware of her? Yes, his reactions were slow, but the drugs had not entirely quenched them. Her hand enclosed him, and even out of the depths of the drugged slumber he was responding. Thalia pushed back the bedclothes and moved astride him, gripping him with her own thighs and supporting her weight on her hands. As she began to move rhythmically, time slipped for her, and the face she saw on the pillow was no longer Dan's, but Edmund's.

Dan was aware now that he had lost large sections of time, and that there were intervals when he slept deeply and not-quite-dreamlessly. Margot stalked those dreams, and sometimes she had Thalia's face and sometimes there was only a blurred pale oval surrounded by black hair. Once or twice Imogen was there as well, wavery and insubstantial. Imogen. Each time the name was like a cool reviving draught of fresh cold water. That's what this is all about, thought Dan, fighting the smothering waves of sleep. That's why I'm here.

The attic was furnished with a narrow bed, and a deal table and chair. At one end was a small kitchen unit, with a lavatory and washbasin through a partition. Dan thought the place had probably been intended as a self-contained flat for a live-in servant, or even an elderly relative or a teen-ager. He could not imagine why Thalia had tricked him up here, or why she was keeping him locked in, unless she was simply keeping him out of the way while she carried out some deep-laid plan against Imogen. The execution of her horrible desires, remember, Daniel?

After the first few days he understood that she was drugging the food she brought him, and he thought she might have been drugging him ever since he got here. He began to work out the pattern in her visits, and he began to see that the food was brought at the same hour each day, and that the strange bed-visits were made exactly two hours after the supper tray. She's only coming into the attic when she thinks I'll be too doped to try to escape, thought Dan.

She's taking a bit of a chance, in fact she's being bloody arrogant. But wasn't arrogance and vanity the hallmark of all genuinely evil people? Dan had no idea whether his villainess was genuinely evil or just plain mad, and by now he was beyond caring.

But she's plotting, he thought, drifting in and out of sleep, occasionally waking to find her in bed with him, appalled at the way she could still coax a response from him. She's plotting all the time – I can *feel* that she is. And when she moves, then I'll move as well.

He studied the food she brought him, with the idea of evading whatever drug he was being fed. Soup could be doctored with crushed tablets and so could the glasses of milk that accompanied most of the meals. Dan tipped all the soup and milk down the loo, and ate only bread, pieces of chicken, and cheese, and was careful to fake drowsiness. At least his villainess was not a mean villainess; Margot would probably have left him to die with a hunk of dry bread and a pitcher of water.

He drank water from the handbasin cold tap, sending up a prayer that it came directly from the mains and not some disgusting septic tank arrangement. And at least Thalia had not tied him up, which Margot certainly would have done.

But despite his care, some of the sedative got through, and he was not completely faking the drugged slumber. The work on the folklore project lay on a small deal table under the skylight window, and at times, by dint of dousing his head with icy-cold water from the washbasin, Dan was even sufficiently awake to spend an hour or two working on it. He thought it might be saving his sanity.

He tried the door at intervals, but it was always locked. He thought it might be possible to break the bolt by smashing a chair against the panel, but so far there was no point. If Thalia was plotting, she was doing so quietly and if Dan broke out now he would never find out what she was planning for Imogen. He would lie low for as long as Thalia lay low, and then, given strength, he would move.

The night he heard the cellar door clang was one of the nights she came into the attic, and it was one of the nights when she was merciless, flicking him into helpless arousal with her fingers and her lips, and then riding him so greedily that when she left, his body felt as raw as if it had been sandpapered.

When she finally left him he heard the church clock in Blackmere striking midnight. After a moment there was the sound of her car revving up outside, and then going down the drive towards the main road.

He was alone in October House. Or was he?

He waited until the sounds of her car faded away into the night, and then got up and pulled on a shirt and trousers and shoes. He ran the cold water tap until the water was icy, and bent over to sluice his face. It did not quite chase the lingering drug fumes away but it helped. He towelled his face roughly dry, and turned to attack the bolt.

It gave more easily than he had dared hope, although the splintering of wood and metal was so loud that he froze, expecting to hear sounds of alarm from below and running feet pounding up the attic stair. But nothing moved and everything was still and quiet. Dan drew in a shaky breath and wiped sweat from his forehead with the back of one hand. His nerves were jangling like tin cans on wires, but at least it would keep him awake.

He went cautiously out on to the tiny attic landing. The strong torch he had originally brought up to the attic had long since died and he thought he would not have dared switch it on anyway. He began to creep down the stairs and through the darkened house, listening all the time for Thalia's return. But no car engine broke the brooding silence. He looked into each of the rooms carefully. His weekend case had been slung into the back of the large hall cupboard. Dan eyed it, and then unzipped the side pocket and found his pencil torch.

The stone-flagged kitchen at the back of the house smelt faintly of cooking and herbs, and a faint warmth came from the Aga. Dan paused, trying to discern whether there was still the feeling of someone else in the house. Someone hiding somewhere? Where would anyone hide in October House? Broom cupboards, pantries, cellars? *Cellars.*

He glanced about him, and then picked up a wooden-handled chopping knife.

There was barely enough light to see the way, but Dan did not dare risk using the pencil torch yet. He certainly did not dare risk trying to find a light switch.

He felt his way down to the cellars, placing his hands on the walls for balance, feeling that they were cold and rough. He had not been down here before and he wondered fleetingly how old October House was; it appeared to have been built around the turn of the century, but it might be a much older building renovated out of recognition, or it might have been built on the site of a much older dwelling. He might be descending to the original cellars this very minute, going down into the subterranean depths of a very old building indeed. As he went down, Dan was strongly aware of the brooding darkness of the house above him.

He was still very conscious of the blanketing effects of the sedatives, and he thought it must surely be that that was making the steps seem so deep. They were the kind of steps where you needed seven-league boots – no, seven-league boots were what giants wore when they strode across the landscape scooping up flavoursome human children as they went. It was a cloak of invisibility that the hapless hero was usually given. Dan would not have minded one now.

With the framing of this thought came others, macabre fragments surfacing and nudging into his consciousness, not just his own essay into the macabre world of faery but the entire netherworld of a hundred sinister romances. The deep, dark enchantments gathered by the Brothers Grimm and Hans Andersen edged into his mind, illuminated by the brilliant grisly perceptions of Arthur Rackham and Andrew Lang, stories given to children to read from the Victorian and Edwardian ages down to the present day.

I'm through the curtain, thought Dan with horror. I really am. I'm not in the real world at all. I've tumbled through into some kind of *Grand Guignol* nightmare and I'm in a fantasy world of giant-killing heroes and blood-quaffing villains and beast creatures with human blood and human creatures with beast blood . . . I'm going down into the dungeons of an ogre's enchanted castle, somewhere in the depths of a lonesome wood . . . No, of course I'm not. Serve you right for reading Perrault's grisly fairy story and pinching his plot!

Of course these were not giant steps cut for giant feet. They were abnormally big and each one felt about two feet deep, but this was unquestionably because his perceptions were dulled or distorted, and also because he was descending in pitch darkness. There was probably a very good reason for them being so deep. Dan wished he could think what it might be.

He reached the bottom, hesitated for a moment, and then flicked on the torch. If anyone was hiding in the house the thin light could not possibly be seen, and if anyone was hiding in the cellar they would have heard his approach by now.

The cellars appeared to stretch under most of October House, and Dan went warily forward. Deeper into the villainess's lair.

To begin with there was not very much to see. Dan made out broken or discarded bits of furniture, a rusting copper boiler and an ancient mangle. There were some plywood cases of crockery and glasses, and a couple of old sea chests; he approached these warily and lifted the lid of the first. It came up with a screech of disused hinges that jarred his nerves all over again. But neither of the chests housed anything more sinister than a pile of old clothes and dis-

332

carded curtains, mostly rotted beyond repair and smelling rather nastily stale. What did you expect to find? Rotting truncated bodies? The poached-eye stare of Edmund Caudle's head? Or a jumble of flesh-stripped bones, ready to be ground into bread? If you aren't careful, Daniel, your imagination's going to derail your sanity. What sanity?

He went forward again, directing the torch carefully, trying not to miss anything. There was a lot of junk down here, but there might be a disregarded fortune as well. First folios of Shakespeare buried beneath the rusting bicycles. Old masters stacked behind the forgotten curtains and back numbers of *Reader's Digest* and freezers. *Freezers*.

Dan stood stock-still and pointed the torch. Set against one wall was a large deepfreeze; a chest freezer, oblong and uncompromisingly angular, and disturbingly reminiscent of a white coffin. It would be another of the household discards, of course, tidily stored down here until it could be taken to a communal tip or scrap metal yard. Nobody would put a workable freezer down here, miles away from the kitchen, especially when the kitchen was more than big enough to house the thing and not notice it. No householder would arrange things so that a long traipse down dark and awkward stairs was necessary each time a packet of frozen chips or a tub of ice cream was wanted. All the time he had been at October House, he had never once seen Thalia come down here.

But supposing the freezer held something much more sinister than food? It was another moment when it was vital to hang on to reality. But it was also a moment to remember the never-forgotten night in a London flat when a deep-freeze had been opened.

Probably the freezer was only part of the jumble down here. Probably it was rusting and faulty. But as Dan went forward he saw that the outside was shiny new, and that a thick cable snaked from one side and ended in a modern electric plug. And the plug was connected to a socket in the wall on the far side. The freezer was switched on and working. It was purring in the way that freezers and fridges did purr, and there was a small light glowing from one corner.

And now every fairy story and every legend ever told about the fatal results of curiosity coursed through Dan's mind. The ladies who looked into chambers forbidden to them, who opened boxes they should not have opened, who used keys strictly prohibited. This is Bluebeard's seventh chamber, it's the box that Pandora should have left closed. So whatever you do, don't open the lid and shine the torch, Daniel.

Dan opened the lid and shone the torch.

Chapter Twenty-nine

It was possible that seen by ordinary daylight, or even by ordinary electric light, the contents of the freezer in October House's cellars would not have sent shock waves scudding through Dan's body. But it was not very likely. Seen in any light it would have been horrific beyond belief.

Dan was half prepared, but there was still a fraction of time when his senses spun in incredulous confusion. He took a tighter hold on the torch and the world steadied slightly, but the thing inside the white coffin was still there.

Lying packed in ice, remote and terrible, was the unclothed body of a human being, either newly dead or in some kind of suspended animation. But even for a dead body there was something very wrong indeed about it.

Dan forced himself to look properly and he forced his mind to analyse what he was seeing. The body was not complete; the arms ended at the forearms, but apart from that it had torso, shoulders, thighs, legs. It had genitals as well – it was unmistakably male. And it was segmented, jointed and hinged as all bodies are jointed and hinged.

But the joints did not fuse and the segments did not match. The shoulders and arms had been aligned with the neck, but the alignment was not quite true and jagged edges of skin overlapped; the hips and thighs lay at unnatural angles to the torso. The body was like a puppet whose limbs had been dislocated, or a human whose shoulders and arms and legs had been twisted out at the roots and left flaccid and useless. The impression of something broken and flung down was inescapable, but also inescapable was the impression of something that might, under certain conditions, animate and sit jerkily up and climb out of the white coffin, and walk disjointedly forward . . . Stop it, Daniel!

There did not seem to be any putrefaction – Dan supposed that this was due to the sub-zero temperature – but here and there the skin was mottled and darkened like raw meat, and frozen blood caked several places. It was impossible not to visualise someone hacking the requisite lump of flesh away, arranging it more or less in place, like building up a model, and disposing offhandedly of the unwanted parts. How? demanded Dan's mind. How did she manage that?

He had recognised the head at once. He recognised the hair that was glistening with white frost but which would normally be golden, and he recognised the eyes – closed now – and the narrow, high-bridged nose. Edmund Caudle. Thalia's dead son, entombed in an ice coffin, provided with this motley collection of human flesh and bone and gristle; waiting to be stitched together in a kind of insane grisly patchwork. Dear God, she's building him up, she's going to recreate him out of human scraps and human lumps of flesh. This isn't Bluebeard's dungeon after all, it's Frankenstein's laboratory.

It was as he straightened up from the freezer that he heard, from overhead, the sound of footsteps crossing the stone floor of the kitchen, and descending the stairs.

Dan had left the outer cellar door open, and although there was not very much light down here, there was some.

He turned to face the door, his heart hammering against his ribs. Someone coming . . . Something wicked this way comes . . .

A wavering light shone on the wall of the stairs, showing up the crumbling stonework and the cold dankness. Dan backed against the wall, searching for the knife he had picked up in the kitchen. But if it's Thalia, would you really use a knife on her? Could you? After all those nights together? And what if it isn't Thalia?

Her shadow appeared before she did; impossibly elongated, the shadow of a thing barely human, a massive, fantastic creature prowling down into its dungeons at dead of night, sniffing out the scent of human meat . . . Dan shut the thought off before it could grow into something even more monstrous, and clenched his fists, ready to spring.

And then she was there, framed in the sullen light trickling down from the moonlit kitchen, holding aloft a square old-fashioned oil lamp that flickered in the slight current of air and showered her with its eerie glow, so that for an incredible moment it was as if she wore a rippling crimson cloak.

There was a moment when she stared at him, and Dan waited. Then she said, very softly, 'Daniel.' There was a pause, and then, 'My dearest boy, what a fool you've made of me.'

She stepped aside, and there was a scrambling, scuttling sound on the stairs and a second figure joined Thalia and stood at her side, grinning horridly. Dan, his mind by now ready to accept anything that might materialise down here, saw that even in this Thalia was conforming to the traditional villainess pattern: she had her familiar, and it was the obligatory ugly hunchbacked dwarf.

Between his hands, the hunchback held a massive iron spanner and a length of thin chain.

Dan was aware of his mind working on several levels all at the same time.

On the topmost level was simple self-preservation, and he was already trying to assess the hunchback's strength and the swing he might give the heavy spanner. But what about Thalia? If Thalia came just a little further into the cellar he could probably grab her and use her as a hostage. He remembered he still had the kitchen knife, and he began to reach stealthily into the pocket where he had put it.

On another level entirely, he was acknowledging at last that Thalia was mad, she was madder than any of the mad ladies born into the Ingram family put together, and he was aware of strong revulsion at the knowledge.

At the deepest, most primeval level of all was a crawling fear, because the emotions and the compulsions that were swirling around in this shadowy cellar were very dark and very dreadful, and they had nothing to do with grief for a dead child. They were born out of ancient rituals learned at the black heart of pagan midnights, time-crusted rites celebrated beneath a sickle moon, Devil worship and men's futile attempts to outwit death . . .

He became aware that Thalia was saying something about a renaissance, even, incredibly, a resurrection. Her eyes rested on the white coffin, and there was the terrible light of the fanatic in them. 'He is almost ready, you see,' she said. 'He is waiting only for hands and heart. And the hands will be artist's hands.'

'And then?'

Thalia looked back at Dan in surprise. 'And then Edmund can live again,' she said.

I don't believe any of it, thought Dan, staring at her. It's pulp horror fiction. Or I'm still suffering from whatever drug she was giving me, and I'm hallucinating.

He said, carefully, 'How did you do it, Thalia?' And thought that if he could keep her talking, if he could lull her into a false sense of security, he could inch forward and pounce. He found himself flinching from the thought of striking her, of using violence towards her. But if he could grab her and put the knife against her throat, he might be able to use her as hostage to keep the hunchback away.

He said, 'You took the head, didn't you? Somehow you stole Edmund's head out of his coffin and used it to make everyone think Imogen was insane.'

A smile curved her lips. 'Edmund . . .' she said, her

voice blurred and slurry with terrible passion. 'Yes, Dan, I took his head. It was so easy – the undertakers were so trusting. So sympathetic to the poor bereaved mother. The last private farewell, the closing of the coffin.' Her eyes, which had been unfocused, suddenly snapped back into awareness. 'And it was so easy,' said Thalia. 'It was so very easy to get the bitch locked away.'

'Why did you hate Imogen so much?'

'Because she lived when Edmund died,' said Thalia, sounding surprised that Dan should ask this. 'Because she would have had everything that should have been Edmund's. I couldn't allow that to happen. I wanted her punished. I wanted them all punished. Most of all, I wanted Edmund back.'

'Resurrection,' said Dan, softly.

'Yes.' The word came out eagerly, as if she was pleased to find him so instantly comprehending. 'He came to me every night, after he died, Dan. I used to wait for darkness because it was when he would be with me. Sometimes when I couldn't wait for darkness, I went to the flat and drew the curtains and locked the door . . .'

Dan, feeling sick, said, 'Because you had part of him there already.'

'I could stroke his poor mutilated face. I could talk to it. It was all I had left of him. And after a while I knew what he wanted.' She paused, and Dan waited, hardly daring to breathe in case the spell was broken.

He said, 'You used your charity work, didn't you? That was where you found your victims.' Keep talking, Thalia, because the more I can find out before I jump on you, the better.

'That's intelligent of you, Dan. Yes, it was almost all through the charity work, although I never saw them as victims, you know. They were sacrifices. Libations. But yes, they all came from the boring endless charity work. Committees to help drop-outs, misfits, homeless. Everyone thought I was so good, so selfless. And perhaps at the beginning I was. But after Edmund died . . .

'You killed the most suitable,' said Dan with mounting horror.

'Yes. But I've only taken four, no more than that. Counting Quincy, there will only be four.' There was a note almost of placation, as if she was saying, only that small number. Nobody could blame me for so few.

'Quincy?' said Dan.

'Imogen's friend. I need her hands. *Artist*'s hands,' said Thalia. 'And I could easily have taken more. You would be surprised how many of the homeless or the drug addicts or the drunks were once young people of great promise.'

'I wouldn't.' This had to be the maddest conversation anyone had ever had. 'It's often the truly gifted people who crack.'

Thalia said, 'I took only the best. Only those in Edmund's image. The first was a young man who was a student of law, but a keen athlete in his spare time. He was lean and lissom.' A pause, and a small, secret smile. 'He took to drugs though, that young man. I found him through one of my very early committees – a counselling service for one of the student bodies. The heroin was already starting to destroy him by then, and he was easily lured,' said Thalia, and again there was the travesty of a smile. A lady remembering a past and pleasant lover. Dan wondered if she would remember him like that. No, she would not, because he was not going to die.

He said, with cold politeness, 'I hope he wasn't HIV positive, Thalia.'

She laughed. 'Of course he was not, Dan. None of them were. Do you think I wouldn't have checked that? The counselling service was very particular about its records.'

'Who else?'

'Oh, next was a young French boy who had been studying dancing with the Ballet Rambert. His ankle was badly broken in a car crash, and he had to give up dancing. He became clinically depressed as a result. Again that was the student counselling service.'

'A useful source,' said Dan, politely.

'Very.' She paused, and then said, 'The last was a young Irishman, a Roman Catholic ordinand struggling with the vow of celibacy.' This time the smile was wolfish and Dan thought: she enjoyed that one! 'Ironically he came to talk to the French boy,' said Thalia. 'We met over discussions about the boy's rehabilitation.' A quick gesture with one hand. 'You see? Only the very, very best. Strength and beauty and music and philosophy. And art.'

Dan said, 'Quincy?'

'Yes. Edmund must be given every gift and every grace, exactly as the bitch-creature Imogen was given. And Quincy is immensely talented. Edmund will have artist's hands, sensitive and gifted.'

So Quincy, whoever she is, is not yet dead, thought Dan. 'Yes, I see,' he said. His mind was still racing, but he asked, very softly, 'And what about the heart, Thalia?'

Thalia took a moment to reply, but when she did, Dan felt as if he had been plunged neck deep into a freezing cold lake of black water.

'The heart,' she said, softly. 'The final ingredient. A fresh, warm, *living* heart. Tomorrow night I shall extract the sweetest revenge of all on Imogen, who lived when she should have died in Edmund's place. Tomorrow at midnight Imogen will be brought here and as dawn breaks I shall remove her beating heart so that Edmund can live.'

'You're mad,' said Dan, staring at her in horror. 'You're absolutely mad. You do know that?'

'Tomorrow, Dan, we shall see which of us is mad and which is sane,' said Thalia, and nodded to the hunchback. 'Knock him out,' she said. 'And then tie him up and leave him down here.' She paused, and the smile lifted her lips again, but now it was the cruel, thin smile of the ogress. Margot, thought Dan. 'Because since we have him,' said the

341

ogress, in her attractive, slightly husky voice, 'it would be a pity not to make use of him.'

It had afforded Thalia a degree of pleasure to relive, however briefly, those weeks before she left London, searching for the young men who would make fitting sacrifices. There had been such dark, sensuous pleasure in luring them to bed. She thought that no one had guessed and even if anyone had, there was nothing criminal about ladies of a certain age lusting after the sweet young bodies of boys.

She had loved all three of the young men who had died. The young lawyer so hungry for heroin that he would do anything to get it, hiring his body to women – or men – who would pay enough. He had been easy to lure to the London flat, and easy to kill while he was fathoms down in the drug-induced visions.

The dancer had been easy as well. He had been embittered and sunk deep in self-pity, but he had possessed sufficient vanity to be flattered at the half-shy, half-voracious suggestion. Thalia had known that he had been framing in his mind how he would tell this story to his contemporaries: the lonely older woman, greedy for satisfaction, but I satisfied her. Thalia had been proud of her performance with that one. He had never once guessed what lay behind the invitation, and he had died still not knowing.

The young priest had been the sweetest conquest of all. He had come to bed with a kind of helpless anger. He had been inexperienced but violently passionate, as if he had banked down his body's needs for many years and could not keep them banked down any longer. He had wept in her arms afterwards, praying for forgiveness, and Thalia had held him to her while she pushed the glinting point of the skewer into the base of his skull. His God would probably deal harshly with him for dying in what he himself had considered mortal sin.

After she had done what there was to be done to each of them – after she had taken what she had to take and laid it lovingly in its place in the deepfreeze – she had simply bundled the remains in black plastic bin liners and taken them down in the lift of the Great Portland Street block, using a small wheeled trolley, the kind that airport and railway staff used for transporting large suitcases and cabin trunks. The car park was in the basement, and she had been careful to park in a deserted corner, and to make this trip not at dead of night, which might have been noticed, but in the middle of the afternoon, three o'clock, when practically everyone in the block was out at work. It had been easy to deposit the bags in the boot of her car, lock it, and go innocently back to the flat. If anyone had chanced to see her, they would have assumed she was disposing of some unwanted household rubbish.

That night, or the next, she would drive her car to one of the deserted quayside areas of London, where she could tip the bags into the Thames. That part she had done at dead of night, keeping a careful eye out for watchers. She had weighted the grisly sacks so that nothing would rise to the surface, using large bags of garden compost bought innocently and openly at garden centres. Nobody had suspected anything, and nobody ever would suspect anything because she was invincible.

And Edmund had been with her all along; guarding her from inquisitive eyes and awkward questions. It was nearly unbearable by this time to look on the thing that Edmund was becoming: the once-smooth skin blotched and mould-spotted, the body leaking decay, but Thalia did look, because it was better by far to have even this of Edmund than to have nothing of him at all. He brought the aura of death with him a little more strongly each time, and it was an aura of oozing putrescence and wormy filth and rotting flesh. She could not escape him, but she did not want to escape him.

She would manage to dispose of Dan Tudor's body as easily as she had disposed of all the others. She locked and bolted the cellar, and went back upstairs, considering how she would use him. Tomorrow she would order the Harris creature to fire the potter's kiln for the disposal of the remains. Dan. Quincy. Imogen . . .

Imogen.

Her mind leapt ahead to tomorrow, to the hour when Harris would bring Imogen out of Thornacre and down to the cellars of October House.

It was going to be rather tedious to get through all the hours of daylight before that could happen.

Chapter Thirty

Leo found it difficult to gather up the threads of Thorn-acre's everyday life again.

His reaction when Imogen finally opened her eyes and looked up at him had been so fierce that for a moment it had nearly overwhelmed him. But he quenched the soaring emotion at once, and called the duty nurse in to make up a mild sedative. 'To make you sleep, Imogen.'

She said, in the same far-away voice, 'More sleeping?' and Leo smiled because even like this there was a faint irony in her voice.

'Yes, but this time it'll be real sleep.'

'No dreams?'

'Not this time. I promise you, Imogen. And someone will be here with you all the time.'

She managed a smile, and Leo touched her cheek for a moment and then turned away, forcing himself to make notes on her chart. Only when he was satisfied that the sedative had sent her into drifting dreamless sleep did he go out, leaving the nurse seated by the bed. Because if he left now he might be able to master his feelings. But as he went to his own rooms his mind was singing with such wild emotion that it almost blotted out everything else. I brought you out, Imogen, and I know hardly anything about you, but I'm beginning to suspect that you've spoiled me for any other female . . .

His own sleep was filled with darting disturbing glimpses of Imogen's silent secret woodland, and when he woke the next morning, Thornacre seemed unreal and blurred.

He went along to her room, to find her eating breakfast. 'A huge breakfast,' she said, smiling. 'They think I've got a lot of time to make up. It's rather a drastic method of slimming, isn't it?' She gave him a cup of coffee from the tray and Leo sipped it and watched her eating scrambled eggs and toast. There were dark smudges under her eyes, but she ate with the hungry appetite of a starving wood-nymph. The image formed in his mind unprompted.

They would arrange for a CT scan later in the day, but Leo did not think it would reveal anything sinister. Imogen was not quite back in the real world, not wholly, but she almost was. The lingering aura of other-worldliness would dissolve quite naturally.

The medical side of Leo scoffed at the concept of other worlds and of the unconscious wandering through them like wraiths, but the mystical side of him was fascinated. Imogen had dwelled for a time in one of the strange lands closed to most people; she had visited some distant, probably chimerical realm, but whether it was the Aegia with its fire-streaked skies or the perfumed fields of Elysium, or Dante's ironstone hell or Milton's dungeon-encircled furnace, or even the enchanted forests of darkly romantic fables, there was no way of telling. At her age she was more likely to have dreamed about pop stars anyway. This was a supremely depressing thought.

Once during his carefully casual questionings, she said, 'I dreamed some odd things—' and then stopped abruptly.

'Go on.'

'I'm not sure which was dreaming and which wasn't.' She frowned.

'Your memory will probably be a bit fragmented for a while,' said Leo at once. 'A slight degree of amnesia is almost inevitable. Your memory will come back although probably not at an even pace. You'll get pieces all in a rush and then nothing for a while, and then more pieces.'

'I feel a bit distant. As if I'm seeing things through a glass wall or under water.'

'That's to be expected as well.' He studied her. 'You said you dreamed some odd things.'

'Yes, but telling dreams is the last word in egotism.'

'Not to me.'

Imogen stared at him. 'One day I will tell you,' she said, after a moment. 'But not yet.'

'Is it that you fear talking about it might spoil it? The dream-world?'

'Not to you.'

The silence lengthened, and Leo thought: at least it doesn't sound as if it was pop stars. I believe I could force her to tell me. I believe I could reach out to her mind again and compel her. Would that be Svengali or Baron Frankenstein? jeered his mind. You're really crossing the line now! If you haven't crossed it already.

He was about to speak – although he had no idea what he was going to say – when there was a timid knock on the door and a scared-looking nurse put her head round.

'Sorry for interrupting, Dr Sterne,' she said, 'but please could you come to Matron's office on account of one of the patient's gone wandering off again.'

Leo said, 'Harris?'

'Well, yes.'

'Curse him. All right, I'll come.' Leo turned back to Imogen. 'I'll hold you to the promise,' he said. 'About the dreams.'

'All right.' The grin showed. 'In the meantime,' said the wood nymph, 'do you think they'd bring me some more toast?'

The news that Snatcher Harris had awarded himself a night out again and only returned in time for breakfast looking slyly pleased dragged Leo nearer to reality. He forced himself to concentrate on this problem, because if the Snatcher had really been out all night it was likely to be connected with Quincy's disappearance. It was possible, as well, that he might have inflicted harm somewhere, and it was devoutly to be hoped that it was nothing more than slight harm. Leo felt the beginnings of anger. Could these wretched nurses not keep a better watch?

He entered Freda Porter's office, banging the door impatiently back against the wall and demanding to know what had happened in such abrupt tones that Freda was thrown into quite a flutter.

'Well, I'm afraid our Llewellyn had been out all night, Dr Sterne.'

'I know that already. What happened?'

'It was my evening off, you know.'

'Yes?'

'I shall make a full inquiry, naturally. These girls don't realise the importance of—'

'*What about Harris?*'

'He was left to his own devices for a little too long, Dr Sterne. He returned,' said Freda, plainly unaware of black humour, 'with the milk.' She thinned her lips disapprovingly and Leo's anger was tinged with amusement for a moment. He repressed the urge to say, 'We've all done that at times, Matron.'

'And now he's bragging about females again.' There was no need to describe the obscene gestures Harris had been making. Freda said, primly, 'In his own fashion, you understand.'

'Revolting little tomcat,' said Leo. 'But we'll hope it's no worse than an attack of flashing. Flashing's about all he's capable of anyway, poor little sod. There's no news of Quincy, is there? No, I thought not. Well, you'd better tell them to bring Harris to my room, Matron. I'll see if I can get anything out of him.'

Freda told him that nothing of any value had been elicited from the Snatcher, even though several of them had tried to talk to him. Freda had actually tried herself, approaching

Harris with calm, sensible questions, which had had the unfortunate result of provoking what had been really a most unpleasant incident. She had managed to get herself out of the room without calling one of the nurses, because it would have been very embarrassing indeed if the disturbance – really very trivial – had become known. Freda could very well imagine the nurses saying to one another, 'And then he got Matron down on the bed and there she was yelling for help, all sprawled out, her skirt round her waist . . .'

This was not an image Freda wanted conveyed to Dr Sterne, and anyway Dr Sterne knew all about Harris. Quite fierce he'd looked earlier on. Freda was glad to have been able to exonerate herself from blame so early on.

'If Harris has had anything to do with Quincy's disappearance I'll get it out of him if I have to beat him!' said Leo, and saw Freda's start of surprise. He grinned inwardly, and with a half-mischievous idea of testing the woman, said, 'Didn't you think I was capable of violence, Matron?' And waited, curious to see her response. Anyone with a genuine interest in this job, or with any kind of imagination at all, would have said something like, 'It's generally held that we're all capable of violence under certain circumstances.'

Freda said, 'Oh dear me *no*, Dr Sterne! Everyone knows how dedicated you are. My word, violence from you, my word, *what* an idea!' She gave a light, deprecatory laugh.

She'll have to go, thought Leo, making his way to his own office.

Snatcher Harris was not going to tell any of them where he had been last night. It was a secret. Secrets were not things you could have very easily inside Thornacre, but they were good to have if you could get them; they made you feel warm and excited and sometimes they gave you power over other people. He collected secrets, storing them up inside his mind.

They all asked a lot of questions about where he had been all night and what he had been doing but he was not letting on about any of it, not him! He knew exactly how to deal with them when they kept on at him like this, and he grunted and blubbered his lips and made obscene gestures. When it came to Matron asking him, primming up her lips and putting on a silly voice, he enjoyed himself very much, pushing the stupid old bitch on to his bed and upping her skirts over her face. She had let out a screech, and he had pretended to lunge between her legs, although really he would not have touched her with a barge pole, ugly old thing. But it had done him a lot of good to see her sprogged out like that, with her fat thighs and knickers all on display. Snatcher would laugh like anything at the memory when he was on his own. He would enjoy reminding her about it when they met. She would hate that. You could do a lot with a few gestures.

Dr Sterne was not so easy to trick, of course, and he was better than most of the others. He usually tried to understand the gruntings, but he did not try this morning because he was angry. There was a policeman there as well, who pretended to understand what was said and wrote a lot of things down in a book, which was silly because he, Snatcher, was deliberately grunting nothings. He knew all about policemen, stupid creatures, and he was not going to tell any policeman anything. He was certainly not going to tell Matron anything, even though she stood there frowning at him, and he was not going to tell Dr Sterne anything either. He gave them all his lopsided idiot grin and lurched around the room making rude waggling motions with his hips and clenching his fist and thrusting his bent arm upwards, until Dr Sterne said furiously, 'Oh, stop it, Harris!' And then, to Matron, 'Take him back to the dayroom. No, I don't want to see him again. I don't care what you do with him. You can drop him over the side of the cliff, for all I care!'

The policeman said something about Harris not being able to understand what was being asked of him, and Dr Sterne said impatiently, 'Of course he understands! He understands everything very well, don't you, Harris? He's being deliberately awkward!'

Matron said in her silly voice, 'Now then, Llewellyn, if you don't behave it'll be the locked room with the cardboard furniture for you!'

Harris turned his back on Matron and bent over so that his bum was sticking up, facing her, and made a loud farting sound. It was a pity that they hustled him out of the room before he could hear what happened next.

He was not very worried about the locked-room threat because Dr Sterne, as far as anyone knew, hardly ever used it, but he had not yet weighed up Matron's exact degree of authority. It occurred to him that it might be as well not to do anything that might upset tonight's plans, and so he went out more or less obediently.

The Lady – Harris thought of her like that – had made it all very clear. She had seemed to understand about secret things, because she said the secret they were going to share was the biggest, most important secret anyone could have. She had been looking for the exact right person, she said, someone who could understand properly, and she thought that he was that very person. She called him 'Mr Harris' which was not a form of address anyone had ever used to him as far as he could recall.

If he would help her, said the Lady, he would be very well rewarded. He could have anything he wanted; she might even be able to see that he was taken out of Thornacre and allowed to live somewhere much nicer.

That would need thinking about. Snatcher did not want to live anywhere where he might have to do work or where he might have to pay for things; he liked Thornacre where other people did the cooking and the cleaning and the paying, where there were all kinds of opportunities, and where he knew to a whisker what he could get away with. And so he had looked slyly out from under his tufty eyebrows, rolling his lower eyelids down so that the crusted red rims were more noticeable than usual. This was something that females never liked; they fidgeted and their eyes slid away, because they were uncomfortable if they had to look at him for very long.

The Lady did not look away and she did not seem to be uncomfortable. She returned the stare coldly, as if she was seeing straight into his mind and picking over what she found there. There was a bad moment when he could very nearly feel her hard, bony fingers sorting through his secrets. But after a moment she said they should talk more; was there somewhere they could be private? What about the grounds? Was Mr Harris allowed out into the grounds? Then she would meet him in about twenty minutes' time, halfway along the drive.

The drive was a long, gloomy stretch of road, fringed by overgrown shrubbery and bushes. There was a thick briar hedge on one side and it was a place that most people avoided. One or two of the nurses who had been here for several years told how it was said to be one of the places where Sybilla Campbell's ghost walked; you could hear her sometimes throughout the hot summer nights: you could hear the tick-tick of her fleshless bones grating together as she searched for a new victim. People argued that the sound was nothing but crickets in the long grass, but the older nurses knew differently.

Snatcher did not mind the drive at all; it was a place where you could hide and watch people coming up to the house without them knowing you were there. It was astonishing the things you could find out that way.

The Lady was there very soon; Snatcher's idea of time was not very precise, but he thought she was early. She parked her car and walked towards him, and for the first time – possibly for the first time in his whole life – Snatcher

Harris felt a prickle of fear. She was taller and thinner than she had seemed in the dayroom. As she came towards him, the shadows of the darkening afternoon twisted about her so that for a moment it looked as if she was wearing a long, swirling black cloak and a hood, with dark pits where her eyes should have been, and scooped-out black caverns where her nostrils were. Llewellyn Harris did not recognise many figures of authority –he would do what Leo Sterne told him and he would more or less do what the nurses told him, although he generally pretended not to understand them – but this was different. This was something he had never before encountered. Power. She glowed with it.

He listened to what she wanted, and when she asked if he would do it and then if he could get out of Thornacre without anyone knowing, he gave the grunting nod which meant, 'Yes.'

Getting out was the easiest thing in the world. There was a disused culvert in the grounds, near to the main road; Snatcher had found it it by accident and it had been worth all the furtive prowling around the grounds. It was over-grown with ivy, and because it was almost bang up against the brick wall, no one else had discovered it. It looked as if it had once been some kind of drain. Snatcher did not trouble his head about it too much because drains were other folks' concern, but what he did know was that it formed a tunnel that went under the brick wall and under the road and came out in a clump of trees on the other side. Once there would have been huge metal covers at both ends and you would have needed a proper turning tool to get them up, but now all you had to do was pull the ivy to one side and let yourself down. It smelt a bit strong in the culvert because foxes and weasels got down there, and it was dark and narrow, but once you were through and out the other side you were free and there were all kinds of things you could do. There was a bit of a pull-in in the trees and cars often parked there. Snatcher enjoyed himself very much watching for cars – Friday and Saturday nights were best – and watching the things that people did on the back seats. Stripped bollock-naked, some of them did, and went at it like stoats!

Sometimes Snatcher stayed silent and still, watching and gloating, but sometimes he went right up to the car windows and tapped the glass and leered in at them. Doing that, it was better to wait until it looked as if the man was on the short strokes, because that spoiled it properly for them. They'd drive off like scalded cats, the engine revving and the girl screeching, and of course they never told, on account of not being supposed to be in the woods and doing it in the car in the first place! He knew what he was about, Snatcher Harris.

And so it had been very easy to get out through the tunnel on the night in question, and very enjoyable indeed to help the Lady carry Quincy into the old coach house with the brick ovens. Tonight they were going to chop off her hands. Snatcher Harris was looking forward to that.

He was looking forward even more to taking Imogen to October House and seeing the Lady dig out her heart.

Dan emerged from the stifling darkness that followed the hunchback's blow to the realisation that he was still in the cellars below October House and that although his hands were not tied, a loop of thin chain circled one ankle and embedded itself in the wall. There was a padlock. He took all this in and then sat up gingerly and attempted to assess his injuries.

He felt a bit sick and dry-mouthed and he thought there would probably be a lump like an egg on his head in a few hours. But all things considered, he did not feel too bad. The blow seemed to have landed on the back of his skull where his hair was thickest, which had probably afforded some protection. And although it was no doubt impossible to diagnose concussion in yourself, he did not think he had any of the symptoms. Slight amnesia and double vision, wasn't it? He was pretty sure he was remembering everything that had happened, right up to the minute he had been struck, and he was certainly seeing everything with perfect clarity. No concussion, then, or at least not so far.

He got up experimentally, encountering only slight dizziness, which might be from Thalia's drugging anyway. After a moment he took a deep breath and carefully made his way to the door, testing the length of the chain. It slithered rather nastily across the cellar floor, and brought him up with a jerk about two feet short of the door. The door would almost certainly be locked anyway. What else did you expect, Daniel? A light over the door saying Exit and a car waiting to drive you back to civilisation? He returned to his corner and sat down again to consider the situation.

There was absolutely no way he could see of escaping from the cellar and its grisly occupant. There was only one door out, and the place was too far below ground to have any windows. The floor was solid concrete. If he had been a smoker he might have had matches or a lighter which might have started a fire and created some kind of diversion, but he did not. If he had had a little more knowledge of electricity he might have found a way of short-circuiting the power supply and done the same thing. But it was a risky thing to do; down here he had no means of knowing whether Thalia was in the house or not, and it would be sod's luck if he started a fire when she was out and he ended up trapped.

Face it, Daniel, you've absolutely no idea what to do, and absolutely no plan for rescuing Imogen Ingram. Impotent fury gripped him. You're within hours of dying alongside the girl who inspired you to write what'll probably be your best piece of work ever, and you can't think up a way of saving either of you! So much for romance, Daniel. So much for all those fictional heroes –including Adam Cadence – who snatch their ladies from under the noses of the villains. Or, in this case, villainess.

It was important to remember that this was reality and not his book, and it was vital not to start thinking he had slid over some kind of invisible line. In any case, the plot seemed to be diverging: Margot was supposed to be thwarted before her evil machinations could reach their culmination and Thalia was not being thwarted at all. In fact she was so far from being thwarted that she seemed to be flourishing like the bay tree in the wilderness, and her accomplice seemed to be flourishing as well. Dan felt the back of his head again where the hunchback had struck him, and winced.

He settled down to think, trying not to look at his watch too many times. It was a digital one, and the figures were faintly luminous. If he started to check it every five minutes he would end up counting the strips of wood making up the roof joists, and getting cross because they did not make an even number. Or he would start imagining that he could hear sounds from inside the freezer . . . Stop it, Daniel.

It was unlikely that Thalia would return before nightfall. She had said that the hunchback would fetch Imogen at midnight, but there would presumably be some preparations before that time. Dan thought he had probably got until nine or ten o'clock tonight before things started to happen. A good twelve hours in which to do something. But what? He got up and prowled around the cellar as far as the chain would stretch in every direction, searching every corner.

But it was not until he sat down on the floor facing the freezer again that the nucleus of an idea began to form, tenuously and lightly, like a bubble about to break in a pan of boiling water.

Chapter Thirty-one

Leo was becoming increasingly concerned about Quincy. She had been missing overnight now, and immediately after breakfast they had called the police again. A detective inspector had come out, and he had not been quite so reassuring.

'We'll find her, of course, Dr Sterne,' he said. 'But I'm bound to say it's beginning to look a bit more serious than it did yesterday. We're searching all the obvious places, and we've alerted railway stations and motorway cafes now. Oh, and we're questioning all strangers to the area.'

The thought of Quincy in the hands of some murderously-intentioned abductor or some prowling pervert was a spade in Leo's guts. He said, abruptly, 'She's an unworldly child, Inspector. She's had to suffer a good deal of ill-treatment.' And, half to himself, 'I promised her she would be safe here.'

'Well, we'll do all we can, Dr Sterne. I'll question the nurses again as well. They might recall something unusual that would give us a bit of a lead.'

The nurses were plainly upset, but Leo, sitting in on the questioning, thought they were truthful. There had been absolutely nothing out of the ordinary about Quincy yesterday, they said, and there had been absolutely nothing out of the ordinary about the outing with Mrs Caudle. Patients were taken out by relatives from time to time, depending on their condition. The fact that Quincy had never been taken out was only because she had no family. Everyone had thought it kind of Mrs Caudle, and everyone had been pleased for Quincy to have the small treat.

Nurse Carr who had helped Quincy to get ready said she thought the girl had been a bit nervous about going out to tea, but no more than you would expect. She wasn't used to the world, said Nurse Carr, that was the trouble. In response to the inspector's next question, she said firmly that Quincy had been happy in Thornacre, or as happy as anyone could be inside a mental institution, and there was no reason to suppose she might run away. In fact there was every reason to suppose she had wanted to stay. She had been helping Dr Sterne with some new treatment on another patient, said Nurse Carr, and sent a covert glance to Dr Sterne to be sure he understood that she was not intending to breach patient confidentiality any further than this. No, she had no idea whether Dr Sterne had genuinely needed Quincy's help or whether it had been a ruse to help Quincy herself. It did not matter; the point was that Quincy had felt important and wanted by doing it, and because of that she had been about as likely to run away as that chair.

'Thank you very much, Nurse,' said Leo, and Nurse Carr took herself off, thinking, yes, and when Fatso Freda comes in, she'll tell you a different tale entirely, but if you've got only half the sense I credit you with, you'll see through it.

Freda Porter was about as irritating as Leo had ever known her, and it was only with a massive effort that he kept his temper. She made it clear at the outset that no blame could possibly be apportioned to her, and gave a list of alibis by way of back-up. She had given the staff explicit instructions. She could not be everywhere at once, and you couldn't trust any of these girls nowadays.

Leo said angrily, 'Matron, if you can't stand the heat up here, you'd better get out of the kitchen.' And added, 'Before you're asked to get out anyway.'

It was very understandable that Dr Sterne's nerve endings should be so frayed; Freda was in a state of nerves herself. Quite a shock it had given them all to find a patient missing, not that Freda could be blamed for any of it, not that Dr Sterne would think of blaming her, even though he had spoken so sharply for a second or two. There was in fact a school of thought that maintained that people only lashed out at those whom they trusted and felt at home with. Dr Sterne would apologise later, and Freda would be gracious about it. You had to make allowances.

You did not have to make allowances for the slapdash slipshod methods of the staff, however, and Freda set about dealing with the miscreants forthwith. They'd all say afterwards that she was a bit of a tartar, the new matron, but it could not be helped; when you had been appointed to a position of authority and trust, you had to be firm. They were all the same, these girls; trying to slide out of trouble and you simply could not have it. That Nurse Carr was a flighty piece if ever she had seen one; she would have to be watched.

Oliver was disturbed to hear that a young girl was missing from Thornacre, and horrified to realise that the police sergeant who was so painstakingly asking questions in the landlord's office at the Black Boar was more than a little suspicious of him.

But it was understandable that they would check on all strangers to the area, and it would be remarkable if they did not look a bit askance at a single man apparently spending Christmas on his own. With this in mind, Oliver answered the police sergeant's questions patiently but guardedly. There was a policewoman with him, which was presumably standard practice in the case of a missing girl.

There was no reason not to be truthful. Oliver explained that he had travelled up to London from Oxford a couple of days before Christmas Day, and by way of credential and confirmation gave the phone number and address of Oriel College's bursar, and also that of the head of the history faculty. For some reason this seemed to disconcert the two police officers.

He had been going to spend Christmas with his brother in London, he said, only they had somehow missed one another. But there had been some mention of his brother coming up here, and so he had driven up here by himself. No, he had no idea why his brother would have come here, it might have been research of some kind. His brother was a writer, it could have been anything. And no, he had not reported his brother as missing because he was not at all sure yet that Dan really was missing. It was possible that he, Oliver, had misunderstood the arrangements, he said.

'Do you often misunderstand arrangements, sir?' said the sergeant.

'Oh yes, frequently. I expect everyone does, don't they?'

'It varies,' said the sergeant cryptically, and made a note. The policewoman asked if Dr Tudor had ever heard of Thornacre.

'Yes, of course I have. I should think everyone in England has after the publicity it's had. I think I drove past it on the way here, as a matter of fact. A grim, bleak-looking place, set a bit above the village?'

The sergeant said, yes, that was Thornacre, and added that a lot of nasty tales had been told about the place down the years, but you shouldn't believe all you heard.

'I never believe anything I hear, Sergeant.'

'It's always been the subject of gossip, that place.'

'I never listen to gossip either,' said Oliver.

'What about Dr Sterne, sir? Dr Leo Sterne. Have you ever met him?'

'Not as far as I know. I suppose I might have met him somewhere and forgotten.'

'I think you'd have remembered him, sir. Now then, would you mind giving us your own movements yesterday?

From around two o'clock onwards. Just a matter of routine, you know.'

Oliver had in fact spent most of the afternoon and evening reading Dan's manuscript and trying to decide if it was a good time to make a second assault on October House, and perhaps leave a careful note for Thalia Caudle. He told the sergeant that he had been working in his room for most of the day – the landlord would probably confirm this. He had had some lunch in the bar – ham and cheese rolls and a half pint of lager, if they wanted chapter and verse – and then he had taken a turn around the village afterwards, just to get a breath of fresh air. No, he had not taken his car out, he had left it in the car park here, and no, he had certainly not been as far as Thornacre. He had spent the evening in the bar where he had eaten the Black Boar's idea of beef stroganoff for dinner.

The sergeant wrote these blameless details down and thanked Oliver for providing them. Probably, he added, buttoning his notebook into an upper jacket pocket, the missing girl would turn up of her own accord. This was what often happened. The policewoman added that they were not treating the disappearance as suspicious.

'Not yet,' said the sergeant doomfully. 'But she's been missing all night now, which makes it a matter of concern. If you think of anything that might help, I hope you'll give us a call, Dr Tudor. I'll give you a card with the station's phone number and the—'

'Have one of mine, Dr Tudor,' said the policewoman. 'WPC Morrison. That's my extension number.'

'Thank you very much.' Oliver pocketed the card. 'I hope you find the girl,' he added.

'The inspector thinks she's most likely gone off on a little expedition on her own account,' said the sergeant. 'She was taken out just after lunch yesterday by a lady visiting one of the other patients at Thornacre – a Mrs Caudle staying in Blackmere village – and she was dropped off at the gates at about five o'clock.'

Oliver had been about to make good his exit. He stopped in the doorway and said, very carefully, 'Really? And that all checks out, does it?'

'Oh yes. This Mrs Caudle was quite clear. Apparently the girl, Quincy, had befriended Mrs Caudle's niece in Thornacre and Mrs Caudle arranged a little outing to thank her. There was some plan of going to an art exhibition somewhere but it didn't come off, and so she drove the girl back.'

Oliver wondered whether he should say that his brother had known Thalia Caudle in London, and decided against it. Better not appear too familiar with anything up here. He said, 'Is it possible that Mrs Caudle didn't take the girl as near to Thornacre as she's claiming? If she was in a hurry perhaps she dropped her off somewhere on the road, and the girl – what did you say her name was? Quincy? – wandered off in the wrong direction.'

'Wandered a bit too far and got lost?'

'Well, yes.'

'Mrs Caudle didn't strike me as the kind to tell lies, sir. She's been up here for two or three months. Quiet lady. Recovering from the death of her son. Well thought of, it seems.'

'Oh, I see. Well, anyway, Sergeant, if I see or hear anything that might help, I'll let you know. Or WPC Morrison.'

'Very kind of you, Dr Tudor. You, er, aren't planning on leaving the area yet, you said?'

'Not for a few days. But you've got my Oxford address in any case.'

'Oh yes, sir.'

Oliver went back up to his room. It was the middle of the morning and there was a dry, hard whiteness everywhere that heralded a frost-ridden night to come. The girl who had vanished from Thornacre might be somewhere out there, lost, frightened, shivering with cold.

Or locked up and helpless?

He had finished Dan's manuscript after breakfast that morning, which was to say he had read as far as Dan had written. There was a rough draft of a conversation between Adam and the hotel manager's daughter, in which a seldom used, semi-secret tunnel into and out of the ancient sea fortress was mentioned. Oliver supposed that the idea had been for Adam to sneak in via this route, and could not decide if this was a clumsy plot device or not. It looked as if Dan had not been able to decide either, because the manuscript ended at this point. Had Dan abandoned it? Or been forced to abandon it?

Oliver sat back and considered October House and Thalia Caudle again. There was probably no connection at all. But it was curious, yes, it was very curious indeed that the girl from Thornacre, Quincy, had vanished on the very afternoon she had gone out with Thalia. Probably she was no longer missing. Probably she was already safely back inside Thornacre.

And however much all this was mirroring Dan's book, you could not go creeping around the gardens of other people's properties. For one thing you would be caught. You might, if you were sufficiently foolhardy, get away with doing it at midnight, but if anyone was going to commit the classic folly of prowling around October House at midnight it was not going to be Oliver.

But there was something else he could do. He could go up to Dan's nightmare mansion and talk to Leo Sterne.

It gave him an odd, through-the-looking-glass feeling to find himself shown into the black and white tiled hall and to smell the faint, lingering cooking scents and the miasma of illness that characterised most hospitals and that Dan had described so well. Dan's asylum had had dark red tiles and chipped marble floor, but that was about the only difference.

Dr Sterne was younger than Oliver had expected – he was

probably in his late thirties – and he was tall and rather thin, with the thinness of people who possessed a great deal of mental energy. He had very clear eyes and although he looked as if he might not suffer fools gladly, he also looked as if he could be extremely gentle. Oliver, who had been trying to dismiss the leering image of Dan's Dr Bentinck, liked him at once. This was no Bentinck; this was someone he could talk to. He remembered that Sterne was a psychiatrist and supposed it was a talent that went with the territory.

He thanked Leo for seeing him without an appointment, and told his story, careful not to omit anything, scrupulous not to over-emphasise. He explained about Dan's brief relationship with Thalia Caudle in London, which might or might not be significant; Dan's subsequent disappearance, and the threadbare but convincing clues that had led Oliver himself to Northumberland.

'The police have questioned me about your missing girl,' he said. 'I can't be sure that there's any connection, of course, but it's a bit suggestive, I think. It raises a few questions about Thalia Caudle.'

'I think it does as well.' Leo frowned, considering this, and remembered his own fleeting distrust of Thalia.

Oliver said diffidently, 'You do believe me, do you?'

'What? Oh, good God, yes, of course I believe you. You're clearly in your right mind – at least as much as any of us are these days – and Thalia Caudle was the last person to see Quincy. That makes her the most suspicious. I can't begin to think what her motives for kidnapping the child would be, though. Even if she's mad – I mean really, clinically mad – she'd need a motive.'

'Really?' Oliver had wondered about this.

'Mad people need motives more often than you'd think,' said Leo wryly. 'In fact there's almost always a thread of astonishingly convincing logic running through what they do. It's warped logic, of course, but not to them. That's the point. One of the most stubborn cases of persecution mania I ever had was a young man who was absolutely convinced that he was an IRA target. He refused to go outside the house for six months because of it, and to prove his argument he even compiled a file of all the evidence. He recorded the times that suspicious cars were parked outside his house and took Polaroid photos of people he claimed were watching him. He even produced threatening letters.'

'Was he really an IRA target?'

'No, of course not. He'd written the letters himself and the watchers turned out to be newspaper boys or leaflet distributors. His only connection with Ireland was drinking its whiskey. Listen, what are we going to do about Thalia Caudle? What can we do?'

'I'm not sure we can do anything,' said Oliver slowly. 'She hasn't, as far as we know, actually committed any crime yet.'

'Thank God for a collaborator with a logical mind,' said Leo. 'You're right, of course. I don't know a great deal about police procedure but I don't think what we've got adds up to very much. I'd guess the police would need far more evidence before they could search October House.'

'And,' said Oliver, 'if the lady is up to something questionable, we shouldn't risk the law galloping up there with sirens blaring and trumpets sounding. It'd alert her and she'd bolt.' He paused, and then said, 'But there's no law I can think of that stops me from calling on her myself.'

'Now?'

'Well, actually,' said Oliver, 'I was thinking of a little later in the day.'

'How much later?'

'About midnight.'

It was actually a quarter to eleven that night when Oliver crept out of the Black Boar. Driving to October House was the last thing he wanted to do, but he knew he would not be able to sleep until he had made sure that neither Dan nor Leo Sterne's missing girl was there.

His car started with reasonable obedience this time, but the inside was like a fridge. As the engine warmed up, Oliver scraped a thick coating of ice from the windows. The roads were icy as well, black and treacherous. In this temperature it would take at least half an hour for heat to trickle into the car, and by that time he would either be back in his room at the Black Boar, or pounced on by Thalia Caudle as a trespasser, or even incarcerated in the nearest gaol. In view of the police sergeant's suspicious attitude, this last seemed the likeliest fate.

As he parked in a patch of deep shadow, he was beginning to think he should have risked calling in the police after all. But it was too late to back out now, so he took off his glasses which were apt to fall off at unpredictable moments and climbed cautiously over the tall iron gates.

As he made his way furtively up the tree-lined drive, he saw that the house was not in darkness this time. A chink of light showed from the large bay window on the left of the porch, where the curtain had not quite been fully drawn. Oliver eyed it. It would be spine-tinglingly risky to go up to that window and look inside, but now he was here he might as well see what he could. He began to inch forward. The house was surrounded by a wide gravel path and the gravel was loose and crunchy underfoot. Oliver was wearing rubber-soled shoes, but he had the horrid feeling that every step could be heard for several miles and that the walls of October House were tissue thin. He wondered how much Dan's book had influenced him, or even whether he was suffering from delusions. The possibility that some of his students had secretly laced his toothpaste with whatever disgusting drug was currently in fashion occurred to him as perfectly feasible.

The uncurtained section of window cast a narrow triangle of light across part of the garden. It was necessary to avoid standing in the beam of light, but it was also necessary to get as close as possible to the window if he was going to see anything. The gravel was a problem but Oliver had by this time discovered that if he went very slowly, letting his weight down gradually with each step, it made only the faintest of sounds. He approached the window in this fashion, hardly daring to breathe, expecting at any minute to see lights blaze all over the house and people come running out to question his presence. Supposing he had got it all wrong? Supposing this was the wrong house? But when, after what felt like a hundred years, he reached the window and crouched under the sill, peering in, he saw that the house was unquestionably the right one.

The room beyond the bay was large and lit by an over-head light and by rather dim wall lights on each side of the chimney breast. They looked as if they were the original gas brackets, adapted to take electricity. A fire burned in the hearth, and the room was comfortably furnished although it was not the last word in luxury. Set against the far wall was a glass-fronted bookcase and a round table of rather florid Victorian design, and drawn up to the fire were several deep armchairs with glazed chintz covers.

In one of the chairs sat a thin-faced dark-haired lady whom Oliver instantly recognised from the photograph in *Women in Business*, and then recognised on another, deeper level. Thalia Caudle. Dan's greedy, unscrupulous Margot. In the other chair was a thin girl who looked about eighteen but who had eyes that might have been any age. She was not very pretty and she was not at all attractive, but she had a face you would find it difficult to stop looking at. She was sitting bolt upright in the chair, her knuckles white where she was gripping the chair arms, and her eyes were fixed on Thalia with the most abject fear Oliver had ever seen in any living creature. Quincy?

His first instinct was to bang down the brass knocker on the door and demand admittance, and then to grab the girl and beat it out of Thalia Caudle's reach, trusting to God or the Devil to let him get clear. But you don't know that it is Quincy, said his mind sharply. And although she doesn't look very happy, she isn't tied up or under any kind of duress.

As Oliver watched, Thalia leaned forward. The leaping firelight fell across her face, and although she was smiling, it was the mad smile of the possessed and her eyes glittered. Oliver felt a shiver of fear. This was a creature drained of all humanity, as mad as the moonlight that showered its eerie radiance into the night, as malignant as Margot when she lured the trusting Anne-Marie into the dank outhouse.

Thalia stood up and moved to the girl's chair, and the girl shrank back. Thalia smiled, as if this was pleasing, and then reached out to touch the short, rough hair. She said something that Oliver could not catch, but whatever it was, it brought a sudden look of resignation to the girl's face. She stood up and began to undress. The firelight lit her thin, immature body to soft radiance, but even at this distance, even viewed through the chink of rain-spattered window, the cynicism in her eyes was apparent.

She's hating it, thought Oliver, torn between disgust and compulsion. She's hating it, but she's not really surprised by it. But I'm surprised. Did I misunderstand about Dan and Thalia that night? Or maybe she's one of those females who likes men and women. I don't think I want to see any more of this. It's supposed to be most men's ultimate fantasy, two females making love to one another, naked in front of a leaping fire, but there's nothing seductive about this. It's grotesque. There's something evil and wrong about it.

There was a moment when he thought a ghost image moved at Thalia's side – a lady a little younger, a little sharper of cheekbone and a little redder of lips. She crossed in front of the hearth, a phantom silhouette, caught and held by the leaping firelight. Oliver blinked and the image vanished.

Thalia was standing in front of the girl, running her hands over her body; her eyes were half-closed and there was an expression of extreme concentration on her face. She's *savouring* her, thought Oliver. This isn't about sex or lust, I was right about that; this is something much deeper and much darker.

And I'm no nearer to finding out what Thalia's aim is in all this, or whether she's got Dan, and I haven't the remotest idea what I'd better do next.

Chapter Thirty-two

Snatcher Harris had hugged his secret to himself all through the day.

There had been a lot of hours to get through but once they had stopped bothering him with their silly questions he had passed the time thinking about tonight; about taking Imogen out of her white bed, hugging her to him, feeling the soft, warm flesh through the thin nightgown she would be wearing, and then hiding her away for the Lady to come and fetch. He knew exactly where he was going to hide her; he had pointed to the place when the Lady had asked about this, and she had nodded and looked pleased.

He waited until everyone was safely asleep in the long dormitory where he had his bed and his locker, and then crept out, pausing by each of the beds. It gave you power to look at people while they were asleep; Harris liked doing it. Most people looked horrible. He stood over them all in turn, looking at their faces, seeing how they blubbered their lips in a snory way. When he left the dormitory, he did so carefully, shutting the door so that it did not click and wake anyone, and then scuttled along the corridor to Imogen's room.

Imogen did not look horrible while she was asleep. He knew this because he had crept into her room several times while there was no one about and stood looking down at her. It would have been nice to think she had been aware of him. It would have been very satisfying to think he might have got into her dreams, whatever they had been, and been frightened.

★ ★ ★

Imogen was not exactly asleep while Snatcher Harris was making his way towards her room, but she was not quite awake either. She thought that fragments of the strange forest place clung to her mind, and once or twice over the past two days she had been aware of the sick twilight still hovering on the outer rim of consciousness. Other things hovered there as well, but Imogen had not yet managed to sort them out properly. Her parents dying and something about Aunt Thalia, and something else about Quincy. She thought, vaguely, that it was odd that Quincy had not come to see her. Or had Quincy been at Briar House? The two places still got mixed up in her mind, but Dr Sterne had said that would get better. He had told her not to worry. He had a nice way of saying her name, *Imogen*, so that you thought about smoky-looking glasses and images reflected in fathomless pools. And his eyes were like melted silver merged with ebony. If you saw him in the dark they would glow.

She was falling deeper into sleep now. If she half closed her eyes she could just make out long, reaching shadows, like purple fingers, like melted bruises, oozing forward. It was like a travesty of that poem about Christopher Robin – 'If I open my eyes just a little bit more, I can see nannie's dressing gown on the door . . .'

But I have to *close* my eyes, thought Imogen, and if I do, I can see not the dressing gown on the door but the door itself, and it isn't a door into anywhere cosy and safe like Christopher Robin's nursery, it's the door into the dark world. And it's still partly open. But this was such a terrible thought that she pushed it down and buried it at once. You're supposed to be safe and sane, Imogen. If you start talking about creeping shadows slithering up out of fantasy worlds and doors opening up into evil forests, they really will put you in a padded cell!

She was just on the borderlands of genuine sleep when there was a sound outside her room. She did not immediately pay it any attention. It's your stupid imagination again,

371

Imogen. Doors into other worlds and bridges across to dream places . . . She was lying with her back to the door, and she was not even going to turn round to see . . .

And then the sound came again, and this time Imogen did turn round. The door of her room was being slowly inched open from the other side, and as the gap widened, a shaft of light from the dimly-lit corridor beyond slid across the floor. She was not immediately worried. This was a hospital of sorts and people came in and out all the time in hospitals. It was probably one of the nurses with something to be drunk or swallowed, or just to check her pulse or temperature. It might even be Leo Sterne, come to hear about her dream world.

No. Whoever was opening the door was certainly not Dr Sterne. Whoever it was was being much too furtive. Imogen propped herself up on one elbow to watch. There was another, different sound – something scuttling, something dragging one foot? – and fear began to well up. Imogen shrank back in the bed, clutching the sheets about her as if for protection. The door opened wider and standing there looking in at her was a grinning, drooling hunchback, its eyes glinting with red lust.

There was a moment when she thought he was not real. He's come up out of the dark forest to get me! flashed frighteningly across her mind. It was followed, almost at once, by: don't be stupid! It's an intruder, someone who's got out of one of the wards. Yell for help at the top of your voice!

Barely a heartbeat passed between these two thoughts, but in that time Snatcher Harris moved, loping across the room to the bed and clapping a hand smotheringly across her mouth. Imogen had drawn breath to scream, and the scream was choked. She struggled and fought but she was still infuriatingly weak from the long sleep. Harris had the advantage and he was stronger than he looked. He pinned her down on the bed and leaned over.

At any minute someone would come running. Imogen cast a frantic glance towards the door. Weren't there night staff here? Wasn't there an alarm bell? She could see the push button that Dr Sterne had indicated, but she could not reach it. Oh, blast you, let go of me, you disgusting creature! He was crooning to himself, not singing and not speaking but breathing rapidly with a dreadful wet, snuffling sound.

Different terror surfaced. He's going to rape me! And with the thought, Imogen aimed a desperate blow at his face. He dodged her hand easily as if he had been expecting it, grinning down at her. His lips were scabby and his teeth were disproportionately tiny, but the inside of his mouth was red and wet so that it was like seeing too ripe fruit split and leak rotten juices. This was disgusting, and Imogen struggled all over again, anger mingling with the fear, because she was damned if she was going to let this revolting little creature frighten her and she was damned if he was going to rape her either! She brought her knee up sharply, jabbing him hard in the groin. He let out a guttural grunt and his eyes – nasty, mean little eyes – bulged for a moment. Triumph surged in Imogen – got you! – and with it a spurt of strength, but the stifling hand did not relax its pressure, and the creature dug one hand into a jacket pocket and produced a thick scarf which he twisted round her mouth. It tasted of dirty wool and dried spittle and it was very nearly worse than his hand had been.

He pushed her on to her front, placing a knee in the small of her back to keep her down, and tied the scarf behind her head. Then, bringing out a second scarf, he tied her hands together as well. His fingers lingered over her tumbled hair, and then over the uncovered skin of her arms and Imogen felt dizzy and sick. This was appalling. None of it could be happening. But Imogen knew it was real. She was awake this time. If he touches me anywhere else I'll kick him again, she thought furiously. I'll kick him anyway when I can get a bit freer.

But he gave her no chance. He bent over and, lifting her up with ease, carried her to the door. She felt the iron muscles of his arms and shoulders again, and there was a dreadful moment when she was pressed against the concave chest. Imogen twisted her head back and forth, trying to bite through the gag or at the very least dislodge it enough to scream. No good. The gag held, and so did the knotted scarf round her hands.

Her captor paused at the door, peering out, and then, nodding to himself as if satisfied that no one was about, he carried her out into the corridor.

Lights burned out here, but they were the deliberately dim lights that you saw in hospitals at night. They were like the bluish glow you sometimes saw on films about night trains – *wagons-lits* and the midnight express. It was cold, rather eerie light, but it was enough for the hunchback to see his way and it was enough for Imogen to see where they went – along a couple of passageways and across a wide hall with a shallow staircase. There was the lingering smell she remembered in Briar House: sick people and yesterday's cooking.

Imogen was by now very frightened indeed, but she thought there would surely be a moment when she could get free. There would be a moment when she could tear away the gag and the scarf round her hands and yell for help. She would do it somehow, even if it meant she had to scratch the monstrous creature's eyes out.

They went through an oak-panelled door leading off the large hall. Imogen was still fighting to get free and hampering her captor's progress as much as possible, but she had the sudden impression of light shutting off, and of clustering darkness and dirt-crusted walls and floor. There was a stench of hopelessness and despair as well, and there was a sick unhappiness everywhere.

For a moment she was confused, because this was surely not part of Thornacre. Oh God, am I plunging into that cobwebby forest again after all? Is this the place at the black core where the slavering evil peered through the trees and rubbed its bony hands together?

As the hunchback went up a wide staircase with a scarred but beautiful oak banister, she caught sight of what looked like the remains of a printed notice. It was fixed to the wall and it was dim and age-spotted, but a shaft of moonlight lay across it and it was still readable.

... no attempts should be made to touch the Lunaticks, for although the Diet is extraordinary Good and Proper, yet they may be subject to Scurvy and Other Disease ... the Lunaticks may not be viewed on Sundays ...

Knowledge surfaced in a cold wave of terror, because even though Imogen had not been inside Thornacre for long – and for nearly all of that time she had been unconscious – she knew its history probably better than the people working here. None of the nurses had said anything, but Imogen knew about Thornacre, and she knew where the hunchback had brought her.

This was the haunted east wing. The place where the ghost was said to walk – Sybilla Campbell. Only she was once Sybilla Ingram, thought Imogen in horror. I don't suppose anyone here knows that. But I know it. And I know that this was the place where the madness surfaced and swamped her, and where she finally died in lonely, raving desolation.

There was just time to realise this, and to feel the ancient emotions and the long-ago terror and shut-away despair that had left their imprint here as plainly as if their symbols had been carved into the stones and the bricks. Then the hunchback took her through to a smallish room with a stone floor and a deep, square, old-fashioned sink. A small grimy window was set above the sink, and next to it was a huge copper boiler nastily crusted with green verdigris around the waste pipe. Imogen thought it might be a disused scullery or an old wash house. Her captor put her down on the floor, which felt cold and rough through the thin stuff of her nightgown, and then stepped back. Imogen tensed. Was this the moment when he would spring on her? But he did not. He looked about him, gave a satisfied little nod, and went away. There was the sound of the key turning in the lock and then of dragging footsteps going away. No one could possibly have heard them. No one could have heard him bringing her here.

She was huddled against one wall, just beneath the window. She stayed quite still and listened to the old wing settle back into silence. There was an occasional creak as a floorboard or a roof joist expanded or contracted, and the faint rustling of trees outside the window. She brought her knees up to her chest and braced her back against the wall, levering herself upwards until she was standing.

And then somewhere quite close by, somewhere that might have been at the end of a corridor or maybe up a short flight of stairs, there was a sound that was not timbers expanding or trees sighing. It was the sound of a massive door being opened and clanging back against the wall with a dull echo. The impression of something heavy and iron-banded printed itself on Imogen's mind. She shivered and pressed back into the concealing shadows. The hunchback returning?

She could see that beyond the window were the dark grounds of Thornacre. A rather horrid smell of clogged-up drains and mice and sour dishcloths wafted up from the sink beneath the window. Whoever was responsible for improving Thornacre either was not very efficient or had not got as far as this place.

Imogen was just trying to calculate if she could get herself on to the sink and break the window when she heard a sound that brought her heart lurching upwards and knocking against her ribs in sheer terror.

Somewhere quite close by several people were whispering.

It was the eeriest, most fearsome thing she had ever heard. To crouch helpless in the dark evil-smelling wash house and hear the whispering voices sent her heart thumping so wildly that for a second it almost blotted the sounds out altogether. Imogen took as many deep breaths as the gag allowed and fought to remain absolutely still and absolutely silent. She strained every nerve to listen.

And now she could make out isolated phrases. Things like, *'We're free, my dears . . .' 'We can leave . . .'* And then, *'Let's go this way . . .' 'But quietly so that no one hears us . . .'* There was a rather horrid sibilance as well, as if the whisperers might have lisping speech impediments, or as if the night stillness of Thornacre was picking up all the s sounds and giving them an echo, so that Imogen heard them as, *'This-s-s way, my dears-s-s . . . Quietly s-s-so that no one hears-s-s . . .'* For some reason this was unspeakably sinister.

Whoever the whisperers were, they were coming nearer. They were creeping slowly and stealthily towards this room; she could make out heavy padding footsteps now, and harsh, laboured breathing.

'This-s-s way . . . Into the darkness-s-s and away . . .'

It was impossible to avoid thinking that the dull, hollow, clanging door she had heard had been the door to some kind of prison being opened. He's let them out, whatever they are, thought Imogen in panic. The hunchback has let something out – several somethings –and they're coming towards me. Maybe they're coming *for* me! Maybe the hunchback left me here for them. As a sacrifice? As a present?

The door was locked from the other side, and she could see nowhere that would hide her, not even a cupboard under the sink into which she could squeeze. But whoever the people were – she must keep remembering that they could only be people and nothing more sinister – she could not just wait for them to come in. They might be friendly and helpful; they might untie her and help her back to her own room and raise the alarm. But they might not. They might be in league with the hunchback. It had sounded, in fact, as if they were escaping themselves – '*We're free, my dears-s-s* . . .' It would have to be the window.

She surveyed it. It was small but it was not as small as all that. It was grimy with the ingrained dirt of decades and very cobwebby but the panes looked large enough to get through, which was all that mattered. If she could get up on to the sink, she might manage to lever herself on to the narrow sill and break the glass. With her hands? Oh God, no, she would never do it, not with her hands still tied. And her feet were bare and anyway she could not risk cutting them because she might need to run. Was there something in here she could use to break the glass? What about the bit of waste pipe protruding from the copper boiler? If it would unscrew, it would be exactly right.

The copper waste was so corroded that it refused to budge. Imogen, hampered by having her hands tied behind her back, struggled fruitlessly for what felt like an eternity. And then, without the least warning, it snapped clean off and she was so startled that she almost dropped it. All right; now for the window.

If the hunchback had tied her ankles together she could never have done it. But although it was a bit awkward not having her hands for balance, she swung first one leg and then the other up into the sink until she was perched awkwardly on the narrow wooden draining board. The sink was brown pitted earthenware, with rusting taps, and the smell was disgusting. There were spiders and beetles. Imogen felt her feet brush against the plughole and shuddered, and then caught the whispers again: '*Through here, and then we'll be s-s-safe* . . .' Get on with it, girl.

Smashing the glass was not going to be very easy; even

using the copper pipe she would probably cut her hands quite badly and fragments of glass might have to be removed later on. But Imogen did not care if she had to be stitched up in fifty different places if it meant getting out before the whispery creatures reached her.

The scarf round her wrists gave unexpected protection. Her fingers were not very free but they were free enough for her to pull a piece of the cloth firmly over one hand. Here I go, thought Imogen, and lifting the pipe as far up as she could and tensing every muscle in her body, she cracked it hard against the glass. It shattered at once and Imogen thought it was not impossible that someone would hear it and come running. If she had been a housebreaker wanting to be silent and stealthy, the sound would no doubt have roused half of Thornacre and she would have been caught and hauled off to justice. But there were no welcome shouts and no friendly running feet, and if she had done anything at all she had probably let the whisperers know she was here. So you'll have to move quickly, you'll have to get out of here like a bat escaping hell.

Most of the glass seemed to have fallen outwards on to the ground outside, which was a mixed blessing because while it should mean she could get through without too much danger from the broken glass, she might land on it with her bare feet. Working more or less by guess, she swung the copper pipe twice more, and then twisted round to see how much of an escape hatch she had made. Yes, if she was careful she could get through. And quickly. Oh God, yes, she had to be very quick indeed. The creatures had heard the glass breaking, they had stopped dead and there was a moment of silence. But then the sounds reached her again, more clearly now.

'*What was-s-s that?*'

'*Better find out.*'

'*Better go and s-s-see, my dears-s-s.*'

'*Look in there . . . No, in there.*'

There was the sound of a door being stealthily opened

and then another. They're searching, thought Imogen in horror, and she flung herself forward to the window in a half-slither, half-crawl. The rough, old-fashioned drainer scraped her legs agonisingly and it felt as if a million splinters were jabbing into her flesh, but this did not matter any more than the broken glass mattered.

And then, '*There's-s-s s-s-someone in the old wash hous-s-se!*' said one of the voices and suddenly the voices were much nearer.

'*A girl! It's-s-s a girl!*'

'*How do you know?*'

'*I s-s-smell s-s-scent!*'

'*S-s-scent on the air, we s-s-smell it as-s-s well!*'

The sibilance of this last remark hissed malignantly through the darkness, and Imogen felt a new fear send her heart pounding again because there was something impossibly sinister about that last remark; there was something terrifyingly macabre about creatures who could smell you. It smacked of things not quite human, and the fee-fi-fo-fum hunting cry of giants.

They were already at the door, Imogen could hear them scrabbling at the lock. Sobbing with panic and the effort to breathe through the horrible gag, she swung her legs through the window, praying she had knocked out enough glass and there was not much of a drop outside.

She was halfway through the jagged hole and spiders were scuttling everywhere and dropping into her hair and it was disgusting and repulsive and she would never feel clean again – but let me get out and let me get free.

She was bracing herself for the drop to the ground when the wash-house door was pushed open. Framed in the opening, silhouetted against the dim light of the passage behind was the most fearsome sight Imogen had ever seen: several huge-headed, huge-framed people with great meaty faces and overhanging brows and thatches of ragged hair. *Huge. Giant-like . . .*

Imogen gave another gasping sob and slid through the broken window. She landed on the ground with a breath-snatching thump.

Chapter Thirty-three

Getting Snatcher Harris to release the acromegaly patients as cover for Imogen's abduction had been a master stroke. Thalia was not going to waste valuable energy or emotion on being pleased, and she was certainly not going to fall into the trap of complacency, but she thought that if she had searched for a hundred years she could not have found anything better suited to use as a diversion.

Leo Sterne had been evasive, but to anyone with even a shred of understanding the situation had been clear. To anyone who had listened carefully to local gossip and interposed the occasional shrewd question, it was very plain indeed that Thornacre still had its secrets. Thalia had looked up the word acromegaly, using the small but well-stocked library in Blackmere, which was one of the places she had used to establish her innocent and worthy persona here, and where she had become acquainted with the head librarian. The small reference section had yielded only a brief entry on acromegaly, but it had been clear enough. The word derived from the Greek: *akron* meaning topmost, and *megas* meaning large. The description of the disease was as Leo Sterne had said.

Thalia had folded the information away; it might become of use or it might not. And now, tonight, it had been of very good use indeed.

It had meant trusting the Harris creature a bit further, but Thalia thought it was not so very much of a risk. As she sat in her car, parked in the deep shadows a little way from Thornacre's iron-sheeted gates, excitement was coursing through her and she was so strongly aware of Edmund's hovering presence that it was almost as if he was in the car with her. Soon now, my lovely boy . . .

As the tiny green figures of the dashboard clock ticked away the minutes, a faint curl of unease brushed her mind. Had Harris done it? He was taking longer than she had calculated. She had allowed an hour for him to carry Imogen to the deserted east wing and lock her in the disused wash house, and then set free the grotesque things in the barred room. With the freaks lumbering around on the loose and the alarm given, the confusion would allow her and Harris to carry Imogen out of the wash house and through the culvert tunnel. From there they would bundle Imogen into the car and be back in October House within fifteen minutes.

From this part of the road the house was hidden from view by the brick wall and the thickthorn and briar. Had she found accurately the place that was Harris's culvert entrance? Supposing she had missed it? Supposing she had misunderstood, or he had been caught? Worst of all, supposing he was less sane than she had judged him? The tunnel might not exist outside the creature's mad fantasy world.

And then he was there, lurching grinningly out of the clump of trees, clearly pleased with his own cunning. Thalia wound the window down and said sharply, 'You've done what I told you? Imogen's locked in the east wing? And the freaks are loose? Good, well done. You know what to do next. Go back inside and wait by the culvert entrance until I come.'

The next part was easy, and it would be enjoyable because it involved fooling people again. Thalia drove to the phone box she had picked out days earlier; it was a little further away than was absolutely ideal but you could not have everything. It had been necessary to use a box which was not on the main road, and which was not too conspicuously well lit. At this time of night most phone boxes were like a lit stage and any passing motorist might see and remember her.

She did not meet any other cars, and it took barely five minutes to drive to the phone box. She dialled the Thornacre police station and as soon as someone answered she reported in a frantic voice that several potentially dangerous patients had escaped. It was easy to flatten her voice a little and shorten the vowel sounds to sound faintly northern. It was easy to send the pitch up several octaves to suggest slightly hysterical panic. She did not overdo it. She was not sure if they would be able to tell that she was using a pay phone, but it was a reasonable bet that a small, remote police station would not be equipped with the latest technology. And even if they could tell it was a pay phone and suspected a hoax, even if they could trace the exact phone box, they would still have to check the story. And find that it was true. Either way, she could not possibly be connected to any of it.

'We're very concerned,' she said. 'We don't know how far outside Thornacre they've got. Can someone come right away?'

It was a different voice to the one who had asked the questions about Quincy, which was not surprising since this was the middle of the night. 'How dangerous?' it asked. 'Violent?'

'Well, yes. Potentially.'

There appeared to be a hasty consultation, and then another, more authoritative, slightly older voice came on. 'Sergeant Pomfret here. How long is it since the patients got out? Do you know?'

'Not precisely. But we think not very long.'

'All right, we're on our way to you. Are the gates shut? Have any of them actually got out of the grounds?'

384

'I don't know, we're checking on that now. We're in a bit of confusion here.'

'We'll be with you at once,' said the voice. 'Can I have your name?'

Thalia had been ready for this. She said, 'I'm the sister in charge of them.' Her tone had a strong flavour of 'Who did you think I was, you fool?' 'I'm sorry, someone's calling, I'll have to go. Please hurry. We won't unlock the gates, but if you call through the intercom we'll let you in.'

Saying she was the sister was another risk, but like the others it was not a very big one. People at Thornacre would ask one another who had phoned the police and no one would know and everyone would assume that somebody else had done it. It did not matter. The important thing now was to get into the grounds unseen through Harris's tunnel, and get Imogen out to October House.

Imogen had missed the broken glass, but the drop from the window had jarred her heels and sent a shuddering pain up her spine and into the base of her neck. She almost over-balanced because of not having the use of her arms, but she managed to keep upright.

The obvious thing to do now was to go round the side of the house to the front and somehow rouse them. She had no idea whether there would be a bell or how entry was gained, but there would presumably be something.

She had landed in a patch of half-cultivated garden, probably once a small kitchen or herb garden which had been neglected. This was lucky because to have landed with bare feet on concrete or even gravel would have been pretty nasty. She stood in the darkness for several minutes, trying to get her bearings, and then set off, trying to close her mind to the shadows which might be hiding the appal-ling things who had broken into the wash house and trying not to think about what she had seen. I'll face that one afterwards, thought Imogen. When I'm safe and when this is all over. Then I'll face it.

The night was filled with little stirrings and rustlings and it was unbelievably eerie to be creeping towards the house's front like this. Imogen expected at any minute to be confronted by one of the grotesque creatures who had broken into the wash house. If that happened, she would run like the furies into the night and hide in the undergrowth and the trees. But of course it would not happen; she would reach the front quite safely and ring the bell or manage to sound the door knocker and people would come running. Dr Sterne would certainly come. She would hold on to the thought of Dr Sterne getting her out of this.

Twice she froze because surely there had been the sound of someone creeping along behind her, and once she thought there was a flicker of movement on the edge of her vision, as if something huge and lumpish was lumbering silently out of the clump of trees fringing the carriageway.

She went warily on, staying close to the side of the building, keeping in the deep shadow that it cast. Another twenty steps and she would reach the corner; she would only have to turn to the left and surely, oh surely she would be at Thornacre's front. Eighteen steps, fifteen . . . Almost there. Nothing's happened, no one's come lunging out at you, Imogen. Keep going.

She had actually reached the corner, and there ahead of her was the blessed sight of a deep porch like a church, with an old-fashioned bell pull on one side. She could not reach either hand to it, but if she could get to it, she could lean on it and keep leaning until someone came.

She was within a dozen steps of the porch when the darkness suddenly and terrifyingly coalesced, and coming towards her with a horrid lurching, shambling gait were two – no, three! – of the macabre creatures who had broken into the old wash house. They were blocking her way to the house's front.

A wave of panic engulfed Imogen and she backed away at once, stumbling in the other direction, into the safe darkness. The ground sloped down, and several times she slipped and almost fell, but each time she managed to right herself and keep going. She thought she must be on Thornacre's main driveway; she could make out immense gates up ahead, backed with sheets of iron so that no one could see in or out. On each side of the gates was a high brick wall, and in the thin, cold moonlight it was possible to see that the bricks were old and dry-looking and covered with lichen and moss.

Coming up out of the ground, seeming to rise up from the bracken and undergrowth and wreathed in shadows and twining ivy, was the thin, hungry outline of a woman.

The last person Imogen had been expecting to see. Her aunt, Thalia Caudle. And at her side was the hunchback.

The hunchback grabbed her at once, and this time there was no doubt about the lasciviousness of his embrace. He clutched her to him, grunting repulsively, and a dribble of saliva slobbered on to Imogen's neck, wetting her skin and the edge of her nightgown. She shuddered and tried to kick him, but he had a firm hold and he half carried, half dragged her into what looked like an ancient gully sunk deep into the ground near the old wall. There was a rising stench of dirt and dead or decaying things and as he carried her along, Thalia ahead of them, Imogen felt a wave of nausea. If the hunchback came this way often it was no wonder he smelt so disgusting.

The walls and the ceiling of the tunnel were rounded; it was probably an old drain. Their footsteps echoed hollowly as they went, and Thalia's torch showed up the rusting iron of the drain and the cracks where tree roots had forced through. They looked like pale, blind worms and Imogen shuddered.

She was just starting to think they had been down here for ever and that she could not bear it much longer when the tunnel ended abruptly. In front of them was an iron ladder

387

nailed vertically into the wall. A dim dusk-light filtered down, and as Thalia grasped the lower rungs and climbed up, she was silhouetted blackly against it. The hunchback waited for her to reach the top, and then slung Imogen over his shoulder and swarmed after her. This time Imogen did not dare to struggle in case he dropped her and she went tumbling down on to the tunnel floor. As he went up the ladder her face was pressed against the hump of curving bone on his back.

They came out into a small copse where a car was parked. The hunchback bundled Imogen into the back and got in next to her. As Thalia drove away, there was just time to catch a glimpse of Thornacre in the wing mirror, and to see that after all someone had raised the alarm, because lights were blazing in almost every window.

As the car drove away from Thornacre, the hunchback turned suddenly and stared through the rear window. In the dim light, his face wore a look of gloating triumph.

The tenuous, fragile plan that Dan had concocted had to be put into operation at once. It would not be a very pleasant thing to do, but it would be even more unpleasant to die at Thalia Caudle's hands and the hunchback's, knowing that his body would be used in some gruesome ritual involving the resurrection of the thing lying inside the freezer.

The thing lying inside the freezer . . .

The plan was based on a mixture of trickery and black-mail and barefaced effrontery – what in Adam Cadence might have been described as 'dash' but what in Dan was sheer desperation. It might work spectacularly well or it might fail ignominiously, but even failure was preferable to simply sitting here, hands folded, waiting for night to fall. Dan refused to consider the prospect of failure, ignominious or otherwise.

Thalia or the hunchback had judged the chain precisely. Dan had already tested its length in every direction, and discovered that he could reach quite a large section of the cellar. He could not reach the door, and he could not reach the electric socket and plug powering the freezer itself because they were on the far side and the chain brought him up short. But he could reach the freezer lid.

He propped it wide open, having first plundered the boxes of household jumble and found a couple of old pewter jugs that were about the right height and size. Adam Cadence would have been able to knock up a super-structured contrivance, or make a block and tackle out of a couple of spent matchsticks, but Dan thought the jugs were pretty effective for the job, which was to hold the lid to its widest extent so that there was no risk of it descending unexpectedly on his head. Thalia had left him his torch, and he propped it so that the thin beam would shine straight on to the freezer's interior. And then he reached inside.

It was excruciatingly difficult. The freezer was lined with its own ice, and Dan's fingers and wrists were aching with cold within the first couple of minutes. The cuffs of his jacket were absorbing the freezing moisture as well, and he pushed them back impatiently and gritted his teeth. *If you get out of here in one piece, you can lie in a scaldingly hot bath for five hours.*

The thing that had once been Edmund Caudle, and that had also been three hopeful, slightly lustful young men, was wedged tightly into the freezer and packed with ice. There was a bad moment when Dan felt the handless arms. Revulsion scudded across his skin, and he remembered that there was still a grisly final operation to be carried out. Quincy, Thalia had said. Imogen's friend. Then this was as much to save the unknown Quincy as anyone. Dan forced himself to go on.

The ice would plainly have to be chipped away. Dan looked around for something to use for this. What about the steel strips banding both the sea chests? A section from

389

one, six or eight inches long, snapped free of the dry, brittle wood easily enough, and he returned to the task.

There was a cracking sound as the last layer of ice splintered and in the enclosed cellar it echoed like the crack of doom. Dan cast a quick look over his shoulder. It would be exactly like Thalia to have crept down the stairs unnoticed and be standing there watching. But nothing moved and nothing stood watching him, and the shadows were quiescent.

Slowly, inch by careful inch, Dan got the appalling thing out. It came stiffly and awkwardly like a wooden doll, and it felt exactly like a monstrous piece of frozen butcher's meat. Don't think about that! Think of it as simply an instrument of escape. But beneath the forced calm, Dan's mind was skittering. Up you come, Edmund, upsadaisy now. Let's sit you in the chair and dust off the nasty bits of ice . . . Dan suspected that he was not wholly sane at the moment, but for heaven's sake, who could be sane prising a frozen body – lumps of frozen joined-together bodies – out of a deepfreeze!

There was a truly horrific moment when the thing was out of the container and standing vertical, with Dan holding it in the travesty of an embrace, keeping it upright. His hands slithered down over the glazed skin and the body rocked and almost fell back. Dan snatched at it but his fingers were numb from the cold, and it slithered back from him, crashing to the floor. A flurry of ice splinters flew out from the skull and shoulders. Dan shuddered and set himself to drag the thing back up and then to prop it up in the chair facing the cellar steps.

The longer Thalia left it before coming back down here the better. The more the body could thaw out the better as well. The instant Thalia saw it, the instant she saw that Dan had tampered with her grisly plan, she would be across the cellar like a wild cat. And if Dan was quick, and not squeamish about striking a female, he could surely overpower her, get the key to the chain and escape.

He switched off the torch to save the batteries – he could flick it on the second he heard her coming. The darkness closed down, absolute and stifling, and pitchier than the pitchiest black night. There was no sound except the steady drip-drip of the ice melting as the body began to thaw.

Chapter Thirty-four

As Harris carried Imogen down the stairs of October House, she had the feeling that the dark evil of the ancient enchanted dream forest was returning. Wherever this place was, it had the same clotting malevolence.

Thalia had taken down an old-fashioned oil lamp from a hook in the large, stone-flagged kitchen, and she was leading the way down, holding it aloft as she went. Her shadow flickered grotesquely on the stone walls, and the long, dark mackintosh she was wearing swirled around her ankles like a cloak.

Imogen was very frightened indeed by now, but she was managing to maintain a semblance of calm. The situation was so wildly unreal that she was no longer sure if it was really happening. It was entirely possible that she was still partly in the forest nightmare.

Thalia unlocked a small door at the foot of the steps, and as it swung open, a sour stench of age and mildew and mice gusted out, and with it something else. Something rotten and tainted. Imogen's stomach began to churn and for a truly terrible moment she was back in the Hampstead graveyard with Dr Sterne and the others, uncovering her mother's coffin. She was smelling the appalling breath of corruption as the lid came up, and then seeing the twisted, screaming thing inside . . . Don't think about it. Concentrate on what this is all about and on getting free. I can't believe that Thalia has brought me down here like this. Clearly she's mad – oh God, yes, Sybilla and Lucienne . . .

Oh God, then this might be even worse than I thought.

Thalia had stopped dead on the threshold of what seemed to be an inner cellar, and drew in a deep, shuddering breath. Even before she screamed like a scalded cat and bounded forward, Imogen understood that something had gone very wrong. Whatever her aunt's plan had been, whatever mad, warped logic lay behind all this, something had gone wrong. And then the hunchback pushed Imogen forward and she skidded several feet and came up against the left-hand wall in a confused tumble. It was a moment before she managed to sit up, but when she did sit up, she saw everything with terrible clarity.

At first sight it looked as if there were two people imprisoned down here. One of the two was a young man with untidy dark hair and intelligent eyes. He was seated on the ground quite near to where Imogen had fallen, his back against the wall, his knees drawn up. His eyes were on Thalia, and with a jolt of shock Imogen recognised him. The young man at Edmund's funeral. The dark-haired, good-looking young man who had come to help her while everyone else was staring in stunned, stupid silence, not knowing what to do. She had wanted to phone him, or write a little note to thank him for being so kind, only she had never done it because it had been the next day that the nightmares had started. And I don't think they ever stopped, not really. I think this is another nightmare down here, or maybe it's the same one. The nightmare continuing . . . It sounded like one of those screamer captions you saw splashed across posters for horror films and books. Scarlet blood-dripping letters on a black background and an exclamation mark. She stared at Dan over the scarf gag because for some reason he seemed to be a point of gravity in a dangerously rocking world, and then she looked back at the thing at the cellar's centre that had caused Thalia to give that single, agonised scream.

The nightmare continuing, and deepening . . .

It was sprawled across a broken bentwood chair, and it was the most macabre thing Imogen had ever seen. It was the body of a young man, plainly most dreadfully dead, but it was not so much the death look that was macabre; it was that everything about the body was wrong. It was so utterly wrong and so fearsomely out of proportion that it made Imogen feel dizzy and sick to look at it. But there was a terrible compulsion about it; once you had looked you had to keep looking, to make sure you had seen right. Or perhaps to hope you had seen wrong.

She had not seen wrong. The body appeared to have all the right number of arms and legs and shoulders, but the arms did not quite join up with the shoulders, and the shoulders themselves had a dislocated look. The hips and legs were at a sickeningly wrong angle to the torso, and she saw that the wrists ended in jagged stumps. And the head . . .

The ancient cellar with the appalling too-sweet stench and the steady glow of light from the oil lamp blurred and threatened to start spinning her into sick darkness again, because the head, *the head* . . .

Her cousin Edmund, his face and head dripping with icy moisture. Not decomposing, but *thawing*. Imogen stared. Yes, it *was* Edmund. Oh God, yes, I remember it all now. The afternoon of the funeral. Someone took his head out of the coffin and hid it under the dish. He's deteriorated a bit since then, thought Imogen, in panic. But it was Thalia all the time. She stole Edmund's head. Has she kept him all this time? Then I was right, and she really is mad, she's a million times madder than Sybilla and Lucienne put together. I'm locked in with a madwoman and a hunchback. No, there's this young man as well. She glanced at Dan once more, almost as if to reassure herself that he had not disappeared, and then looked helplessly back to the Edmund-thing on the chair.

Edmund's once-bright hair was plastered to his head,

matted and darkened. His eyes were closed, the lashes beaded with moisture, but even like this it was possible to make out the mean craftiness. He died with the sly mood on him, thought Imogen. And if you discount the awful *warped* look, he doesn't look very dead after all. He looks as if he might open his eyes at any minute, as if he might jerk himself to his feet and come walking across the floor . . . But with this thought she twisted her hands behind her back until she could dig the nails of one hand into the palm of the other, because she would not let herself fall back into that terrible haunted forest, she absolutely would not.

It was then that the unknown young man moved across to her, and with angry impatience tore the scarves away, freeing her wrists and her mouth. Imogen gasped and took a grateful shuddering breath of ordinary air for the first time in what felt like hours, and said, a bit indistinctly, 'Oh, thank you. What—'

'We'll go into the *what* all in good time,' said the young man. 'At the moment it's a question of the *when*. As in, when do we get out of here.' He glanced at Thalia, and then looked back at Imogen and grinned suddenly. 'At the moment your aunt's holding centre stage, I'm afraid,' he said. 'It's a good performance, although she's going a bit over the top for my taste.'

The sense of having fallen into somebody else's dream increased, but trying to match his coolness, Imogen said, 'She always did go over the top.' Her voice came out a bit better this time.

'With any luck she'll burn herself out and we can do something to get free. I don't suppose you've got any ideas on that score, have you?'

'Well, no, but I'm working on it.'

'Good girl. I'm Dan Tudor, by the way.'

'I wish I could say I was happy to meet you, Mr Tudor, but—'

'But you'd really rather not be here. I'd really rather not be here either.' He sent another speculative glance to Thalia and Imogen saw a hard anger show briefly in his eyes.

'I saw you at Hampstead that afternoon,' she said, tentatively.

'Yes. We weren't introduced, were we?' Again the smile. 'But I know who you are, Imogen.'

Dan had thought he was prepared for the sight of Imogen – he had known Thalia intended to bring her here – but when she half walked, half fell into the cellar, white and dishevelled, his heart had lurched painfully.

When she managed to make that slightly ironic rejoinder, he felt something soft and inexorable fasten itself about his mind and his guts, and even with the appalling danger closing all around them, he knew a sudden sense of fatalism. Until now he had been equating Imogen with his own Rosamund, and Rosamund, it had to be said, was not possessed of the quality known as irony. She was beautiful and gentle and kind, but ironic, no. Dan stared down at Imogen's pale, smudged face and thought, I was really rather hoping that if I ever did meet you properly, you'd turn out to be a pretty nonentity –well, all right, a *beautiful* nonentity – so that I could dismiss you; say thanks, Imogen, for providing the inspiration for my book, see you around sometime. But I don't think I'm going to be able to walk away from you, always assuming we get out of here and I can walk away anywhere.

He turned back to where Thalia was standing over Edmund. After that first tormented cry she had not spoken, but Dan saw now that she was dabbing the monstrous head with a handkerchief, blotting up the trickling water, stroking the dead flesh.

And so much for plans about setting traps and jumping on villainesses and wresting the keys from their hands. When Thalia had moved, the hunchback had moved with her and he was standing between Thalia and Dan, holding a fearsome-looking iron bar threateningly. It was no consolation to Dan to think that the world was probably littered with people who had overreached and underestimated, and to realise that he was now one of them. For a split second he considered bounding forward and trusting to luck that he could take the hunchback by surprise, but even as the idea formed he discarded it. The creature was deformed and apparently more or less dumb, but his eyes showed a cruel intelligence, and they had never once left Dan. In the brief time it would take him to get to his feet, the hunchback would have brought the iron bar crashing down. And this time he might not recover so easily. And supposing it was not him at all but Imogen that the creature attacked? He thought, well, at least I've disrupted their plans by hauling that thing out of its bizarre coffin. They might have to rethink and that might give me an opportunity.

Thalia stood behind the chair holding the body and fixed her eyes on Dan. He only just managed not to flinch because there was such blazing hatred in her expression. But when she spoke her voice was controlled and soft.

'It was a clever idea,' said Thalia. 'Although it's a pity for you that it wasn't quite clever enough. You intended me to come near enough for you to get the key and then escape, didn't you?'

Dan said, equably, 'It seemed a reasonable assumption.' He glared at the hunchback, who leered and brandished the iron bar. 'But even so, I've screwed up your plans, Thalia,' he said. 'What are you going to do now with that lump of half-decaying flesh over there? What *can* you do, except burn it or bury it?'

There was a sudden silence and Dan thought he had miscalculated or misjudged, and that she would simply order her familiar to kill them both there and then. He tightened his arm about Imogen.

Thalia said, 'You haven't screwed anything up at all, Dan. In fact you've helped me. You've brought things forward by several hours.' She regarded them both for a moment, and then brought out of the pocket of her jacket a small, silver-mouthed pistol. The smile that Quincy had seen as an ogress smile showed as she levelled it at the two prisoners.

'I was going to sacrifice you both at dawn,' she said. 'Along with Quincy. But instead, I'm going to do it now.'

And then, looking across at Harris, she said, 'Help me get them up to the studio. Chain them up with Quincy. And then we'll fire the kiln.'

The essence of all the best plans was simplicity, and Thalia employed simplicity now, keeping the pistol levelled as Harris unlocked Dan's chain. 'Don't try to escape, Dan,' she said coldly. 'And don't try any ridiculous chivalrous rescue bid either.'

'Heaven forfend. What do you want me to do?'

'Carry Imogen up the stairs,' said Thalia. 'Harris will go first, carrying the lamp, and you'll follow him. I'll bring up the rear. And remember, I've got a gun. If you try to escape I'll shoot you in the stomach and leave you down here to die.'

'Always the feminine touch, Thalia,' said Dan.

The potter's small kiln was already heating and the studio was filling up with the hot-iron scent as Harris and Thalia chained their captives to the wall. It was a good scent, a purging, cleansing scent. It would consume the remains very efficiently. Thalia had studied the kilns carefully in preparation of her plan; there were three of them and they were all electrically fired, but tonight Thalia was firing the one called a burning kiln, used for glazing earthenware objects, which reached a temperature high enough for vitrification.

She turned to survey her three prisoners. Dan and the bitch-girl were both safely chained and at least twelve feet separated them so that there could be no collaboration, no mad attempt at an escape.

Quincy was lying in one corner where Thalia herself had put her. She had enjoyed the girl's body earlier tonight; she had savoured Quincy's fear and it had lent an edge to all the things she had made Quincy do. But it was time now for Quincy to be sacrificed to Edmund, just as the young men who had gone before her had been sacrificed.

Harris had tied Quincy's hands and feet and he was playing his part very well indeed. Quincy was plainly terrified, and she was trying to crawl towards the door and escape. Harris stood watching her, playing cat and mouse with her. Each time he waited for her to get within a few feet of the door, watching with a drooling leer, and then pounced and brought her back. It was good to see Harris so zealous; Thalia had sensed a brief rebelliousness from him while they were inside Thornacre earlier on. But it was all right.

Harris had remembered what he had to do with the kiln as well. As its temperature began to rise, he picked up the long iron spline that secured the circular door and slotted it into the horizontal grooves on the door's front. The handle protruded on the right-hand side, and Harris grasped it and bore his weight down on it, rotating it through 360 degrees. The grotesque shape of his distorted back was cruelly outlined against the kiln, which was beginning to glow with inner heat. As the spline turned the full circumference, the locking mechanism ground home. Harris nodded to himself as if satisfied, and came loping back.

Thalia's lip curled with contempt as Imogen called out to Quincy, telling her not to be afraid, and Dan said something about escape, about how they would all get out of here. This was all so stupid as to be not worth even listening to, and in any case she wanted them afraid. She wanted them to die knowing what was being done to them; most of all she wanted Imogen to die knowing. If they continued to call out to one another, they would have to be gagged.

Only when she was absolutely sure that everything was in

place and that nothing had been forgotten did she help Harris to carry Edmund's body up and to arrange it on the potter's long, bare table. She hated seeing the hunchback's grubby horny hands on Edmund, but it was unavoidable. Once Edmund's body had been arranged on the scrubbed table top, she dismissed the hunchback to the shadows; only her own hands would touch Edmund from now on.

As she went about her final preparations, careful to keep her distance from all three prisoners, Thalia felt the golden inner strength filling her mind. Exultation welled up. This was how high priests had felt as they prepared for ritual sacrifice; it was how the flamens and the druids had felt. And the next few minutes should see a life for a life.

The potter had installed bright, soulless, fluorescent strip lighting in his studio, but Thalia ignored it and lit candles, scarlet ministers of light that made pools of gentle radiance, soft blurry circles that overlapped in places. As she placed them at each end of the long table, they cast their warm, gentle light over Edmund's body, and their scent mingled with the sweet scent of Edmund's flesh and skin and hair. The longing for his presence was so strong that it was physical agony. Thalia paused to stroke the poor dead face, and then took up the ceremonial position in front of the long table. Harris went to and fro, remembering all he had been told, laying a clean white cloth over Edmund's lower body, bringing forward the finely-honed knives. The blades caught the light and glinted redly.

Exultation was filling Thalia like a fiery golden river, and the blood of all the high priestesses was coursing through her veins. She was Deborah of the Old Testament, stirring up Barak to march against Sisera; she was Flaminica of the ancient Roman Dialis. She was Sibyl of Cumae guiding Aeneas through the underworld, and she was the Delphic Pythia. She understood now what she had not fully understood before: there was a link, a chain of power, passed down and passed on. Her ancestresses had known it and they had harnessed it and then channelled it. Sybilla (mark the name!) and Lucienne had done it. The others, further back, whose names had faded or been lost or forgotten, had done it as well. People had thought them mad, people might think she herself was mad, but they were very far from mad. They were the keepers of the ancient flamelike power. The knowledge that in another few minutes she would use that power to bring Edmund back to her was like a heady draught of champagne to her brain.

As Sibyl had guided Aeneas through the underworld, so Thalia would now guide Edmund up from the death-sleep and into the world again. She looked down at him, at the golden hair, at the white alabaster skin that would shortly be filled with warm, flowing blood; at the closed eyes that would soon open and see her once more.

Chapter Thirty-five

The discovery that the acromegalic patients in the east wing had somehow got out and that the police had been summarily called angered Leo, but he banked his feelings down as much as possible.

The police inspector was the one who was in charge of Quincy's disappearance, and Leo thought he was intelligent and efficient. He explained that when the acromegalics were found they would have to be treated with caution.

'Most of them have been in one institution or another for the better part of their lives,' he said. 'Two or three of them in Thornacre itself, in fact. I'm afraid they were quite badly treated by my predecessor. He kept them half comatose on huge doses of largactil for years – that's an appallingly old-fashioned treatment – and they were in a pitiful condition when I came here. I've been trying to reduce the medication and gradually bring them nearer to the real world. We've tried to give them their own quarters – the nearest thing to a self-contained flat that Thornacre can provide—'

'They were kept in the east wing?'

Leo saw the inspector's mind silently frame the words 'haunted wing', and he said quickly, 'Yes, it worked quite well. It wasn't precisely a halfway house, but it meant they could be introduced to a semblance of normality. The therapists have been teaching them some social skills. Most of them had never so much as made a cup of tea, poor things, or even watched a television programme.'

'And there was nothing out of the ordinary about them tonight?'

'No. As far as I can make out, the nurses gave them supper as usual and locked the wing up at half past nine.'

'Well, somebody must have done something out of the ordinary somewhere,' said the inspector. 'Left a door unlocked, or a window. We'll check. But I'm bound to say there are a few suggestive facts about all this, Dr Sterne.'

'What kind of suggestive facts?'

'It looks as if there might have been a bit of inside help given to your acromegalics. We've searched the grounds pretty thoroughly now, but so far we haven't found hide nor hair nor whisker of them.' He paused, and then said, 'You've got a fairly sophisticated electronic locking system on those main gates, Dr Sterne.'

'We need it. There are several acute cases here. What about it?'

'If your missing patients got as far as the gates, could they have understood how to open them?'

'Of course not. I doubt they could manage to change a light bulb.'

'Then, Dr Sterne, somebody helped them to get through, either by explaining how the gates worked or by opening them, or . . .' He hesitated.

Leo said, 'Go on.'

'Or there's a way out of Thornacre we haven't found yet. I suppose there aren't any hidden exit routes, are there?'

'Secret tunnels?' said Leo, with a brief smile. 'You've been listening to village gossip, Inspector.'

'Yes, I have, and you'd be surprised how useful it can be at times, sir.'

'I wouldn't,' said Leo. He frowned, thinking. 'I don't know of any hidden tunnels or secret passages,' he said. 'But that doesn't mean there aren't any. I haven't been here very long, and we're still working on the renovations. Some of the older nurses might know if there's anything. I daresay you'll want to question them.' He paused, and then added wryly, 'Again.'

'Yes. You've had a run of bad luck here, haven't you, sir?' said the inspector non-committally. 'Tell me about these acromegalics. How disturbed are they?'

'They have some intelligence,' said Leo. 'And also some sensitivity. But they certainly won't be able to cope with the outside world, although they won't realise that. They'll be a bit like children; they'll think they can cope until they're brought up against something out of their experience. Faced with a battery of policemen and bright lights they might react.'

'Violently?'

'Abruptly.' There was no need to give details about oculogyric crises involving obsessive behaviour patterns, or about the nightmares and 'daymares' that sometimes reached hallucinatory proportions.

'We could use nets to catch them,' said the inspector. 'Or tranquillising darts.'

'Not nets,' Leo said at once. 'I'll get you some chlorpromazine and diazepam from the dispensary. By the way, who phoned you?'

'We didn't get the name but she said she was the sister in charge of the wing.'

Leo started to say, 'But there isn't a—', realised that this was only wasting time and could be gone into later, and went through to the dispensary to write up the order for the sedatives.

On the way back he made two discoveries. One was that Snatcher Harris had apparently gone on one of his tomcat wanderings again. The other was that Imogen had vanished.

Leo passed this new development on to the inspector at once, answered what appeared to be a string of totally unrelated questions, and returned to his office. His mind was churning and his whole body felt as if it was a mass of

404

raw, exposed emotion. Imogen, his beautiful enigmatic wood nymph, had vanished.

He had no means of knowing if she had gone out into the night of her own accord, or if Harris or the acromegalics had taken her, or if someone had taken the acromegalics. Or if it was a combination of any of these things, or none of them. But he could not believe that Imogen had gone voluntarily. His mind presented him with the picture of her creeping out of Thornacre under cover of darkness, and he repudiated it at once. She would not have done it; she would not have gone like that, leaving him prey to agonised concern. Oh, wouldn't she, though? jeered his mind. Why do you imagine she'd give you a second thought? You're forty to her seventeen; that's a gap of twenty-three years and it's verging on the indecent. Svengali was a dirty old man if you analyse it and Frankenstein was a megalomaniac. She's probably been thinking of you – if she's been thinking of you at all – as a father figure. The nice doctor who helped her out of an illness. Probably there was a boyfriend all along only you never found out, and probably she got a message from him and now she's gone to meet him and they're at it somewhere in the bushes, or on the back seat of his car.

The thought of Imogen helpless and afraid somewhere beyond Thornacre's boundaries was like a knife turning in his guts, but the thought of her with some eighteen- or nineteen-year-old boy dug his guts out and flung them on to a blazing pyre.

He could hear the police still searching the grounds outside and he supposed he should be out there with them, but it seemed more important to remain in one place so that news would find him without any delay. Twice there was a timid tap on the door and he looked up in sudden hope, but the first time was only a request to know if he was all right or wanted anything, and the second was to bring in a tray of sandwiches and coffee. He ate and drank with the uninterest of an engine refuelling.

The disappearances had to be linked; it was stretching coincidence beyond credibility to believe anything else. Quincy, Imogen, Harris and the acromegalics. There had to be a common denominator. The thought lodged in his mind, but it was a maddeningly elusive thought and it was infuriatingly formless. It was like trying to grasp quicksilver or a piece of a rainbow. Harris was the most suspect of the lot, but Leo doubted that the Snatcher had sufficient intelligence to spirit away so many people. Oliver Tudor had believed Thalia Caudle was involved, but how? And why? Had she made an accomplice of Harris? Would anyone make an accomplice of Harris? And what could possibly be the motive?

Leo tilted his chair back and stared up at the ceiling. Imogen, Harris, Quincy, the acromegalics. Thalia Caudle. Did anything link them? *Think*, Leo. He rearranged the names in his mind to see if a different pattern formed. Thalia, Harris, the acromegalics. Quincy, Imogen. Like playing put and take. Like a child's game where you built up brightly-painted blocks to make a house or a picture. Paint. Pictures. *Quincy*.

He moved without thinking, going swiftly through the old house to the ward where Quincy had slept. Pictures. The police had already searched her things, but they would not have been looking for what he would be looking for.

The ward was deserted, and Leo knelt in front of the flimsy locker. It had been unlocked for the inspector's men earlier with the master key, and it was still unlocked. Leo began to go through the locker again. She had pitifully few possessions, poor child. Brush and comb, a small pile of underclothes. A couple of sweaters and pair of cheap cotton jeans. There was an expensive box of talc on a shelf by itself, probably given to her, probably by Imogen. The paints he had himself bought for Quincy were tucked in one corner as if she had feared they might be stolen, and next to them was the plastic wallet of aquarelle crayons that Thalia Caudle had brought on Christmas Day. And there, at the very back, was what Leo had been looking for: the block of drawing paper. He lifted it out carefully and sat on the nearest bed, turning the pages, despite himself smiling with wry amusement at the depiction of Matron Porter. And then he turned to the last sketch and felt as if someone had struck him between the eyes.

All of Quincy's work had more than a touch of the macabre, but her last drawing was the most disturbing of them all. It was vividly reminiscent of the old Flemish diableries – Hieronymus Bosch or Brueghel, whose works Quincy had surely never seen – and she had drawn in a thick, decorated border crammed with tiny creeping goblin figures and sneering dwarfish ghouls and hag-featured spectres, like a travesty of the illuminated proscenium frames of Victorian theatre posters, or the illuminated manuscripts of the medieval monks.

The central figure was recognisably Thalia Caudle, but it was a Thalia hugely tall and icily commanding. Quincy had cloaked her in rippling crimson silk, and every sculpted fold suggested corruption and menace. For foreground detail she had drawn a scattering of half-rotting human skulls and bleached finger bones. Crouching nearby, leering out of the macabre frame, was a familiar lumpish figure, and Leo stared at it and thought, Harris! Dear God, she's drawn Thalia as a kind of ogress witch figure, with Harris as the dark satanic familiar! The face, the pose, was familiar from a dozen different dark fairy stories. The scuttling hunchback servant, the frog prince, all denizens of that almost real fantasy world where deformity equated with evil. *Snow White* and *Rumpelstiltskin* and their kin. Leo stared at the figure and felt, as he always felt when confronted with human deformity, the guilt of being normal. But are you sure you're so entirely normal yourself? demanded his mind. Remember that not all deformities are visible. What about that quirk of the spirit, that kink in the mind that

407

enables you to spin up the coruscating power like the miller's daughter set to spin straw into gold?

Clustering against the lowering clouds in Quincy's drawing were several brutish-featured beings, with great meaty hands and mean, red-glinting eyes. Leo stared at it, and even though he knew perfectly well what Quincy must have seen to have drawn this, and even though his physician's mind knew the medical terms and the medical palliatives, a prickle of fear scudded through his mind. *Because there were giants on the earth once* . . . Because they strode across the world in seven-league boots, and they prowled through the dark pages of Grimm and Andersen and Perrault. And they had names. They were called Blunderbore and Brobdingnag, and Pantagruel the ever-thirsty or Cyclops the angry-eyed, and they devoured children and ground the bones of men to make bread.

The shadows of Thornacre seemed suddenly to gather and rear up to confront him. Leo shut the sketch book with a snap and returned it to the locker, and the ghosts and the darkness receded.

But he had the denominator. Quincy had seen through Thalia's smooth, urbane mask – he had nearly seen through it himself. She had seen through to something she had believed to be fearsome and menacing. She might have been wrong, but Leo did not think she was. This was her last drawing, clearly done on the night before she went out with Thalia, and it was filled with fear.

He was straightening up from the locker, the drawing still in his hands, when Nurse Carr came into the room to tell him that there was a Dr Tudor on the phone and it was a matter of extreme importance.

Oliver had driven back to the Black Boar, his mind working at top speed. The most obvious thing to do now was phone the police and haul them out here, but there were several aspects to this that had first to be considered, the most worrying of which was the dialogue that might ensue. Oliver could imagine it only too well:

'I think the missing Thornacre girl could be at October House after all, Sergeant.'

'Really, sir? And what makes you think that?'

'Because I've just been out there. I crept into the garden, and peered in through a window.'

'Did you now? What exactly did you see while you were peering through the window?'

'Well, Thalia Caudle was with a young girl and the girl was undressing. It looked as if they were about to have it away together on the hearth rug.'

'Really? And do you make a habit of peering through windows and watching that kind of thing, Dr Tudor?'

It was a shudderingly awful prospect.

They would presumably have to check his story, even if they did write him off as a voyeur, but they would be distrustful. They were distrustful already. They might uncover the fact that Dan had known Thalia in London. Why the devil hadn't he admitted to that at the outset! They might do the checking by telephone. Oliver could easily visualise some fed-up night duty sergeant delegating the task. 'Just ring up this number, Fred, and check that Caudle woman's story again. There won't be anything in it, but the inspector says we've got to.' Whatever they did, the outcome would be that that odd child with the wise-ancient eyes would no longer be inside October House when they got there.

It was only when he heard the slightly startled voice answering the Thornacre phone that he realised it was now after midnight. But it could not be helped; as soon as Leo came on the line, Oliver said without preamble, 'I've been out to October House, and I think your missing girl's there.'

'Yes?'

'Well, it makes rather bizarre telling,' said Oliver hesitantly, remembering his estimation of the police reactions.

'I'm a psychiatrist, I'm used to bizarre things.'

Leo listened without interruption as Oliver briefly described the strange scene he had witnessed in the lamplit, firelit room of October House. 'And I can't be sure that it was Quincy,' Oliver said. 'But the police sergeant who questioned me described her, and it matched near enough. Small, not pretty, with wary eyes and short hair. A kind of urchin look.'

'Yes, urchin describes it very well.'

'And she had a rather old-fashioned air. I don't mean she had old-fashioned clothes or hairstyle, I mean her face. She looked as if she belonged to a different century. The mid-nineteenth, for choice. The *poor* mid-nineteenth.'

'It's Quincy all right,' said Leo. 'But since we talked, Dr Tudor, something else has happened. I don't know how much bearing it has on your brother's disappearance, or whether it has any at all, but six patients are missing, and so is Thalia Caudle's niece.'

There was an abrupt silence. 'I'm sorry,' said Oliver, 'but did you say *six* patients?'

'Yes,' said Leo shortly. 'Six patients suffering from acromegaly –I'll explain what that is some other time. And with Imogen Ingram it's seven.'

'Do the police know?'

'Yes, of course they know, they're crawling all over Thornacre at the moment, for God's sake. But if you mean do they know about Thalia's involvement, no, they don't.'

'You haven't told them?'

'No, I have not, and the reason I haven't is that Caudle's involvement is still only my deduction and yours,' said Leo. 'There's nothing tangible to connect her with this, any more than there was this morning. And the logic we applied then still holds.' He paused. 'Exactly how eminent are you, Dr Tudor?'

'I'm not eminent at all. What's that got to do with anything?'

'I was wondering how much of a professional reputation

410

you had, and whether you were prepared to risk it.'

'I don't give a damn for my professional reputation, such as it is. What have you got in mind?'

'A little exercise in housebreaking,' said Leo.

'October House?'

'Yes. I expect I can do it on my own, and if I have to I will. But it'd be easier with two of us.' He paused, choosing his next words with care. 'The thing is if we're caught it'll be straightforward breaking and entering. We won't have a leg to stand on. If you want to opt out now, I shan't blame you. In fact I'd think you were behaving very sensibly.'

'Stuff common sense, and as for professional reputations, isn't your own far more at risk than mine, Dr Sterne?'

'If I ever had one, I lost it years ago,' said Leo.

'And I never acquired one,' said Oliver. 'I'll meet you outside October House in fifteen minutes.'

Chapter Thirty-six

Quincy knew that she was in the ogress's lair and that the ogress was going to kill her. That was what this was all about. The ogress had crawled up out of her dark hiding place when no one was watching, and she had caught her. She had also caught Imogen and the young man called Dan. There would not be any escape, even though Imogen was calling to her to be brave, and Dan was telling her that he would get them all to safety somehow.

Quincy was lying on the floor. There was a fiery glow from the ovens, and the stench of evil everywhere. The ogress was leaning over her, and flaring candles lit her from behind, so that you could see that her eyes were red and glaring. Her lips were drawn back in a snarl.

The evil-smelling place was beginning to spin round Quincy in a huge, whirling storm. There were immense crimson streaks in the storm, like blood, and there were jagged lights that hurt your eyes and made you feel sick. Quincy thought Imogen was crying, and she could hear the young man swearing at the ogress. She tried to call out to him that it would not do any good; you could not kill ogresses because they were not like humans, and this was the most evil ogress there was; this was probably the queen, like you had queen bees who led the others. But there was something brave-making about the young man, and Quincy was grateful to him. He might be able to get Imogen out later on, and then they would be together. He was exactly the kind of person you could visualise Imogen being with.

Quincy held on to the idea of Imogen getting free and being with Dan, because it was a good thought.

The ogress gave a scream of fierce delight and triumph, and lifted her hands above her head. There was a scalding sizzling sound, like a whiplash curling through the air, and then a flash of steel, glinting in the candlelight.

Pain tore through Quincy's hands and exploded up into her arms and shoulders, and through her whole body. It was so fierce and so enormous that the red-lit place wavered and blurred, and she felt as if she was plummeting down and down into a deep, deep ocean. Someone was screaming and there was the choking feeling of agony closing over her head. She was swimming through the agony in her hands, and it was becoming difficult to see and difficult to hear. Imogen was still talking – yes, Imogen was still with her – and Dan was shouting, telling her to hold on, to hold on, Quincy, because they would not let her go . . .

As Thalia severed Quincy's hands with that single terrible blow, Dan felt the horror engulfing him. His mind shuddered in disbelief because nothing, not the worst waking nightmare, not the most warped vision, could be as bad as this.

Thalia was straightening up, holding the two jagged-edged lumps of flesh above her head, and Dan caught the white glint of bone and saw the frill of blood-dabbled flesh. The blood was dripping sluggishly to the ground, and Thalia immediately cupped her free hand under it. Cradling the severed hands carefully, she leaned over the white, still form on the table, and began to arrange the hands in place. Her eyes were rinsed of all sanity, and blood smeared her cheek. At intervals she laughed, and once or twice she crooned Edmund's name. In his corner, the hunchback was gibbering with delight, scuttling back and forth over the same few inches of ground, like a monstrous human-faced spider busy about its web.

Quincy lay in a little huddle on the floor, surrounded by clotting pools of her own blood. She looked tiny and frail, and her skin had a waxy look, like tallow or old polished ivory. Dan looked across at Imogen and saw that she was crying, and trying to reach Quincy. But the chain held firm and she could only stretch a foot or so into the centre of the room.

Quincy's eyes were filmed over with pain and exhaustion, but as Imogen dragged furiously at the chain, she seemed to hear. She lifted her head and Dan saw that she was still conscious. Her eyes rested on Imogen for a moment and then turned to him, and she moved, holding out her mutilated arms to him in dreadful entreaty. The pity of it clutched at Dan's guts, because her hands, her poor hands . . . The wrists were soaked in blood, and splinters of bone and muscle and tendon protruded. And she's dying, he thought; she's bleeding to death there on the floor, and there's absolutely nothing I can do to help her.

Incredibly she was trying to speak. She was almost beyond sight and hearing, but she was not yet beyond feeling, and she was trying to reach him, pitifully trying to reach his arm with the bloodied stumps that were her wrists. Dan swallowed the choking knot of emotion and sickness, and even though the chains brought him up short, as Imogen's had done, he reached towards her as far as he could get. There was an appalling moment when the dripping, truncated arm brushed the tips of his fingers, and he only just managed not to flinch. 'It's all right, Quincy,' he said. 'In another few minutes we'll all be free, and we'll get you to a hospital and you'll be fine.' And God forgive me for the lie, because I don't think any of us are going to get free, and this poor child is dying fast.

Quincy said, 'Don't let her – get Imogen . . .'

'She won't get Imogen. I promise you she won't. It's all right.'

'Look after . . . Imogen . . .'

'I will look after Imogen,' said Dan.

'So beautiful . . .'

Their eyes met. Dan said, very softly, 'Yes. The most beautiful thing I've ever seen. I understand. I'll look after her, Quincy.'

The filmed eyes focused on him with difficulty. 'Promise?'

'On my word of honour.'

He thought she nodded and gave a little sigh. Her head fell back on the ground, and Dan saw her eyes flutter and close. He looked up to meet Thalia Caudle's mad red-lit eyes, and braced himself for what was ahead.

Thalia said, 'In a little while we will burn what's left of that one. But now it's time for the bitch-whelp. It's time to dig out her heart and give it to Edmund.'

Imogen had managed to hold on to a shred of courage while Quincy was killed, and this was mainly because of Dan. It was important not to let either Thalia or Harris know how frightened she was, but it was much more important not to let Dan know.

When the hunchback dragged her towards the table, she fought him for all she was worth, but he overpowered her, grinning and mumbling to himself. Imogen said, very clearly, 'Take your disgusting hands off me, you repulsive insect,' but the creature only gave a snuffling chuckle and lifted her on to the table, arranging her limbs caressingly.

Lying next to the thing that had been her cousin almost dissolved the last fragments of Imogen's courage. There was a dreadful sense of finality about this and a stifling feeling of anticipation in the old coach house now. As if something unseen was pressing down from above. As if something huge and dreadful hovered nearby, waiting its chance . . .

Imogen stared up at the ceiling and terror swept over her, because it was really beginning to look as if this was it. She was about to die; there was not going to be any eleventh-hour rescue; the seventh cavalry riding in or the knight on the white charger. But I can't die like this! she thought wildly. I can't die in some disgusting warped ritual, before I've found out anything about the world and before I've done anything! She turned her head to one side to look at Dan, and as she did so she saw him look sharply towards the small, rather grimy windows as if he had caught a sound from outside. A flicker of hope surfaced. Had Dan heard something? Imogen strained to listen. The sense of something unseen, waiting and watching just outside the old coach house, brushed her mind, but nothing moved, and neither Thalia nor the hunchback seemed to be aware of anything.

It was obvious Dan had no idea how to get them out, and by this time Imogen's heart was racing so fast she could hardly think at all. She thought she might faint, and she began to hope she would because then she would not know what was being done to her. It was as she was willing unconsciousness to close down that an angry little inner voice suddenly sounded inside her mind. You wimp! said this unexpected, unfamiliar voice. Why should he be the one to think of something? What's wrong with you? Well, because I can't. Because nobody ever expected me to think before. Well, start thinking now, said the voice. You got out of the wash house in Thornacre, so get out of this place as well, because if you don't, it's a sure thing you never will experience anything and you never will find out about the world!

Harris had left off the mouth gag, probably because out here you could scream for all you were worth and nobody would hear you. If there really had been something outside Imogen would have screamed until her throat was in tatters, but she did not think there had been anything.

She was so close to Edmund's body that she could feel the cold wetness of the dead flesh, and little puddles of thawing ice were soaking her nightgown. She could smell the faint stench of corruption as well, and if she turned her head, she would see the dead face . . . But she would not look.

There *was* something outside. Thalia and Harris were bending over the knives and moving the candles, and the knives were scraping and clattering a bit, and Thalia's whole attention was on what she was doing. But Imogen heard the sound this time: soft, rather heavy-sounding footsteps, as if someone was moving in the dark garden. You're imagining it. You're hearing what you want to hear. No, there it is again. Traffic? How near was the house to the main road? Imogen could not remember. What about thunder? It might easily be thunder. It might even be her own heart pounding with terror. Don't think about hearts, Imogen. Don't think that in a very short time this mad creature is going to try to cut your heart out and plunge it into the grotesque corpse next to you. The anger she had felt a few minutes earlier boiled up more strongly. I *will* get free! cried Imogen silently, and now she did turn her head, searching for a means of escape.

Thalia's eyes were glittering, her face white and thin, and Imogen could feel the mad power emanating from her. For a truly terrible moment she thought she was paralysed in every limb, as if Thalia had spun a sticky, mesmerising web round her, holding her fast. Imogen reached for the anger again, and took hold of it properly this time, because anger could send the adrenalin pumping; it could make you capable of performing the most extraordinary feats –fighting madwomen, overpowering hunchbacks, creating diversions so that you could get free . . .

Diversions.

Like Imogen, Dan had thought there was someone prowling through the garden but, also like Imogen, he had eventually discounted it.

As the hunchback arranged the table, his mind was working furiously on several levels. Thalia was clearly so wildly insane that any attempt to bargain for Imogen's life would be pointless. And Thalia would be physically very powerful; not only had she the gun and the hunchback, she had madness on her side as well.

But Dan was blowed if he was going to sit meekly here and let Thalia kill Imogen in some mad ritual, the climax of which was intended to give Edmund Caudle back his life. He would get Imogen free if he died in the attempt – he was probably scheduled to die shortly anyway.

When Thalia finally waved Harris back from the table, Dan saw that the hunchback went back to the corner on the other side of the kiln. Thalia was at the table, facing the room, her gaze unfocused, her lips moving silently, as if she was praying. Dan's heart leapt with hope. The kilns had been partly built into the whole back wall of the studio, but the front portion of the one fired tonight jutted out by a couple of feet; Harris, on the far side, was for the moment out of his line of sight. But was he out of Harris's? Was it possible that he could inch along the wall towards the kiln and not be seen? It was worth a try.

Harris had not tied Dan's hands behind his back, as he had Imogen's; he had tied them in front, probably because it was quicker. It would make an attack easier. Dan had not quite sunk down to the floor after Harris had tied him up; he had remained in a half-kneeling position, resting lightly on his heels and facing the room, thinking it would be easier to spring upright if any chance presented itself. He stayed in the same position now and, keeping his eyes on Thalia, began to move towards the kiln in a kind of sideways crawl. If Thalia looked round or Harris scuttled out from the other side of the kiln, Dan was ready to freeze into immobility. But neither of them looked in his direction, and by dint of moving slowly and tortuously, Dan was eventually up against the jutting side wall of the furnace. It cast deep shadows on each side, and only a thread of scarlet showed round the rim of the door, but heat pulsated outwards. Dan was relying on being able to get level with the edge of the door and reach the handle of the iron locking spline and twist it free. The door was about four feet across, and the iron key was a little longer. Four and a half feet? If he could wrench it free it would make a good weapon.

His skin was already flinching from the heat, but he had seen instantly that this was a potter's studio and he was working on the assumption that a furnace used as a kiln would need to be opened easily and frequently. It was not unreasonable to hope that the handle of the spline would be cool enough to grasp.

Thalia bent over Imogen; there was no sign of movement from the hunchback. Now? There might not be a better moment. Dan took a deep breath and reached out, grabbing the spline's round handle between both hands. It was warm but not blisteringly so and it came free easily.

Thalia spun round at once, with a little hissing sound of anger, and Harris came darting out of the shadows and launched himself straight at Dan. Dan was holding the spline a bit awkwardly, but he had a firm grip on it, and as Harris came towards him, he swung his bound hands as far to the left as possible and brought the iron shaft hissing across the air at waist level in a scything movement. The heavy iron slammed into the hunchback's spine and Dan actually felt the sickening crunch of bone as the iron connected. Harris let out a yelping grunt and half fell to the ground, rolling in agony.

Imogen had not waited for the blow to connect. The instant Dan moved, she brought her knees up to her chest and kicked out hard against Edmund's body. It yielded at once, slithering to the edge of the table, and then fell to the ground with a soft, squelching thud. Thalia screamed and lunged towards it, unheeding of anything else, and crouched over her son.

Imogen rolled off the table and landed heavily, several of the knives and what sounded like the gun clattering after

419

her. Her hands were still tied behind her back, but she rolled over a bit more and by dint of twisting and slithering managed to get one of the knives between her hands. Dan crawled towards her and took the knife.

'Turn round.' There was the feel of the knife slicing through the scarf, and then Imogen's hands were blessedly free. She grabbed the knife back and sliced the twine round Dan's hands. Dan was just freeing his ankles and Imogen's, when they both looked up involuntarily. The sounds they had both thought they heard earlier were there again.

This time there was no doubting them. This time Thalia and Harris heard them too. Whispering. And huge, heavy footsteps. Ice and fire formed lumps in Imogen's stomach, and memory skittered backwards. Giantish creatures that lumbered through the night, whispering as they came . . . She looked across to the door and let out a gasp of horror.

Peering through the small, multi-paned windows on each side of the door were the brutish creatures from Thornacre.

Chapter Thirty-seven

The four people in the old coach house – Dan and Imogen, Thalia cradling Edmund's head in her lap, Snatcher Harris squirming on the floor – all froze, staring at the window.

With the glow of the candle flames flickering across them and the dark trees of October House's grounds as a backdrop, the acromegalics looked like creatures out of the time-foxed pages of Middle European fairy stories; they were the beings who walked through every dark legend and every macabre folk tale ever whispered before a chimney corner or told around a roaring fire with the doors double-locked against the night. They were terrible and pitiable; they had no place in the twentieth-century world, no place in any world other than that of nightmares.

The whispering came clearly through the night.

'*This-s-s is-s-s the way, my dears-s-s.*'

'*This-s-s is-s-s where the hunchback s-s-showed us-s-s.*'

Harris was lying on the floor, still grunting in pain, but at the sound of the whisperings, a curious blend of fear and sly triumph showed on his face for a second. Imogen had just time to think: he brought them here! Somehow he showed them how to get here and told them to break in. How did he do that? The whispering voices said, '*Through the door, my dear-s-s. This-s-s is-s-s the door he s-s-said . . .*'

The studio door was dealt a heavy blow from the other side.

Imogen saw Thalia lift her ravaged face from Edmund

and stare at the door. For the first time, real fear showed on her face.

The creatures were pounding on the door, and against her will Imogen remembered how, a million years ago in Thornacre, they had hissed to one another about smelling the scent of a girl. She shivered and shrank back into the corner of the studio, gripping the knife in her right hand as if it was a talisman that could banish the intruders to whatever dark subterranean twilight they had emerged from.

The door was quivering under the repeated blows. Dan remembered how Thalia had directed the hunchback to lock it, but he thought the lock would never hold against such an onslaught.

It did not hold. It snapped suddenly, with a sharp metallic sound, shocking in the listening silence, and the door burst open and flew back against the wall with a deafening crash. In the same instant, jarred by the impact and freed of its locking iron spline, the kiln door swung wide, and scorching heat belched outwards.

Thalia was the first to move, darting forward to the door like an eel. Imogen drew breath to shout, 'No!' but the giants barred Thalia's way, their great hands reaching out. They began to back her into a corner of the studio, greed in their brutish faces.

'*A hos-s-tage for us-s-s!*'

'*Take the hos-s-tage!*'

'*Back to Thornacre with her!*'

Thalia was standing against the far wall, the pulsating light of the furnace showering over her, so that for a moment it looked as if she was wearing a rippling crimson mantle of fire and blood and heat. Imogen blinked and shuddered and the image vanished.

Harris was lying where he had fallen, but at the giants' approach, he squirmed nearer to the furnace door, one hand flailing desperately for the iron key.

'I think his back's broken,' said Dan softly as he and Imogen shrank back into the shadows, trying to see their chance to reach the door. And despite himself, he added, 'Poor sod. God Almighty, he's trying to close the kiln door. He'll never do it.'

'He's not trying to close it, he's trying to reach the iron thing you used on him,' said Imogen.

Harris was hauling himself to a standing position by means of the furnace wall, using it for support. He dragged himself almost upright, so agonisingly slowly that despite herself Imogen suddenly wanted to run across the room and help him. At her side, Dan said shortly, 'Don't do it, Imogen. Just try to reach the door without those things turning their attention to us.'

'Dan – how did they get here?'

'God knows. We can't think about it yet. Concentrate on getting out.'

'What happens if they turn on us?'

'I've got the gun,' said Dan.

Thalia had backed up against the wall, alongside the yawning furnace, her palms pressed against the wall, her eyes darting to and fro seeking a way of escape. And then her eyes fell on Harris, still struggling to reach the iron key. His fingers were within inches of it as Thalia pounced, snatching it up and thrusting the thick key end deep into the glowing heart of the kiln. She's heating up a weapon to use on them, thought Imogen in horror. She looked unwillingly back at the acromegalics, and for the first time saw the rather childlike expressions.

Thalia was pointing at the helpless Harris.

'If you want a hostage take that creature!' she cried, her face white but her eyes blazing with madness. 'Take him! Do whatever you want with him! And then,' said Thalia slyly, 'I'll help you to get free!'

There was a sudden silence, and Imogen held her breath. The giants hesitated, and turned to look at Harris. They're

423

trying to understand, thought Imogen. I don't believe they're evil at all; they're bewildered and they don't fully understand what's happening.

Thalia moved forward until she was standing over the crouching hunchback. 'You failed me,' she said, staring down at him, speaking as if no one else was in the room with them. 'You failed me, you miserable worm, and now you've betrayed me as well. You brought these monsters here, didn't you? Why? To have more repulsive mutants on your side? To ruin my plans? Did you show them the tunnel under the road? Did you tell them my secrets?' Her eyes narrowed to glittering slits, and her hands curved into claws. 'For that – for all of that – you must be punished,' she said, on a soft hissing note.

Harris's face was twisted and almost unrecognisable with fear and pain, and he was holding up both his hands as if to ward off an attack. He shook his head wildly back and forth and a stream of unintelligible grunting sounds issued from his mouth.

As the giants stood irresolute, Thalia moved again, taking up a stance near the open kiln, silhouetted blackly against the glowing interior. She pointed again to the hunchback. 'He's a traitor! He brought you here to trap you!'

The heavy dull-eyed faces turned to the squirming figure half on the ground, half clinging to the side of the kiln.

'*Traitor!*'

'*Brought us-s-s here to trap us-s-s.*'

'*The Lady s-s-said s-s-so.*'

'*But he pretended we would be his allies-s-s, s-s-showed a picture of this-s-s hous-s-se where we would live. A nic-c-ce hous-s-se . . .*'

'*But he tricked us-s-s-s . . .*'

Harris, stark terror in his face, began to drag himself across the floor in a last desperate attempt to escape. As the giants circled about him, he tried to draw himself up, holding out his hands in a gesture of dumb entreaty.

424

Imogen gasped and bit her lip in sudden unwanted sympathy. He was trying to stand and he couldn't. It was gut-wrenchingly pitiful.

Harris staggered backwards against the open kiln and let out a scream of agony as his shoulders and the upper part of his damaged back fell against the burning iron surface. Thalia darted forward, between the acromegalics, and pushed him hard. He clutched at her hands, vainly fighting her off. The two figures struggled together for a moment, and Thalia screamed, 'Traitor! You brought them here! You intended to ruin my plans! You intended to stop me from reaching Edmund.' And then, on a terrible note, '*Edmund!*'

The lumpish, squat figure of the hunchback tumbled backwards straight into the open furnace. The flames leapt at once, like hungry mouths, like greedy tongues, and for the count of half a dozen heartbeats Dan and Imogen both saw the blazing, burning shape still moving inside the furnace.

Thalia snatched up the linen cloth that had been used to cover the makeshift altar, and using it to protect her hands seized the iron rod and withdrew it from the furnace depths. The key end was white-hot from the fierce heat, and as the acromegalics advanced, she swung it through the air, much as Dan had swung it to disable Harris earlier. The glowing iron smashed into the face of the nearest giant. He yelped with a dreadful childlike squeal and half fell, and the rest cowered back, throwing up their hands to cover their faces. Thalia turned on them, and Dan grabbed Imogen's hand and pulled her through the open door and into the safe darkness beyond.

As they ran through the garden, they heard the frightened, pain-filled squealing of the giants as Thalia attacked them.

Nothing had ever felt as good as the cold sharp night air in their lungs, and the freezing rain stinging their faces.

As they ran towards the house, Imogen said breathlessly, 'What are they? Those things?'

'I haven't the remotest idea. Are you all right?'

'Yes. Is the hunchback—'

'Dead within seconds,' said Dan abruptly.

'And the giant things?'

'God knows. But we're not going back to find out, Imogen. We're going to beat it out of here and get you to safety. Can you get down to the road dressed like that?'

Imogen had forgotten that she was wearing only her nightgown and that her feet were bare. But she said, 'I can walk as far as Land's End if it means getting out of here.'

'All right,' said Dan. 'But let's see if there's a coat somewhere. You're not escaping from that mad creature only to die of pneumonia straight afterwards. Come into the house with me.'

'Well, I'm not staying out here on my own.'

He sent her a sudden grin. 'Good girl. Stay with me, Imogen.'

They half fell through the rear door of October House, and Dan snatched an elderly duffel coat from what looked like an old garden room, and flung it round Imogen's shoulders. It was warm, and although there was a faint smell of paint and of what might be brick dust, it felt unexpectedly friendly. There were rubber boots as well; they were several sizes too big, but they would serve the purpose.

Dan went swiftly through the hall, switching on lights as he went. 'We haven't much time,' he said. 'We don't know what Thalia might do. But I think we have to risk phoning the police.' He glanced back at her. 'And then we'll beat it out of here and go down the drive to the main road.'

'All right.' Imogen followed Dan into the big sitting room at the front of the house and stood in the centre, wrapping her arms about her for warmth and comfort, listening for sounds from outside.

Dan had already dialled 999, and Imogen heard him say impatiently, 'No, of course it isn't a hoax! Yes, I bloody am being serious! Just get out here with all the king's horses and all the king's men, will you! No, we daren't stay put! We'll get on to the main road as quickly as possible.'

He banged the phone down and crossed the room, grabbing Imogen's hand on the way. 'We've got two options, Imogen. We can search for the keys to Thalia's car and drive to Blackmere, or we can just make a run for it.'

They looked at one another and as they did so, they heard a burst of sound from the garden. Somebody started screaming, and there was the banging of the studio door. Dan said, 'No contest. Let's run for it.' Together they went out through the front door and down the dark drive.

They had got as far as the main road when they saw the arcs of car headlights slicing through the night and coming towards them.

Driving through the darkness to October House, Leo had been obeying instincts that had nothing to do with logic or rationale.

He *knew*, with his heart and his guts, that Thalia had taken Imogen and that she had got Quincy as well, and he knew with his blood and his bones that Imogen's life was balanced on a knife edge. He drove through the night at a frantic pace, the sense of urgency and desperation filling him to the exclusion of everything else. I might not be in time. Imogen might already be dead.

As he drove through Blackmere village, he slowed down, his eyes raking the darkness, trying to pick out October House, trying to see Oliver Tudor's car. It did not look as if Oliver was here yet.

Ahead of him, on his right, was a building with lights burning at the downstairs windows. October House? He changed gear and drove towards it, peering into the darkness, seeing the tiny dancing shapes of insects caught in the headlights' beams, seeing the spangling moisture from the December night mist everywhere. *Imogen, where are you?*

And then she was there, as abruptly as if she had materialised out of that night mist, coming towards him from out of the spindrift veil, beads of moisture clinging to her hair. And at her side was a young man whom Leo had never seen before.

The night mist had graduated to a steady downpour, and even through the tightly-drawn curtains in the bay-windowed sitting room it was possible to hear the steady soft patter. Imogen tucked the potter's duffel coat more tightly round her, grateful for the warmth and the lights and the company of the others.

Two police cars were still parked outside, and they could hear the occasional buzz of the patrol radios and the voices of the policemen still going through the old coach house. It was a reassuring sound.

Imogen was curled into the deep, comfortable chair at the side of the fire, with Dan and Leo Sterne facing her, one on a matching chair, the other on a low stool. Oliver had arrived minutes behind Leo, and he was sitting on the deep sofa, facing the fire. He had not said much, but there had been a moment when he and Dan had embraced in a brusque, faintly embarrassed masculine fashion. He had said something about Dan looking like a fugitive, and Dan had said they were lucky he didn't look like a corpse. It was clear that they were very fond of one another. Oliver looked a lot like Dan – at least, how Dan would look with the disreputable beard removed and his hair cut, but he seemed gentler and more hesitant. Imogen thought he was rather nice.

It was somehow typical that Dr Sterne should take the armchair and sit upright in it in a more or less conventional fashion, and that Dan should sprawl untidily against the chimney breast. The chair gave Dr Sterne authority, and yet . . . Imogen sent a covert look towards Dan. *Stay with me, Imogen*, he had said.

They were all drinking the potter's whisky, which had been unearthed from a cupboard and which Dan had said they might as well plunder on the grounds that they could replace it tomorrow – 'Or maybe it's already today.'

'I don't suppose the police are taking an inventory,' said Leo as Dan splashed a good measure into four glasses and added soda.

Despite the low stool, Dan had retained a fair share of authority. When he said, 'What were those creatures, Sterne? And how on earth did they get out here?' Imogen thought that by using Dr Sterne's surname Dan had somehow put himself on a level with the other man. She thought he had done it naturally and unthinkingly, but she thought that for some reason it had brushed a raw nerve in Leo Sterne. This was odd, because Oliver had used the same form of address and it had not called up the same reaction at all; in fact Dr Sterne seemed to be regarding Oliver as a collaborator and a friend.

Leo took a minute to reply to Dan's question. 'They're sufferers from a fairly unusual condition called acromegaly,' he said at last. 'I won't bore you with the technicalities, but it results in excessive growth of bones – especially the limbs and quite often the face.' He paused. 'Thornacre had several acromegalic patients,' he said. 'And tonight someone – Harris, from the sound of it – let them out.'

'And he told them how to get here,' said Dan.

'Why? How?' asked Imogen, leaning forward.

'I don't suppose we'll ever know,' said Leo. 'But it might be that he promised them some kind of reward. And it might very well be that he wanted to enlist their help on his own account.'

'How? I mean,' said Oliver, 'how would he get them here?'

'Several ways,' said Dan.

'Yes, and it wouldn't have been very far for them to walk,' put in Leo. 'It's a straight route. It might have taken an hour, or even a bit less, but certainly no more.'

'Would they have understood a map? Can they read?' asked Oliver.

'They can't manage the complete works of Shakespeare, but they can read plain things. It's possible they could have understood a simple map.'

'There you are then,' said Dan. 'Harris could have drawn a map for them. Or he could have given them the house agent's details of the place – Thalia had a couple of copies here, I remember, so that's a good contender. Or Harris might have secretly brought one of them here last night. Or painted marks on the roadside with luminous paint – or given them a ball of twine to unwind as they went, like Ariadne going into the Minotaur's den— Any of those do you, professor?'

'May heaven preserve me from the runaway imaginations of writers,' said Oliver, rather dryly. 'Any one of those will do nicely. On balance, I'll go for Harris's map-drawing.'

Dan grinned and got up to pour himself another whisky and soda.

'I wonder what Harris had in mind for them?' said Imogen thoughtfully. 'Will they be all right, Dr Sterne?'

'Yes, Imogen,' said Leo, gently. 'Yes, they'll be all right. I shall take them back to Thornacre where they feel safe and where we understand them. And we'll keep trying to bring them a little bit more into the world.'

And then Imogen said, 'Thalia's car's still here. And all her things are upstairs.' She looked at them in silence for a moment, and then said, 'What's happened to Thalia?'

What indeed?

The three men had gone back to the studio with the Thornacre police inspector, leaving Imogen in the warm, well-lit sitting room. The dull glow of the furnace-kiln still

430

illuminated the studio, and there was the same scent of hot iron and a whiff of something that might almost be sulphur. How appropriate, thought the detached part of Dan's mind. Brimstone and sulphur, and scuttling hunchbacked demons— He shut off the rest of the thought.

As the two police officers pushed wide the door the stench of heat belched outwards, and wrapped inside it was another stench: blood and sadness and fear. Leo said in a voice of the utmost horror, 'Dear God, what went on here tonight?'

'Something that would take a year to tell you,' said Dan.

The two of them stood for a moment in the doorway, and unwittingly shared a thought, nearly identical. Dan thought: cold and efficient evil did this. Leo thought: mad and efficient evil did this. Oliver, a little behind his brother, found himself remembering Milton's lost paradise, where the flames of the great furnace flamed round the iron-hued dungeon, discovering the sights of woe.

The acromegalics were seated in a circle in front of the kiln, like obedient children left by a nursery fire, their huge faces watching the flames with absorption. Two of them were lying against the wall, bruised and cut from where Thalia had attacked them and one had a scorch-mark, but Dan thought the injuries were not serious. He looked back at the silent figures ranged before the kiln, and ice began to close about his heart.

The door was propped open, and the flames burned up greedily. And the giants are watching them, thought Dan. They're concentrating on something deep inside the furnace. Something burning.

He looked frantically round the studio, half-expecting to see Thalia Caudle unconscious or dead in the shadows; certainly expecting to see the thing that had been Edmund lying on the ground where it had fallen. The icy horror hardened as he looked back at the yawning furnace door and at the intent faces of the acromegalics watching the leaping flames.

431

Epilogue

Dan leaned back against the bar and surveyed the crowded room with pleased detachment. When you looked like being a success – when pre-publication sales were already gladdening the heart of your bank manager and your agent, and your publishing house had set up an extravagant launch at a princely West End hotel – you could afford to feel pleased, although it was better not to show it too much.

He had been introduced to, and shaken the hands of, what felt like several dozen people, most of whose names he had not caught, none of whom he was likely ever to meet again. He had listened politely to several earnest young females who appeared to be seeing things in his plot which he had never seen for himself. After the fifth gin and tonic he told them there were no deep-seated, subtly-suggested analogies or parallels; all he had set out to do was write a story to entertain people and make some money – in that order. This was not very well received, and it was doubtful if it was believed.

Several people from writers' groups wanted a date for him to go along and talk to their members, which was probably something that would have to be done. Dan wondered what he would find to say, because you did not write books by talking about them.

'And the inspiration?' said a solemn reviewer from a magazine whose name Dan had forgotten.

He said, warily, 'What inspiration?'

'Oh, but surely—' she pushed her glasses back on to the bridge of her nose, 'you must have had some secret inspiration for your book.'

'The inspiration was seen through the bottom of an emptying whisky bottle most of the time,' said Dan, blithely, and it was at this moment that the inspiration for the book – the real gut-clutching, heart-scalding inspiration – walked into the room.

Dan said, 'Excuse me – could we discuss this later,' and went straight to Imogen.

It was over a year since he had seen her, well, all right it was thirteen months to be exact. The book had been finished exactly three weeks from that remarkable episode in Blackmere, and Dan's agent had liked it very much. He had got an almost immediate contract from a publishing house who liked it very much as well. Hence tonight. Hence the five gins and the sycophantic reviewers.

His feelings about her had been complicated. He held long arguments with himself as to whether it mightn't be wiser to keep her as part of that strange out-of-the-world experience they had both shared.

One of the aunts had taken her on a protracted cruise straight after the extraordinary episode in Blackmere – the Greek islands, apparently – and then there had been some kind of intensive cookery course in Paris. *Cordon bleu* level from the sound of it. I'm losing her, Dan had thought in panic, reading the letters Imogen wrote him. She's simply being polite because of what we shared. She'll dazzle them in Paris, and she'll be scooped up by some rich French businessman with a taste for good food and a beautiful female to cook it for him, and I'll never see her again. The letters will get shorter and more infrequent and eventually they'll dwindle to a Christmas card with a note saying 'Hope all is well with you' and listing how many children she's got.

Writers seldom met their inspirational heroines or heroes in real life, and if they were honest, probably did not want to. Dan thought that for heroines or heroes to step out of whatever visionary-realm their creators had built for them and appear against a workaday backdrop might fracture the dream and shatter the inspiration. You did not really want everyday life to intrude on your dreams. Would Imogen be less Imogen if she turned out to be – well, say humourless? No, not humourless, there had been that wry humour when they were both in October House. And the letters she had sent from Paris were far from humourless, they were witty and descriptive. Mean, then. Or spendthrift. Or addicted to chocolate or pop music or in love with a rock group. Remember she's only nineteen or so even now, and according to Juliette she was kept a bit cloistered. Supposing she's broken out and taken to drink, or drugs, or to sleeping with bikers or New Age travellers? The thought of Rosamund sniffing crack or with mauve hair and a nose-stud was not to be borne.

But in the end he rang Ingram's offices, who eventually put him in touch with Aunt Dilys. Aunt Dilys was charmed to hear from Dan, whom she remembered *perfectly* she said, and yes, certainly Imogen would be back in time for his book launch, and why not send the invitation c/o the Battersea address. And how very nice to hear from him.

After thought Dan sent an invitation to Leo Sterne and Juliette Ingram as well. Juliette with her publishing and publicity connections would probably accept and be instantly at home, and Dan thought they could meet with complete equanimity. Juliette was the kind of girl who would attend an ex-lover's wedding and grin conspiratorially at him across the church.

But he was unsure about Leo Sterne on several levels. He was unsure whether Leo would be in London and free, and he was very unsure indeed about whether he wanted him there at all. He knew perfectly well that under any other circumstances he would have rather liked Leo, but . . .

But he brought Imogen out of the long sleep, thought Dan, and that argues a degree of mental intimacy between them. Mental intimacy was a very powerful thing indeed – the welding of minds could be far more compelling than the welding of bodies – and older and more experienced females than Imogen had fallen into less charismatic arms than Leo Sterne's because of it. Dan admitted crossly that he was as jealous as hell of Sterne, but sent the invitation anyway.

Everyone agreed with Dilys that it was so nice of Mr Tudor to invite Imogen to the launch of his book. Dilys had apparently had quite a long chat with him on the phone; a *very* nice voice he had, she said, and he had been so polite. Rosa recalled how resourceful Dan had been on the terrible afternoon they were all trying to put behind them, and said she did like a man to *be* a man.

Flora Foy, informed that Dan was a writer, said, 'Ho, a writer, is he?' and gave a sudden reminiscent chuckle. When pressed, she would only say that all the writers she had ever known were inclined to be extremely passionate when not writing.

'Didn't somebody once see him with Juliette?' demanded Rosa, suddenly.

'Oh yes, but I don't think there was anything in it, Rosa. And Juliette's involved with somebody in banking at the moment.'

'God help the City,' said Flora.

Elspeth thought it was very nice that Imogen should be coming back to London, but said what a pity that she apparently did not intend to live in Battersea with Rosa and Dilys. But that was the way of the world now, of course. George had said only the other day that he did not know what modern girls were coming to.

'If he doesn't know, no one does,' said Rosa. 'I hear his new girlfriend is twenty years his junior.'

Leo had accepted the invitation with a very divided mind.

He was curious about Dan Tudor. Half of him liked Dan very much and rather admired him; the other half was aware of boiling envy, because of what Dan had shared with Imogen in October House. He rescued her, thought Leo. She was about to be butchered by that mad creature Thalia Caudle, and Dan rescued her. Any girl – any female, come to that – could be pardoned for feeling a touch of hero-worship for someone who had done that.

Imogen had ceased to be his patient after that amazing night in October House, save for a few more or less routine checks straight afterwards. But Leo had known long before the results came in that there was absolutely nothing wrong with her; this was a girl as normal as it was possible for anyone to be. Except that to Leo she would always be extraordinary.

She had written to him from Paris several times, and she had asked about his news: about how the revamping of Thornacre was progressing and whether he had set up any convention-defying treatments, and what had become of Matron Porter. Leo had written back, telling her that Freda had left Thornacre for the stultifying gentility of a home for retired army officers on the south coast, and Imogen's comment had held the gentle irony that Leo remembered. 'Her spiritual home I should think,' she had said. She scribbled a postscript to say that she was loving the course here, but she was looking forward to coming home. Next time he was in London she would cook him a gourmet dinner.

She was normal and bright and intelligent and she was starting to take her place in the world at last; the trouble was that it was a world that was a million light years away from Leo's own world. You're going to have to let her go, said his mind. You'd better face it, you know. She's not for you, she never was. She's for some bright, clever, *younger* man who's just starting out in life, and who'll be eminently suitable and who'll think she's a knockout.

Dan Tudor?

Imogen had not, of course, turned into any of the things Dan had been visualising.

She looked very nearly the same as his private, remembered vision, although she had scooped her hair up in a kind of loose chignon, which made her look older, and she was wearing a dark red dress that turned her skin into translucent ivory. Dan was so abruptly and so completely glad to see her that he forgot about milksop heroines and headed across the room.

She was exactly and precisely as he remembered her, in fact, she was better. She came towards him, her face lighting up with delight, and she held out her hands, and Dan wanted to grab her and run off with her there and then.

Imogen did not seem to notice. She was still holding his hand, and talking to him. It was tremendous to see him, she said; she had so looked forward to it. Letters were no substitute, were they? And she had read his book, and it was terrific; she had not been able to put it down. Was he working on another? The same thing or something different this time?

She was real and she was good to talk to, and she had no affectations or mannerisms. She accepted a glass of wine and sipped it with enjoyment, asking about his work. They progressed to the food that was set out, and Dan, who was by now recovering his equilibrium, asked what she was intending to do now that she was back in London.

'Well, it's possible that I can join forces with a friend of my cousin Juliette's. They run a small catering firm. Dinner parties in your home and boardroom lunches. I'd have to start on the bottom rung, and I think it'll be hard work, but it's what I'd like to do.'

'Not the board room at Ingram's?'

Imogen grinned. 'Ingram's can run itself without me. I've taken a flat in Juliette's block, you know. The family nearly had a fit.' She studied him for a moment, wondering if she could invite him to the tiny flat. She had been planning it all the way here, but now that they were actually face to face it was not quite so easy. What could she say? 'Maybe you'd like to act as guinea pig for one of my cookery experiments one evening . . .' It was the kind of thing she could have said to Dr Sterne without there being the least suggestion of anything – well, physical – but with Dan it was very different.

They looked at one another. After a moment Dan said, 'If you'd like a busman's holiday, perhaps we could have dinner some evening.'

'I'd love to.'

'Really?'

'Oh yes, really.'

He stared at her. She had accepted almost before he finished asking. It was possible to believe that she meant it. As a further test of that, he said, 'Tomorrow evening?'

'That would be terrific. I'll give you my address.' She wrote it down, and smiled at him and then looked beyond his shoulder. 'Oh, there's your brother with Juliette.'

'So it is. I don't know if he cornered Juliette, or if it was the other way round.'

'I'm afraid it's likely to have been the other way round.'

'I think you're right.' Dan was amused. It looked as if this time Oliver was not going to get away.

'Oh, and Dr Sterne's just come in,' said Imogen, with sudden pleasure. 'Dan, it's almost as if we're all together again—'

And stopped abruptly, her mind remembering and her eyes clouding with pain.

The three of them stood together in front of Quincy's last, remarkable drawing.

It had been used for the book jacket, and the framed blown-up illustration was on display as part of the publicity campaign. It was striking and disturbing, and every time Dan looked at it he felt a deep sadness for the fey child who had died. But far beneath that was a snaking thread of fear, because Quincy's sketch was so utterly and completely Margot; it was Margot shrouded in voluptuous evil. How did Quincy get it so right? he wondered uneasily. How did I get it so right, as well? I anticipated very nearly every step that Thalia took.

Leo, studying the illustration, vividly aware of Imogen at his side, felt his mind loop back to the night when he had sat in the deserted dormitory, staring down at Quincy's sketch. He had not forgotten Quincy, and he thought he never would forget her. Even at this distance he still felt anger at the waste of her life, and he was deeply grateful to whoever had made the decision to use the sketch for Dan's book.

Seeing Imogen with Dan had brought sharply home to him that she was indeed moving into a different world and on to a different plane. Even that bright remark in her last letter – 'next time you're in London I'll cook you a gourmet dinner' – even that had a filial air about it. *Filial.* The very last emotion I want from her. I'm losing you, my darling girl, thought Leo. But even though I'm losing you, for a very short time you were wholly mine. While we were in Thornacre, while you were locked in that twilit greenwood shade . . .

Thornacre. The word rippled across the surface of his consciousness, and he thought, at least I still have Thornacre.

Thornacre, with those dark, sad corners, but with those abrupt sunlit splashes of happiness as well. If Imogen's twilit forest truly existed anywhere, it would exist inside Thornacre. Because it was there, said his mind, at the heart of that chimerical woodland dusk, that she really did belong to me. Belonging, like sleep, like life, like love, has many levels and many existences, and in that unknown, un-named world, she was all mine. He glanced down at her, and felt the bitterness again. Yes, I think you're going to haunt Thornacre for me, Imogen.

He understood now that Dan, too, had had his dreams of Imogen and that they might not have been very far removed from Leo's own. That's how he wrote that remarkable book, thought Leo. Yes, of course! Does Imogen see that? No, I don't think she does, not yet. But she will see it one day. He'll tell her one day. And in the meantime – yes, in the meantime I still have Thornacre.

Imogen was not thinking about dreams-made-real or lost loves, or even future loves. She was thinking about Quincy, and how tragic it was that Quincy could not be here. It occurred to her for the first time that Dan and Quincy both had a little of the ability to see things hidden from everyone else. With the thought came a sudden chill, as if something had breathed corruption into her mind, or as if something sly and malevolent was watching her. She shivered and half turned round, and at once Dan turned with her.

'What's wrong?'

Imogen scanned the room, frowning slightly. But there was nothing there to disturb her. Juliette was moving in on Oliver; she had placed one hand on his arm, and she was wearing the expression that meant that at any minute she would say, purringly, that it was time they left, and her flat was only a few minutes away.

Imogen looked back at Dan. 'There's nothing wrong,' she said. 'It's just that for a moment I thought I saw someone I knew. But I think I must have been wrong.'

As Imogen got ready to go out – taking a long scented bath, deciding which outfit to wear – delighted anticipation was welling up inside her.

It was probably pretty unsophisticated to read too much into a dinner date: people went out to dinner all the time without it having any significance, but there was still the feeling of something special about tonight.

She flipped the radio on while she brushed her hair. Classic FM and a programme of Tchaikovsky was just starting. Nice. Imogen liked modern music, but she liked this kind of music as well. It depended on the mood you were in. She dabbed on scent, and crossed to the window to look down into the street. It was probably the last word in naivety to look out of the window for your escort, but she would pretend that it was to save Dan from bothering with parking and with the intercom downstairs. She stood in the shallow window recess, one hand drawing the curtain aside a little, watching the traffic snailing its way towards Kensington High Street.

As for that odd disquieting moment at yesterday's party – and how remarkable that Dan had sensed it! – Imogen had decided to ignore it. The likeness had been astonishing for a second or two, and the man had stood watching her, and then he had gone. But there had been just that second when Imogen had caught the glint of hair that was molten gold and of blue eyes that were sly and cruel, and she had thought: Edmund! Edmund? *He's going to live again*, Thalia had said. *I'm going to dig out your heart and give it to Edmund* . . . Impossible! said Imogen's mind firmly. So way-out as to be absurd! Start thinking about the good things; the real, positive things. Meeting Dan tonight – yes, that was a very good thought indeed. They might talk a bit about Thalia and October House, but they would probably not talk much about it, because it was all over, and Imogen had the feeling that there were more exciting, more interesting things to be discussed. Dan's work – she would like to hear about that. She wanted to talk to him about the truly amazing way his plot had mirrored what had happened last year. And she might tell him a bit about Paris, which had been fun but hard work. She might even be able to talk about Thornacre itself, which was not something she had

441

yet been able to do with anyone, not even Leo Sterne. The realisation that she was going to be able to talk to Dan about all these things, about everything and anything, made Imogen suddenly feel safe and warm. Something good was starting tonight. Something absolutely *tremendous* was starting.

Dan's ramshackle car turned the corner and bounced down the road, and Imogen picked up her coat and went out of the flat, locking the door carefully. It was not until she was crossing the landing outside that she realised she had left the radio on. It did not really matter, in fact it would fool potential house-breakers into thinking there was someone at home. The radio was not very loud, but she could just make out the music.

Tchaikovsky's finale to *Sleeping Beauty* was just beginning.

Imogen grinned and began to descend the stair.